# KILLING PATTERN

Kristi picked her words carefully. "I think whoever's behind the girls' disappearances is into something really dark. Evil."

"Evil?" Jay repeated.

She nodded and he saw her shiver. "I think we're dealing with something so vile and inherently depraved that it might not even be human."

"What are you saying, Kris?"

"I've been doing a lot of research. On vampires."

Jay laughed. "Okay. You had me going there."

"I'm dead serious."

"So whoever's behind the girls' disappearances believes in vampires. Is that what you're saying?"

"What I'm saying is this guy believes in vampires or maybe he believes *he's* a vampire. I don't know. But a person like that, Jay? someone deluded or obsessed . . . They're dangerous. This guy is dangerous."

A whisper of something slid over Jay's skin. Fear? Premonition? "Maybe you've let your imagination carry you away," he said, but she could hear the uncertainty in his voice . . .

Books by Lisa Jackson

SEE HOW SHE DIES
FINAL SCREAM
WISHES
WHISPERS
TWICE KISSED
UNSPOKEN
IF SHE ONLY KNEW
HOT BLOODED
COLD BLOODED
THE NIGHT BEFORE
THE MORNING AFTER
DEEP FREEZE
FATAL BURN
SHIVER
MOST LIKELY TO DIE
ABSOLUTE FEAR
ALMOST DEAD
LOST SOULS
LEFT TO DIE
WICKED GAME
MALICE

Published by Zebra Books

# LOST SOULS

## LISA JACKSON

ZEBRA BOOKS
KENSINGTON PUBLISHING CORP.
http://www.kensingtonbooks.com

ZEBRA BOOKS are published by

Kensington Publishing Corp.
850 Third Avenue
New York, NY 10022

All Kensington titles, imprints, and distributed lines are available at special quantity discounts for bulk purchases for sales
promotion, premiums, fund-raising, educational, or institutional
use.

Special book excerpts or customized printings can also be
created to fit specific needs. For details, write or phone the
office of the Kensington Special Sales Manager: Attn. Special
Sales Department. Kensington Publishing Corp., 850 Third
Avenue, New York, NY 10022. Phone: 1-800-221-2647.

ISBN-13: 978-0-8217-7938-5
ISBN-10: 0-8217-7938-9

First Kensington Books Hardcover Printing: April 2008
First Zebra Books Mass-Market Printing: March 2009
10  9  8  7  6  5  4  3  2  1

Printed in the United States of America

# Acknowledgments

I would like to thank everyone who worked on this book. As always, my insightful editor, John Scognamiglio, helped with the book from the time it was a germ of an idea. With his help I was able to make a vague concept into a complete plot, and I can't imagine how many hours he spent on the manuscript. Before the finished book ever reached New York, my sister, author Nancy Bush, helped with the editing and compiling of the manuscript—a daunting task, believe me. Behind the scenes, a legion of people helped with the research and promotion. I can't thank them enough: Ken Bush, Alex Craft, Matthew Crose, Michael Crose, Kelly Foster, Ken Melum, Roz Noonan, Ari Okano, Joan Schulhafer, Mike Seidel, Larry Sparks, and Niki Wilkins. If I've forgotten anyone, my apologies. Can I blame it on the age-thing?

## Author's Note

For the purposes of this story, I've bent some of the rules of police procedure and also created my own fictitious police department in the city of New Orleans.

# PROLOGUE

*All Saints College*
*Baton Rouge, Louisiana*
*December*

*Where am I?*
   A rush of icy air swept across Rylee's bare skin.
   Goose bumps rose.
   Shivering, she blinked, trying to pierce the shifting darkness, a cold dark void with muted spots of red light shrouded in a rising mist. She was freezing, half lying on a couch of some kind and . . .
   *Oh, God, am I naked?*
   Was that right?
   No way!
   Yet she felt the soft pile of velvet against the back of her legs, her buttocks, and her shoulders where they met the rising arm of this chaise.
   A sharp needle of fear pricked her brain.
   She tried to move, but her arms and legs wouldn't budge, nor could she turn her head. She rolled her eyes upward, trying to see to the top of this freaky dark chamber with its weird red light.
   She heard a quiet cough.
   *What?*

She wasn't alone?

She tried to whip her head toward the sound.

But she couldn't. It lolled heavily against the back of the chaise.

*Move, Rylee, get up and friggin' move!* Another sound. The scrape of a shoe against concrete—or something hard—reached her ears. *Get out, get out now. This is too damned weird.*

Her ears strained. She thought she heard the softest of whispers coming from the shadows. What the hell was this?

Her insides shriveled with a new fear. Why couldn't she move? What in the world was happening? She tried to speak but couldn't utter a word, as if her vocal cords were frozen. Frantically, she looked around, her eyes able to shift in their sockets, but her head unable to swivel.

Her heart pounded and, despite the chill in the air, she began to sweat.

This was a dream, right? A freakin' nightmare, where she, immobile, was positioned on a velvet lounge and naked as the day she was born. The chaise was slightly raised, it seemed, as if she were on a weird stage or dais of some kind, and surrounding her was an unseen audience, people hiding in the shadows.

Her throat closed in terror.

Panic swept through her.

*It's only a dream, remember that. You can't speak, you can't move, all classic signs of a nightmare. Calm down, shut this out of your mind. You'll wake up in the morning. . . .*

But she didn't heed the suggestions running through her mind, because something was off here. This whole scene was very, very wrong. Never before when she'd been terrorized by a nightmare had she had the insight to think she might be dreaming. And there was a realness to this, a substance that made her second-guess her rationale.

What did she remember . . . oh, God, had it been last night . . . or just a few hours earlier? She'd been out drinking with her new friends from college, some kind of clique that was into the whole Goth-vampire thing . . . no, no . . . they insisted it was a *vampyre* thing. That old-fashioned spelling was supposed to make it more real or something. There had been whispers and dares and blood-red martinis that the others had insisted were stained with real human blood. It had been some kind of "rite of initiation."

Rylee hadn't believed them, but had wanted to be a part of their group, had taken them up on their dares, had indulged . . . and now . . . and now she was tripping. They'd laced the drink, not with blood, but with some weird psychedelic drug that was causing her to hallucinate—that was it! Hadn't she witnessed the hint of hesitation in them when she'd been handed the blood-red martini and twirled the stem in her fingers? Hadn't she sensed their fascination, even fear, as she'd not just sipped the drink but tossed it back with a flourish?

Oh, God. . . .

This initiation—which she'd thought had been a bit of a joke—had taken a dangerous, unseen turn. She remembered vaguely agreeing to be part of the "show." She'd drunk the fake "blood" in the martini glass and yeah, she'd thought all the vampire stuff her newfound friends were into was kind of cool, but she hadn't taken any of their talk seriously. She'd just thought they'd been screwing with her head, seeing how far she would go. . . .

But within minutes of downing the drink, she'd felt weird. More than drunk, and really out of it. Belatedly, she'd realized the martini had been doctored with a potent drug and she'd started to black out.

Until now.

How much time had elapsed?

Minutes?

Hours?

She had no idea.

A nightmare?

A bad trip?

She hoped to God so. Because if this was real, then she really was situated on a couch, on a stage, wearing nothing, her long hair twisted upon her head, her limbs unmoving. It was as if she were playing a part in some eerie, twisted drama, one that, she was certain, didn't have a happy ending.

She heard another whisper of anticipation.

The red light began to pulse softly, in counterpoint to her own terrified heartbeat. She imagined she could see the whites of dozens of eyes staring at her from the darkness.

*God help me.*

Gritting her teeth, she willed her limbs to move, but there was no response. None.

She tried to scream, to yell, to tell someone to stop this madness! Her voice made only the tiniest of mewling noises.

Fear sizzled through her.

Couldn't someone stop this? Someone in the audience? Couldn't they see her terror? Realize the joke had gone too far? Silently she beseeched them with her eyes. Slowly, the stage became illuminated by a few well-placed bulbs that created a soft, fuzzy glow punctuated by the flickering red lamp.

Wisps of mist slid across the stage floor.

A rustle of expectancy seemed to sweep through the unseen audience. What was going to happen to her? Did they know? Was it a rite they'd witnessed before, perhaps passed themselves? Or was it something worse, something too horrible to contemplate?

She was doomed.

*No! Fight, Rylee, fight! Don't give up. Do not!*

Again she strained to move, and again her muscles wouldn't obey. Vainly she attempted to lift one arm, her head, a leg, any damned thing, to no avail.

Then she heard him.

The hairs on her nape raised in fear as cold as the Northern Sea. She knew in an instant she was no longer alone on the stage. From the corner of one terrified eye she saw movement. It was a dark figure, a tall, broad-shouldered man, walking through the oozing, creeping mist.

Her throat turned to sand.

Panic squeezed her heart.

She stared at him, compelled to watch him slowly approach. Mesmerized by terror. This was the one. The man the vampyre-lovers had whispered about.

She almost expected him to be wearing a black cape with a scarlet lining, his face pale as death, eyes glowing, glistening fangs revealed as he drew back his lips.

But that wasn't the case. This man was dressed partially in black, yes. But there was no cape, no flash of red satin, no glowing eyes. He was lean but appeared athletic. And sexy as hell. Wraparound mirrored sunglasses covered his eyes. His hair was dark, or wet, and was long enough to brush the collar of his black leather jacket. His jeans were torn and low-slung. A faded T-shirt had once been dark. His snakeskin boots were scuffed, the heels worn. Something about him was familiar, but she couldn't place his face.

Eager anticipation thrummed from the darkness surrounding the stage.

Once again she thought this was a far-out dream, a weird nightmare or hallucination that was now as sexy as it was frightening.

Oh, please . . . don't let it be real. . . .

He reached the couch and stopped, the scrape of his

boots no longer echoing through her brain, only the hiss of expectation audible over her own erratic heartbeat.

With the back of the lounge separating their bodies, he slid one big, calloused hand onto her bare neck, creating a thrill that warmed her blood and melted a bit of the fear that gripped her. His fingertips pressed oh-so gently against her collarbones and her pulse jumped.

A part of her, a very small part of her, found him thrilling.

A hush swept through the unseen crowd.

"This," he said, his voice commanding but low, as if addressing the shrouded viewers, "is your sister."

The audience released an "ahhh" of anticipation.

"Sister Rylee."

That was her name, yes, but . . . what was he talking about? She wanted to deny him, to shake her head, to tell him that what was happening was wrong, that her nipples were only stiff from the cold, not from any sense of desire, that the throb inside the deepest part of her was *not* physical lust.

But he knew better.

He could sense her desire. Smell her fear. And, she knew, he loved her for her raging emotions.

*Don't do this,* she silently pleaded, but she knew he read the warring signals in the dilation of her pupils, the shortness of her breath, the moan that was more wanting than fear.

His strong fingers pushed a little more forcefully, harder, hot pads against her skin.

"Sister Rylee joins us tonight willingly," he said with conviction. "She is ready to make the final, ultimate sacrifice."

What sacrifice? That didn't sound good. Once again Rylee tried to protest, to draw away, but she was paralyzed. The only part of her body not completely disengaged was her brain, and even that seemed bent on betraying her.

*Trust him,* a part of it whispered. *You know he loves*

*you . . . you can sense it. . . . And how long have you waited to be loved?*

No! That was crazy. The drug talking.

But she wanted to succumb to the feel of his fingers, slipping a little, edging lower, a hot trail along her breasts, ever-closer to her aching nipples.

Deep inside, she tingled. Ached.

But this was wrong. Wasn't it . . . ?

He leaned closer, his nose against her hair, his lips touching the shell of her ear as he whispered so quietly only she could hear, "I love you." She melted inside. Wanted him. A warm throb rose through her. His fingers rubbed the skin beneath her collarbones a little harder, pressing into her flesh. For an instant she forgot that she was on stage. She was alone with him and he was touching her . . . loving her. . . . He wanted her as no man had ever really wanted her. . . . And . . .

He pushed hard.

A strong finger dug into her flesh, jabbing against her rib.

A jolt of pain shot through her.

Her eyes widened.

Fear and adrenaline spurted through her bloodstream. Her pulse jumped madly, crazily.

What had she been thinking? That he could seduce her?

No!

Love? Oh, for the love of Jesus, he didn't love her! *Rylee, don't be fooled. Don't fall into his stupid trap.*

The damned hallucinogen had convinced her that he cared for her but he, whoever the hell he was, intended only to use her for his sick show.

She glared at him and he recognized her anger.

The bastard smiled, teeth flashing white.

She knew then that he reveled in her impotent fury. He felt her heart pumping, the blood flowing hot and frantic through her veins.

"Hers is the untainted blood of a virgin," he said to the unseen crowd.

*No!*

*You've got the wrong girl! I'm not a—*

She threw all her concentration into speaking, but her tongue refused to work, no air pushing through her vocal cords. She tried fighting, but her limbs were powerless.

"Don't be afraid," he whispered.

In horror she watched as he bent downward, ever closer, his breath hot, his lips pulling back to show his bared teeth.

Two bright fangs gleamed, just as she'd fantasized!

*Please God. Please help me wake up. Please, please . . . !*

In the next heartbeat she felt a cold sting, like the piercing of a needle, as his fangs punctured her skin and slid easily into her veins.

Her blood began to flow. . . .

# CHAPTER I

So far, so good, Kristi Bentz thought as she tossed her favorite pillow into the backseat of her ten-year-old Honda, a car that was new to her but had nearly eighty thousand miles on the odometer. With a thump, the pillow landed atop her backpack, books, lamp, iPod, and other essentials she was taking with her to Baton Rouge. Her father was watching her move out of the house they all shared, a small cabin that really belonged to her stepmother. All the while he was glaring at her, Rick Bentz's face was a mask of frustration.

So what else was new?

At least, thank God, her father was still among the living.

She hazarded a quick glimpse in his direction.

His color was good, even robust, his cheeks red from the wind soughing through the cypress and pine trees, a few drops of rain slickening his dark hair. Sure, there were a few strands of gray, and he'd probably put on five or ten pounds in the last year, but at least he appeared healthy and hale, his shoulders straight, his eyes clear.

Thank God.

Because sometimes, it just wasn't so. At least not to Kristi. Ever since waking up from a coma over a year and a half earlier, she'd experienced visions of him, horrifying images that, when she looked at him, showed he was a ghost of himself, his color gray, his eyes two dark, impenetrable holes, his touch cold and clammy. And she'd had many nightmares of a dark night, the sizzle of lightning ripping through a black sky, an echoing split of a tree as it was struck, then her father lying dead in a pool of his own blood.

Unfortunately, the visions haunted more than her dreams. During daylight hours, she would see the color leach from his skin, witness his body turning pale and gray. She knew he was going to die. And die soon. She'd seen his death often enough in her recurring nightmare. Had spent the last year and a half certain he would meet the bloody and horrifying end she'd witnessed in her dreams.

These past eighteen months she'd been worried sick for him as she'd recovered from her own injuries, but today, on this day after Christmas, Rick Bentz was the picture of health. And he was pissed.

Reluctantly he'd helped lug her suitcases out to the car while the wind chased through this part of the bayou, rattling branches, kicking up leaves, and carrying the scent of rain and swamp water. She'd parked her hatch-back in the puddle-strewn driveway of the little cottage home Rick shared with his second wife.

Olivia Benchet Bentz was good for Rick. No doubt about it. But she and Kristi didn't really get along. And while Kristi loaded the car amidst her father's disapproval, Olivia stood in the doorway twenty feet away, her smooth brow wrinkled in concern, her big eyes dark with worry, though she said nothing.

Good.

One thing about her, Olivia knew better than to get between father and daughter. She was smart enough not to add her unwanted two cents into any conversation. Yet, this time, she didn't step back into the house.

"I just don't think this is the best idea," her father said . . . for what? The two-thousandth time since Kristi had dropped the bomb that she'd registered for winter classes at All Saints College in Baton Rouge? It wasn't like this was a major surprise. She'd told him about her decision in September. "You could stay with us and—"

"I heard you the first time and the second, and the seventeenth and the three hundred and forty-second and—"

"Enough!" He held up a hand, palm out.

She snapped her mouth closed. Why was it they were always at each other? Even with everything they'd been through? Even though they'd almost lost each other several times?

"What part of 'I'm moving out and going back to school away from New Orleans' don't you get, Dad? You're wrong, I can't stay here. I just . . . can't. I'm way too old to be living with my dad. I need my own life." How could she explain that looking at him day to day, seeing him healthy one minute, then gray and dying the next, was impossible to take? She'd been convinced he was going to die and had stayed with him as she'd recovered from her own injuries, but watching the color drain from his face killed her and half convinced her that she was crazy. For the love of God, staying here would only make things worse. The good news: she hadn't seen the image for a while, over a month now, so maybe she'd read the signals wrong. Regardless, it was time to get on with her own life.

She reached into her bag for her keys. No reason to argue any further.

"Okay, okay, you're going. I get it." He scowled as clouds scudded low across the sky, blotting out any chance of sunlight.

"You get it? Really? After I told you, what? Like a million times?" Kristi mocked, but flashed him a smile. "See, you are a razor-sharp investigator. Just like all the papers say: local hero, Detective Rick Bentz."

"The papers don't know crap."

"Another shrewd observation by the New Orleans Police Department's ace detective."

"Cut it out," he muttered, but one side of his hard-carved mouth twitched into what might be construed as the barest of smiles. Shoving one hand through his hair, he glanced back at the house to Olivia, the woman who had become his rock. "Jesus, Kristi," he said. "You're a piece of work."

"It's genetic." She found the keys.

His eyes narrowed and his jaw tightened.

They both knew what he was thinking, but neither mentioned the fact that he wasn't her biological father. "You don't have to run away."

"I'm *not* running 'away.' Not *from* anything. But I am running *to* something. It's called the rest of my life."

"You could—"

"Look, Dad, I don't want to hear it," Kristi interrupted as she tossed her purse onto the passenger seat next to three bags of books, DVDs, and CDs. "You've known I was going back to school for months, so there's no reason for a big scene now. It's over. I'm an adult and I'm going to Baton Rouge, to my old alma mater, All Saints College. It's not at the ends of the earth. We're less than a couple of hours away."

"It's not the distance."

"I *need* to do this." She glanced toward Olivia, whose wild blond hair was backlit by the colored lights from the Christmas tree, the small cottage seeming warm and cozy in the coming storm. But it wasn't Kristi's home. It never had been. Olivia was her stepmother and though they got along, there still wasn't a tight family bond between them. Maybe there never would be. This was her father's life now and it really didn't have much to do with her.

"There's been trouble up there. Some coeds missing."

"You've already been checking?" she demanded, incensed.

"I just read about some missing girls."

"You mean runaways?"

"I mean missing."

"Don't worry!" she snapped. She, too, had heard that a few girls had disappeared unexpectedly from the campus, though no foul play had been established. "Girls leave college and their parents all the time."

"Do they?" he asked.

A blast of cold wind cut across the bayou, pushing around a few wet leaves and cutting through Kristi's hooded sweatshirt. The rain had stopped for the moment, but the sky was gray and overcast, puddles scattered across the cracked concrete.

"It's not that I don't think you should go back to school," Bentz said, leaning one hip against the wheel well of her Honda and, today, looking the picture of health—his skin ruddy, his hair dark with only a few glints of gray. "But this whole idea of being a crime writer?"

She held up a hand, then adjusted some of the items in the back of the car, mashing them down so that she would be able to see out her rearview mirror. "I know where you stand. You don't want me to write about any of the cases you worked on. Don't worry. I won't tread on any hallowed ground."

"That's not it and you know it," he said. A bit of anger flashed in his deep-set eyes.

Fine. Let him be mad. She was irritated as well. In the last few weeks they'd really gotten on each other's nerves.

"I'm worried about your safety."

"Well, don't be, okay?"

"Cut the attitude. It's not like you haven't already been a target." He met her eyes, and she knew he was reliving every terrifying second of her kidnapping and attack.

"I'm fine." She softened a bit. Though he was a pain in the ass often enough, he was a good guy. She knew it. He was just worried about her. As always. But she didn't need it.

With an effort she tamped down her impatience, as Hairy S., her stepmother's scrap of a mutt, streaked out the front door and chased a squirrel into a pine tree. In a flash of red and gray, the squirrel scrambled up the pine's rough bole to perch high upon a branch that shook as the squirrel peered down, taunting and scolding the frustrated terrier mix. Hairy S. dug at the trunk with his paws as he whined and circled the tree.

"Shh . . . you'll get him next time," Kristi said, scooping up the mutt. Wet paws scrabbled across her sweatshirt and she received a wet swipe of Hairy's tongue over her cheek. "I'll miss you," she told the dog, who was wriggling to get back to the ground and his rodent chasing. She placed him on the grass, wincing a little from some lingering pain in her neck.

"Hairy! Come here!" Olivia ordered from the porch, but the intent dog ignored her.

Bentz said, "You're not completely healed."

Kristi sighed loudly. "Look, Dad, all my varied and specialized docs said I was fine. Better than ever, right? Funny what a little time in a hospital, some physical therapy, a few sessions with a shrink, and then nearly a year of intense personal training can do."

He snorted. As if to add credence to his worry, a crow flapped its way toward them to land upon the bare branches of a magnolia tree. It let out a lonely, mocking caw.

"You were pretty freaked when you woke up in the hospital," he reminded her.

"That's ancient history, for God's sake." And it was

true. Since her stay in ICU, the whole world had changed. Hurricane Katrina had ripped apart New Orleans, then torn through the entire Gulf Coast. The devastation, despair, and destruction lingered. Though Katrina had raged across the Gulf over a year earlier, the aftermath of Katrina's fury was evidenced everywhere and would be for years, probably decades. There was talk that New Orleans might never be the same. Kristi didn't want to think about that.

Her father, of course, was overworked. Okay, she got that. The entire police force had been stretched to the breaking point, as had the city itself and the beleaguered and scattered citizens, some of whom had been sent to far points across the country and just weren't returning. Who could blame them, with the hospitals, city services, and transportation a mess? Sure there was revitalization, but it was uneven and slow to come. Luckily the French Quarter, which had survived virtually unscathed, was still so uniquely Old New Orleans that tourists were again venturing into that part of the city.

Kristi had spent the past six months volunteering at one of the local hospitals, helping her father at the station, spending weekends in city cleanup, but now, she figured—and her shrink insisted—that she needed to get on with her life. Slowly, but surely, New Orleans was returning. And it was time for her to start thinking about the rest of her own life and what she wanted to do.

Detective Bentz, as usual, disagreed. After the hurricane Rick Bentz had fallen back into his overly protective parental role in a big way. Kristi was way over it. It wasn't as if she was a child, or even a teenager any longer. She was an adult, for crying out loud!

She slammed the back of her hatchback shut. It didn't catch, so she readjusted her favorite pillow, reading lamp, and the hand-pieced quilt her great-aunt had left her, then tried again. This time the latch clicked into place.

"I gotta go." She checked her watch. "I told the land-lady that I'd take possession today. I'll call when I get there and give you a complete report. Love ya."

He seemed about to argue, then said gruffly, "Me, too, kiddo."

She hugged him, felt the crush of his embrace, and was surprised to find she was fighting sudden tears as she pulled away from him. How ridiculous! She blew Olivia a kiss, then climbed behind the wheel. With a snap of her wrist the little car's engine sparked to life and Kristi, her throat thick, backed out of the long, narrow driveway through the trees.

At the country road, she reversed onto the wet pavement. She caught another glimpse of her father, arm raised as he waved good-bye. Letting out a long breath, she felt suddenly free. She was finally leaving. At long last, on her own again. But as she rammed her car into drive, the sky darkened, and in the side view mirror she captured a glimpse of Rick Bentz's image.

Once more all the color had drained from him and he appeared a ghost, in tones of black, white, and gray. Her breath caught. She could run as far away as possible, but she'd never escape the specter of her father's death.

In her heart she knew.

It was certain.

And, it would be soon.


Listening to an old Johnny Cash ballad, Jay McKnight stared through the windshield of his pickup as the wipers slapped the drizzling rain from the glass. Cruising at fifty-five miles an hour through the storm with his half-blind hound dog seated in the passenger seat, he wondered if he was losing his mind.

Why else would he agree to take over a night class for a friend of a friend who was on sabbatical? What did he owe Dr. Althea Monroe? Nothing. He'd barely met the woman.

*Maybe you're doing it for your sanity. You damned sure needed a change. And anyway, how bad could one term of teaching eager young minds about forensics and criminology be?*

Shifting down, he guided his truck off the main drag and angled along the familiar side streets, where rain fell through the naked branches of the trees and the streetlights were just beginning to glow. Water hissed beneath his tires and few pedestrians braved the storm. Jay had cracked the window and Bruno, a pitbull-lab-bloodhound mix, kept his big nose pressed to that thin sliver of fresh air.

Cash's voice reverberated through the Toyota's cab as Jay slowed for the city limits of Baton Rouge.

"My momma told me, son . . ."

Jay angled his Toyota onto the crumbling driveway of the house on the outskirts of Baton Rouge, a tiny two-bedroom bungalow that had belonged to his aunt.

". . . don't ever play with guns. . . ."

He clicked off the radio and cut the engine. The cottage was now in the process of being sold by his ever-battling cousins, Janice and Leah, as part of Aunt Colleen's estate. The sisters, who rarely saw eye-to-eye on anything, had agreed to let him stay at the property while it was being marketed, as long as he did some minor repairs that Janice's do-nothing wanna-be rock star husband couldn't get around to making.

Frowning, Jay grabbed his duffel bag and notebook computer as he hopped to the ground. He let the dog outside, waited as Bruno sniffed, then lifted his leg on one of the live oaks in the front yard, before locking the Toyota. Turning his collar against the rain, he hurried up the weed-strewn brick path to the front porch, where a light glowed against the coming night. The dog was right on his heels, as he had been for the six years that Jay had owned him, the only pup in a litter of six who hadn't been adopted. His brother had owned the bitch, a purebred bloodhound who, after going into heat, hadn't waited for the purebred of choice. She'd dug out of her kennel and taken up with the friendly mutt a quarter of a mile away whose owner hadn't seen fit to have him neutered. The result was a litter of pups not worth a whole helluva lot, but who'd turned out to be pretty damned good dogs.

Especially Bruno of the keen nose and bad eyes. Jay bent down, petted his dog, and was rewarded with a friendly head butt against his hand. "Come on, let's go look at the damage."

"Folsom Prison Blues" replayed through his mind as he unlocked the door and shouldered it open.

The house smelled musty. Unused. The air inside dead. He cracked two windows despite the rain. He'd spent the last three weekends here, repainting the bedrooms, regrouting tile in the kitchen and single bath, and scraping off what appeared to be years of dirt on the back porch where an ancient washing machine had become the home to a nest of hornets. The rusted washer along with its legion of dead wasps was now gone, terra cotta pots of trailing plants in its stead on the newly painted floorboards.

But he was far from finished. It would take months to get the house into shape. He dropped his bags in the small bedroom, then walked to the kitchen, where an ancient refrigerator was wheezing on cracked linoleum he had yet to replace. Inside the fridge, along with some cheese that had dried and cracked, he discovered a six pack of Lone Star that was only one bottle shy, and grabbed a long neck. It was strange, he thought, how Baton Rouge, of all places, had become his haven away from New Orleans, the city where he'd worked and grown up.

Had it been the aftermath of Katrina that had drawn

the lifeblood from him? The crime lab on Tulane Avenue had been destroyed by the storm and the work the lab did scattered to different parishes and private agencies as well as to the Louisiana State Police crime lab in Baton Rouge. Sometimes they worked in FEMA trailers. It had been a nightmare—the extra hours, the frustration of evidence that had been collected, only to end up being compromised. And then there was the volunteer time spent helping with victims of the storm, as well as the cleanup after the floodwaters receded. He doubted few people on the police force hadn't thought about quitting, and a lot had, leaving the force understaffed in a time when it needed more dedicated officers, not less.

Not that Jay blamed anyone for leaving. Not only were they helping victims of the hurricane, many officers, too, were dealing with the loss of their own homes and loved ones.

He, too, needed a change. It wasn't just the horrendous hours he'd worked. Witnessing the horror of the hurricane and watching the city struggle to recover while the Feds pointed fingers at each other was bad enough. But then knowing that so much evidence, painfully collected over the years, had literally been washed away—that had settled on him like a weight. So much waste. So much to do to bring things back.

At thirty, he was already jaded.

And something—some last piece of tragedy—had sent him on this journey away from New Orleans.

Had it been the looters—those who were desperate or criminal enough to take advantage of the tragedy?

The victims trapped in their own homes, or nursing homes?

The lack of a quick response by the federal government?

The near-death of a city he loved?

Or was it the fact that his own home had been to-

taled by the screaming wind and flood that had torn his
rented cottage from its foundation, ruining nearly
everything he'd owned?

And how much of the disaster could he blame for his
ill-fated romance with Gayle? Had the demise of their
relationship been his fault? Hers? The situation?

He gave the dog fresh water in an old saucepan, then
opened his beer. As he took a long swallow from the long
neck, he stared through the grimy, rain-spattered window to the backyard. Through the panes he saw a bat
swoop near the branches of a solitary magnolia tree.
Dusk was falling rapidly, a reminder he had work to do.

Twisting his head, he heard his vertebrae crack and
adjust as he walked to the second bedroom—still painted
a nauseating shade of pink—where he'd set up a desk,
lamp, and small file cabinet. A dog bed was in the corner
and Bruno found an old half-chewed rawhide "bone"
and started working on it. Jay took another swallow of
his Lone Star, then set the beer down. He opened his
notebook computer and set it on the chipped Formica
desktop before hitting the power button. With a whirr,
the PC started and images appeared. Seconds later he
was on the Internet, eyeballing his e-mail.

Imbedded in the spam and mail from coworkers and
friends was another note from Gayle. His gut clenched
a bit as he opened the missive, read her quick little
cheery e-note, and found no humor in the joke she'd
forwarded to him. No big surprise. They'd agreed to be
civil to each other, remain friends, but who was kidding
whom? It wasn't working. Their relationship was dead.
Had been dying long before the storm hit.

He didn't respond. It was as pointless as the diamond ring that sat in his bureau drawer in New Orleans. His lips twisted at that. He hadn't had much luck
in the ring department. Years before he'd given a "promise
ring" to his high school sweetheart, and Kristi Bentz had
promptly gotten involved with a TA when she'd gone

off to school up here, at All Saints College. How about that for a bit of irony? Years later, when he'd finally offered a ring to Gayle, she'd accepted the diamond and begun to plan their life together—his life—to the point that he'd felt as if a noose had been draped over his neck. With each passing day the rope drew tighter until he hadn't been able to breathe. His attitude had rankled Gayle, and she'd become all the more possessive. She'd called him at all hours of the night, had become jealous of his friends, his coworkers, even his damned career. And she'd never let him forget that he'd wanted to marry Kristi Bentz long before he'd met her. Gayle had been certain he'd never stopped pining for his high school sweetheart.

Which was just damned stupid.

So he'd asked for his ring back.

And had it hurled at his forehead, where it had cut his skin and left a small scar just over his left eyebrow, evidence of Gayle's fury.

He figured he'd ducked a bigger missile when he'd called off the wedding.

So much for true love.

Grabbing the remote for the small television balanced upon the filing cabinet, he skimmed through his e-mail. Half listening to the news as he waited for a sports report and an update on the Saints, he'd started reading through a dozen other pieces of e-mail when he caught the end of a news report on the television.

". . . missing from the campus of All Saints College since before Christmas, the coed was last seen here, in Cramer Hall, by her roommate on December eighteenth around four-thirty."

Jay swung all of his attention to the screen, where a female reporter in a blue parka, battling wind and rain in a threatening sky, was staring into the camera. The report had been taped in front of the brick edifice of the dorm in which Kristi Bentz had lived years ago as a freshman. An image of Kristi as she was then, with her long, auburn hair, athletic body, and deep set, intelligent eyes, sizzled through his brain. He'd been stupid about her back then, certain she was "the one." Of course since that time, he'd learned how wrong he'd been. Thankfully she'd broken it off, and he'd avoided a marriage that would've certainly ended up a trap for both of them. Talk about a screwed up family!

". . . Since that day, a week before Christmas," the reporter was saying, "no one has seen Rylee Ames alive." A picture of the twenty-ish girl flashed onto the screen. With blue eyes, streaked, blond hair, and a bright smile, Rylee Ames looked like the quintessential "California girl," a cheerleader type, though the reporter was saying that she'd attended high school in Tempe, Arizona, and Laredo, Texas.

"This is Belinda Del Rey, reporting for WMTA, in Baton Rouge."

*Rylee Ames.* The name sounded familiar.

Bothered, Jay quickly logged onto the college's Web site and checked his class list, one that was updated as students added or dropped classes from their schedules. The first name on his roster was Ames, Rylee.

His cop radar was on full alert and he had to slow his mind from reeling onto one horrifying scenario after another. Rape, torture, murder—he'd seen so many violent crimes, but he tried not to leap to any conclusions, not yet. There was no evidence that she'd met with foul play, just that she was missing.

Kids her age dropped out, changed colleges, or took off on ski vacations or to rock concerts without telling anyone. For that matter she could have eloped.

But maybe not. He'd worked at the crime lab in New Orleans long enough to have a bad feeling about this student he'd never met. He took another swallow of beer and read lower on the roster.

Arnette, Jordan.

Bailey, Wister.
Braddock, Ira.
Bentz, Kristi.
Calloway, Hiram.
Crenshaw, Geoffrey.
*Wait! What?*
*Bentz, Kristi?*

His eyes narrowed on the screen, zeroing in on the familiar name that still had an impact that sent his blood pressure soaring.

*No way! She was haunting his thoughts!*

Kristi Bentz *couldn't* be in his class! *Could not!* What kind of cruel twist of fate or irony would that be? But there her name was, big as life. He wasn't foolish enough to think it might be another student with the same name. He had to face the fact that for three hours each week on Monday nights, he'd see her again.

*Crap!*

The rain pummeled the windows and he stared at the class roster as if mesmerized. Images of Kristi flitted through his mind: Long hair flying as she ran from him through a forest, the play of shadowy light catching her through the canopy of branches, her laughter infectious; emerging from a swimming pool, water dripping from her toned body, her smile triumphant if she'd won the meet, her frown deep and impenetrable if she'd lost; lying beneath him on a blanket in the back of his truck, moonlight shimmering against her perfect body.

"Stop it!" he said out loud, and Bruno, ever vigilant, was on his feet in an instant, barking gruffly. "No, boy, it's . . . it's nothing." Jay promptly shut out the stupid, visceral images of his horny youth. He hadn't seen Kristi in over five years and he figured she'd changed. And for all his romantic fantasies about her, there were other images that weren't quite as nice. Kristi had a temper and a razor sharp tongue.

He'd figured long ago that he was well rid of her.

But the truth was, he'd read and heard about her brushes with death, about her dealings with madmen, about her long stint in the hospital recovering from the latest attack, and he'd felt bad, even going so far as to call a florist to send her flowers before changing his mind. Kristi was like a bad habit, one a man couldn't quite shake. Jay was fine as long as he didn't hear about her, read about her, or see her. All those old emotions were locked away under carefully guarded keys. He'd been interested in other women. He'd been engaged, hadn't he? Still, having to see her on a weekly basis . . .

It would probably be good for him, he decided suddenly. "Character building" as his mother used to say whenever he was in trouble and had to pay the price of punishment, usually at the hands of his father.

"Hell," he muttered under his breath as the truth of the matter sank in. His jaw slid to one side and for a second he let himself fantasize about teaching a class where Kristi was his student, where she would have to be under his scrutiny, his control. Jesus! What was he thinking? He'd decided long ago that never seeing her again was just fine. Now it looked like he'd be staring at her face for three hours once a week.

Draining his beer, he slammed the empty bottle onto his desk. He hadn't altered his whole damned work schedule, started working ten-hour shifts, gone through the headache of changing his whole life only to have to see Kristi every week. His jaw clenched so hard it ached.

Maybe she'd drop his class. The second she realized he was stepping in for Dr. Monroe, Kristi would probably alter her schedule. No doubt she didn't want to see him any more than he wanted to deal with her. And the thought that he would be her teacher would probably really bug her. She'd resign from his class. Of course she would.

Good.

He read the rest of the class list of thirty-five students interested in criminology—make that thirty-four. His gaze drifted back to the first name on the list: Rylee Ames. Disturbed, Jay scratched at the stubble on his chin.

What the hell had happened to her?

# CHAPTER 2

" . . . No loud music, no pets, no smoking, it's all here in the lease," Irene Calloway said, though she herself smelled suspiciously of cigarette smoke. In her early seventies with a few short wisps of gray hair poking from under a red beret, Irene was as thin as a rail beneath her faded baggy jeans and oversized T-shirt. Her jacket was a man's flannel shirt and she peered at Kristi through thick glasses. She and Kristi were seated at a small scarred table in the furnished studio apartment on the third floor. The place had a bit of charm with its dormers, old fireplace, plank floors, and watery glass windows. It was cozy and quiet and Kristi couldn't believe her luck in finding the place. Irene jabbed a long, gnarled finger at the fine print of the lease.

"I read it," Kristi assured her, though the copy she'd been faxed had been blurry. Wasting no more time, she signed both sets of the six-month lease and handed one back to her new landlady.

"You're not married?"

"No."

"No kids?"

Kristi bristled as she shook her head. Irene's questions were a little too personal.

"No boyfriend? The lease stipulates only one person up here." She motioned to the small loft that had once

been an attic, possibly servants' quarters of the grand
old house now chopped into apartments.

"What if I decide I need a roommate?" Kristi asked,
though whoever that might be would be relegated to the
tired-looking love seat or an air bed.

Irene's lips thinned. "Lease would have to be rewrit-
ten. I'd want to run a security check on any prospective
tenants and, of course, the rent would go up along with
another security deposit. And no subletting. Got it?"

"So far, it's just me," Kristi said, somehow managing
to hold her tongue. She needed this apartment. Housing
was hard to find in the middle of the school year, especially any apartments close to campus. A stroke of luck
helped her discover this loft on the Internet. It had been
one of the only units she could afford within walking
distance to school. As for a roommate, Kristi would
rather fly solo, but finances might dictate trying to find
someone to share the rent and utilities.

"Good. I've no use for nonsense."

Kristi let that one slide. For now. But the older woman
was beginning to bug her.

"You don't have any other questions?" Irene asked as
she folded her copy crisply with her fingernails and slid
it into a side pocket of a hand-crocheted bag.

"Not yet. Maybe once I move in."

Irene's dark eyes narrowed behind her glasses as if
she were really sizing Kristi up.

"If there are any problems, you can also call my
grandson, Hiram. He's in One-A." She waved her fingers as she explained, "He's kind of the manager on
duty. Gets a break on his rent to fix things and take care
of small problems." The furrows over her eyebrows deepened. "Damned parents of his split up and forgot they
had a couple of kids. Stupid." She fished into the pocket
of her jeans and withdrew a business card with her name
and phone number along with Hiram's, then slid it across
the table. "I told my son he was making a mistake tak-

ing up with that woman, but did he listen? Oh, no . . . Damn fool."

As if realizing she was saying too much, Irene quickly added, "Hiram, he's a good kid. Works hard. He'll help you move in, if you want, does all the fix-up. Learned it from my husband, may he rest in peace." Pushing to her feet, she added, "Oh, I'm having Hiram install new dead bolts on all the doors. And if you have any window latches that aren't solid, he'll take care of those, too. I suppose you've heard the latest?" Her gray eyebrows shot up over the tops of her rimless glasses and she scratched at her chin nervously, as if she were weighing what she was about to reveal. "Several students have disappeared here this school year. No bodies found, y'know, but the police seem to suspect foul play. If ya ask me, they're all runaways." She glanced away and muttered, "Happens all the time, but you can never be too careful." She nodded, as if agreeing with herself, tucking her bag under her arm.

"I saw the news coverage."

"Things were different when I grew up here," Irene assured. "Most of the classes were taught by priests and nuns, and the college, it had a reputation, but now . . . ach!" She waved one hand into the air, as if brushing aside a bothersome mosquito. "Now it seems they hire all sorts . . . weirdos, if you ask me, anyone who has a damned degree. They teach classes about vampires and demons and all kinds of satanic things . . . religions of the world, not just Christianity, mind you, and . . . then there are those ridiculous morality plays! Like we're still living in the Middle Ages. Oh, don't get me going about that English Department. A nutcase is in charge of it, let me tell you. Natalie Croft has no business teaching a class, much less running a department." She snorted as she opened the door. "Ever since Father Anthony—oh, excuse me, it's 'Father Tony' because he's so hip I guess, everyone's best friend—ever since he took over from Father Stephen, all hell has broken out. Literally."

Lips compressed, Irene shook her head as she stepped over the threshold onto the porch with its poor lighting. "How's that for progress? Morality plays, for crying out loud? Vampires? It's like All Saints stepped back into the Dark Ages!" She grabbed hold of the railing and headed down the stairs.

Open-minded, Irene Calloway was not. Kristi neglected to mention that some of the classes the old woman had disdained were already on her schedule.

Locking the door after her new landlady, Kristi checked all the windows, including the large one in the bedroom leading to an ancient, rusted fire escape.

The latch on every window in the small apartment was broken. Kristi figured she wouldn't mention the lack of security to her father. Immediately, as she headed down the exterior staircase for her things, she called Hiram's cell. Irene's grandson didn't answer, but Kristi left a message and her phone number, then began hauling her few belongings to her new home, a crow's nest overlooking the stone fence surrounding All Saints College.

Seated at her desk at the Baton Rouge Police Department, Detective Portia Laurent stared at the pictures of the four coeds missing from All Saints College. None of the girls had resurfaced. Just disappeared, not only from Louisiana, but, it seemed, the face of the earth.

As computer keyboards clicked, printers hummed, and an old clock ticked off the final days of the year, Portia eyed the pictures for what seemed to be the millionth time. They were all so young. Smiling girls with fresh faces, intelligence and hope shining from their eyes.

Or were their expressions masks?

Behind those practiced smiles was there something darker lurking?

The girls had been troubled, that much had been ascertained. So they'd been written off. No one, not the other members of the police department, not the administration of the college, not even the missing girls' families seemed to think that any serious foul play was involved. Nope. These smiling once-upon-a-time students were just runaways, headstrong wild girls who had, for one reason or another, decided to take a hike and not reappear.

Had they been into drugs?

Prostitution?

Or were they just tired of school?

Had they connected with a boyfriend who had whisked them away?

Had they decided to hitchhike around the country?

Had they wanted a quickie vacation and never returned?

The answers and opinions varied, but Portia seemed to be the only person on the planet who cared. She'd taken copies of these girls' campus ID pictures and pinned them to the bulletin board of her cubicle. The originals were in the general file of all the recent missing persons, but these were different; these photos connected every girl who had attended All Saints College, disappeared, then left no trail. No credit cards had been used, no checks cashed, no ATMs accessed. Their cell phone usages had stopped on the evenings they'd gone missing, but not one of them had turned up in a local hospital. None of them had bought a bus or plane ticket, nor had there been activity on their MySpace pages.

Portia stared at their pictures and wondered what the hell had happened to them. Deep inside, she believed them all dead, but she hoped against hope that her jaded cop instincts were wrong.

None of the girls had owned a vehicle, and none had

called the state of Louisiana home until they'd enrolled at the small private school. The last persons known to have seen each of them hadn't noticed anything strange, nor could they give the police even the tiniest hint of what each girl had in mind, where she could have gone, whom she might have seen.

It was frustrating as hell.

Portia reached into her purse for her pack of cigarettes, then reminded herself that she'd quit. Three months, four days, and five hours ago—not that she was counting. She grabbed a piece of nicotine gum and found little satisfaction in chewing as she gazed from one picture to the next.

The first victim, missing nearly a year since last January, was an African-American student, Dionne Harmon, with dark skin, high cheekbones, a beautiful, toothy grin, and a tattoo that said "LOVE" entwined with hummingbirds and flowers low on her back. She hailed from New York City. Her parents had never married and were now both deceased, the mother from cancer, the father in an industrial accident. Her only sibling, a brother by the name of Desmond, already had three kids of his own, had skipped on his child support, and when Portia had tried to reach him he'd told her he wasn't interested in "what had happened to the 'ho.' "

"Nice," Portia remembered aloud, recalling the phone conversation. None of Dionne's friends could explain what had happened to her, but the last person to admit seeing her, one of her professors, Dr. Grotto, had at least seemed concerned. Grotto's specialty was teaching classes on vampirism, sometimes using a Y in the spelling—like *vampyrism*—which was a little odd, though people could become intrigued and inspired by the strangest things sometimes. In his midthirties, Grotto was sexier than any college professor had the right to be. The old Hollywood description of "tall, dark, and handsome" fit him to a T, and he certainly was far more interesting than any of the old dusty profs who had been her teachers in her two years at All Saints over a decade earlier.

The other missing girls were Caucasian, though they, too, had disjointed, uninterested families who had written them off as irresponsible runaways, "always in trouble."

How odd they had all ended up at All Saints and subsequently disappeared within eighteen months.

Coincidence? Portia didn't think so.

The media had finally noticed and was adding some pressure. The public was now nervous, the police department receiving more calls.

Since Dionne had disappeared over a year ago, Tara Atwater and Monique DesCartes had also vanished, Monique in May, Tara in October, and now Rylee Ames. All of them took some of the same classes, primarily in the English Department, including the class on vampyrism taught by Dr. Dominic Grotto.

*Slap!*

A file landed atop her photos.

"Hey!" Detective Del Vernon said, resting a hip on her desk. "Still caught up in the missing girls?"

*Here we go again,* Portia thought on an inward sigh, expecting a lecture from the ex-military man turned detective. Vernon had the "three-B-thing" going for him: bald, black, and beautiful. Though he was in his forties, he'd never lost his U.S. Marine-honed build. His shoulders were wide and straight, his waist trim, and according to Stephanie, one of the secretaries for the department, his butt was "tight enough to hold in his bad-ass attitude." And she was right. Vernon had a great body. Portia tried not to notice.

"What's this?" she asked, picking up the file and flipping it open to a crime scene report and the picture of a dead woman.

"Jane Doe . . . throat slashed, from the Memphis PD.

Looks like it could be the same guy who killed the woman we found last week near River Road."

"Beth Staples."

"I want you to check it out."

"You got it," she said, and waited for him to remind her that the girls missing from All Saints weren't known to be victims of homicide and therefore not their concern.

Yet.

But he didn't. Instead Vernon's cell phone rang and he thumped his fingers onto her desk before walking back through the maze of cubicles. "Vernon," he said crisply, crossing the threshold to his private office and kicking the glass door shut behind him.

Portia picked up the Jane Doe file, turning her attention away from the pictures of the coeds. There was a chance that she was wrong, a chance that the missing coeds were, indeed, still alive, just teenage runaways rebelling and getting into trouble.

But she wasn't laying odds on it.


Two days after Kristi moved in, she landed a job as a waitress at a diner three blocks from campus. She wasn't going to get rich making minimum wage and tips, but she would have some flexibility with her shifts, which was exactly what she'd wanted. Waiting tables wasn't glamorous work, but it beat the hell out of working for Gulf Auto and Life Insurance Company, where she'd spent too many hours to count in the past few years. Besides, she hadn't given up her dream of writing true crime. She figured with the right story, she could become the next Ann Rule.

Or a close facsimile thereof.

Twilight had settled as she crossed campus, her backpack slung over one shoulder, her head hunched into her shoulders as the first drops of rain began to

spatter the ground on this, the day before New Year's
Eve. A gust of winter wind stole through the quad, rattling the branches of the oak and pine trees before
brushing the back of her neck with a frosty kiss. She
shivered, surprised at the drop in temperature. She was
tired from the move and her legs felt leaden as she angled past Cramer Hall, where she'd lived her freshman
year of college nearly ten years earlier. It hadn't
changed much, certainly not as much as she had, she
thought ruefully.

Her breath fogged in front of her, and from the corner of her eye she thought she saw a movement, something dark and shadowy, in the thick hedge near the
library. Gaslights glowed blue, casting watery light, and
though she squinted, she saw no one. Just her overactive
imagination.

But who could blame her? Between her own experi-
ences at the hands of predators, her father's warnings,
and her landlady's remarks, she was bound to be jumpy.
"Get over it," she admonished, cutting past Wagner
House, a huge stone edifice with dark mullioned windows and black iron filigree. Tonight, the grand old
manor seemed foreboding, even sinister. *And you think
you can write true crime? How about fiction? Maybe
horror? Or something equally creepy with your imagination! Geez, Kristi, get a grip!*

Hurrying as the rain began to pour, she heard footsteps on the walk behind her. She hazarded a quick
glance over her shoulder and saw no one. Nothing. And
the footsteps seemed to have stopped. As if whoever
was following her didn't want to be discovered. Or was
mimicking her own hesitation.

Her stomach squeezed and she thought about the can
of pepper spray in the backpack. Between the spray
and her own skill in self-defense . . .

*Dear God, get over yourself!*

Hoisting her bag higher, she started off again, ears

straining for the scrape of leather against concrete, the whisper of heavy breathing as whoever it was gave chase, but all she heard was the sound of traffic in the streets, tires humming over wet asphalt, engines rumbling, an occasional squeal of brakes or whine of gears. Nothing sinister. Nothing evil. Still, her heart was hammering and despite her mental berating, she unzipped a pocket of the leather pack and fumbled for the canister. Within seconds it was in her hand.

Again she looked over her shoulder.

Again she saw nothing.

Half running, she cut across the lawn and through the gate nearest her apartment. She'd reached the street when her cell phone jangled. Jumping wildly, she cursed softly under her breath as she reached into her coat pocket. Her father's name lit the screen. Clicking on, and grateful, for once, that he had called, she greeted, "Hey, don't you ever work?"

"Even cops get breaks every once in a while."

"And so you decided to take one and check up on me?"

"You called me," he reminded her.

"Oh, right." She'd forgotten . . . one more little reminder that she wasn't a hundred percent—her damned faulty memory. Every once in a while, she totally blanked out on something important. "Look, I wanted to tell you my new address and that I got a job at the Bard's Board. It's a diner and all the food is named after Shakespearean characters. You know, like Iago's iced latte and Romeo's Reuben and Lady Macbeth's finger sandwiches or something. It's owned by two ex-English teachers, I think. Anyway, I have to learn them all by Monday morning when I start. I guess it'll get me back into the swing of the whole memorizing thing again."

"Romeo's Reuben sounds sexual."

"Only to you, Dad. It's a sandwich. I might not mention it to your partner."

"Montoya will love it."

She smiled and, as she reached the apartment house, asked, "So how're you feeling?"

"Fine. Why?"

She thought of the image of him fading to gray as she'd driven away the other day. "Just checkin'."

"You're making me feel old."

"You *are* old, Dad."

"Smart-ass kid," he said, but there was humor in his voice.

She almost said, "A chip off the old block," but curbed the automatic response. Rick Bentz was still a little touchy when reminded that he wasn't her biological father. "Listen, I've got to run. I'll talk to ya later," she said instead. "Love ya!"

"Me, too."

She started up the exterior stairs only to meet a petite girl at the second-floor landing who was struggling with what appeared to be a leaking garbage bag.

The dark-haired Asian girl looked up and smiled. "You must be the new neighbor."

"Yeah. Third floor. I'm Kristi Bentz."

"Mai Kwan. 202." She gestured widely toward the open door of the nearest unit that occupied the second floor. "Are you a student? Hey, give me a sec while I take this to the Dumpster." Moving lithely, she eased around Kristi and hurried down the remaining stairs, her flip-flops clicking loudly in the rain.

Kristi wondered if she wasn't some kind of kook with her sandals and dripping bag. And anyway, Kristi wasn't about to wait in the cold and rain. Reaching the third floor, she heard the snap of Mai's flip-flops hurrying up the staircase below her. Kristi had just unlocked her door and stepped inside when Mai called out from the darkness. "Kristi, wait!"

*For what?* Kristi thought, but stood just inside the

door as the scent of rainwater swept through her apartment. Mai appeared at that moment and didn't wait for an invitation, just waltzed right in, her sandals making puddles on the old hardwood floor.

"Oh, wow!" Mai said, eyeing Kristi's new place. Her hair, chopped into shaggy layers that ended at her chin, gleamed in the lamplight. "This looks great!" She grinned, showing off white, straight teeth rimmed in shiny coral lip gloss. Her dark eyes with their carefully shadowed lids took in the space.

A small kitchen was tucked behind bifold doors at one end of the long room, which was punctuated with dormers that allowed views over the walls of the campus. Kristi had pushed a small desk into one of the dormer alcoves, and a reading chair and ottoman into the other. She'd cleaned the furniture as best she could and scattered a few cheap area rugs over the floor. One of the lamps, a fake Tiffany, was hers. The other, a modern floor lamp with a shade that was seared from being held too close to a lightbulb, had come with the unit. The walls were covered with posters of famous writers and pictures of Kristi's family, and she'd bought candles and positioned them over the windowsills and scratched end tables. With a mirror she'd purchased at a second-hand store, and a few well-placed pots with growing plants, the place looked as student-chic as she could make it.

"This is great! Geez, you've even got a fireplace. Well, I guess all the units on the north end do." Mai walked to the thick carved mantel and ran her fingers along the old wood. "I love fires. You're a student here, too?" she added.

"Yeah. A junior. Journalism major," Kristi clarified.

"I was surprised when I heard this had been rented." Mai was still walking through the place, glancing at the pictures Kristi had hung on the wall. Squinting, she leaned closer to a framed five-by-seven. "Hey, this is you and that famous cop in New Orleans . . . wait a sec. Kristi Bentz, as in the daughter of—?"

"Detective Rick Bentz, yes," Kristi admitted, a little uncomfortable that Mai had recognized her father.

Mai stepped closer to the picture, eyeing the framed snapshot as if to memorize every nuance in the photograph of Kristi and her dad on a boat. The picture was five years old, but one of her favorites. "He cracked a couple of serial killer cases around here, didn't he? Ones up at that old mental asylum? What was the name of it?" She snapped her fingers and before Kristi could answer, she said, "Our Lady of Virtues, that was it. Oh, wow. Rick Bentz . . . Huh . . . He's kinda like a living legend."

Well, now, that was stretching the truth. "He's just my dad."

"Wait a minute . . ." Mai cocked her head. "And you . . . you . . ." She turned and faced Kristi again and a look of awe passed over her face. "You were involved, too, weren't you? Like almost a victim. Jesus! I'm kinda into the whole serial killer thing. . . . I mean I don't glorify them or anything—they're evil—but I find them fascinating, don't you?"

"No." Kristi was firm on that. However, there was the true-crime book she was considering. In that way, she, too, held more than a passing interest in the deviants whose number seemed to grow more prolific every day. But she didn't feel like going into it with a neighbor she'd met less than five minutes earlier. "You said something about being surprised that I rented the apartment."

"That *anyone* did." Mai glanced again at the picture of Kristi and her father.

"Really? Why?"

"Because of its history."

"What history?"

"Oh . . . you know." When Kristi didn't respond, Mai added, "About the previous tenant."

"You're going to have to fill me in."

"It was Tara Atwater, as in the same Tara Atwater that went missing last spring term?"

"What?" Kristi's heart nearly stopped cold.

"Tara is the third missing girl. The second one, Monique, is the reason the press kind of started nosing around a little more intently. Last May. But it was the end of spring term and people just assumed she dropped out. The story kind of died until this fall when Monique left school before the end of fall term. Where have you been?"

"In New Orleans," Kristi said, pretending ignorance. She didn't want Mai to see how affected she truly was.

"You *had* to have heard about the missing students." Without waiting for an invitation, Mai plopped onto the oversized chair, sitting on it sideways so that her feet dangled over one of the arms. "It's been all over the news . . . well, at least in the last few days. Before then, the administration acted as if each of them had just dropped out or run off or whatever. No one could substantiate that any of them were really missing. But what's really weird is that their families don't even seem to care. Everyone assumes they just took off and poof"—she snapped her fingers again—"vanished into thin air."

*Not everyone,* Kristi thought, remembering her father's worries.

"They turn up missing and it's a big deal. Then the story gets shuffled off page one and everyone seems to forget, until the next girl disappears." She frowned, her smooth forehead wrinkling in frustration.

"And one of them lived here." Kristi motioned to the interior of her new apartment, the "steal" she'd found on the Internet. No wonder it had been in her price range.

"Yeah. Tara. From Georgia. Southern Georgia, I think, yeah, some tiny podunk town. A Georgia Peach, whatever that means. I don't know much about her. No one did. I mean I saw her a few times, but never thought twice. Then she ended up missing; no one really realized she was gone, for a while."

"So that's why no one rented the place?"

"Mrs. Calloway put it on the Internet and stuck the FOR RENT sign up, then Rylee Ames disappears. Now the missing girls are big news again—I can't believe you didn't know!—but by then, you'd rented the place." She plucked a tiny feather off the overstuffed arm of the chair and let it drift to the floor.

The hairs on the back of Kristi's neck raised as she thought about Tara Atwater. Had she really rented a space most recently occupied by a girl who was missing, who could have ended up the victim of foul play? Damn, what were the chances of that? Kristi observed her studio with new eyes. She asked, "And the police, they're sure she disappeared . . . that the others disappeared, too? That they weren't just runaways?"

"'Just runaways,'" Mai repeated. "Like that's okay." She lifted a shoulder. "I don't know what the police think. I really don't think they put the whole thing together until recently." She let out a disgusted sigh. "What's that saying about our culture, huh? *Just* runaways."

Kristi thought about the latches and locks in her apartment that didn't work. "So tell me about Hiram."

"Irene's grandson?" Mai shrugged. "Major geek. Into all things technical."

"He's supposed to fix the latches on my windows and install a new dead bolt."

"In which century? He's like a ghost, you never see him."

"A techno-major geek ghost?"

"Exactly. Hey, if you're not busy on New Year's Eve,

some of my friends and I are going to hang out at the Watering Hole. You could join us and y'know, ring in the new year. 'Auld Lang Syne,' funky little hats, confetti, champagne, and crap. The cover's really cheap. Just enough to pay for the band."

"Maybe," Kristi said, acting as if her social calendar wasn't completely empty. "I'll see."

The first notes of a classical piece Kristi couldn't quite place erupted and Mai reached into her pocket for her cell. She glanced at the screen and grinned. "Gotta run," she said quickly as she climbed to her feet. "Nice to meet ya."

"You, too."

"Seriously. Call me if you want to party and kick in the new year." She pushed a button on her cell phone as she eased to the door and opened it with her free hand. "Hey! I was wondering when I was gonna hear from you. A text? Nah, I didn't get it. . . ." She was out the door and wrapped in her conversation with the person on the other end of the call.

Kristi closed the door behind her and, alone in the apartment, was left with a creepy feeling. "Don't let it get to you," she told herself. The building was centuries old, people could have died here, been killed here. All sorts of atrocities could have occurred here over the years. Tara Atwater's disappearance wasn't even necessarily a crime. She eyed the cozy room but couldn't fight a sudden chill. What had happened to the girl? Was her disappearance really linked to the others? What had happened to all of them? Had they all met some horrid fate as her father seemed to think?

*Find out, Kristi. This is the story you've been looking for. Here you are in the thick of it, in the very damned apartment from which one of them went missing. This is it!*

She picked up her purse and dialed Hiram. True to the history of her previous three calls, she was sent directly to voice mail. "Great," Kristi muttered, grabbing her purse. She wasn't waiting for the dweeb. How tough could it be to install a damned dead bolt? She'd go to a hardware store, buy the hardware she needed, and put it in herself. She figured she'd take the expenses off the next month's rent and Hiram could explain it to his granny himself.

Locking the door behind her, she headed to her car. No one followed her. No dark figure lurked in the shadows. No sinister eyes trailed her every move. At least none she could distinguish in the thick, shimmering, rain-washed shrubbery surrounding the pock-marked parking lot. She climbed into the Honda without incident, and after turning on the headlights and wipers, stared through the windshield, again seeing nothing out of the ordinary. Maybe Mai was just messing with her, jerking her chain.

*Why? Sooner or later she'd be found out. No, Mai Kwan was telling the truth as she knew it.*

"Wonderful," Kristi groused to herself as she backed up, then rammed the car into drive. No one was about but a man walking his dog near the gaslight, and a biker pedaling fast enough to keep the beam of his headlight steady. No criminal was waiting for her. No deranged psycho hiding between the parked cars on the street. All was quiet. All was normal.

But as she drove onto the street, she couldn't shake the feeling that something was about to go wrong.


So she'd returned.

Like a salmon drawn from the sea to a creek to spawn.

Kristi Bentz was a student again at All Saints.

It was fitting somehow, he thought, from his rooftop viewpoint. Through the skeletal branches of the trees near the thick stone wall of the campus, he focused his binoculars at the attic loft she'd rented.

Where one of the others had once lived.

A sign from the Almighty?

Or from the Prince of Darkness?

He grinned as he watched her check her window latches, make small talk with the Asian girl, then fly down the exterior steps to that pathetic little car she'd parked beneath a security lamp in the nearest lot. His view was cut off, of course, once she was down the stairs and below the wall, but he knew what she was doing.

The sound of the Honda's engine firing up was barely audible over the drip of rain and swoosh of traffic on the side streets, but he heard it. Was tuned to it. Because it was she, the prodigal daughter. How perfect.

His throat went dry at the thought of her: long dark hair streaked with red, pert nose, intelligent green eyes, and wide mouth. . . . Oh, what she could do with those lips! He imagined them trailing down his body as she let her tongue slide across his flat abdomen, her breath hot and anxious as she undid the fastening to his jeans.

His groin tightened and his cock grew thick and he knew a minute of regret. He had to deny himself, at least for now. There was another . . .

He slid through the darkness and inside the fortresslike structure within the campus walls. Without turning on any lights, he made his way to the stairwell and eased down the steps, quiet as a cat. His gift was his vision, a gaze that could penetrate the darkness when others couldn't. He was born with the ability, and even in the thick Louisiana nights, when low-lying fog clung to the cypress trees and oozed over the water of the bayou, he had vision. Enough that he could see prey and hunt without the use of night goggles or flashlights.

His ability had served him well, he thought, as he

slipped outside and took in a deep breath of the fresh scent of rain . . . and more. He imagined he smelled the salty scent of Kristi Bentz's skin, but he knew the aroma to be an illusion.

The first of many, he imagined, as he jogged silently and easily through the night. His body was in perfect shape. Honed. Ready.

For the ultimate sacrifice.

She wouldn't be taken easily.

But she would be taken.

And, at first, willingly.

He just had to plant the seeds to pique her curiosity.

And then she wouldn't be able to stop herself.

# CHAPTER 3

**"** . . . This is Hiram Calloway," a thin, reedy voice said over the static of a bad cell connection. "I got your message about the locks. I thought I'd stop by your apartment and see if I could fix them."

"Too late," Kristi said, irritated. Only today, at two o'clock on New Year's Eve, had he decided to return her calls. "I already installed new ones and put in new latches on the windows. I couldn't wait any longer. I'll bill you."

"What?" he shrieked, his nasal voice hiking up a notch. "You can't—"

"I can and I did."

"That kind of thing has to be approved. It's . . . it's in the lease, paragraph seven—"

"I'm just telling you, the apartment wasn't secure and I think there's something about that in the lease, too. Check it. And I don't know what the paragraph is, but I've already taken care of the problem."

"But—"

"I have to get back to work," she said, snapping her cell off. She slipped the phone into the pocket of her apron and walked past two cooks loitering under the overhang of the back porch where they were smoking in their greasy chef coats. The screen door slapped shut behind her as she made her way through a maze of hallways in the thirties bungalow that had been converted to a restaurant years before. The history of the building had been written up in the local paper ten years earlier and was yellowing in its frame that hung between the bathrooms, marked LORDS and LADIES. As if any of the clientele were blue bloods.

Retying her apron, Kristi passed through swinging doors from the kitchen to the dining area and stopped fuming about Hiram. At least he'd finally called back. Kristi had been beginning to think the manager/grandson was a figment of Irene's imagination.

So far, it had been a busy morning and early afternoon, but things were slowing down, thank God. Her feet were sore, her clothes feeling grimy from the grease and smoke that hung in the air and clung to her hair. After a few hours working frantically in her section, she'd wondered why she hadn't taken her father's advice and tried to nail a desk job at another insurance company. After all, it wasn't as if she were getting rich on tips. However, just the memory of hours on the phone with complaining customers of Gulf Auto and Life had reminded her of her goal and her dream of writing true crime.

Her stomach rumbled, reminding her that she hadn't eaten anything since downing a muffin on the fly early in the morning. After her shift she thought she might splurge on a Mercutio melt and a slice of King Lear's key lime pie.

*Happy New Year,* she thought sarcastically as she grabbed a pot of coffee and refilled half-empty cups on the tables in her section.

A group of women strolled in and squeezed into the worn bench seat of a corner booth.

Snagging four plastic-encased menus, Kristi approached. The women hardly noticed, they were so into their conversation, and one of the voices sounded familiar. Kristi couldn't believe it, but as she stared at the

back of a curly head, she realized that she was about to
serve Lucretia Stevens, her original roommate when she
was an undergrad and living in the close quarters of
Cramer Hall. Inside, Kristi cringed. She and Lucretia
had never gotten along and had been as different as day
to night. Kristi, in those days, had been a party girl and
Lucretia a brainiac who, when she hadn't been studying, had spent hours flipping through *Brides* magazine
and munching on Cheetos. She hadn't had any social
life and had been evasive when talking about her boyfriend, who'd gone to another college. Kristi had never
seen the guy and had often wondered if he'd only existed in Lucretia's mind.

*What goes around, comes around,* she thought as she
slid menus in front of the women and asked them what
they wanted to drink.

"Kristi?" Lucretia asked, before anyone answered.

"Hi, Lucretia." Geez, *this* was going to be uncomfortable.

"What're you doing here?" Lucretia's eyes were wide,
probably due to the contacts that, when she'd worn them
in lieu of her glasses, had always made her appear owlish.

"Trying to take your order," Kristi said, offering a smile.

"Hey, everyone, this is Kristi Bentz, my old roommate when I was a freshman, oh, God, a kabillion years
ago." She laughed, then motioned toward a woman of
about twenty-five with narrow-framed glasses and dark
brown hair that fell to her shoulders. "Kristi, this is Ariel."

"Hi," Kristi said, shifting from one foot to the other.

"Oh, hi." Ariel nodded, then glanced past Kristi to
the door, as if she were looking for someone, at least
someone more interesting than Kristi.

"And this is Grace," Lucretia indicated her thin friend
who wore braces and had spiked, reddish hair. The
woman couldn't have weighed a hundred pounds. "And
this is Trudie." The last girl, seated next to Lucretia in

the booth, was heavier-set, had thick black hair pulled into a long ponytail, a smooth olive complexion and white teeth with a bit of a gap. All three managed smiles as Lucretia said, as if surprised, "Geez, Kristi, you look great."

"Thanks."

"Bentz?" Trudie repeated. "Wait a sec. Didn't I read about you?"

*Here we go,* Kristi thought. "Probably about my dad. He makes the press."

"Wait a minute. He's a cop, right?" Ariel asked, twisting her head and squinting up at Kristi. She was suddenly interested. "Didn't he crack that case at Our Lady of Virtues a year or so ago?" She shuddered. "That was soooo weird."

*Amen,* Kristi thought, anxious to end the personal conversation about a time she'd rather forget.

"Weren't you involved?" Lucretia was now serious. "I mean, didn't I read something about you being injured?" Her forehead wrinkled as she thought. "The way the article was slanted it was as if you were almost killed." She was nodding, her hair shimmering in dark curls beneath the overhead lamps. "Like before."

Kristi didn't want to be reminded of her close calls at the hands of sicko perverts. Twice already, she'd nearly been killed by a psychopath, and the shards of memory about those encounters were enough to turn her blood to ice. She needed to deflect the conversation and fast.

"It was a while back. I'm over it. So, the special today is red beans and rice, I mean Hamlet's hash."

But Lucretia wasn't about to be derailed. She had everyone at her table and the surrounding area's attention, and she wasn't going to let go. "I think I read or heard that you *died* and came back or something."

"Or something," Kristi said as all of the women at the table, Lucretia's friends who had been so animated a few minutes earlier, grew silent. The strains of an old Elvis tune ran over the clink of silverware, buzz of conversation, and hiss of the ancient heater as it struggled to keep the diner warm. She shrugged, relegating the story of her past to "who cares" status.

"Kristi's used to it," Lucretia said. "Lives the life."

Ariel asked, "What does it feel like to have a famous father?"

Pen poised over her order pad, Kristi ignored the knot in her gut. "Quasi famous. It's not like he's Brad Pitt or Tom Cruise or even—"

"We're not talking about movie stars." Lucretia interrupted her. "Just local celebs."

"Local celebs like Truman Capote and Louis Armstrong?" Kristi said.

"Dead," Trudie said.

"My dad's just a cop."

Lucretia stared at her as if she'd just said she'd become a devil worshipper. "He's not *just* anything."

Kristi held on to her patience with an effort. That hadn't been what she'd meant, but Lucretia had always had a way of twisting things around. Maybe it was because her divorced parents had hardly had time for her; they'd been so wrapped up in their own problems. Or, maybe it was something else entirely. Whatever it was, it was annoying and always had been.

"You're right," Kristi managed. "He's great, but he'd be the first to tell you he was just doing his job."

"How cool is that?" Trudie asked.

Time to end this. "So, anything to drink?" Kristi asked. "Coffee?"

Thankfully, Lucretia and her group picked up their menus and rattled off their choices.

"Two sweet teas, a Diet Coke, and a coffee. Got it," Kristi said, thankful to hurry back to the kitchen. Who would have thought that Lucretia would have kept up with her, or her father? Kristi and Lucretia hadn't kept in touch over the years; in fact, while living together, they hardly spoke. They'd had *nothing* in common before. Kristi doubted that had changed over the years.

"Old friends?" Ezma, a waitress with mocha-colored skin and impossibly white teeth, asked as she filled plastic glasses with shaved ice from a rumbling ice machine positioned near the soda dispenser. Ezma, barely five feet and a hundred pounds, was a part-time student and full-time waitress, a wife, and a mother of a precocious two-year-old.

"I guess." Kristi took three of the glasses and filled two from the pitcher of sweetened iced tea, then pushed a button on the soda machine and filled the final glass with diet cola, holding the dispenser button a second too long. The soda fizzled over the top. Sweeping a towel from a nearby hook, she swabbed at the spilled cola and topped off the glass. "One of the women"— she hitched her chin toward the table where Lucretia seemed to be holding court—"was my roommate when I first enrolled at All Saints, back before the turn of the millennium."

"Let me guess—Lucretia Stevens," Ezma said, sliding a glance toward the table.

"How did you know?"

"I guess I'm just omniscient."

"Yeah, right." Kristi smiled faintly.

"And"—she lifted a slim shoulder—"I eavesdrop."

"That's more like it."

Ezma laughed as she grabbed the dispenser handle for the water hose and filled the remaining glasses. "Actually, I had her for one of my classes, writing two twelve, I think it was."

"She's a professor?"

"Assistant."

Kristi was stunned. She'd always known Lucretia

was a perpetual student, but she'd never imagined she would actually stick around All Saints to teach.

"And I think she's involved with someone at the university. Another professor."

"Really?"

So much for Lucretia's college boyfriend, whom she'd pined about for the year Kristi had known her.

"Well, I have to admit, if I weren't a happily married woman, I might be interested. Some of the professors are hot!"

Kristi remembered some of her teachers from the past. Weird Dr. Northrup, edgy Dr. Sutter, and crusty, superior Dr. Zaroster. All of them were musty, slightly crotchety academics who suffered from superiority complexes. Definitely not "hot." Not even lukewarm. At least not in Kristi's vocabulary. "You're kidding me, right?"

"Uh-uh. I'm tellin' you, the staff at All Saints is something. At least the English Department. It's as if whoever was recruiting was looking at Hollywood head shots."

"Now I know you're full of it."

"Well, you'll see soon enough." Ezma added a slice of lemon to each glass. "Classes start next week. I bet you'll agree."

Kristi filled her tray. "And so you think Lucretia is dating one of these hotties?"

"Rumor has it. But I don't know which one. Whenever I get too close, she clams up, like she's hiding it or something."

"Why?"

Ezma shook her head. "Don't know. Maybe he's married or engaged or there's some rule about the staff fraternizing. Or maybe it's Dr. Preston." Her lips tightened at the corners. "He teaches writing and he's bad news."

"I think I have him for a class."

"Oh, yeah? My friend Dionne took his writing class and was all about him, but he comes in here and he's just plain rude. Then Dionne went missing."

"Your friend is one of the missing girls?" Kristi asked. "And you think Preston might be involved?"

Ezma was about to say no. But she changed her mind. Kristi could see it in the way her chin slid to the side. "I don't think so, but I wouldn't put anything past that guy. The trouble is, no one really believes anything bad happened to Dionne. They think she just disappeared, probably took off with her boyfriend." Ezma shook her head.

"Then why hasn't anyone heard from her?"

"Exactly! The common theory is that she's with Tyshawn and they've taken on new identities. Tyshawn Jones is also bad news. Into drugs, did time for robbery when he was still a minor. Personally, I never knew what she saw in him. Before Tyshawn, she dated a really great guy, Elijah Richards. Was going to school at a junior college, planning on being an accountant, but Dionne started seeing Tyshawn and that was the end of her relationship with Elijah. A shame."

"What about Tyshawn? Is he missing, too?"

"No one ever mentions that, do they?"

Kristi swept around one of the line cooks as he tossed a handful of sliced potatoes into the fryer and the hot oil sizzled and bubbled. She pushed the swinging doors open with her back, then carried the drink tray to the women's table and heard Lucretia's voice over the piped in music.

". . . I'm telling you, he's *amazing*. Absolutely and undeniably amazing. I've never . . . not ever met anyone like him."

Kristi had to fight from rolling her eyes. Even as a freshman Lucretia had been a hopeless romantic. It seemed as if things hadn't changed. Lucretia was on the verge of adding something else, but quit gushing when she spied Kristi. She sent the other women a silent glance, which they understood, and everyone at the table went quiet.

Kristi got the message—Lucretia did not want her old roommate to know anything about her love life. As if Kristi cared.

As Kristi distributed the cold drinks and poured coffee, Lucretia eyed her old roommate. "So you're enrolled at A. S.?"

"Uh-huh." No reason to lie about it. Kristi poured coffee into a cup.

"Didn't you graduate?"

Kristi wasn't about to be baited. "Just a few credits shy." Jesus, why did Lucretia care?

"I thought you had a thing about writing."

"Mmm. Cream?" she asked the woman who had ordered coffee, ignoring Lucretia's questions.

"Do you have no-fat milk?"

"Sure. Just a sec."

"I'm teaching now," Lucretia said proudly.

"That's great," Kristi forced out as she swept away, refilled half-empty cups at a nearby table, then hurried back to the kitchen, where she filled a small pitcher with skim milk and grabbed a dish with packets of sugar and artificial sweeteners. Tamping down her irritation with Lucretia, she returned to the table. "Here ya go." She set the pitcher and dish onto the table near the coffee drinker. "Now, have you decided?" Forcing a smile, she took their orders without further incident and carefully wrote the instructions on the ticket. One woman wanted diet dressing on the side of her Julius Caesar salad, another insisted on no condiments whatsoever on her King Lear burger, and a third wanted a cup of the Cleopatra clam chowder with a side of fruit rather than coleslaw. Lucretia had recently developed allergies to all shellfish, so she wanted to insure that Tybalt's tuna salad hadn't been tainted with any of Ophelia's oysters or Scarus's scampi.

Hands delved deep inside the pockets of her raincoat, Portia Laurent walked along the sidewalks that crisscrossed the quad at All Saints. It was New Year's Eve and she was on her dinner break. Already, the night was closing in and the promise of revelry was evident in groups of students laughing and talking and hurrying to the local restaurants and bars to ring in the new year.

At least four students wouldn't be among the partiers. Dionne Harmon, Monique DesCartes, Tara Atwater, and now Rylee Ames, whom, Portia believed, had all met with the same bad end. There could be others as well, she thought, though none from All Saints. She'd checked. In three years no other students had been reported missing.

"No bodies, no homicides," Vernon had insisted in their most recent conversation, but Portia didn't believe it. True, there was no proof that anything suspicious had happened to the girls, and while Dionne was African American, the other three girls were white. Serial killers *usually* didn't cross racial lines, but that wasn't always the case.

She thought about Monique DesCartes, from South Dakota. When Monique was fourteen her father had been diagnosed with Alzheimer's disease and Portia knew firsthand how that could ruin a family. Monique's mother had been straight-up pissed that Monique had applied for scholarships and taken off, leaving the mother to deal with a rapidly failing husband and two younger daughters, one of whom was still in grade school. Monique, ever rebellious, had run away twice in high school and so, now, was chalked up as a girl who

gave up easily and took off. She'd been known to drink
and smoke dope and had broken up with her most recent boyfriend a few weeks before her disappearance.
The boyfriend, already in an "intense" relationship
with a new girlfriend, hadn't given a rat's ass what had
become of Monique.

It seemed as if no one did. Except Portia.

She walked past the library, where three stories of
lights glowed bright in the night. The rain had let up but
the air was heavy and damp, leaves of some of the
bushes still dripping as they shivered in the rain. The out-
door lights glowing throughout the campus had the appearance of old gaslamps, a nod to the era in which the
school was founded.

As she headed to Cramer Hall, where she had lived
years ago as a first-year student, she thought about the
missing girls. All English majors. All enrolled in some
basic classes as well as a class in the newer controver-
sial curriculum. They'd each been enrolled in Writing
the Novel, Shakespeare 201, and The Influence of
Vampyrism in Modern Culture and Literature. There
was no evidence that the girls had known each other
and they'd not taken the classes during the same terms,
but they had enrolled and passed each of those three
classes. Maybe it was nothing. But maybe it was. . . .

She found herself directly in front of the dormitory.
The brick edifice looked very much the same, and she
stared up at the room on the second floor that had belonged to Rylee Ames. Rylee, like the other girls, was
estranged from her family but her mother's remarks
hadn't rung true. Nadine Olsen had simply said in her
west-Texas drawl, "You know how it is with some girls,
when the going gets tough, the tough hitchhike to
Chicago and get knocked up." Portia had found no evidence that Rylee had ever given birth, but she had dab-
bled in drugs—ecstasy, marijuana, and cocaine—and

run away several times as a teenager while Nadine tried to hold her brood of three sons together on a cannery worker's salary. Rylee's father, the first of Nadine's five husbands, had only said, "Always knew that kid would come to no good. Takes after her mother."

Great, Portia thought grimly. No one seemed to care what had happened to Rylee Ames.

Which was the same apathy that surrounded the other victims.

"They're not victims until we prove that some crime has been perpetrated against them," Del Vernon had insisted, but Portia knew better. Those girls had been victims from the day they were born. That much they had in common. Along with the fact that they had been English majors at All Saints College and as such, had taken some of the same required and elective courses.

Coincidence?

Portia doubted it.

A cold wind blew across the grounds, rattling the branches of the pines and causing the Spanish moss hanging from the live oaks to dance and sway, like ghosts in the lamplight.

If Portia had been a superstitious woman, she might have felt a chill in her soul or cared when she spied the black cat scurrying across her path. However, she didn't believe in ghosts or demons or vampires. She wasn't even really sure about God, though she prayed regularly. But she did believe in evil. The dark rotting of the soul where malevolence and cruelty resided in a human form.

And she was scared to death that the four girls missing from All Saints had encountered a homicidal maniac of the worst order.

She hoped to God that she was wrong.

\* \* \*

Kristi couldn't stand it. So what if it was New Year's Eve? So what if everyone she knew was out celebrating. She'd had offers, of course. From Mai, just yesterday, which she had no intention of accepting, but also from friends in New Orleans, friends she'd grown up with, friends she'd worked with, and even from her newfound sister, Eve. She'd turned them all down. She wanted to get settled, here, in Baton Rouge, and when it came to the woman who was her half-sister, that was just too weird to think about. For most of her twenty-seven years she'd thought she was an only child and then . . . out of the blue, Eve Renner turns out to be related to her. It was just too bizarre to be contemplated and all wrapped up in a time she'd rather forget.

"One step at a time," she told herself as she lit a few candles and turned on her notebook computer. Besides, she was on a mission. She had no intention of schlepping tables at the Bard's Board forever and she was back at school for a reason—to hone her craft.

She'd found some success writing for *Factual Crime* magazine and had done a few articles for a similar e-zine, but she wanted to write a full-blown book. Since her father had refused to give her access to any of his cases, she'd have to locate her own.

The laptop whirred to life and, with little difficulty, she found an open wireless connection that she could use. Seated at her little writing alcove in the dormer, its pane window overlooking the wall surrounding campus, Kristi began scouring the Internet for information on Tara Atwater, the girl who had lived in this very unit when she'd disappeared. Kristi had become adept at finding information on the net, but this time, she came up with very little, just a few articles that mentioned Tara Atwater. There wasn't much on the other missing girls either, she decided, as she scanned articles on the Web version of the local paper. But this felt like a story.

Maybe the one she'd been looking for. Maybe she'd ended up with this apartment because this was the true-crime book she was supposed to research and write.

*Something* had taken the coeds away.

Girls didn't go missing for no reason. Not four from the same small college within an eighteen-month period. Not four enrolled in the same classes.

Kristi bookmarked a page as she heard steps on the staircase. A second later the doorbell rang, and she rolled her secretary's chair away from the desk, crossed the small room to peer through the peephole. Through the fish-eye she saw a scruffy man in his early twenties or late teens standing under the single dim light mounted on the landing of the staircase meant to be her porch. Damp and dripping, his dishwater blond hair was plastered to his head. He was carrying a toolbox in one hand and wearing an I'm-pissed-as-hell expression that was meant to suggest authority.

No doubt the missing Hiram.

"Who is it?" she called just to be certain.

"The manager. Hiram Calloway. I need to check your locks."

*Oh, now he needed to check the locks? Way to be on it, Hiram.*

He looked as pathetic as she'd expected with his thin beard, ancient bad-ass T-shirt from a Metallica concert, grungy camouflage pants, and sullen ask-me-if-I-give-a-shit attitude.

She opened the door a crack, leaving the chain in place. "I already took care of the locks."

"You can't just go doing all kinds of stuff to the place, y'know. You don't own it. I'm supposed to fix things around here."

"Well, I couldn't find you, so I handled it myself," Kristi stated with finality.

He frowned. His lips, half hidden in what he clearly

was hoping would be a beard someday, curved petulantly over slightly crooked teeth. "Then I'll have to have the key. I mean a copy. My grandma . . . Mrs. Calloway owns this place. She has to have access. It's in the lease."

"I'll see that she gets one."

"That'll just take more time. She'll give me a copy anyway. I have to have a key to every apartment in this building. I might have to get into the unit, you know, if something goes wrong or you lose your key or—"

"I'm not going to lose my key."

"It's for your protection."

"If you say so." She wasn't counting on it.

"Jeez, why are you being such a—" He bit off the epithet at the last moment.

Kristi's temper flared. "I called you and it took you three days to respond. All the locks in the unit were broken or loose and I heard that one of the girls who went missing from the campus lived here, so really, I thought I'd better take the situation into my own hands."

His mouth dropped. "Anyone ever tell you to lose the attitude?"

"Like they've told you?" she snapped back.

He actually blushed and she felt a jab of regret. The kid, though incompetent, seemed to be trying to do his job. Even though he was failing, she really didn't want to tick him off.

"You don't have to be so mean," he mumbled.

Kristi inwardly sighed. "Okay, let's start over. Everything's cool here, okay? I fixed the locks. I'll give your grandmother, Mrs. Calloway, a key and she can see that you have one, though, I assume that you won't come barging in here unless you give me notice . . . I think that's in the lease, too." She slid the chain out of its latch and let the door open wider, then stepped onto the small porch. "I didn't mean to get off on the wrong foot with you, Hiram. I'm just a little nervous, hearing that one of the missing girls lived here last term. Your grandmother didn't mention it and it's a little weird." He stared at the floorboards of the landing. He didn't look a day over seventeen. Hardly man enough to be a manager of any kind. "So, did you know her? Tara?"

"Not really. We talked. A little." He lifted his eyes to meet the questions in Kristi's gaze. "She was nice. Friendly." He didn't have to say "not like you" but the unspoken accusation was there in his dark, murky stare. His features stiffened almost imperceptibly, but enough so that Kristi noticed the tightening of his jaw, the nearly involuntary pinching of the corners of his mouth. In that instant Kristi knew she'd been fooled by his youthful appearance. There was something sinister smoldering in his night-dark eyes, something she didn't like. This was no boy at all, but a man in a boy's gawky body. She hadn't noticed it through the peephole or in the slit of the door when the chain was engaged, but now, face to face with Hiram Calloway, she realized she was standing next to a complex and angry man.

She lifted her chin. "So, what do you think happened to her?"

He glanced over the railing toward the campus. "They say she ran away."

Kristi said, "But no one really knows."

"She did before."

"Did she tell you about it?"

He hesitated, then shook his head. "Nah. She kept to herself."

"You said she was friendly. That you talked."

A funny smile played upon those half-hidden lips. "Who knows what happened to her? One day she was here. The next, gone."

"And that's all you know?"

"I know that her old man is in prison somewhere and that she stiffed my grandmother." He met her gaze deliberately. "Owed her back rent. Grandma says she's a 'flake' and a 'crook like her old man.' Grandma figures she got what she deserved."

"Got what she deserved," Kristi repeated slowly, not liking the sound of that. Far away, laughter crackled through the night.

Hearing his words repeated made Hiram frown. "I'll tell Irene you've got a key for her." And with that he was gone, trudging down the steps and carrying his tools. Kristi stepped back into her apartment and slammed the door shut. She locked the dead bolt and chain and felt her skin crawl. Irene Calloway's "good kid" of a grandson gave Kristi a major case of the creeps.

# CHAPTER 4

*B*ANG!
A sharp gun report blasted through the thick dark
night, the smell of cordite overriding the earthy odor of
the wet grass, the horrible crack reverberating through
Kristi's skull.

In horror, she watched as Rick Bentz went down, falling, falling, falling . . . near the thick stone wall surrounding All Saints College.

Blood flowed. His blood. All over the street. Staining
the concrete. Spraying the grass. Running in the gutters. Draining from him.

"Dad!" she screamed, her voice mute, her legs
leaden, as she tried to run to him. "Dad, oh, God, oh,
God. . . ."

Lightning sizzled through the sky, striking a tree. A
horrid rending noise keened through the night as the
wood splintered and a heavy branch fell with a thud.
The ground shook and she nearly fell.

BANG! BANG! BANG!

More shots! People were yelling, screaming through
the hail of bullets. Someone was howling miserably as if
he or she, too, had been hit.

But her father lay still, his color fading to black and
white.

"Dad!" she screamed again.

*BANG! BANG! BANG!*

Kristi sat bolt upright in her chair.

Oh, God, she'd been dreaming, the nightmare vivid and terrorizing. Her heart was thundering, fear and adrenaline screaming through her blood, sweat breaking out on her skin.

She jumped, then looked at the clock and realized she was hearing the sound of firecrackers. People were ringing in the new year. Muted laughter and shrieking reached her ears. Church bells on campus peeled and over the din she heard the sound of horrible yowling, the noise she'd attributed to someone injured in the attack.

"Dear God," she whispered, her heart still thundering.

Still a little groggy, she pushed herself up from the chair. She'd been reading about a serial killer and the imagined images still danced inside her head as she shoved her hair from her eyes and then walked to the door of her studio. Only her desk light was on, and aside from the pool of light cast from the small lamp, the room was in shadows. Peeking through the peephole in the door, she saw nothing. Just the empty stair landing where the dim bulb in the ceiling offered a hazy blue glow. Still the crying continued. Leaving the chain locked, she slid the dead bolt out of place and opened the door a crack.

Instantly a skinny black cat shot inside.

"Whoa . . . !" Kristi watched as the half-starved creature scurried under the daybed, the bedskirt undulating in the cat's wake. "Oh, come on, kitty . . . kitty . . . no . . ." Kristi followed the scrawny animal, then got down on her knees and peered under the skirt. Two yellow eyes, round with fear, stared back at her. Somehow the damned thing had wedged itself between the top mattress and the lower trundle in a space barely wide enough for Kristi's hand. "Come on, kitty, you really

can't be here." She tried to reach into the tight space but
the cat hissed and flattened itself deeper in the crevice,
its body pressed against the wall. "I mean it, come out."
Again, she was shown a curling pink tongue and needle-sharp fangs. "Great. Okay."

Kristi pulled on the lower bunk and the cat dropped
into the space between the mattress and wall. When she
pushed the trundle back, she thought the cat would
squirt out one end, but apparently the little thing found
a hiding spot. No amount of moving the bed could dis-
lodge the animal and Kristi wasn't about to drag out the
bed and slide into the tight space with a terrorized feline and its sharp claws.

"Please, cat . . ." Kristi sighed. She didn't need this.
Not tonight. Besides, there was some damned rule in
clause five hundred and seventy-six or something about
not having any pets on the premises. She was certain
Hiram could recite it chapter and verse. "Come on . . ."
she said, trying to sweet-talk the frightened feline.

No such luck.

"Kitty" wasn't budging.

"Okay . . . how about this?" She scrounged in her cupboard, found a can of tuna, and opened it. Glancing over
her shoulder, she expected to see a little nose or curious
eyes or at least a black paw peeking from beneath the
daybed.

She was wrong.

She put a couple of forkfuls of tuna into a small dish
and half filled another with water, then set them close
enough to the bed to entice the cat, but far enough away
that Kristi thought she could grab it by the back of its
neck and haul it outside. But she'd have to be patient.

Not her long suit.

She set the dishes on the floor and backed up. Then
waited, watching the digital clock on the microwave as
the minutes dragged by as if they were hours and more
revelry sounded outside: people yelling, horns honking,

fireworks exploding, footsteps on the porches below. Laughter. Conversation.

Inside, the cat stayed put. Probably petrified with all the noise.

Perfect, Kristi thought, fighting a headache. She was bone tired. The minutes dragged by and she finally gave up. She couldn't wait all night.

"Fine. Have it your way." Already in her PJs, she closed the door, locked it, double-checked the latches on the windows, and crawled into the daybed. It creaked beneath her weight and she thought for certain she'd hear the cat slink from beneath the mattress, but not a chance. There were noises outside. Music and laughter filtering up through the floor. Mai Kwan's group back from the Watering Hole, no doubt, but her new house-guest didn't so much as stick his nose out from under the bed.

It appeared that the black cat she'd already decided to call Houdini had settled in for the night.

"It's midnight. Come on, celebrate!" Olivia insisted, and offered Bentz a glass of nonalcoholic champagne. "It's going to be a better year."

"Doesn't it have to be?" He pushed away from the desk in their cottage in Cambrai. Ever since the roads had been repaired from the aftermath of Hurricane Katrina, he and Olivia, along with her scruffy dog and noisy bird, had lived out here. Kristi, too, off and on, had stayed in the spare bedroom upstairs in this cottage Olivia had inherited from her grandmother. Kristi, though, had always been restless in this little cabin on the bayou. Moreover, she'd never really felt comfortable with him and his new wife. For years it had been just the two of them, and though she gave lip service to "liking" Olivia and "loving" the idea that he wasn't alone any longer, that he'd finally gotten over Kristi's mother, that he was living his own life, there was a part of her that still hadn't accepted it all. None of this had escaped his ultraperceptive wife, though Livvie held her tongue on the matter. Smart woman. And goddamned beautiful.

Since living out here they both had to commute to the city, but it was worth it, he decided, once he'd gotten used to living next door to gators and egrets and possum. The distance from the city gave both he and Olivia some peace of mind, a little time away from the chaos that had been New Orleans.

Olivia still owned her shop, the Third Eye, just off Jackson Square, where she sold trinkets, artifacts, and new age stuff to tourists. The store had been spared any serious damage, but the square itself had changed and the tourist business had been slow to return. The tarot readers and human statues, even many of the musicians, had left in the storm's aftermath, as their homes had been destroyed and even now, things were slow.

"Don't be such a pessimist, Bentz," she teased, and he grudgingly took the drink and touched the rim of his glass to hers. "Happy New Year." Her eyes, the color of aged whiskey, gleamed and wild blond curls surrounded her face. She'd aged some in the years since they'd married, but the lines near the corners of her eyes didn't detract from her beauty; in fact, she insisted they gave her character. But there was a sadness to her, too. They'd never been able to conceive and now Bentz wasn't really interested. Kristi was in her late twenties and starting over again seemed unnecessary, maybe even foolhardy. Jesus, he'd be in his sixties when the kid finished high school. That didn't seem right.

Except Olivia wanted a child.

And she would make a damned fine mother.

"I'm not a pessimist," he corrected as Hairy S. trotted into the room and hopped onto Bentz's La-Z-Boy to peer at them through the bush of his eyebrows. "I'm a realist."

"And a glass-is-half-empty-kind-of-guy."

He took a swallow of his tasteless fizzy fruit juice and held it to the light. "Well, I'm right. It is half empty."

"And you're worried sick about Kristi."

"I didn't think it showed."

"You've been a wreck ever since she left." Olivia sat across his lap, wrapped an arm around his shoulders, and touched her forehead to his. "She's going to be all right. She's a big girl."

"Who was almost killed . . . had to have her heart started twice. Almost legally dead."

"Almost," Olivia stressed. "She survived. She's tough."

He rotated the kinks from his neck and drank in the scent of her as Hairy whined from the nearby recliner as if he wanted to join them in the oversized chair. "I just worry she's not tough enough."

"You're her dad. She's tough enough." She took a long swallow from her glass, then twirled the stem. "Wanna fool around?"

"Now?"

"Yeah. You play the big, tough detective and I'll be—"

"The weirdo who can read a killer's mind?"

"I was going to say a weak little woman."

He was taking another drink and nearly choked. "That'll be the day." But he kissed her and felt the warmth of her lips mold over his intimately. Familiarly. Old lovers who still had heat.

His cell phone vibrated loudly, quivering across the desk.

"Damn," Olivia whispered.

He picked up the phone and glanced at the LCD. "Montoya," he said. "No rest for the wicked."

"I'll hold you to that when you get home," she said as he grinned and placed the cell to his ear. "Bentz."

"Happy New Year," Montoya said.

"Back atcha." It sounded as if Montoya was already driving, speeding through the city streets.

"We've got a DB down by the waterfront. Looks like a party gone bad. Not far from the casino. I'll be there in fifteen."

"I'm on my way," Bentz said, and felt a jab of regret when he saw the disappointment in Olivia's eyes. He hung up and started to explain but she placed a finger over his lips.

"I'll be waiting," she said. "Wake me."

"You got it."

He found his jacket, keys, wallet, and badge, then, making sure Hairy S. stayed inside, walked outside to his truck, an ancient Jeep that he kept threatening to trade in. So far he hadn't had the heart, nor the time. Climbing behind the wheel, he heard the familiar creak of the worn leather seats as he jammed the SUV into reverse, backing around Olivia's sedan. Ramming the Jeep into first, he managed to find a pack of gum and unwrap a piece of Juicy Fruit as he nosed his rig down the long lane and across a small bridge. Popping the stick of gum into his mouth, he slowed as he turned onto the two-lane road toward the city, then hit the gas. Olivia was right, he supposed, he had been out of sorts. Worried. He had his reasons and they all centered around his kid. The boles of cypress, palmetto, and live oak trees caught in the splash of his headlights while he thought about Kristi.

Headstrong and beautiful as Jennifer, her mother, Kristi had been described as "a handful," "stubborn," "independent to a fault," and a "firecracker" by her teachers both in LA where he and Jennifer had lived, and here in New Orleans. She'd certainly given him more than his share of gray hairs, but he figured that was all part of the parenting process and it would end once she'd grown up and settled down with her own family. Only, so far, that hadn't happened.

He took a corner a little too fast and his tires skidded just a bit. A raccoon, startled by the car, waddled quickly into the undergrowth flanking the highway.

Kristi seemed as far from getting married as ever and if she was dating anyone, she studiously kept that info to herself. In high school she'd gone with Jay McKnight, even received a "promise ring" from him, whatever the hell that meant—some kind of preengagement token.

Bentz snorted, listening as the police band crackled, the dispatcher sending units to differing areas of the city. Kristi had claimed she'd "outgrown" Jay and broken up with him when she'd attended All Saints the first time around. She'd found an older guy at the school, a TA by the name of Brian Thomas who'd been a zero, a real loser, in Bentz's admittedly jaded opinion. Well, that had ended badly, too.

Gunning the engine, he accelerated onto the freeway and melded with the sparse traffic, most vehicles driving ten miles over the speed limit toward Crescent City.

Now, Jay McKnight had finished college and a master's program. He was working for the New Orleans Police Department in the crime lab and Bentz would defy his daughter to think of Jay as "boring" or "homegrown" any longer. A little turn of the screw was that Jay was going to teach a night class up at All Saints. Maybe Kristi would run into him.

*And maybe he could be convinced to check in on Bentz's daughter. . . .*

He inwardly groaned. He didn't like going behind Kristi's back, but wasn't above it, not if it meant her safety. He'd nearly lost her twice already in her twenty-seven years; he couldn't face it again. Until the Baton Rouge Police figured out what was happening with the missing coeds, Bentz was going to be proactive.

Easing off the freeway, he headed for the waterfront. In the moonlight, the decimated parts of town looked eerie and foreboding, abandoned cars, destroyed houses, streets that were still impassable. . . . This part of New Orleans was hardest hit when the levees gave way and Bentz wondered if it could ever be rebuilt. Even Montoya and his new wife, Abby, had had to abandon their project of renovating their home in the city, two shotgun row houses that they had been converting into one larger home. The house, which had survived over two hundred years, had been in its final phase of reconstruction when the wind and floodwaters of Katrina swept through, destroying the once venerable property. Montoya, pissed as hell, was commuting from Abby's cottage outside the city.

They were all tired. Needed a break.

He sped to the crime scene, where two units were already in position, lights flashing around a roped off area where officers were keeping the onlookers at bay. Montoya's Mustang was parked half on the sidewalk, and he, dressed in his favorite leather jacket, was already talking to the officer who'd been first on the scene.

The body was lying face up on the sidewalk. Bentz's gut clenched and the taste of bile climbed up his throat. The woman was Caucasian, in her early forties. Two gunshot wounds stained a short red dress. There were signs of a struggle, a couple broken fingernails on her right hand and several scratches across her face. Bentz stared at her long and hard. She wasn't one of the missing women who had disappeared from All Saints College. He'd memorized the faces of Dionne Harmon, Tara Atwater, Monique DesCartes, and now Rylee Ames. Their images haunted his nights. This unidentified woman was none of them.

He felt a second's relief and then a jab of guilt. This victim belonged to someone, and whoever it was—mother, father, brother, sister, or boyfriend—would be devastated and grief-stricken.

". . . so I'm thinkin' it was probably a robbery gone bad. No wallet or ID on her," the officer was saying.

*Jane Doe.*

"She was found by those guys over there—" He hitched his chin to a sober group of four, two men and two women, who'd been separated from the lookie-loos wandering by. "They're just partiers on their way home from the Hootin' Owl, a bar on Decatur," the officer said.

Bentz nodded. He knew the place.

The officer continued, "They claim they didn't hear or see anything, just nearly stumbled over her body. But then, they're pretty wasted."

Bentz glanced at the two couples, dressed in glittery clothes and looking suddenly sober as judges.

"I'll talk to them," Montoya said, easing toward the couples, both African American. The girls rubbed their arms as if chilled to the bone, their eyes wide with fear. Their dates were both tight-lipped and tough-looking. The slimmest girl stared at the body, the other looked away, and the tallest of the group lit a cigarette that he shared with his date, the thin one.

Bentz's cell phone rang as the crime lab van arrived with Bonita Washington at the wheel. She double-parked behind a cruiser. Inez Santiago, hauling a tool kit, climbed out of one side, while Washington cut the engine of the big rig.

Bentz glanced down at the digital readout on his phone. Police dispatch. No doubt another homicide.

Crap.

"Bentz," he answered, watching as Bonita, in all her self-important fury, ushered the uniforms and gawkers away from what she considered "her" crime scene. She was an intense black woman with a don't-mess-with-me attitude and an IQ rumored to be in the stratosphere. She loved her job, was good at it, and didn't take flack from anyone. Santiago was already taking pictures of the dead girl. Again Bentz's stomach twisted.

Over the phone, the dispatcher gave him the location and a quick rundown of what looked like a hit-and-run closer to the business district.

"I'll be there ASAP, as soon as I'm done here," he said, hanging up.

"Move away," Washington yelled at one of the uniforms near the yellow tape, waving him off with one hand. "Who the hell has been tromping all over here? Damn it all—Bentz, get these people back, will ya? And you," she said to the uniformed cop, "don't let anyone, and I mean not even Jesus Christ himself, across that line, you got that?"

"Yes, ma'am."

"Good. Just as long as we understand each other." She flashed him a smile with zero warmth and got down to the business of collecting samples, gunshot residue, footprints, and fingerprints as the medical examiner's van pulled up.

"Don't tell me," Montoya said as his phone began to play a salsa melody. "Damn." He checked his watch. "Fifty-three friggin' minutes into the new year and already two DBs."

"There'll be more," Bentz predicted as he glanced once more at the victim. Two hours ago, this woman had been ready to celebrate the new year.

Now she'd never see another day.

His cell phone rang again.

His jaw clenched.

It promised to be a helluva night.


Midnight.

The witching hour.

A time when the last day was done and the next starting, and, in this case, a new year. He smiled to himself as he walked through the rain-washed city streets, hearing the sounds of firecrackers and, he supposed, champagne corks, all sounding like the rapid-fire reports of guns.

Not that he was into that type of weaponry.

Too impersonal.

Being so far from a victim, hundreds of yards in some cases, took away the thrill, the feeling of intimacy that came when the lifeblood drained from the body, the light in the victim's eyes died slowly, and the frantic, fearful beating of her pulse at her neck slowed to nothing. That was personal. That was perfect.

Dressed in black, blending into the shadows, he crossed the campus, smelled the sweet odor of burning marijuana, and watched a couple clumsily fumbling at each other's clothes as they kissed and made their way toward a dorm, and presumably a small twin bed where they'd go at it all night.

He felt a twinge of jealousy.

The pleasures of the flesh . . .

But he had to wait.

He knew it.

Despite his restlessness.

His *need*.

Deep inside he craved release and knew it would only come through the slow taking of a life . . . and not just any life. No. Those who were sacrificed were chosen.

The ache in him throbbed, refused to be denied, and his nerves were strung tight. Electrified. Anxious.

He smelled their lust. Their own special yearning. The blood singing through their veins.

He clenched his fists and cleared his mind of lust, of desire, of the heat that pounded through his skull.

Not now.

Not this night.

Not *them*.

Giving the entwined, stumbling couple one last angry

glance, he clamped down hard on the most basic of urges to follow.

To hunt.

To kill.

*They are not worthy,* he reminded himself. *And there is a plan. You must not stray from your mission.*

On noiseless footsteps he made his way swiftly through the campus gates and along several streets, zigzagging through alleys to the old building that had long been condemned, a once-grand hotel that was locked and boarded, where the only inhabitants were spiders, rats, and other vermin. He made his way to the back of the building, where once there had been a service entrance for deliveries. He hurried down the crumbling stairs and, using his key, unlocked a back door. Inside, he ignored the dripping, rusted pipes, broken glass, and rotting boards that had been part of a previous attempt at renovation. Instead he walked along the familiar hallway to another locked door and spiral steps leading downward. At the base of the steps, he unlocked the final door and stepped inside to an area that smelled of chlorine. Locking the door behind him, he waited a few seconds, headed down a short dark hallway to a large open area, then flipped a switch, where dim bulbs illuminated an Olympic-sized swimming pool, its aquamarine tiles shimmering silently in the ghostly light.

Stripping noiselessly, he cast his clothes into a corner and, once completely naked, walked to the pool's edge and dove deep into the bracing, unheated water. The shock puckered his skin, but he stretched his body and began knifing through the water, breathing naturally, turning at the far end, athletically, then swimming the length again. His body, honed by hours of exercise, sliced through the water as easily as a hunting knife through flesh. He stroked faster and faster, increasing his speed, feeling his heart pump and his lungs begin to strain. Five lengths. Ten. Twenty.

He only drew himself out of the water when he felt the first wave of exhaustion pulling at him, calming him, forcing the bloodlust from his heart. There was time enough for that later. Cool air slid over his wet skin. His nipples tightened. His cock shriveled. But he embraced the cold as he made his way through a dark hallway, his eyes adjusting to the lack of light as he turned two corners and walked into another chamber where his trophies were hidden.

There was a bare writing desk in the room, a squatty black table, and a few thick pillows upon the tired concrete floor. A computer screen from a notebook added a faint blue glow and he considered logging on. He communicated with them over the Internet; on pirated wireless connections throughout the city they knew him by several screen names, but he called himself Vlad. Not particularly clever but fitting for his purposes, he decided. What was the quote from Shakespeare? "What's in a name? That which we call a rose/By any other name would smell as sweet." Well, Vlad smelled sweet and tasted even better, he thought. So, for the purposes of this, his mission, he would be known as Vlad the Impaler. And was he not? Did he not impale each of the ones he chose?

Oh, irony.

Lighting a candle, Vlad sat cross-legged at the stubby Japanese table, opened a drawer within it and drew out the pictures, snapshots taken for student ID cards. He set the first four onto the glossy surface of the table.

*Sisters,* he thought, though not genetically related.

He touched each photo with the tip of his index finger, in the order in which he'd taken them.

Dionne, sweet and supple, her rich dark skin soft as silk. Oh, she'd been ripe and so hot . . . so damned hot and wet . . . Crying out her unwillingness, but her body responding to him as he made her ready, made that perfect body want him. His throat tightened at the memory of taking her, from behind, his hands kneading her abdomen, making her come just before he did.

He swallowed hard.

And Tara, the thin one with her gorgeous breasts. Full and white, with pale rose-colored nipples the size of half-dollars. He felt his prick twitch at the thought of those glorious tits. He remembered suckling them, teasing them, biting them, scraping them with his teeth as she cried out in heated torment . . . again his blood began to sing. He touched Tara's photo, then looked to the next girl.

Monique. Tall and lean, an athlete's body. Muscles that had strained against him as he'd sculpted her with his palms, fingers exploring all her intimate, sweet crevices. He licked his lips as his cock stood at attention.

He glanced to the next photo. Rylee. Small. Frightened. But oh, so delicious. Her pale yellow hair had caught his attention and when she was stripped bare, her white skin had been luminous, her veins visible beneath the surface, her beating heart apparent in the fluttering, frightened pulse throbbing so perfectly within the circle of bones at her throat.

Oh, God, how succulent she'd been . . . the taste of her . . . He turned the photo over where the smear of her blood was still visible on the back of the snapshot. Smiling in pure self-indulgent wickedness, he lifted the picture to his mouth and gently flicked the tip of his long tongue over the dark crimson stain. The taste of her filled his mouth and he sucked in his breath with the euphoria of it.

His cock was rock hard now. Ready.

To impale.

Licking his lips, he laid the picture onto the table

with the rest of his chosen ones, then searched the others . . . hundreds of them tucked into his hiding place.

He'd already pulled those he thought the most likely candidates, the girls who appealed to him. Though he was missing a few. The new ones. The coeds who had signed up for this, the second term, as new students. He didn't have their pictures yet.

But he would.

And soon.

Then they would join those he'd already identified, those who would soon join their sisters.

He smiled, running his tongue over his teeth, savoring the taste of poor, scared-out-of-her-mind Rylee Ames.

In the next batch, though he had yet to procure her photograph, Vlad thought of another, the cop's kid who had rented Tara's apartment. As if she were fated to do so, he thought, conjuring up her image in his mind.

He'd seen her. Watched her. Mentally claimed her. She was a gorgeous woman with just the right amount of spirit and the perfect body for his needs, for his sacrifice. When her time came. She was not slated to be the next, but her time would come soon enough. He could wait. He had no choice. All that was to be, had already been decided.

His blood flowed hot at the thought of taking her and he looked down at the pictures on the table before him.

Though she didn't yet know it, Kristi Bentz would soon join her sisters. . . .

# CHAPTER 5

So this is what everyone was talking about, Kristi thought as she took a seat in the packed classroom on the first day of the term. It was the Monday after New Year's at eight in the morning. Most of the students looked as if they'd just rolled out of bed.

Chairs scraped against the floor, shoes shuffled, voices buzzed with conversation, and in the background the soft strains of Renaissance music drifted from speakers mounted high on the walls of the large, auditoriumlike room. Rows of seats were situated on tiers that funneled down to a barren center stage that held a battered table, podium, and microphone. A stack of books and an open three-leaf binder were situated near a laptop computer on the table.

A man in his mid-to-late thirties, presumably Dr. Victor Emmerson, was already standing behind the table, one jean-clad hip thrown out as he leaned over his notes, his scruffy black leather jacket tossed over a white T-shirt, a pair of reflective sunglasses folded and tucked into the shirt's crew neck. His hair was shaggy, dark brown, and appeared not to have been combed since the day before. About three days' worth of beard-shadow covered a strong jaw. He looked as if he took road trips on a Harley-Davidson. Everything about him oozed "cool, moody biker." A far cry from the stuffy teachers she remembered from a few years earlier.

Maybe the class would be as interesting as she'd heard. She'd signed up because it was required for an undergraduate English degree and it sounded interesting. Even more so now.

Emmerson scratched at the stubble on his chin as he read his notes, flipping through pages, scowling at his own scribbles, only looking up when the door to the room opened and yet another student walked in and searched for a vacant desk.

The remaining spots to sit in were few and far between.

This class on Shakespeare was surprisingly popular and Kristi figured the fascination with the class had more to do with the sexy, unlikely professor than the Bard or his works. She slid her computer onto the desk to take notes and checked out the other students, several of whom looked familiar. Mai Kwan, her neighbor, was seated near the front of the room, several rows below Kristi, and a couple of girls who had been with Lucretia the day she'd come into the diner were huddled together near the windows. But the kicker was that just before class was to start, who should stroll in but Hiram Calloway, Kristi's would-be apartment manager. She turned away quickly, hoping that he didn't notice one of the few vacant seats was next to Kristi. Fortunately, he found another desk, near the back of the room.

Good.

The door slammed shut behind Hiram, and Emmerson checked the clock on the wall, then hit a button behind the podium, killing the music. Straightening, taking the entire class in with one broad look, he said, "Okay, I'm Professor Emmerson, this is Shakespeare two-o-one and if this isn't the class you signed up for, leave now and make room for someone who intended to enroll. For those of you who have heard that this is an easy class, a guaranteed A, you, too, are welcome to exit."

No one moved. The class was silent except for the ticking of the clock.

A cell phone chirped loudly and Emmerson looked directly at the kid in a baseball cap who was fumbling in his pocket.

"That's the next thing. No phones in class, and not just ringing. If I sense one is vibrating, or if anyone looks at his or hers to read a text or even to check the time, you're history. Automatic F. If you don't like the rules, then drop the class and take it up with the administration. I don't care. This classroom is not a democracy. I'm the king, okay? Just like the ones we'll study, only, I hope, not quite as self-serving.

"While you're in here"—he held up two hands to indicate the entire classroom—"with me, we'll be studying good old Willie Boy like you've never studied him before. We're not just going to read his plays and his poems. We're going to learn them. Inside and out. We'll read them as they are meant to be read, the way Mr. Shakespeare—or depending upon your viewpoint, whoever wrote them—meant them to be read. For the purposes of this class, we'll assume they belong to William Shakespeare. If you're one of those Francis Bacon freaks who thinks he did it, even though he wouldn't have had a lot of time, or Edward de Vere enthusiasts, or for those of you who think Christopher Marlowe, even though he supposedly died in 1593, took up the quill in his dead hand under Shakespeare's name, or, for that matter anyone else, again"—he pointed toward the back of the room—"there's the door. I know there's a movement to prove that poor, illiterate William couldn't possibly have written anything so sophisticated or knowledgeable about the upper class and Italy and all that rot. I also know some of academia think that his works were really written by a group of people. We're going to have a lot of lively discussions about Shakespeare's work, don't get me wrong, but the whole 'did he or did he not write them' subject is taboo. I don't care who wrote them, okay? That's for another class. I'm only interested in what you think of the work." He walked around to the front of his desk and rested his jean-clad hips against the edge. "I assume you all received a syllabus via e-mail for this class. If you haven't, double check your inbox or spam folder and only if you really didn't receive one, call my office and I'll shoot another your way. Most of your assignments will come through the Internet and that's why you all have an address ending with allsaints.edu. If you don't have one, or think you don't, check with the registrar or admissions. It's not my problem.

"For those of you who did check your syllabus, you'll see that we're going to begin with *Macbeth*. Why?" His smile was a little wicked. "Because what better way to start off the year than with witches, prophesies, blood, ghosts, guilt, and murder?"

He had everyone's attention now and he knew it. Glancing over the captivated students, his gaze moving from one rapt face to the next, he nodded slowly. His eyes found Kristi's and held for a split second. Was it her imagination or did he linger just a little longer on her than the others?

No way.

It was just a trick of light.

Had to be.

And yet, his grin seemed to shift a little before he looked away, as if he knew a deep secret. An intimate secret.

What the hell was wrong with her? Just because he was good-looking she was thinking all kinds of ridiculous things.

"Besides," he said in his deep voice, "in this classroom, I get to decide what we do. I like *Macbeth*. So—"

He clapped his hands together and half the class jumped. Again the knowing smile. "Let's get started. . . ."


"Kristi!" As she was walking briskly past the steps of the library, she heard her name and her stomach nose-dived. She recognized the voice. Turning, Kristi spied her old-roommate-cum-assistant professor, Lucretia, black overcoat billowing, umbrella held in one fist, hurrying toward her. The skies were threatening a downpour, the wind was kicking up, and the last thing Kristi wanted to do was have a chat with Lucretia Stevens in the middle of the quad. "Hey, wait up!"

There was no escape.

She paused and Lucretia, breathless, half ran to catch up with her. "I need to talk to you," she said without preamble.

"Really."

Lucretia ignored Kristi's irony. "Do you have a minute?" Other students, heads bent against the wind, hurried along the concrete and brick paths intersecting the lawn in the middle of campus. Some were on bikes, some walking, and one zipped by on a skateboard. "We could go into the student union and get a cup of coffee or tea or something." She seemed earnest. Worried.

"I have a class at eleven and it's across campus." She glanced at her watch. Ten thirty-six. Not much time.

"It won't take long," Lucretia insisted, grabbing hold of Kristi's arm and trying to shepherd her toward the brick building that housed the student union, café, and on the other side, the registrar's office. Kristi pulled her arm back, but walked with Lucretia into the cafeteria-style restaurant, where they headed to the coffee counter and waited behind three girls ordering coffee drinks. Kristi perused a display of scones, muffins, and bagels, then ordered a black coffee while Lucretia asked for a caramel latte with extra foam. Kristi tried not to notice the minutes ticking by as they waited for their drinks, but it ate at her that she'd be late for her next class, The Influence of Vampyrism on Modern Culture, taught by Dr. Grotto.

Once they were served, she followed Lucretia through scattered tables where students were clustered, talking, studying or listening to their iPods. She noticed a couple of Lucretia's friends, Grace and Trudie, locked in a deep conversation at a table near the back door, but Lucretia, as if to avoid them, headed for a corner booth that hadn't been cleaned in a while. She took a seat with her back to her friends.

Kristi settled in to her side of the booth and realized she now only had twenty minutes to get to class. She was doomed to be late. "Better make it quick. I don't have a lot of time," Kristi warned as she blew across her steaming cup.

Lucretia let out her breath, then glanced over her shoulder as if she expected someone to be watching them. Satisfied that they weren't being observed or overheard, she leaned over the table and whispered, "You've heard that some of the students—girls—have gone missing from campus."

Kristi pretended only mild interest. She nodded. "Four, right?"

"Yes." Lucretia bit at the corner of her lip. "So far they're just missing. . . ."

"But . . . you think . . . something else?"

Lucretia didn't touch her coffee, just let it sit on the chipped Formica table near some used packets of hot sauce and mustard that someone hadn't bothered to throw away. "Well, I just think something's going on. Something weird." She lowered her voice even further. "I knew Rylee."

"Knew. As in past tense?"

"No," she said quickly. "I mean, I *know* her, but no one and I mean no one has seen her since before Christmas. I think maybe . . . oh, God, this is just so weird."

"What is?"

"I think she might have been a part of some cult."

*"Cult?"*

She was nodding, rotating her small cup and watching the foam slowly melt into her untouched coffee.

"You mean like a religious cult?"

"I don't know exactly what kind. . . . There are rumors about all kinds of weird things going on. The big thing seems to be some interest in vampires."

"Like in *Buffy the Vampire Slayer* or *Dracula* or—?"

"I mean in real live vampires."

Kristi gave her a look. "Vampire bats . . . or the Count Dracula kind? Oh, wait, I get it. You're putting me on."

But Lucretia was serious. "This isn't a joke! Some of the kids run around with fangs and vials of blood hanging from their necks, and they are so into Dr. Grotto's class that it's almost like an obsession. Totally out of line."

"But they don't really believe there are vampires who sleep in coffins during the day and run around and drink human blood at night. The kind that are only killed by wooden stakes or silver bullets and can't look into mirrors."

"Don't be that way."

"What way?" Kristi asked.

"So . . . harsh. And I don't know what they believe." Almost guiltily, Lucretia played with a gold chain encircling her neck. Between her fingers a small diamond-encrusted cross dangled.

"So, Rylee was into this vampire thing," Kristi said skeptically.

"Yes. Oh, yeah . . ." The diamond cross glittered under the huge suspended lights of the dining hall.

"What do they do? This vampire cult?"

"I don't know. Rylee was . . . secretive."

"What do you know about her?"

"Well, I wouldn't call her the most stable girl on the planet," Lucretia admitted. "She had quit college once before, maybe in winter or spring term of last year." She cleared her throat. Looked away. The cross winked.

"And—" Kristi prodded, sensing there was more.

"And, well . . . she was . . . is a bit of a drama queen. Well, not just a bit, I would say. She did try to commit suicide once."

"Suicide?"

"Shh!" Lucretia lowered her voice and quit playing with her necklace. "I know, that's a cry for help and I'm not sure she ever got it. Her mother spent so much time worrying that Rylee would get pregnant, she never saw how much pain Rylee was in."

"Her mother ignored her suicide attempt?" Krista asked incredulously.

"The way Rylee told it, she gave her mom a lot of trouble as a teenager—staying out late, partying, the wrong crowd, drugs, boys, you name it. So she washed her hands of her, turned her back on her own kid. How about that?" Lucretia said the last phrase bitterly and Kristi was reminded of Lucretia's own disengaged parents. At least disengaged emotionally.

Lucretia cleared her throat. "Anyway, from what I understand, her mother thinks Rylee's disappearance is just one more of her 'stunts,' a clamor for attention."

"But you think it's this . . . cult."

"Yes."

"And that she got mixed up with something or someone evil within the cult."

Lucretia swallowed hard. "I hope I'm wrong."

"You think she took this vampirism thing too far, really believed it, and got in over her head."

Lucretia was obviously turning it over in her mind. "Yes . . . yes . . . I think it's possible."

There was something off about the conversation, something Lucretia wasn't saying, something worrisome. Here they were in the middle of the damned cafeteria of the student union, surrounded by kids and adults, talking, laughing, joking, or studying, some listening to iPods, some eating or drinking coffee or sipping on sodas, and she and Lucretia were actually talking about vampires and cults. Something soulfully evil? She eyed her ex-roommate and wondered what had happened to her over the past few years. "What about you, Lucretia?" she asked, watching for the tiniest reaction. "Where are you on the whole vampirism thing?"

Lucretia glanced at the window to the gloomy day beyond. "Sometimes I don't really know what's real and what's not."

A shiver of apprehension slid down Kristi's spine. "Seriously?"

"Do I believe in vampires? As in the Hollywood archetype? No." Lucretia shook her head slowly. Thoughtfully. As if she were wrestling with the idea for the first time. Almost unconsciously, she began shredding her paper napkin.

"Let's take Hollywood out of it," Kristi suggested. She should probably drop the entire conversation. It was too weird. Too unreal. But she couldn't help herself. Her curiosity had been whetted with the mystery of the missing coeds and she'd already decided to look into their disappearances; maybe Lucretia could help. She certainly seemed as if she wanted to.

Lucretia thought hard, then said, "Philosophically, I believe that you can make your own truth. People who hallucinate, whether from drugs or medical conditions, see things that are very real to them. It's their truth, their frame of reference, though it isn't, maybe, anyone else's. My grandmother, before she died, saw people

who weren't in the room, and she was certain she'd
gone places that she couldn't have, because she was
stuck in a hospital bed in a nursing home. But she described her 'trips' with amazing clarity, to the point she
nearly convinced us. Was she dreaming? Hallucinating?" Lucretia shrugged her shoulders. "Doesn't matter. Her reality, her *truth* was that she had been there."

"So you're thinking that the students who are in this
cult, they've altered their reality. Through what? Mental
problems? Drugs?"

"Or maybe desire."

Kristi felt an icy wind cut through her soul. "Desire?"

Sighing, Lucretia finally brushed the pieces of her
napkin aside, piling the tiny bits with the gooey used
packets of condiments. "They want to believe it so
badly that it's real. You know what I mean. Wanting
something so badly in your life that you can almost
taste it. Wanting something . . . *something* you would
do anything to get." Her dark eyes zeroed in on Kristi
and she grabbed her hand, holding it so tight her knuckles showed white. "We all want something."

A moment later she let go of Kristi's hand. Kristi
found that her heartbeat had accelerated. "But this particular fantasy . . . Why would anyone want to think
that there are vampires?" Kristi asked, truly mystified.

"It's hot. Sexy."

"Really? Drinking blood? Living in darkness? Being
undead for centuries? That's hot? Who in their right
mind would want—"

"No one said anything about them being in their
right minds." Lucretia stared at her again, then finally
picked up her coffee cup and took a sip. "These—believers—their lives are empty, or boring, or so goddamned awful that any kind of magic, or sorcery, or
alternative existence is better than what they're living."

"That's whacked. You're saying there's a whole cult of these people who believe in this creature of the night fantasy."

"It's whacked to you. But not to them. Oh, there are probably some who participate just for the thrill of it. There's an allure to the whole vampire culture. It's dark. It's sexual. In some ways it's very romantic and visceral. But to some people it's not a fantasy. Those are the ones that really, and truly, believe it."

"They need help," Kristi said.

When Lucretia stared at Kristi her eyes had darkened again. With worry? Or her own Stygian dogma? How weird was this? Kristi and Lucretia had never been friends, so why had her old roommate sought her out? Why were they even having this discussion? At a nearby table two jock-type guys scraped chairs from the table and set down a tray loaded with hot dogs and fries. They were joking and talking, grabbing at the mustard and ketchup packets. It was all so normal.

Was she really having a conversation about vampires with Lucretia?

"So what about Dr. Grotto?" Kristi asked, envisioning the tall sardonic man with such dark hair and intense eyes. "Do you think he promotes it with his classes on vampirism? Is he the cult leader?"

"What? God, no!" She set down her cup so hard that some of the foam and coffee beneath sloshed over the rim.

"But he teaches the classes—"

"Not on *being* a vampire, for Christ's sake, but on the influence of the whole vampire, werewolf, shapeshifter, monster myth in society. Historically, and today. He's an intellectual, for God's sake!"

"That doesn't mean he's not into the whole thing—"

"You're missing the point. It's not about Dominic. . . ." Lucretia shook her head vehemently and actually paled at the thought. "He's a wonderful man. Educated. Alive.

Look, this was a mistake." Ashen-faced, she stood, and she was actually trembling as she gathered her things. "I thought because you'd been through a lot, because your dad is such a crack detective, that you might be able to help, that you might be able to convince your father to check into what happened to Dionne, Monique, Tara, and Rylee, but forget it."

"Your friends are still missing," Kristi pointed out, as she, too, got up from the table.

"They're not 'my friends,' okay? Just some girls I knew. Part of a study group."

"They knew each other?"

"Peripherally, I guess. I'm not sure. They were English majors and all of them, I think, were kind of troubled, lonely kids, the kind who could've gotten caught up in the wrong thing. But I should have known you'd twist it all around." She rolled her eyes as she tossed the wet napkin into a nearby trash can.

"Did you tell this to the police?"

"No—I—I'm an assistant professor here now, but I'm not tenured, and I don't have access to all the records as I'm not a full professor yet and . . . damn, it's complicated. I can't go spouting off about cults on the campus, but then I ran across you and . . . so, I'm telling you now. Because I thought your father could look into this quietly, without getting me into any hot water. Before, I wasn't convinced that there was anything wrong. Dionne and Monique, they were pretty wild and always talked of just hitchhiking away, but now . . . I don't know. Tara was unhappy, but Rylee?" She shoved her hair out of her eyes, caught sight of the boys at the nearby table, and lowered her voice. "Maybe I'm imagining all this. You know, the whole blur between what's real and fantasy. I don't know why I even told you about it."

Neither did Kristi. She'd never seen someone go from ice cold to red hot in a matter of seconds. Obviously she'd hit a nerve bringing up Professor Grotto, who just happened to be the teacher of Kristi's next class, the one she was late for, the one on vampires. Kristi decided she'd keep that information to herself for the moment. She gulped the last of her coffee and tossed the cup away while Lucretia gave the table one last swipe.

Kristi couldn't help but notice the ring on Lucretia's left hand. "Are you engaged?" she asked, and remembered the conversation Lucretia was having about the guy who was absolutely "*amazing*." Could she have meant Grotto?

Lucretia stopped mopping for a second, looked down at her fingers, and her white face instantly flushed scarlet. "Oh . . . no . . ." she stammered. "It's . . . it's just . . . nothing." Quickly she wadded the napkins over the old packets of sauce and dropped the whole mess into the trash bin. She added quickly, "And it's not a 'promise ring' or whatever you called it when you were a freshman." A little smile crawled across her lips. "Remember?"

"Yeah."

Lucretia was wiping her hands on a fresh napkin. "Isn't that a hoot? To think that the guy you tossed over when you were first here is now on the staff. Talk about a twist of fate."

Kristi stared, trying to make sense of Lucretia's comment. "You mean Jay?"

"Yeah, Jay McKnight."

Her stomach dropped to the floor. Whatever she and Jay had shared was long over, but that didn't mean she wanted to bump into him. No, Lucretia had to have gotten bad information. "He works for the New Orleans PD," Kristi argued, then started to get a really bad vibe when she saw a glint of triumph in Lucretia's gaze as she slung the strap of her purse over her shoulder.

"But he's teaching a class here. A night class, I

think. Filling in for a professor who had family problems and had to take a leave of absence or something."

"Really?" Kristi couldn't believe it, but wasn't about to argue. Lucretia was just plain wrong or yanking on her chain just to bug her. She wasn't about to give it any credence until she saw Jay McKnight with her own two eyes. Then she was hit by another bad feeling. "What class?"

"I don't know . . . something in criminology, I think."

Kristi's stomach tightened. "Introduction to Forensics?"

"Could be. As I said, I'm not sure."

*Oh, God, please no.* She couldn't imagine Jay being her instructor—that would just be too much to deal with. She flashed on how she'd so callously broken up with him and cringed. Even though it had been nearly a decade, she didn't want to think there was a chance she could run into Jay on campus. Or that he could be her teacher. That would be torture.

"See ya around." Lucretia was already heading for the door when Kristi noticed the big clock mounted on the back wall of the building over the doors leading to the admin offices.

She noticed the time.

It was three minutes to eleven.

No way could she make it across campus. No doubt, she'd be late. But maybe it was worth it. Lucretia's fears, her theories about a cult here on the campus, were definitely interesting. Worth checking out. But really—vampires?

"Don't make me laugh," she muttered to herself, then was annoyed by the involuntary shiver that slid down her spine.

# CHAPTER 6

The double doors of the student union clanged shut behind Lucretia, then opened again as a wave of students, talking and laughing, dripping from the rain, pushed their way inside and headed for the counter to order.

Wasting no time, Kristi gathered her notebook computer and purse, then hurried outside and down the steps as the bells from the church tower began tolling off the hour. "Great," she muttered, noticing how few people were still hurrying across the quad.

*Because everyone's already in class.*

Even Lucretia, who had left just moments before Kristi, was nowhere to be seen, as if she'd vanished into the gloomy day.

*This is no way to start the term,* she told herself as she half ran along a brick pathway that led out of the quad and cut past the chapel and around Wagner House, the two-hundred-year-old stone mansion where the Wagner family, who had donated the land for the college, had once lived. Now a museum, and rumored to be haunted, the towering manor rose three full stories and was complete with mullioned windows, gargoyles on the downspouts, and dormers poking out of the steep, ridged roof.

Raindrops began to fall as Kristi dashed past the

wrought-iron fence that separated the gabled house from
the edge of the campus, then cut behind a science building. She rounded a corner and nearly crashed into a tall
man dressed all in black who was standing with his
back to her. He held a hand to his forehead, as if pro-
tecting his eyes from the rain. He was deep in discussion
with someone Kristi couldn't see, but as she dashed by,
she caught a glimpse of his white clerical collar and
etched, grim features. He was talking to a small woman
in an oversized coat. Her face was turned up to him as
she lowered her voice when Kristi passed, but Kristi
recognized Lucretia's friend, Ariel. Her hair was pulled
into a ponytail, she was holding a bag of books, her
glasses were splattered with rain, but even so, she
looked as if she were on the verge of tears.

"...I...I just thought you should know, Father
Tony," Ariel said, flipping the hood of her jacket over
her head.

*Father Tony.* The priest Irene Calloway had griped
about being too hip. Kristi had seen his name in the
school catalogue, where he'd been listed as Father Anthony Mediera. In the All Saints information packet the
priest had been smiling and calm, wearing a cassock as
he stared into the camera with large eyes. Now those
blue eyes were dark and guarded, his jaw set, his thin
lips flat in repressed anger.

"Don't worry," he said with the hint of an Italian accent, also lowering his voice as Kristi passed. "I'll handle it. Promise."

Ariel's smile was tremulous and adoring, until she
spied Kristi. Her expression changed quickly and she
hurried away, as if hoping Kristi hadn't recognized her
like she'd obviously recognized Kristi.

Which was fine.

Kristi was late. Whatever Ariel was confessing to Father Tony had nothing to do with her.

She zigzagged behind the religious center and finally,

nearly ten minutes late, reached Adam's Hall, where she took the exterior steps two at a time. Inside the old building she clamored her way to the second floor, where the doors to her classroom were already closed.

*Damn,* she thought, yanking open the door to a room so quiet she was certain anyone within could hear a pin drop let alone her bold entry.

The windows were draped in thick dark velvet, the rectangular classroom lit by fake candles. A tall man stood at the podium. Her heart nearly stopped as he stared at her with near-black eyes, then glanced at the clock over the door.

She found one of the few empty seats and told herself he wasn't glaring at her with eyes like embers, dark but threatening to glow red. It was all just a matter of lighting and her own vivid imagination. Because the classroom had been converted to a creep-a-thon, and the image that was cast behind him on the chalkboard from a slide projector plugged into his computer was of Bela Lugosi, dressed as Dracula, in white shirt and cape.

Bela's picture disappeared, changed to another image, one of a horrible, hissing creature with needle-sharp teeth and blood dripping from his lips.

"Vampires come in all shapes and sizes and have varying powers," Dr. Grotto said, glancing at the next picture, an old comic book cover with a cartoon image of a lurking vampire creature about to lunge at a fleeing, scantily clad blonde with a figure that would make Barbie envious.

Kristi tried to meld into the other students, but no such luck. Dr. Grotto seemed to single her out, to glower at her as she opened her notepad and laptop computer. Finally, he cleared his throat and glanced down at his notes. "We'll start the term with Bram Stoker's *Dracula,* discuss where he found his inspiration. In cruel

Vlad the Impaler, as most people believe? In Romania? Hungary? Transylvania?" he asked, pausing for effect. "Or perhaps in other historical monsters such as Elizabeth of Bathory, the countess who tortured servant girls, then bathed in their blood to protect her own waning beauty? Myth? Legend? Or fact?" Grotto went on about the course itself and what he required. Kristi took notes, but she was more interested in the man than his lecture. He walked catlike from one side of the room to the other, engaging students, seemingly to mesmerize them. Tall and lithe, he embodied his subject matter.

The images kept changing behind him, from campy to cruel. As a trailer for the television series *Buffy the Vampire Slayer* appeared behind him, Grotto hit a button on his desk. The overhead lights glowed and the curtains retracted. Buffy and the gang's image faded and the room transformed into a normal classroom. "Enough of the theatrics," Grotto said, and the class groaned. "I know, we all like a stage show, but this is a college credit course, so, I trust you have all received a syllabus through your e-mail and you know that you're to read Bram Stoker's *Dracula* by the end of this week. If not, see me after class.

"So, let's start the discussion. . . . What do you know of vampires? Are they real? Human? Do they really feast on human blood? Morph into a variety of creatures? Sleep in coffins? Today we'll discuss what you know about vampires, or think you know." He smiled then, showing off glistening fangs, only to remove the false caps and set them on the desk. "I said I was done with the theatrics, didn't I?"

From that second on, Dr. Grotto held everyone's attention for the rest of the lecture. The class was lively with Grotto asking questions as well as answering some, and it was obvious why the class was one of the most popular at the college.

Dominic Grotto could transform as easily as the mythical creatures he studied. One minute dark and thoughtful, the next animated and witty. He had an easy manner and used the entire front of the classroom as his stage, walking from one side to the other, making notes on the chalkboard, pointing to students to speak their minds.

Kristi recognized several students in the class, a couple of kids who had been in her Shakespeare class with Dr. Emmerson, including Hiram Calloway—was there no getting away from the creep? Again, she spied Lucretia's spiked-haired friend Trudie, and Mai Kwan, the girl who lived downstairs from Kristi.

*Small world,* Kristi said to herself, then corrected herself, thinking *small campus.* With less than three thousand students in the entire school, it wasn't that surprising that she'd see familiar faces in her classes.

Within seconds, the door opened again and the professor glared as Ariel slipped into the room, grabbing the first empty seat she found near the door. Ariel looked as if she wanted to do nothing more than melt into her seat. Kristi sympathized. Ariel caught Kristi's glance, but turned her attention to her notepad, flipping it open as the professor continued to speak.

An odd girl, Kristi thought, wondering about Lucretia's mousy friend. Ariel seemed shy, even needy, the proverbial wallflower who wanted to disappear into the background. Kristi glanced at the girl again, but Ariel had lifted the book up, to hide most of her face.

Was she still crying?

Why? Homesickness? Something else?

Whatever it was, Father Tony had promised to "take care of it," so Kristi focused all of her attention on the front of the room.

She listened raptly to Dr. Grotto, taking in the man's appearance. He was tall with thick, expressive eyebrows, a strong jaw, and a nose that looked as if somewhere along the way it had been broken a couple of times. His eyes weren't red or black, but a deep brown, his lips thin, his body honed, as if he worked out. There was an arrogance about him, but an affability as well, and Lucretia's words rang through her brain. *He's a wonderful man. Educated. Alive.*

As opposed to dead? No . . . as in *animated*, Kristi berated herself. All this vampire talk was getting to her. Lucretia was certainly quick to defend Dr. Dominic Grotto, despite her suspicions. She'd acted as if the man were nearly a god, for crying out loud, and then there was the matter of the ring. . . .

Kristi watched the professor's hands. They were large. Strong looking. Veins apparent when he wrote on the board. But his left hand was bare. No wedding ring. No tan line or indentation suggesting he'd recently removed it. What had Ezma at work said? That Lucretia was rumored to be involved with one of the professors? A big secret? Hmmm.

She studied Dr. Grotto and tried to imagine him with Lucretia. It just didn't fit. Grotto was smart enough, that much was evident, but he exuded an innate sexuality in his beat-up jeans and casual black sweater. Lucretia was the egghead's egghead. Not unattractive, just socially a step off, almost snooty in her pseudo-intellectuality, but then, maybe that air of superiority was what had attracted him to her.

Stranger things had been known to happen.

Kristi settled back in her desk chair and scrutinized her new professor.

As Ezma had warned, Grotto was definitely "hot." Was he involved with the missing coeds? The man who'd maybe inspired the vampire cult that had attracted Rylee?

When Kristi had first driven to Baton Rouge, her father's warnings had fallen upon deaf ears, but now that she was here, on the campus of All Saints, she was beginning to think there might be some merit in Rick Bentz's fears. Four girls were missing. Maybe dead. All had taken Grotto's class on vampires.

Coincidence?

Kristi didn't think so.

In fact, she was going to find out. She'd start calling the family, friends, and neighbors of the girls today, in between classes, if she had to. Something had happened to the missing students. Something bad.

Kristi was damned well going to find out what it was.


Jay stepped out of the shower and toweled off after a weekend of ripping off paneling and repairing the tears to the plaster that had been beneath the wooden facade. His muscles ached from hours with a chisel and hammer, but the house was taking shape. Most of the deconstruction was about finished. He had only a bit of linoleum to rip up and then he'd be ready to rebuild. He threw on boxers, a pair of khakis, and a cotton sweater, then yanked on a pair of socks and stepped into his shoes as he checked his watch. Less than an hour until his first class. With Kristi Bentz. He'd had no notes of anyone, including Kristi, dropping out, so he expected to see her.

*Brace yourself,* he thought, then chided himself for being childish. They were both adults now. So they'd gone together as teenagers. So what? Time had marched on and other relationships had come and gone.

The phone rang and he recognized Gayle's number. What the hell did she want and why now, when he was just getting ready to deal with Kristi, did he have to talk to her? He almost didn't answer. But the thought that she might really be in trouble, might really need him, caused him to take the call. Good old trusty Jay.

"Hi," he said, without preamble. They both knew about Caller ID.

"Hi, Jay, how're you?" she asked in that soft, dulcet drawl he'd once found so intriguing.

An interior designer who adored antiques and New Orleans architecture, she'd grown up in Atlanta, the only daughter of a judge and his wife. Jay had found her cultured, smart, beautiful, and fun-loving. Until they'd gotten serious. Then he'd recognized her strong, unbending will and almost obsessive attention to detail. How many times had she insisted his tie hadn't matched his shirt and jacket, or that his shoes were out of style, or that his jeans were far too "ratty to even be considered hip, darlin'?" Her temper, too, had come to the fore. What did it say about his personality that he always picked hardheaded, smart, sassy women who could blow at any minute. For a half a second, he thought of Kristi Bentz. Talk about a temper! Kristi's was practically legendary. Jay figured his choices in women were a major character flaw.

"I'm doin' fine, Gayle," he said, realizing she was waiting for a response. Tonight, he didn't have time for niceties. "How 'bout you?"

"All right, I guess."

"Good, good." He was gathering up his keys and wallet, making certain he had everything he needed. His gaze scraped the interior of the cottage as he made certain he was leaving everything secure.

"But I have to be honest. Sometimes I get lonely. Sometimes I miss you," Gayle said, drawing his attention back to the telephone conversation.

His gut tightened. "I thought you were dating someone—an attorney, right? Manny or Michael or something?"

She hesitated, then said, "Martin. But it's not the same."

"Nothing ever is. It's always different, sometimes

better, other times worse." Why the hell was he even having this conversation?

As if she knew she'd pushed him too far, she said, "I know this is the night of your first class and I wanted to wish you luck."

Yeah, right. "Thanks."

"You'll do great!"

The woman did know how to stroke his ego.

"Hope so."

"Believe me, those kids will be enthralled with all that creepy forensic stuff."

"Yeah?" He checked his watch. Time to go. Where the hell was the leash? He didn't want to take Bruno anywhere without it. Oh, maybe in the truck!

"Oh, yeah, honey. I've heard you speak. You know, I was wondering—"

Here it came, the real reason for her call.

"I know you spend most of your weekends up there at your cousins' house, but when you're back in the city, give me a call. I'd love to go out for a glass of wine or dinner or something. . . . You know, no strings attached."

The no strings part, he didn't believe.

"I doubt I'll have any time before the end of the term," he said. "Pretty busy."

"I know, Jay. You always are. That's the way I like it."

Again, a fairy tale. She liked a man she could boss around. That's where most of their problems began and ended. "Listen, Gayle, I gotta run. Take care."

"You, too," she whispered as he hung up and whistled to the dog. He was not going to be pulled into the trap of dating Gayle Hall again. Not ever. He'd learned his lesson and had the scar above his eyebrow to prove it.

He double-checked the lock on the back door, then gathered his notes and stuffed them into his banged-up briefcase. He had samples in the case as well. Examples of evidence that he'd share with his class. The science of forensics had become a big deal since the airing of the *CSI* shows and their knock-offs on television, and Jay figured part of his job was to point out the difference between fiction and fact, between wrapping up a drama in forty-odd minutes, and doing the legwork and lab work that required hours and hours in real life. Even the shows on Court TV were somewhat misleading with days, weeks, months, and even years of detective work wrapped up in under an hour. Though the detectives and criminalists and even the announcers would remind the viewer of the time that passed, the case was always solved within an hour, including time for advertisements. It was all part of the quick response/action/reaction short attention span television programming that viewers had come to expect.

If only they knew the truth about all the fancy television-inspired crime labs that could get DNA evidence back nearly instantly. The extraction of body fluid, the dropping of a sample of the fluid into a test tube, a flick of a switch and the spin of some centrifuge, and voilà, DNA results. In truth it took weeks and months to process, and then there was the matter of all the evidence that had been destroyed by the hurricane. Not only evidence that could convict a criminal, but evidence that might exonerate an innocent man. Or woman. It made him sick to think about it.

He locked the front door behind him, whistled to the dog, then with Bruno at his heels, walked briskly to his truck. The rain that had pummeled this part of Louisiana all day had stopped, leaving sodden ground and the air heavy with a thick mist that seemed to rise to the skeletal, bone white branches of the cypress trees.

A perfect night to discuss the subject of murder.

\* \* \*

Hoisting himself easily from the pool, Vlad stood at the edge of the shimmering depths and felt the water cool upon his skin. The lamp beneath the water's surface and the monitor of his small computer gave off the only light in this, his special retreat. He loved the kiss of the cold air against his wet flesh but had little time to savor it.

There was so much to do.

And one problem that nagged at him. He'd tried to ignore it, had spent months telling himself it was of no consequence, but with each passing day, he felt a little more irritated, a bit more compelled to correct his stupid mistake.

He'd hoped that the taking of the last girl would have calmed him, but it hadn't. Not completely. Though Rylee's ultimate submission and death thrilled him, the fact that he'd erred gnawed at him. Distracted him. Even now, he found himself biting his nails and spitting them into the pool, then forced himself to stop the disgusting habit he'd had since childhood, when he was certain his father would return, discover that he'd gotten into trouble, and lock him into the old outhouse.

At that thought his stomach convulsed, so he pushed all images of his childhood aside. After all, the old man had gotten his, hadn't he?

Vlad smiled as he remembered the bloody tines of the pitchfork in his father's freak farming accident. He'd spent hours relating the horror of finding his father on the barn floor, how the old man had fallen from the hayloft and onto a broken bale where the pitchfork had been left. Vlad had admitted to leaving the tool where it wasn't supposed to be. And had the pitchfork not hit the femoral artery, how his father might have survived. Instead, the old man had lain on the pitchfork like a turtle on its back, his pelvis shattered, his screams unheard until Vlad had returned from the neighbor's house and found the man who had sired him in a pool of coagulating blood. How unfortunate it had been on the weekend when his mother had been away, visiting her sister.

But the old man's death couldn't help the situation now.

Vlad prided himself upon his perfection, and the fact that he had made one mistake bothered him.

He walked to the far end of the pool and into a small alcove where a bank of metal lockers still resided. They were empty save for the one he'd reserved for his treasures, those he'd locked away. Deftly, in the semidark, the smell of the chlorine he'd added drifting to him, he flipped the combination of the lock and opened the rusting door.

Inside were several rows of small black hooks. Three, on the upper row, saved for the elite, the ones he thought of as royals, had been marked with the name of the owner and held a gold necklace from which a tiny vial dangled. Carefully, he extracted one of the gold loops and held it to the light so that he could see the deep red color within the bit of glass . . . like expensive wine, he thought. Gently twisting open the vial, he held it under his nose. He inhaled the sweet, coppery scent of Monique's blood. Closing his eyes, he remembered how she'd struggled. A natural athlete, she'd fought the effects of the drugs, and as he'd restrained her, she'd gone so far as to spit in his face.

He'd laughed and licked it into his mouth and that's when he saw her fear. It wasn't that he could hold her wrists or pin her weight with his legs, it was that he enjoyed the fight in her and that scared her to death.

He'd seen it in the dilation of her pupils, felt it in the rising and falling of her chest as he'd held her down waiting for the cocktail she'd been given to completely take effect. He'd witnessed her struggles on the stage before she'd ultimately succumbed to him. He'd suspected she would be difficult, a fighter. And she hadn't disappointed.

Hers was a life not quickly given.

Thinking of Monique now, he licked his lips. Draining her blood had been exquisite, watching her breaths become shallow and bare, seeing her skin whiten, feeling her heartbeat slow and finally stop all together, then staring into her open, dead eyes. . . .

He shuddered, reliving the moment, but it wouldn't be enough. Memories faded all too quickly.

Fortunately the bloodlust would be fulfilled.

He capped the teeny bottle and watched it dangle and sparkle for just a second before returning it to the locker.

The empty hooks mocked him, especially the one marked for Tara Atwater. Old rage burned through him when he thought of how that little bitch had tried to defy him, had hidden the treasure meant for him. No amount of urging or force had been able to loosen her thick tongue and she was dead quickly, almost willingly, with little fight in her.

But she had managed the tiniest of smiles as the blood had drained from her and she'd released her soul, as if she had somehow won their battle.

His teeth clenched as he considered the imperfection.

The vial was out there. He just had to find it.

He'd tried of course, to no avail.

But he wouldn't give up.

He slammed the locker door shut. *Bam!* The sound ricocheted off the walls and he stormed still naked into the cavernous room with the pool and alcove he used for an office. The water reflected in shifting shades of blue upon the walls and ceiling, his computer hummed faintly.

The vial was most likely in Tara's apartment, hidden away somewhere. Until now, he'd been careful to stay away from the empty unit with the old busybody of a landlady. But now he had more than one reason to return. Not only was he certain that the precious vial of Tara's blood was secreted somewhere on the premises, but now Kristi Bentz occupied the very apartment he had to search.

Which was perfect.

# CHAPTER 7

"Wasn't Grotto's class the best?" Mai gushed as Kristi climbed the stairs to her apartment. Carrying an overflowing basket of laundry, Mai met her on the landing of the second floor. Almost as if she'd been waiting for her and peering out between her living room blinds. "I saw you come into the class a little late."

"Everyone did," Kristi said, silently groaning. She'd wanted to talk with the vampirism prof after class but had failed in her efforts. But she was determined to meet with him and see what he knew about campus cults.

"Was the whole experience cool, or what? The dark classroom, the drapes drawn, and fake candles lit? All of those images of vampires? Some of them were so scary, I actually got goose bumps, and the others were so camp. I mean, Bela Lugosi? Really? But I gotta say, I about freaked when Grotto took out his false fangs."

"You didn't think it was a little much?" Kristi kept hiking up to the third floor. She didn't have a lot of time. She'd taken over part of Ezma's shift at the Bard's Board from twelve-thirty until six and now she had less than forty-five minutes to get to her night class.

"I think it was imaginative, and interesting, and so much cooler than a musty old professor in a tweed jacket with suede patches on the elbows up at the podium lecturing while we, all bored out of our minds, flipped through pages of a textbook written in the eighties."

"Like that was going to happen."

"Hey, I just admire the guy for bringing some life, or, well, maybe death into the classroom!" Animated, Mai hauled her basket and followed Kristi upstairs. As Kristi entered her apartment, Mai was on her heels and through the door. She set her laundry basket on a table near the kitchen alcove as if she and Kristi were best friends now.

Houdini, who ventured from his favorite hiding spot when he felt Kristi wasn't looking, jumped from the windowsill to the daybed, then quickly slunk into the small space he'd made his home.

"Friendly," Mai observed dryly. "So what's with the cat? I thought pets were a definite no-no."

"He's not a pet. Just a stray I can't seem to get rid of."

Mai glanced to the area in front of the bifold doors hiding the kitchen. There upon a small mat was a pet dish that held food and water, one Kristi had picked up at the local grocery market when she'd been buying coffee, milk, peanut butter, bread, and half a dozen tins of cat food. "You're feeding it. Mrs. Calloway will freak."

"She can come and catch him then. I don't even have a litter box."

Mai wrinkled her pert little nose. "Then . . . how . . . where?"

"He's toilet trained."

"What?" She whipped her head around toward the doorway leading to the closet-sized bathroom. A beat passed as Kristi took off her coat. Mai caught her faint smile. "Oh, you're kidding."

"I leave the window open a crack and he slips through, outside onto the roof. It's amazing how small a space he can get through, but so far, no accidents."

"You're not trying very hard to get rid of him," Mai

observed, and Kristi shrugged. "So he goes on the roof?"

"I think he climbs down the magnolia tree."

"I won't tell . . . but if Mrs. Calloway sees him, there'll be hell to pay." Mai's almond-shaped eyes took in the room, just as she had the last time she'd visited. It was almost as if Mai were looking for something, or trying to memorize every nook and cranny of Kristi's private space.

"If she sees Houdini, I'll deal with it then," Kristi said.

"Houdini?" Mai repeated. "You *named* it?"

"He had to have a name."

"You're sure it's a he?"

"I haven't got that close."

Mai looked at her as if she'd lost her mind. She walked to the table that Kristi used as a desk, the space where Kristi had left her notes about the missing girls.

Suddenly Kristi felt uncomfortable with Mai's prying eyes. "You've been here since last year, right?" Kristi asked to divert her.

"Uh-huh."

"So you know a lot of people."

"My share, I guess."

"Have you heard anything about a cult, maybe on campus? One that believes in vampires?"

"You're kidding, right?"

Mai's fingers touched the back of Kristi's chair. A moment passed and Kristi got the impression she was giving herself time to think.

Kristi pressed, "Is it possible that the girls who went missing were involved in some kind of secret society?"

"That's kind of a reach," Mai said.

"Is it?"

"Do you know something?" Mai asked.

"*You* know something," Kristi guessed. "Tell me."

Mai glanced at the photos of the missing girls lying face-up on Kristi's makeshift desk and she bit her lip. Shaking her head, she picked up the picture of Rylee Ames. "I don't want to sound crazy."

"I just want to know."

She dropped the photo. "There's always been an interest in the vampire thing, y'know? I mean, if you look it up on the Internet, you'll find all kinds of parties and groups who purport to really be vamps. It's this big counterculture. Some people get into it for cheap thrills, I think, but others, they have all these rituals and they sleep in coffins and drink blood, I think even human blood."

"And there's a group here on campus. People who are into it," Kristi added.

Mai lifted a shoulder. "I've heard rumors, sure."

"You think Grotto's involved?"

Mai glanced away. "Grotto? It seems far-fetched. I mean, if it's all so secret, why would he flaunt it? You know, call attention to himself? His class probably just adds to the interest, the allure of it all. My guess? At least some of the students who take his classes are part of the group. But I don't think that just because kids show some interest in vampires and try to hook up with others that I'd call it a cult."

"Maybe it's just the extremists," Kristi said, "a faction that takes things further. Maybe that's the cult part."

"If there even is one. People tend to label things they don't understand." She glanced again at the pictures on the desk. "What are you doing with these?"

"I don't know yet. Just thought I'd do some checking," Kristi said. That much was true enough. Already she'd spoken with two family members of the missing girls. She didn't tell anyone that she thought she'd write a book about them, because, truth to tell, if the girls did end up being runaways, she had no story. Until there was actually a crime, she couldn't very well start penning a true-crime book.

Of course, she hadn't shared that information with Dionne's purportedly great, once-upon-a-time boyfriend Elijah Richards, who was sure he'd see his name in print like some sort of urban hero. In her conversation with him, he'd been all about Elijah, barely able to focus on the girl he supposedly loved. Maybe there was a reason Dionne left him for Tyshawn Jones, even with Tyshawn's criminal tendencies.

Kristi bit her lip, thinking of the other family members she'd reached—Tara Atwater's mother, who had been a real piece of work. Angie Atwater had spent most of the conversation ranting about how her "no-good daughter" was following in her father's path—straight to the Georgia State penitentiary. Poor Tara.

With each conversation, Kristi was becoming more convinced that something awful, something evil had happened to the four missing girls. There was a chance that through her digging, she could find a link between them, a reason they'd gone missing, and turn over whatever she found to the police. Maybe they'd get lucky and find the coeds alive. At the very least she could help prevent any more girls from disappearing.

"Did you personally know any of the missing girls?" Kristi asked Mai.

"No," Mai said quickly. "I didn't really talk to Tara." She lingered over the desk as if intrigued . . . connected. She seemed about to say something more, but changed her mind.

Suddenly, Kristi realized the time. "Look, I've gotta run. I've got a night class in"—she glanced at the clock hung over the fireplace—"fifteen minutes!"

Mai picked up her laundry. She looked away from Kristi's desk and managed to shake off the pall that had settled over her. "Yeah, I gotta get at this"—she held up the basket of dirty clothes—"or it'll be midnight before I'm done. The laundry room here—" She shuddered. "It's just plain creepy. I don't think anyone's cleaned that basement since the Civil War. Pardon me, the War of Northern Aggression, as it's called by some of the natives around here. There are tons of spiders down there and some might even be poisonous, and there are probably rats and snakes, too. . . . I put off washing my clothes until the last minute."

Kristi didn't argue. The basement laundry room was dark and dingy. The ceiling was low, the concrete walls looking as if moisture seeped through the cracks, the exposed beams filled with cobwebs. The odors of mildew and mold were ever present, even when Kristi added bleach to her wash.

"Creeps me out," Mai said. "Anyway, I just wanted to tell you that you missed a *great* party."

"Next time."

"You mean next year?" Mai asked, her gaze skating once more across the room to the desk where the pictures of the missing girls were strewn. "I'm probably not going to throw another party until next New Year's Eve. If then. The party itself was fun, but the mess the next day—forget it!" Mai made her way to the door, and holding the basket on her hip, waved and said, "See ya," before leaving.

Kristi made a beeline for the bathroom, where she took a two-minute shower to rid herself of the smell of grease, onions, and fish that still clung to her from her hours at the diner. After toweling off, she snapped her wet hair into a ponytail and pinned it loosely on her head. Throwing on a clean bra, panties, jeans, and a T-shirt, she then smudged on some lip gloss without checking the mirror. At the front door she stepped into boots, pulled a sweatshirt from a peg and tossed it over her head. She picked up her backpack again and was out the door bare minutes behind Mai.

If only she'd brought her bike from home, the fifteen-speed she'd bought after losing her racing bike to the hurricane, she thought as she clattered down the stairs, cut through a back alley, and jogged across the street separating the apartment house from the campus. Once through the massive gates, she headed toward Knauss Hall, which was primarily used for the biological science curriculum, but now held the new criminology department.

Silently she prayed that Jay McKnight was not her teacher. Surely someone would have told her, right, if there had been a change in instructors?

*No way. You sign up for a class; the school registrar/computer decides where you'll end up.*

"Not Jay," she said aloud, then felt foolish, as if she were fourteen instead of twenty-seven. *Get a grip, Kristi. You can handle this. No matter what.*

"You know, Baton Rouge is not your jurisdiction," Olivia said as she entered the alcove in the guest room on the second floor of their cottage.

Bentz had set up his laptop on a TV tray in the room Kristi had occupied when she'd lived here. The makeshift desk wasn't much, but he did most of his work at the station. He was now hunched over the small computer.

Glancing over his shoulder he spied his wife leaning in the doorway, one shoulder propped against the jamb as she cradled a cup of tea in her hands. Though a smile caused her lips to twitch, she assessed him with serious eyes that seemed to see past his facade and into his very soul.

"How do you know what I'm checking into?"

"I'm psychic, remember?"

That he did. When he'd first met her, he'd thought her a bonafide nutcase. She'd shown up at the station, ranting about seeing murders as they'd been committed, and he'd written her off. At first. He hadn't wanted to believe that this woman with her wild blond hair and gold eyes could read the mind of a cold-blooded killer. But she'd proved him wrong. He still felt sick inside to know what she'd experienced as she'd witnessed the most macabre and brutal of crimes. "You were only a psychic on one case," he reminded her. "Since that time you've proven yourself utterly useless."

"Oooh, low blow, Bentz," she said, but chuckled deep in her throat. "So, okay, I'm lying about being able to read your mind, but I know you, Detective, and I do know how you think." She walked into the room and propped that tight little butt of hers against the arm of an overstuffed chair that was pushed into a corner, opposite a twin bed covered with an aqua-colored spread. "You're worried about Kristi."

"You don't have to have ESP to know that."

"But it's because of the missing girls and hence my warning that Baton Rouge is not your jurisdiction."

"I know. But who cares about lines on a map when girls have gone missing?"

"Oh, yeah, like you would be thrilled if someone from another jurisdiction showed up and started nosing around your cases. Face it, Bentz, you don't like it when the FBI shows up, and you're not even crazy about sharing your cases with some of your own men. I don't know how many times you've complained about Brinkman."

"He's a pain."

"Hmm . . . I won't argue that one," she said, dunking her tea bag in the steaming water within her cup. The scent of jasmine wafted over to him as he stared at the images on the screen—pictures of the four missing girls.

"Brinkman might be resigning."

"Really?" She looked up, letting the tea bag settle.

"Because of the storm."

"It's been over two years."

"He lived in the Lower Ninth Ward, had a couple of rentals there, too. All gone. His parents lived in one. They got out," he said, not adding that their cats hadn't. They'd hidden during the storm and when the rescuers had come, couldn't be found. Weeks later, when the floodgates had receded, Brinkman had returned to his family home and found the house marked with an X by the searchers. The other note said only: "Two dead cats inside." Brinkman had gotten to dispose of the animal carcasses and inform his mother. Since then, he'd packed up his parents, who now lived in Austin, and was talking of getting the hell out of Dodge himself.

"It's too bad."

"Yeah. So I'm not going to let some government-drawn lines stop me from looking into the disappearances on my own time. I've got a call up to the Baton Rouge PD."

"Because you don't have enough to do." She lifted the tea bag from the cup and dropped it, dripping, into a nearby trash basket.

"I said it was on my own time."

"Time you could be spending with your family."

"Kristi is my family."

"I was talking about me," she said.

He smiled. "I know."

Sipping the tea, she said, "I could put on my sexiest negligee and we could . . ." She let her voice trail off.

He cocked a brow.

"Interested?"

Pushing his chair away from the TV tray, Bentz growled, "Always. But you don't need a negligee."

"No?" She looked up at him over the rim of her cup.

"Waste of time." He took the cup from her hand and

set it on the window ledge. "So tell me, Mrs. Bentz, is this attempt at seduction because you're so hot for me you can't think straight, or is it because it's the right time of the month to conceive?"

"Maybe a little of both," she admitted, and it was like a douse of cold water.

"I told you . . . I don't think I want any more children."

"And I told you, I need a baby."

He rested his head against hers and saw the desperation in her eyes. He'd give her anything. But this . . .

"Being a cop's kid is no picnic."

"Neither is being a cop's wife. But it's worth it. Please, Rick, let's not worry about this, okay. If it happens, it happens, if it doesn't, then we'll see."

"Meaning?"

"Meaning let's not worry about *that* now."

He pulled her more tightly against him, feeling her warm body pliant against his. To his knowledge, he'd never fathered a child. Not biologically. Kristi's mother, Jennifer, had cheated on him. Plain and simple. And she'd gotten pregnant. That could have been the end of it, as Jennifer had owned up to the fact that the baby in her womb wasn't his in the eighth month of her pregnancy. But Bentz had taken one look at Kristi seconds after she'd been born and had claimed the baby as his own. Even now, twenty-seven years later, he remembered the moment she'd come into the world, the moment that had changed his life forever.

In all the years since, neither Jennifer nor anyone else had gotten pregnant by him, whether by luck or incredibly good birth control. He'd never been tested, hadn't really worried about it. Never felt the need for another kid, but now Livvie wanted a baby, when he was facing the big five-o. If she got pregnant now, Bentz would be pushing seventy when the kid finished high school. If he didn't get killed in the line of duty first.

Was that fair to the child?

His wife stood on her tiptoes and kissed him. She tasted of jasmine and desperation and damn it, he gave into her. As always.


Kristi took off across campus.

The air was thick. Heavy. A wisping fog rising from the damp ground. She wasn't alone. Other students, too, were heading this way and that, cutting across the quad. They passed her on bikes, skateboards, or on foot; knots of kids talking, solitary students walking briskly to the various old brick buildings that made up All Saints College.

It was weird to be back.

Most of the undergrads were nearly a decade younger than her. There were the grad students, of course, in much smaller numbers, and a few adults who'd returned to school in midlife or beyond. Though the campus with its vine-clad, hundred-year-plus buildings and neatly trimmed grounds seemed fairly unchanged, the feel of being at All Saints was quite different from her freshman year.

At the library, she veered away from the heart of the school as Knauss Hall was at the edge of campus not far from the large old mansions that had been converted to sorority and fraternity houses. Hurrying as the night closed in, she looked down the narrow, tree-flanked street lined by estatelike houses. Her gaze landed on a pillared white plantation-style mansion, home to the Delta Gammas, a sorority she'd pledged at her father's insistence all those years ago, but the whole Greek thing had never worked for her. To this day she didn't know where even one of her sorority sisters was, nor

did she care. She'd never felt like a "DG" while here.
Not only had Rick Bentz insisted she join what she'd
later referred to as "the sisterhood," but he'd also laid
down the law and forced her into tae kwon do lessons as
well as teaching her all about the use and safety of
firearms. Although the sorority thing hadn't taken, she'd
gotten a black belt in her martial art of choice. She also
knew her way around guns and was a decent-enough
shot.

She noticed a car moving steadily up the street,
creeping along, as if the driver were looking for something, or someone. The hairs on the nape of her neck
rose. She squinted, unable to make out the driver.

Most likely, it was nothing. He was probably just lost
and searching for an address, she decided, though all
the talk about missing girls and possible foul play made
her a little suspicious.

*Maybe some of your dad's paranoia is finally rub-
bing off on you!*

The glare of the car's headlights reached Kristi and
the vehicle slowed even more, tires crunching. The low-
lying mist rose over the fogged windows, making it
even more difficult to see who was behind the wheel.
Was the driver a man? A woman? Was someone in the
passenger seat?

Church bells tolled the hour, reverberating chimes
reminding her of the time.

"Hell," she whispered. *Late again!*

She kicked into a jog, leaving the slow-moving car
and its mystery driver behind. Running easily along the
walkway, she cut through the grass and trees lining the
brick and stone building that housed the science labs.

She heard the car pick up speed, then slow again to
the point where the engine was only idling. Kristi
glanced over her shoulder, still unable to see who was
in the darkened vehicle. She wished she was close

enough to get the license number. All she saw was that it was a dark domestic-looking sedan, probably a Chevy, but she couldn't be sure.

*So what? A car is going slow. Big deal. What does it matter if it's a Ford, a Chevrolet, or a friggin' Lamborghini? Get over it.*

She had a more pressing problem: there was a chance that the high school boyfriend she'd so callously tossed over might be her professor.

Groaning inside, Kristi dashed up the steps of the vine-clad hall and yanked open a heavy glass door.

Another student shot through ahead of her and she recognized Hiram Calloway as he swept past. She almost said something because she felt as if the guy were following her. When she'd needed his help with the apartment building, she couldn't scare him up to save her life. But now that she was starting classes, he was everywhere she turned on campus. She had a bad feeling that he, too, might be signed up for Dr. Monroe's Monday night class. . . . Geez, didn't guys work their schedules so that they could stay home on Mondays and watch football?

Let him get to the classroom first so she could avoid sitting anywhere next to him.

As the door swung shut behind her, Kristi headed for the stairwell, where the smell of some pine-scented cleaner couldn't quite hide the odor of formaldehyde that seeped through the hallways. Many of the floor tiles had cracked, and the light green walls had grown dingy with age. The stairs, too, were worn, the banister polished smooth by thousands of hands.

The staircase opened to a wide landing. Several hallways angled off the main corridor, making the area seem more like a rabbit warren than a science lab building.

She followed signs around a corner that led to a long

corridor. At the far end of the hall a door was open and a few students, including Hiram Calloway, were walking into a large classroom.

Crossing her fingers that she wasn't about to see Jay again, Kristi walked briskly to catch up with the crowd. She stepped through the doorway with the last of the stragglers.

Once inside, Kristi's worst fears were founded.

Beneath the glow of fluorescent lights, Jay McKnight stood at the front of the windowless room. Several life-sized charts of the human body were pulled down over a chalkboard behind him.

Kristi's heart sank. What had started out as a bad day just nose-dived. She caught his eye and he didn't so much as smile, but he didn't look away. The worst part of it was that the fates of aging had been more than kind to him. At six foot two inches, he was tall, fit, with a strong clean-shaven jaw and razor-thin lips. His light brown hair was longer than she remembered and uncombed, either because he didn't care or because he was making a stab at being hip. Eyes somewhere between brown and gold met hers and she thought she caught the faintest narrowing at the corners. He had a new tiny scar that cleaved the top of one eyebrow, but other than that one slight imperfection, he looked none the worse for wear. In fact, he'd filled out slightly, his beard shadow darker than it once was, and there was a new air of confidence about him that increased his appeal.

Not that she cared.

She was over him. Had been for a long, long time.

She dropped into one of the few empty chairs and didn't immediately realize that she'd taken a seat directly in front of Hiram Calloway.

*This is just getting better and better,* she thought without a drop of humor, then reminded herself it was no big deal. She was in college, not fourth grade. It's not as if the seats were assigned.

*It's only about ten weeks, for God's sake. Thirty-odd hours. You'll live!*

But tonight, staring at Jay McKnight, the first man she'd ever loved, she wasn't so sure about that.

# CHAPTER 8

Jay wasn't going to let her distract him.

Of course he noticed Kristi the second she stepped into the room. How could he not? And he'd been primed, seeing her name on the class roster.

She was taller than he recalled, probably because her long legs were accentuated by slim jeans and boots with at least two-inch heels. She had an athletic build, her shoulders defined by years of swimming, her abdomen flat, breasts on the small side but still firm, hips slim.

Even dressed down in old jeans and a sweatshirt, she could turn some heads. Not because she had runway model beauty, but because she was a little bit more than pretty and she wore an air of confidence that was natural, easy, and compelling.

As she started toward the rear of the room, she glanced at him, but somehow he hung onto his cool, not even acknowledging her as the rest of the would-be next generation of forensic scientists found their seats. Jay was certain that these students assumed his job was like *CSI*, glamorous and slick, in cities as cool as Las Vegas, New York, and Miami, with sexy, smart police officers and clever, if quirky, crime scene techs working against sly crooks. They probably imagined investigators who were always able to determine the perpetrator and send him away for good. Jay figured his job here was not so much to disavow the television image as to give them all a cold dose of reality.

"Some of you are probably wondering who I am," he began, rounding the desk and balancing his hips upon its edge as the final stragglers slid into their seats. The classroom had seen better days and the worn flooring, scarred desks, and undulating fluorescent lighting suggested the last time it had been revamped was in the Eisenhower administration. "I'm Jay McKnight and I work for the New Orleans Police Department. I've got a double degree, one in criminology and another in clinical laboratory science, then a master's in forensic sciences, the last from the University of Alabama. I also work for the New Orleans crime lab, which, as you probably guessed, since Katrina, has been a struggle. We lost our lab and more than five-million dollars worth of equipment in the storm. Evidence was destroyed and will never be regained. We've had to work out of space provided by other parishes' sheriff's offices or through private agencies, which has slowed things down incredibly. We've lost technicians, too, who got tired of living out of FEMA trailers and working in FEMA trailers and collecting evidence at FEMA trailers."

He had their attention. Their eyes, serious now, were trained on him, and no one was talking or so much as chewing gum.

"But things are getting better. Slowly. We don't have the offices and labs portrayed on television shows like *CSI,* but we do have our own facility now at the University of New Orleans at the lakefront campus."

He glanced at Kristi. She, like the others, was regarding him soberly. If she felt any emotion other than studious regard, she sure managed to hide it.

Good.

"I know most of you thought the class would be taught by Dr. Monroe, but due to an illness in her family, she had to take some time off and so you're stuck with me.

"So, for the next nine weeks we'll be discussing criminology in three-hour segments. We'll hit the major topics and rather than say I'll lecture, we'll say I'll lead the discussion on the science of forensics and evidence. During the last hour and a half, we'll have whatever quiz I think is appropriate and then there'll be a question and answer period. We'll discuss crime scenes and how to protect them, how to gather evidence and what we do with that evidence when it's collected. We'll cover everything from blood spatter patterns to firearms, entomology, and forensic biology, both plant and animal. We'll talk about cause of death and autopsies."

One boy, sporting a soul patch and several earrings, shot a hand into the air, "Is there any way we can go to an autopsy?"

That caused a few whispers, some excited, some disgusted.

"Not this term, I'm afraid," Jay said.

"But how cool would that be?" Soul Patch wasn't giving up.

"I don't know, how cool would it be?" Jay asked the class, and some of the kids actually hooted while others groaned. "As I said, it's not scheduled and this is a pretty large group. There are rules about that kind of thing, contamination issues, timing issues, and as cool as you think it might be to see, the medical examiner is a busy person, as is everyone who works for the examiner's office.

"However, to make things interesting, each week I'll discuss a specific case that the department solved, then show you the evidence that was collected, and we'll see what you can tell me about the crime. Afterward, we'll compare it to what the police actually discovered."

He still had their attention. Everyone seemed tuned in. At least for now. He made eye contact with Kristi again, as he did with the other students as he continued to lecture. It was easy for him because he loved his job. Examining evidence and linking it to a crime and a suspect was exhilarating as well as frustrating. He was animated as he talked, though it was difficult not to notice that Kristi still had that same vibrancy about her that had attracted him years before, when she was still in high school and he'd just started taking a few college classes while still working for his dad. Then, Jay had found her to be smart, sassy, stubborn, and tough as nails, sometimes even foolhardy, but Kristi Bentz had never been boring. Athletic and brave almost to the point of idiocy, Kristi exuded a raw energy that had been missing in most of the women he'd dated in his lifetime, including Gayle Hall.

Now, sitting in the back of the room without any makeup, her big, green eyes staring at him, her dark coppery hair twisted away from her face to reveal a clean jaw, straight nose, and high cheekbones, Kristi watched him intently. She sat low on her back, arms folded over her chest almost insolently, as if she were daring him to teach her anything she didn't know.

Or maybe he was imagining things.

He barely let his gaze touch hers before he turned toward the other side of the room and focused on a tall boy with thick glasses and a scrawny black beard that didn't cover his case of acne.

"I'll send each of you a syllabus tonight via e-mail, and my office hours are Friday afternoons from four to six. I know, that's a bummer for those of you who like to take off for the weekend, but it's the best the department could do as they have to work around my schedule. You can e-mail me at anytime; my e-mail address is on the syllabus.

"So, let's start with a little basic anatomy. Tonight, we'll talk about how a person can be killed, and what the body might show in an autopsy. After the break we'll discuss the crime scene and collection of evidence. This might seem a little backward, but I thought for our first 'case' we'd go at it from the body back to the scene. Next week, we'll take another case and do it in just the opposite manner, which, of course, is usually the normal procedure, though, not always. Can anyone tell me why?"

One arm shot up and waved frantically as if she could barely contain herself. She looked to be less than five feet tall and couldn't weigh a hundred pounds. Her light blond hair fairly shivered as she tried to get his attention.

He nodded at her. "Yes?"

"Sometimes the crime scene evidence doesn't make sense because the body might have been moved. In that case you would have the dump site but you'd also find evidence from the place where the attack or killing actually occurred."

"That's right," Jay said, nodding to the girl, who smiled smugly and beamed at being correct.

"Now, let's take a look at these—" Jay hopped off the desk and walked toward the charts of the human body he'd hung on the wall. One was skeletal, another was muscular, another showed the organs, and the fourth was a blowup of the sketch of a human body with the marks and notations added by a coroner from an actual case. He told the class this crime had occurred over ten years earlier, when a killer who called himself Father John was stalking the streets of New Orleans. The ligature marks around the victim's neck, as indicated by the ME's notes, were unique to Father John, or the Rosary Killer as he'd been called, who had strangled each of his victims with a rosary he'd created just for that purpose.

Father John had been a twisted serial killer, someone the kids would find macabre and fascinating.

Jay had not only a copy of the drawing from the autopsy, but photographs of the victim, which he would show later, then demonstrate how the science of forensics had helped lead the police to their killer. This case, he thought, would interest his class as the murderer had been familiar with All Saints Campus. Of course, Kristi Bentz might find it all a little more personal as her father had helped unmask the killer's identity. He noticed that she straightened in her chair.

"Now we'll look at a murder and work backward. You'll see we have a photograph of the victim and the medical examiner's notes." He reached for a stack of papers and began passing them out. "We'll look at the body the way the ME did. Start on page one, it's a smaller version of the medical examiner's notes. . . ."

*Tonight,* Vlad thought, from his perch on the third floor. Tonight would be a perfect time for his next abduction. He glanced upward through the highest limbs of the trees to the sheer outline of the moon, barely visible through the slowly moving clouds.

But, of course, that was not how the process worked. He couldn't just take a victim on her way home from a late class or the library or her job. He wasn't allowed to hide in the backseat of their cars at night, nor stalk them as they went unknowingly about their business. No . . . he was required to wait, to play the game, to make certain everything went as meticulously planned. He could take a life tonight, but it would not be one of the elite, one of the "chosen." Those who had been screened so carefully, those he deemed the royal ones. The privileged and college-educated. He had to be careful with them. They were being watched. But the others. *Those* he could maraud at will; though as ever, he must be careful. Always careful.

He heard the chime of the chapel bells and his pulse quickened. It was time.

*Bong, bong, bong . . .*

As they tolled off the hours, he felt a surge of excitement. Students began to pour out of the buildings, dashing hither and yon, talking, laughing, hurrying through the night, not realizing he was watching, that here, from his hiding spot, he could, if he were so inclined, pick them off one by one with a rifle, or a bow and arrow, or even a wrist rocket, a weapon he'd used as a child, sighting on birds and squirrels, even bats at night. His vision and hearing were so acute, even his sense of smell honed, that he could easily kill the prey of his choice, not that he needed a weapon.

But that was not the way it was to be.

That would be breaking the rules.

Tonight All Saints could not be his hunting ground.

His gut tightened as he spied several coeds, girls he'd seen on campus, students whose pictures he had tucked away. Several he knew by name and he smiled when he realized that one of them would be the next of the chosen ones. He rubbed his fingertips together and imagined their unwitting paths to him, which they themselves created, as they were the catalysts of their own demise . . . mistresses of their very own fates, the prophets of their own deaths.

*Soon,* he thought as a shadow passed over the moon and the air changed slightly. He smelled her scent first, then, turning, caught sight of her, Kristi Bentz, walking swiftly, her long legs eating up the concrete path leading from Knauss Hall. She was following someone . . . no, chasing him down as he strode to a parking lot at the edge of campus.

Even from this distance, he recognized the man.

The new professor.

Of course. His lips twisted as he eyed Jay McKnight, newest addition to the staff of All Saints.

The cop's daughter waved and, hair streaming behind her, caught up with McKnight.

Hidden in the shadow of the tower, he felt his blood

begin to run hot. From passion? Desire? Or anger? The
night seeped through his skin and into his bones as his
pulse elevated. His heart was thundering now, his muscles taut, his nerves tight as stretched rubber bands. He
imagined what it would be like to touch her . . . to feel
her respond to him, to slowly pull away each stitch of
her clothing until she was bare to him. In his mind's eye
he saw her long limbs, muscular yet feminine . . . supple legs that would wrap around him as he leaned forward, his breath hot over her breasts, his teeth and tongue
sliding over her nipples as he nipped. . . .

His muscles became taut and his genitals responded,
an erection growing rock hard.

No! He couldn't allow himself to go too deep into
the fantasy. Not yet. He had to save himself. Without a
sound, he closed the window.

Slowly, on silent footsteps, he backed away from the
glass panes to the stairs and, as he descended the well-
worn steps, he tamped down his need.

He could not be rash.

He could not give in to quick judgments.

He had to follow the plan.

Meticulously.

Or all would be lost.


"Jay! Professor McKnight! Hey, wait up!" Kristi
walked as fast as she could, trying to catch up with him.
She'd left right after class and started home, then decided they needed to clear the air, so she'd retraced her
steps, only to spy him heading out a back door. By the
time she'd gotten close enough to call to him, he'd
reached a staff parking lot. In the watery pool of illumination cast from a security light, he was loading his books
and briefcase into the cab of a beat-up old pickup.

He looked over his shoulder and his jaw slid to one
side. "Kristi Bentz."

"Hi." She nearly slid to a stop a good ten feet away from him. "I, uh, I was surprised that you were taking over Dr. Monroe's class. . . ."

"I bet."

She inclined her head, feeling her face flush. "This is awkward. Look, I know we—I—didn't leave things very good between us, and I thought—"

"Ancient history, Kris."

She'd forgotten he'd called her that. He'd been the only one in her life who had shortened her name. "Okay." She nodded. "But who knew we would be in the same classroom, or that you would be my professor, or—wait a minute," she said as the truth suddenly dawned on her. "You knew. You had to have known."

"As of a few days ago, yeah." He nodded and opened the door a little wider.

A deep "woof" escaped from the darkened cab and a huge, muscular dog leaped to the ground. In the streetlight, the animal's muscles rippled beneath a coat that looked like burnished copper.

Kristi took a step backward.

"This is Bruno," he said.

"He's mammoth!"

"Nah, just a little guy." Leaning down, he stroked Bruno's big head. "Gentle as a fawn unless you piss him off."

"I won't be doing that."

Jay flashed a smile and scratched the big dog's floppy ears. "Hurry up," he said to Bruno. "Take care of your business." Jay motioned to the edge of the lot where crepe myrtles lined the flower beds separating the campus from the parking area.

Bruno complied, sniffing the moist ground, then lifting his leg on a shrub while staring at Jay with baleful eyes.

"Good boy," Jay said as the dog finished relieving himself and began to sniff the ground. "Later. Come on, load up."

Bruno glanced at Kristi, then sprang into the passenger seat of the cab.

"So . . . why are you teaching here?" she asked.

"Change of pace. Things at the PD are still rough, never been right since Katrina, but I bet you know that."

She nodded, thinking of her father and his long hours, frustration, and disintegrating attitude. She'd even overheard him talking about retirement, which was years off. It was odd because Rick Bentz had been born to be a cop. He was most alive when he was on the job. That dedication and work-above-all-else ethic had cost him his job in LA and his marriage to her mother. Ultimately, she feared, it would cost him his life. But lately, since the mother of all hurricanes and the storm's aftermath, he'd been overworked, overstressed, and disenchanted.

"So, opportunity knocked and I answered."

"And now I'm in your class."

"Appears so," he drawled, and for the first time she saw beyond his own frustration to a bit of amusement at the situation. Oh, great. Just what she needed.

"Well, I just wanted to be sure that there were no hard feelings."

He lifted a shoulder. "No feelings period."

That stung a little bit, but she let it go. "Then we can go about this as if I'm just a student and you're the prof."

"Right."

"Good." She was still uneasy with the conversation; there seemed to be a million things they should be talking over, but why drag up all the old, hard feelings? If she could believe what he was saying, then they didn't have a problem.

"So, can I give you a lift?" he asked.

"Oh—uh, no . . . I'll cut across campus." She hooked her thumb in the opposite direction.

"It's late," he said.

"I'm fine. Really."

"Some girls have disappeared."

"Yeah, I know, but I can take care of myself. Tae kwon do, remember?"

The smile broadened. "Oh, yeah," he said.

A quicksilver memory slashed through her brain. She'd been a senior on a night not unlike this. They'd been alone in her father's apartment and she'd made the mistake of telling him that with her martial arts skills she could take down any man who tried to bother her. She'd assured him, then said: "I can take care of myself."

A don't-give-me-any-of-that-feminist-crap smile had crossed his face. "Yeah, right."

"I *can*."

She'd insisted that with her skills, she could handle anyone who came near her. He'd called her on her bragging and the discussion had elevated into a dare. Then, before the terms had been hammered out, he'd grabbed her, swept her feet from her, and taken her to the ground, using a technique he'd learned as a high-school wrestler. Within seconds he'd pinned her and she'd been unable to twist away from his weight.

She remembered lying on the living room carpet, staring into his triumphant face, breathing hard, so furious she wanted to spit at him. Nose to nose, hearts pumping, they'd lain wedged between her father's recliner and the television, each waiting for the other to move. Muscles tense. Ready. He'd known if he were so much as to shift his weight, she might be able to twist away; she was waiting for just that opportunity.

"Give?" he'd asked.

"No."

"You sure?"

"I'm sure."

"I pinned you."

"For now."

He grinned, taunting her. "I've got to be heavy."

She glared up at him and tried vainly to ignore her racing heart. The truth was he'd been crushing her, but there was more to it than that. She had to fight to keep from glancing at his lips, so near hers. Her blood pumped hard through her veins and she wondered what it would be like to make love to him. Right then. Right there. While they were still sweating and breathing hard from their wrestling. She saw his eyes darken, his pupils dilate as his own thoughts possibly mirrored hers. "Come on, Kris, I win," he said, his voice low.

"It's temporary . . ." She licked her lips and heard him groan, felt the hardness between his legs. She let out a little moan in reply and he lost control and kissed her. Hard. With a hot lust that spread from his bloodstream to hers. It was glorious.

And then she bit him.

Drawing blood.

He sucked in his breath in pain, his weight shifting just a bit. He swore, too, softly but dangerously as she started to wriggle free, struggling to gain enough room to twist and kick him as she'd learned in her last class.

But she stopped cold when she heard footsteps on the stairs outside the apartment door.

"Get off!" she ordered.

"What?"

Keys jangled on the other side of the door.

"It's Dad! Get off!"

In one fluid motion, Jay rolled off her and onto his feet. Before she could tell him what to do, he sprang over the couch, landed in the hall, and slipped into the bathroom as Kristi quickly adjusted her clothes and threw herself in her father's chair. She clicked on the remote just as the door swung open, revealing her father.

"Kristi?" Rick Bentz called as he spied her. "Oh . . ." Dropping his keys, wallet, and badge onto the entry hall table, he glanced at the television that was flickering on to a sports station. As if she'd ever been interested in a golf match. Cripes!

"Hi," she said brightly, with more enthusiasm than she'd ever greeted him. She knew her face was red, her hair sweaty, guilt written all over her expression, but she pretended that everything was normal and that her father, a detective who'd spent his life being suspicious and who was an expert in recognizing when someone was lying, didn't notice anything unusual.

"What's going on?" he asked casually.

About that time Jay flushed the toilet loudly, ran water in the sink, and walked out of the bathroom. He, too, was red in the face and his lip was discolored, a bit of dark blood visible where she'd bit him. Kristi wanted to drop through the floor and disappear.

"Hi, Detective," Jay said, and reached for his jacket, which had been slung over the back of the couch. "Gotta run. Work."

"Good idea," Rick Bentz said, his eyes narrowing on Jay. "You know there's a rule in my house. One my daughter seems to have forgotten, so I'll tell you. It's archaic, I know, but hard and fast. There are to be no boys in this place when I'm not here." He glared at Jay, then at Kristi.

"Sorry. Just bringing her home."

"And ending up with a split lip?"

"Yeah. Kristi can explain," Jay said, shooting her a look. "'Night, Kristi. Detective Bentz." And then he left her to deal with her father and "the talk" in which her father asked her if he needed to make an appointment with a doctor; if she needed to be on the pill, or should he be buying her condoms. She explained about the wrestling match, about biting him to gain control, and her father exploded, telling her that she was pushing it, that boys don't have any control, that she was asking for trouble.

"Way to go off the deep end, Dad," she declared, furious. "For your information, not that it's any of your business, I'm fine. I don't need pills or anything yet and when I do, believe me, I'll take care of it. Myself."

And she had. Six months later.

So now, here she was, in the dead of night, declining a ride from Jay McKnight, the boy to whom she'd given her virginity, then tossed over. The boy who was now a man and her college professor.

"I'll see you next week," she said, and moved away from the truck.

"I'd feel better if you'd let me drive you."

Shaking her head, she half smiled. "I can take care of myself," she said, echoing the phrase from so long ago once more, then turned on the heel of a boot and headed toward Greek Row and the Wagner House.

"Call my cell if you need anything," Jay threw after her, rattling off his number. Kristi lifted an arm but didn't turn around as she headed toward the library. From there, she cut to the gate near her apartment house, aware that she was memorizing his number against her better judgment. She didn't need Jay in her life.

She didn't look behind her, but heard the sound of a truck's engine cough, then catch. Good. She'd cleared the air with Jay and she was okay with it.

A second later, she heard the pickup drive out of the lot and she was on her way, hurrying across the dark campus, feeling the wind pluck at her hair.

There were a few other students out, but not many, and the shadows between the security lamps were thick and gloomy, seeming to shift with the rattling of the branches and the turn of the wind. The rain had stopped sometime during the past three hours, but the smell of damp earth was heavy in the air, the grass covered in dewy drops that shimmered in the moonlight.

Kristi angled toward the other side of the campus, to the gate near her apartment building. She cut behind

Wagner House and saw a movement . . . something out
of the ordinary. Red flags went up in her mind and she
flipped open the flap of her purse, her hand sliding into
the pocket where she kept her pepper spray.

*Don't be silly,* she told herself, *it's probably just a
dog.*

But she felt nervous sweat gather at the base of her
spine. It wasn't so much what she could see as what she
couldn't. She moved rapidly, on the alert, her pepper-
spray canister clutched tight in her fist. She hated being
a wimp. *Hated* it. She'd worked hard to be observant, to
pay attention to her surroundings, to trust her feelings,
and she'd been trained in self-defense so that she
wouldn't have to rely on anyone but herself.

But there was no reason to be foolhardy.

She thought of the weird sensation she'd gotten from
the dark car rolling down the street before class, and the
feeling every so often that she was being observed,
watched by unseen eyes.

The result of all her research on the missing girls.
The disturbing conversations she'd had with their families—people who truly didn't care—were getting into
her psyche.

She studied the shadowy shrubbery as she rounded a
corner and cut across the quad. A person in a dark
hooded jacket was walking in her direction. Kristi tensed,
her muscles suddenly tight, her senses honed on the approaching figure.

Until she realized the person approaching her was a
woman. A slight woman.

Kristi let out her breath as they passed. She caught a
glimpse of a face in the dark hood and recognized
Ariel, who, upon spying Kristi, veered a step away.

Kristi was about to say something when Ariel looked
directly at her and in that moment, all color drained
from Ariel's face, her complexion turned ashen, her vis-

age in shades of gray. Was it a trick of light? The silvery glow from a cloud-covered moon? The sheen from incandescent security lamps flickering in the mist?

"Ariel?" she said, turning, but the girl had headed down a brick path near the Commons and disappeared into the gloom.

But that draining of color . . . so much like the vision of her father. . . . Kristi's heart pounded hard.

She sensed, with cold certainty, that Ariel was doomed.

# CHAPTER 9

"Idiot," Jay muttered under his breath. He wanted to kick himself five ways to hell and back as he drove through the empty streets surrounding the campus. Bruno gave a soft woof, his nose at the crack in the passenger window, drinking in the smells of the night.

Jay flipped on the radio, hoping the sound of the Dixie Chicks would drown out any thoughts of Kristi. Instead, the song about getting even with an ex-lover only made him grip the wheel even tighter. "Son of a bitch." He'd kept his cool through class and beyond, when she'd chased him down to set things straight and clear the air between them, but it had backfired. At least for him. As mule-headed and reckless as she was, he still found her damned fascinating.

It was a sickness.

Like a death wish for his soul.

"Stupid, stupid, stupid," he grumbled, and switched stations to a local radio station where Dr. Sam, a radio psychologist, was dispensing advice to the lovelorn or confused in a special extended program. He figured there must be a lot of loonies in the dead of winter. He slapped the radio button off as he flipped on his wipers to swat away the mist that had collected. It wasn't raining, but the fog was dense and he wondered if he should have insisted on driving Kristi home.

*How? By bodily restraining her? You offered. She declined. She didn't want to ride with you. End of story.*

"Unless she ends up missing," he said, squinting through the windshield and stopping at an amber light about to turn red. A couple of teenaged boys zipped across the dark street on skateboards, their wheels grating on the pavement. Laughing, one dialing a cell phone as he rode, they turned toward a convenience store sizzling with neon lights but guarded with bars on the windows. A few cars crossed the intersection before the light changed again, glowing green in the mist.

Jay started, only to slam on the brakes as a cat sprinted across the street. "Damn!"

Bruno, spying the speeding tabby, started baying and scratching madly at the dash.

"Stop!" Jay ordered the dog as he eased through the intersection.

Bruno twisted, paws on the back of the passenger seat as he glared through the window of the cab at his adversary. He was still growling and whining. "Forget it," Jay advised, increasing his speed to thirty. "It's gone."

The hound wasn't about to give up but with a final "Leave it," from Jay, he gave a single woof and curled up on the seat again. "Good boy," Jay said, then spying something in his headlights, slammed on the brakes again. "Jesus!"

His truck skidded, frame shimmying, tires squealing. Bruno was nearly dumped into the dash as the truck's grill barely missed the man in black who leaped to one side and hazarded a quick glance at the pickup, his clerical collar showing white, his glasses fogged and reflecting the headlight's glare. His washed-out face was twisted in anxiety, as if he were in fear for his life. He kept running, his cassock billowing behind him. "Are you nuts!" Jay yelled, adrenaline shooting through his bloodstream.

Jay's heart was beating like a drum. He'd nearly

struck the guy! But the priest didn't so much as break stride. Half running, he disappeared into a park that backed up to one side of the campus.

"The guy's out of his mind," Jay muttered furiously, mentally counting to ten as he eased off the brakes and once again started driving through the night. "What the hell is he doing crossing the damned street in the dark? Moron! What's wrong with the crosswalk?"

What the hell was going on . . . ? The holy man looked as if he'd just seen a ghost, and he seemed to want to avoid anyone seeing him.

Jay let out his breath but he was still tense, muscles drawn, nerves stretched thin, fingers clenched over the steering wheel. Within three minutes he'd nearly hit a cat and a man.

The priest had looked familiar. It had been dark, yes, but there was something about him that made Jay think they'd met before. Here. In Baton Rouge. And it wasn't because Jay hightailed it to mass on Sunday mornings. No . . . it had to have been on campus or at an All Saints event of some kind.

Letting out a shaky breath, Jay shook his head. He cautiously stepped on the gas again, his eyes narrowing on the quiet road. "Third time's a charm," he said, wondering if he were cursing himself. Few cars passed him, nor were any following him as he turned onto the winding street leading to his cousins' bungalow.

He glanced in the rearview mirror, though he didn't know why. No one was following him. "Better keep your eyes on the road, McKnight."

He was still trying to place the priest. It hadn't been Father Anthony Mediera, the priest who, for all intents and purposes, was in charge of the college, but someone else he'd met on campus. Who? When?

He turned into the driveway of Aunt Colleen's small house, wondering what the hell the priest had been running from.

*Mathias Glanzer!*

That's who it was. Father Mathias, Jay was certain of it, and yes, he was associated with the college in some way. *Huh,* Jay thought. *What's the deal?*

Jay parked, pocketed his keys, and dragged his brief-case and computer into the cottage. With Bruno at his heels, he walked into the kitchen, where he studiously ignored the exposed sheetrock and lack of countertops. As Bruno sloppily drank from his water dish, Jay pulled a beer from the refrigerator and followed a short hall-way to his pink office. Bruno, water dripping from his snout, tagged after him.

"I *really* have to paint in here," Jay advised the dog as Bruno curled into his dog bed in the corner of the room, where once Janice's—or had it been Leah's?—twin bed had been positioned under a canopy of posters and album covers of the sisters' favorite rock stars. David Bowie, Bruce Springsteen, Rick Springfield, and Michael Jackson came to mind.

He sat down at the makeshift desk, then hooked up his laptop, waiting for an Internet connection. Logging on to the Web site for All Saints College, he browsed through the list of instructors until he found a picture of Father Mathias Glanzer, head of the drama department.

Twisting off the cap of his Lone Star, he took a long swallow. In the photo Father Mathias looked almost be-atific, his expression warm, friendly, at peace. He sat wearing a white alb with a gold-embossed overlay stole. His hands were folded and his blue eyes, behind rimless glasses, stared straight into the camera's lens. His chin was sharp, his lower lip slightly larger than the upper, his nose narrow. The entire photograph gave the viewer a sense that they were staring at a composed, calm man of conviction.

Far from the vision Jay had experienced earlier, when the priest had seemed rattled—or furtive—as if a demon straight from hell had been on his tail.

Why?

Jay shook his head. He'd had a long day and had to get up at the crack of dawn to drive to New Orleans. Shoving all thoughts of the holy man from his mind, he found the e-mail addresses of the students in his class and attached his syllabus. He saw Kristi Bentz's name again and frowned.

Bad luck, that.

He grimaced. Maybe Gayle had been right when she'd charged him with never really being over his high school girlfriend. It had seemed ridiculous at the time, the ranting of a jealous woman.

But . . .

After seeing Kristi again, he realized she was still under his skin. It wasn't as if he wanted to get back together with her. No way. But he couldn't deny that there was something about her that caused him to think stupid thoughts and remember forgotten moments in sudden sharp clarity, memories he'd considered long forgotten.

He exhaled heavily.

The smart thing—the only thing—was to leave her alone as much as he could.

Wasn't it bad enough that she thought she could predict her father's death? Did she have to bear this onus for other people as well?

Kristi unlocked the door of her apartment and stepped inside. To the rooms that had been occupied by Tara Atwater, one of the missing students. *Get over it. The apartment had nothing to do with Tara vanishing. She went missing from the campus and that didn't keep you from signing up for classes. Wouldn't you have taken this apartment anyway, even knowing?*

"Not on a prayer," she murmured, unable to stop the goose bumps from rising on her flesh. She double-checked the dead bolt as Houdini, who must've been waiting on the roof, hopped through the partially opened window, climbed over the kitchen counters, and disappeared.

"My stepmother would have a heart attack if she ever saw you on the cabinets," Kristi said. The cat peeked out at her. Houdini still wouldn't let her get close, but he was starting to seem to want to interact.

She filled the cat's bowl, made herself a bag of microwave popcorn, and spent the next hour and a half organizing her desk, not only for her schoolwork, but also to organize her notes on the book she hoped to write, the book about the missing girls, if it turned out they all had come to bad ends.

She looked around the small space where Tara Atwater had lived. Had Tara, like Kristi, slept on the trundle bed? Had she noticed the small closet smelled of mothballs? Had she complained about the lack of water pressure? Had she made popcorn here, used the same microwave, experienced the uncanny feeling that someone was watching her?

Kristi plugged her laptop into her printer, logged on to the Internet and began downloading and printing any article she could find on the missing girls. She located their MySpace pages and looked for any hint of them belonging to a cult or being interested in vampires. She thought there were some veiled references in their likes and dislikes columns, and decided to check them out further later. Tonight she'd gather information; later, she'd sort and analyze it.

Barely touching the popcorn, she searched cults, vampires, and cross-referenced them to All Saints College. She found that there was a surprising number of groups into the vampire/werewolf/paranormal thing. Some of the Web sites and chat rooms were obviously just for those with a passing interest, but others were more intense, as if whoever created the spaces actually believed demons walked among the living.

"Creepy," she said to the cat as he tiptoed to his food. He scurried away at her voice. "Definitely creepy." And Lucretia knew more about it than she was saying. "I guess we'd better stock up on garlic and crosses and silver bullets," she said . . . "or wait, are the bullets for werewolves?" Houdini froze, tail switching. Then he ran across the floor, up to the counter, and out the window. "Something I said?" Kristi muttered as she walked to the counter and stretched.

She gazed out at the night, over the wall surrounding the campus to the buildings beyond. A few stars were visible through shifting clouds and the layer of light from the city. Again she had the disturbing sensation that she was being watched attentively, that unseen eyes were observing. Calculating. She lowered the blinds, leaving only enough space for the cat to return if he so deigned.

Returning to the computer, she wondered if Tara Atwater had experienced the same odd sensation that someone was surveying her from the cover of darkness.


It was time.

He had to dispose of the bodies.

As Kristi Bentz snapped the blinds shut, Vlad checked his watch. It was after one in the morning. Perfect timing. He'd been watching her for over two hours and wishing that she was next. He'd caught glimpses of her breasts as she'd pulled off her sweatshirt and unhooked her bra. The mirror over the fireplace was positioned so that if the bathroom door were ajar, he had a view of the shower stall, sink, and even a bit of the toilet. He'd observed Tara from this very spot as she'd spent so much time painstakingly applying makeup or cocking her head as she inserted her earrings, struggling with the backs. He'd held his breath as he'd watched her lift her arms. She'd been unaware that she was also moving her breasts, giving him a better view of those gorgeous, sexy globes and the vial of her blood hanging from a chain surrounding her neck, nestled in her cleavage. Where the hell had she hidden it?

*You'll never find it,* he imagined her taunting him from the other side of the pale. Her tinkling laughter slid through his brain and his fists clenched so hard the skin over his fingers stretched taut.

"I'll find it," he muttered, then realized he was talking to no one, a ghost, the figment of his imagination.

*Just like his mother.*

Clenching his jaw, Vlad snapped back to reality. He couldn't stand here indefinitely and remember Tara. Nor did he have time to fantasize about what it would be like to watch Kristi as she showered and toweled dry, her wet hair clinging to her white skin. His teeth ground together and he pushed aside the want that always snaked through his blood. He knew that his lust was only one part of his life, and the girls he so lovingly sacrificed were only a means to an end.

Without wasting a second, he hurried down the stairs and out a back door. On quiet footsteps he made his way through the alleys and streets, always taking a different path, never allowing himself the luxury or trap of using the same route, one where he might be seen over and over again.

Noiselessly he unlocked the door to his private space and entered. He was restless and knew the bracing cold water of the pool would settle him, but there was no time. He'd spent too long at the window, watching Kristi Bentz, trying to decipher what it was she was doing at her desk so long. She'd spent hours on the Internet and he doubted that she was studying for any of her classes.

Already dressed in black, he spent a few minutes applying dark face paint, pulled on a wig of light brown, then covered his features with a nylon stocking . . . just in case. He already had lifts for his shoes, so he appeared taller than he was . . . no one would recognize him and he'd been careful in his dealings with the women, so that there would be no way to link him to them.

He walked quickly, past the shimmering pool and further to the space beneath the old hotel's kitchen. He unlocked a heavy door and carefully pushed it open, feeling the cold breath of winter against his skin, the kiss of Jack Frost. He snapped on a light. The single bulb illuminated the interior of the freezer in a glaring light that reflected in the thick bands of ice crystals lining the frigid room and sparkling, almost giving life to the open, dead eyes of the four women who hung on meat hooks, their skin frozen and pale as snow, the muscles of their faces solidified into expressions of sheer horror.

He hated to let them go.

He enjoyed visiting them after a long swim.

He'd walk between their cold bodies feeling the icy air on his own naked flesh. He would rub against them, feeling an erotic high, his white-hot blood almost boiling in his veins, the arctic air against his skin and the hard, smooth frozen muscles of these, the first of what would be many.

Licking his cracked lips, he leaned forward and ran his tongue over Dionne's breast, darker than the others, the nipple taut in icy death.

"I'll miss you," he breathed, before suckling a bit and feeling his erection strong as he rubbed it against her hanging legs. One hand cupped her buttocks and he remembered the hot joy of entering her. . . .

"In the next lifetime, my sweet," he vowed, turning his attention to Rylee . . . perfect, petulant Rylee. He hadn't had enough time with her. Her perfect, icy body called out to him and he thought of saving her, playing with her bloodless body, but he knew it was best to take her away as well.

He kissed her frozen, twisted lips and stared into her open eyes. Then he smiled as he viewed her neck, so perfect, arching back, the icy strands of her hair falling away to show the two perfect holes at the base of her throat, and he imagined the taste of her blood. Salty. Warm. Satisfying.

Yes, it would be difficult to let her go.

But there would be others . . . so many more.

He smiled in the darkness as their faces came to him.


Kristi couldn't sleep. The clock at her bedside table told her it was nearly one in the morning and the events of the past few days had been swirling in her mind. Over and over again, the pictures of the missing girls revolved and she remembered the phone calls she'd made between classes and work and a few face-to-face meetings with students who had known the girls who disappeared.

"Always knew she would come to no good . . . bad blood just like her father." It was Tara's mother's words that kept her awake the most. "He's in jail, y'know. Armed robbery, not that it's any of your business. My guess? She took off with some boy and somehow I'll end up having to pay the loans she took out to go to school. You just wait and see. And me with two other kids to support. . . ."

But Monique's mother had been no better, seemingly pissed off that her daughter had gone away to school and left her to deal with a husband with Alzheimer's disease. "She couldn't deal with it . . . not that she could deal with anything. That girl!" Monique's mother had snorted from somewhere in South Dakota.

Dionne's brother had thought she was a "cheap-ass ho," while her last boyfriend Tyshawn Jones was still MIA, or so it seemed. Dionne's coworkers at the pizza parlor had insisted they didn't get to know her and that she'd kept to herself.

Rylee's mother was a nightmare, inferring her daughter would just get herself "in trouble" as if that were the worst thing that could happen.

Kristi threw off the covers, disturbing Houdini, who had ventured close to the bed as she was sleeping. "Sorry," she said as the cat scrambled to his hiding place. She padded barefoot into the kitchen area, flipped on the faucet and, holding her hair away from her face, took a long swallow of the tap water.

*How many times had Tara done this?*

Kristi twisted off the tap and wiped her lips by turning her head, using the shoulder of the oversized T-shirt she used as pajamas. She leaned her hips against the counter and stared into the room where she and the ghost of Tara Atwater resided. The desk chair had come with the place, probably used by Tara to study for the same classes that Kristi was now taking.

She listened as the clock ticked off the seconds, the refrigerator hummed, and her own heart kept a steady beat. It was almost as if she was tracing Tara's life, walking in her footsteps, becoming the girl who had just left class one day and never shown up again.

It didn't make any sense.

Tara had no car, but she did have a credit card, a computer to log on to the Internet, a MySpace page, and a cell phone, none of which had been used since. The last person Tara had seen was the head of the English Department, Dr. Natalie "No comment" Croft. So far Kristi hadn't been able to get through to her.

Kristi's mind jumped to Rylee. The last person she'd met with was Lucretia Stevens, something Kristi's ex-roommate had failed to mention. "Curiouser and curiouser," she said to Houdini, who'd slunk to the far side of the room, luminous eyes focused on Kristi. Closing her eyes and rotating her neck, Kristi took in five deep breaths; then knowing that sleep would be far too elusive, she rolled out her desk chair, sat down, turned on her computer and, ignoring the charts she was making, logged on to the Internet. She'd found several vampire sites and some of the kids were chatting with her anonymously.

Maybe tonight she'd get lucky chatting with people who had names like ILUVBLUD, or FANGS077, or VAMPGRL or whatever. She hadn't had much luck with getting information about a cult or whatever, nor had anyone yet admitted to knowing any of the missing girls. Either they knew something and were keeping it secret, didn't recognize the coeds' real names as opposed to their screen names, or were totally clueless. Kristi was betting on the last, but she still kept up a conversation while checking out the missing girls' MySpace pages, reviewing their "groups" and pictures, trying to find a clue that she might have missed before.

Surely she'd find something.

People didn't just vanish off the face of the earth.

Even if they did believe in vampires . . .

Right?


The Mississippi rolled by thick and dark as he stood on the levee downstream from New Orleans. Ghostlike, Spanish moss drooped from the branches of the live oaks planted near the river's banks.

Vlad drew in a deep breath, smelling the damp earth mingling with the overpowering odor of the slow-moving water.

He was alone on this remote stretch of riverbank, yet he felt it still too exposed. If the bodies were to float to

the surface, to be discovered, things could get dangerous, and he still had so much work to do.

For her.

Always for her.

He closed his eyes and thought of her.

So perfect.

So beautiful.

A woman who, beyond all others, heated his blood.
He could hardly wait until he saw her again . . . watched
her from a distance, feeling himself grow hard at the
thought of her warm body and the blood . . . always the
blood.

He ran his tongue across his teeth in anticipation. A
surge of excitement sped through his veins and need
coursed to his soul.

Discarding this spot as his dumping ground, he
walked swiftly from the rise, through the long grass,
and into the trees where his van was parked. He climbed
behind the wheel and turned around, then drove out the
long lane and onto a back road that cut into the bayou.

Here, the sound of crickets chirping and toads croak-
ing cut through the stillness. Every once in a while there
was the soft, nearly inaudible splash of an alligator slipping into the water.

He parked by the dilapidated cabin, walked to the
back of his van, and pulled on hip waders. He slid a
miner's helmet onto his head, then switched on its light.
In the bright beam, he worked quickly, yanking on a
pair of gloves, then pulling out each body from the back
of the van. Wrapped in tarps, weighted with bricks
strapped to their torsos, they had begun to thaw, but
each was a deadweight as he carried her firemanlike,
over his shoulder. Down a deer trail to the edge of the
water. He unwrapped the first and stared down at her
face and her naked, frigid body for just a second. In the
harsh glare of his light, Dionne stared sightlessly up at

him, her black skin taking on a bluish tinge, ice crystals in her hair beginning to melt.

He hadn't wanted to leave them all together. That would make things too easy should anyone discover one of the bodies, but he was running out of time. He'd waited too long, putting off this part of his mission. He'd wanted to keep them near him forever, but, of course, could not. "Eternal rest," he said as he pushed Dionne's smooth body into the water. Once she submerged, the bricks ensuring that she sank to the bottom, he returned to the van.

Next he pulled out the tarp wrapped around Tara. The third. He'd watched her from his hiding spot as she'd walked nude around her apartment, the same upstairs studio Kristi Bentz now occupied. *How fitting,* he thought as he lugged Tara's frozen body to another point a little further downstream, opened the tarp and viewed her again. Her skin was pale, though tan lines that hadn't quite faded from summer were still visible. Her big breasts with their incredible nipples were puckered, begging for him to kiss them, lick them one last time. Yet he resisted. She, too, was pushed into the motionless water to be found by the creatures of the night.

He made two more trips, first with Monique. Tall and statuesque in life, an athlete, and now heavy and stiff, unbending. He untied the tarp with his gloved fingers and noticed that even in death, her muscles were defined. Her long red hair fell stiffly past her shoulders and was mimicked by frosty curls at the juncture of those long, incredible legs. His gut tightened as he looked at her before rolling her body into the water.

Finally he carried the last, smaller tarp far from his parking spot, where he untied the lashings, let the plastic fall free, then gazed long and hard at Rylee, with her cheerleader good looks and blue, sightless eyes. Even in the harsh beam of the headlamp, she was still beautiful. Her curves were perfect, her tiny waist nipped in beneath the globes of round breasts with pale pink nipples. A butterfly tattoo was frozen on the inside of one thigh and he remembered licking the icy decoration with his tongue as he'd explored her.

Yes, he would miss her and was irritated that he hadn't had longer to view her, touch her, feel her icy smooth skin against his own.

*There will be others . . . give her up. Make room for the next.*

His heartbeat quickened. He had but a week to wait and then . . . oh, and then . . .

With renewed energy, he pushed her body into the shadowy swamp water. With the beam of his light cutting through the inky depths, he saw her staring up at him through the wavering current as the water slid over those pale features.

Her blood, he'd thought, had been pure.

Perfect.

Slowly she disappeared from view.

# CHAPTER 10

Ariel knelt in the chapel.

Her knees ached and her shoulders were tight as she bowed her head and asked for guidance. Again. As she had every morning this week.

Ariel had always had a strong faith, hoping it would carry her through the tough times in her life: the death of her older brother Lance; her parents' divorce; her new stepfather and the string of boyfriends who had left her from the time she was fourteen, boys whom she'd given her heart and so much more before they all moved on.

No one had stayed.

Even her mother, after the divorce, had lost a ton of weight, started coloring her hair, and dating men who, like her, all tried to look younger and more hip than they really were. Eventually Claudia O'Toole had remarried. Tom Browning, a long-haul trucker, was nice enough, but he'd destroyed Ariel's tiny dream that her parents would get back together.

So, Ariel had turned from her family to her faith . . . until college.

"God forgive me."

From her knees she glanced up at the life-sized crucifix hanging between two tall stained-glass windows.

The statue of Jesus, wearing his crown of thorns, his head, hands, and side bleeding, arms stretched wide, stared benevolently down upon her.

*I am the light. . . .*

She could hear the words He told all of those who believed in Him.

"Dear Lord." She squeezed her eyes shut against her tears. Why, if Christ was so near, so caring, was she always so lonely? Why did she feel abandoned?

"Be with me," she intoned. "Please, Father."

Never before had she been so confused about her religion. Never before had she questioned the tenets of the church, never had she been so tempted . . .

She made the sign of the cross deftly, as she had thousands of times in her life.

She'd never been away from home before . . . well at least not for any length of time. Sure, she'd stayed with her father every other weekend for a while, then less often. And yes, there had been the time she'd run off with Cal Sievers when she'd found she was pregnant . . . even that precious little baby hadn't survived. Ariel, unfit to be a mother, had miscarried in her third month.

Now she bit down on her lower lip and felt her shoulders shake. She'd wanted that baby, that small little life who would love her, but even the infant, whom she sensed was a girl and had named Brandy, had left.

Knees aching, she swallowed hard, tasted the salt of her tears in her throat, and thought about the group she'd joined, those who had willingly embraced her.

No questions asked.

No judgments made.

And the leader . . . She stared up at the crucifix, felt that Christ could see into her soul, notice the tarnish around its edges.

She loved God. She did.

But she needed friends. A family here on earth.

Her own parents weren't interested.

The girls in the sororities were a bunch of shallow, self-indulgent snobs.

But her new friends . . .

She made the sign of the cross and stood, turning only to spy Father Tony standing in the balcony, gazing down upon her. Dressed in black, his clerical collar in stark contrast to his black shirt and slacks, he was a tall, handsome man. Too handsome to be a priest. She glanced away, sniffing and self-consciously dashing her tears from her eyes, but she heard his tread on the staircase, knew she couldn't make it out the carved doors of the chapel without facing him, talking with him, maybe even being persuaded into the confessional.

She sent up another small prayer and hurried past the rows of pews and was nearly to the front doors when he rounded a corner on the stairs and descended the last few steps into the vestibule, where candles had been lit, their small flames flickering as he passed.

"Ariel," he whispered, the hint of an Italian accent discernible. His dark hair gleamed in the candlelight, the expression on his even, handsome features solemn and concerned. "You are troubled," he said softly. Knowingly. Gently, he touched her hand with his warm fingers.

"Y–yes, Father." She nodded, unable to keep the tears from running down her cheeks.

"So many are. You know you're not alone. You must trust in the Father." Dark eyebrows drew together and his eyes, a pale ethereal blue, searched hers. She noticed the tightness in the corners of his mouth, the fact that his nose had obviously once been broken. "Talk to me, my child," he suggested, softly, almost seductively.

Ariel swallowed hard. Dare she trust him? Her private thoughts were so personal, her dilemma one no mortal man would understand, and yet she was tempted. Staring into a gaze that could surely see into her soul,

she wondered how much she could bare her soul and
how far she could stretch her lie.

Kristi gulped down her final swallow of coffee and
left her cup in the sink, then made sure the window was
open a crack for Houdini to enter and leave at will. Sunlight filtered into her apartment, the first time there had
been a cloudless day since she'd moved in. And the clear
skies had a way of lifting her spirits, a welcome change
after she'd immersed herself in cults, vampires, and missing girls, doing research, making charts, logging in hours
on the Internet searching news articles and personal
pages. She was beginning to understand the missing girls,
getting a sense of their dysfunctional family lives.

Didn't anyone care?

Kristi had approached the dean of students and had
received a frosty "none of your business" indicating to
her that the school was covering its ass, worried about
bad press.

Frustrated, stretched thin, and running on only a few
hours of sleep each night, Kristi barely had time to
breathe. She'd taken on a few hours working at the registrar's office to gain access to files regarding the missing girls' addresses and families, and insight into the
inner workings of their jobs and backgrounds. She was
still working at the diner, taking a full load of classes,
and struggling to keep up with the mounds of homework assigned.

And the missing girls were forever with her.

On her mind during class, or walking across campus,
or while she was working. She'd started making a few
social inroads, meeting friends of the girls, but they
were few, far-between, and extremely closemouthed. Of
the girls she'd tried to interview, no one had any idea
about a special group to which any of the coeds had belonged, but she sensed they had been hiding something.

Something she damned well was going to uncover.

Even if she had to enlist help from someone on staff. She'd been fighting the idea, but was tired of hitting her head against a brick wall.

Today, in the sunlight, she felt uplifted. For over a week the overcast days had seeped into her bones, the thickness of the night had made her want to curl up by the fire and double- and triple-check the locks on her doors.

She'd never had serious issues with fear, not after her mother died, not even after the attempts upon her life. It was odd, she thought, that she wasn't one to experience panic attacks considering all she'd been through. But lately, in the dead of winter, in this apartment from which a woman had vanished, on the campus where she had few friends, things had changed. At times she felt as paranoid as her cop father, who, even though he hadn't left New Orleans, seemed to be breathing down her neck.

But not today. Not with the January sun chasing away the clouds.

Grabbing her backpack with her laptop computer, she headed out of her apartment.

It was Thursday of the second week and already she was caught on the horns of several dilemmas. First, there was the matter of Jay and her conflicted feelings for him. During the second class he'd been all business, his gaze never touching on hers for more than an instant, no more than anyone else's as he'd reconstructed the evidence of a crime scene involving the serial killer Father John. Jay had been coldly clinical in his analysis of the differing pieces of evidence that the police had found. During the break, he'd been besieged by interested students as he had been after class. He hadn't seemed to notice when she'd left.

So what? Big deal. All for the better, she'd tried to convince herself. *He's your professor. End of story.*

And yet the fact that he'd basically ignored her had bothered her more than she wanted to admit. But then, she knew she was about to fix that, for like it or not, she had to approach Jay, talk to him, engage him and hopefully enlist his help.

"That should be a lot of fun," she said to herself.

Her other quandary was more difficult to deal with, she thought as she found a jacket and threw it on. For the past ten days, off and on, Kristi had caught glimpses of Ariel O'Toole, Lucretia's friend. Once at the bookstore, another time in the student union, a third time near Wagner House, and each and every time Kristi had seen the girl, Ariel was pale, washed out, her skin the color of cold ashes.

Was she ill?

Or about to meet with an accident?

Or was this all a figment of Kristi's imagination?

No one else seemed to notice. Could Ariel's appearance be all in her mind? Very much like the death she was certain she'd seen in her father's features time and time again? Should she approach Ariel? Talk to her? Mention it to Lucretia?

She frowned at that thought as she stuffed her cell phone into her purse. If she told anyone about her newfound ability to predict a person's death, she'd be considered a kook. And did she have any proof of this "gift"? Well, a little. One woman she'd seen on a bus who'd turned gray before her eyes had died a week later. But then she'd been, according to the obituary, when Kristi had looked it up, ninety-four.

She tried to shake off her worries but she didn't even have time to relax. On today's schedule was Creative Writing with Dr. Preston, another hunky instructor. He had the looks of the quintessential California surfer dude, complete with shaggy blond hair and hard, sculpted body, which he didn't bother to disguise in his tight jeans and old T-shirts. During class he had the habit of pacing across the room, looking at the class, all the while tossing a piece of chalk up in the air and catching it. He never broke stride, never quit lecturing, and never dropped the piece of chalk, which he kept at the ready in case he had to scribble some inspiration on the chalkboard before starting his pacing again. Ezma had labeled him rude, but he was definitely eye-candy.

If Dr. Preston was sun and surf, Professor Deana Senegal was at the other end of the spectrum. Since Althea Monroe had taken a leave, Professor Senegal was Kristi's only woman instructor. Senegal, who taught journalism, was a woman around forty who spoke in rapid-fire sentences and stared through sleek, rectangular glasses. Deana Senegal was pretty, smart, and had worked at newspapers in Atlanta and Chicago before getting her master's and accepting a position here at All Saints three years earlier. She'd taken a sabbatical for the birth of her eighteen-month-old twins, but now was back to work. With thin lips stained a deep wine color, porcelain skin, and green eyes that snapped fire behind those designer frames, Senegal was all business. She'd barely cracked a smile for the entire class period.

Kristi made her way down the stairs, thinking how she'd met several people who resided in the building. A married couple lived next to Mai on the second floor, and on the first, in the unit abutting Hiram's, was another single man, maybe a student, but one who kept odd hours; she'd only seen him late at night, either coming or going. He was tall and usually wore a dark coat, but she'd never seen his face well enough to decipher his features.

Today, as Kristi grabbed a textbook she'd left in her car, she spied Mrs. Calloway's PT Cruiser roll into the lot. The white car with its convertible top was distinctive, and not what Kristi had expected the older woman to drive.

Kristi reached her driver's door just as Irene was

climbing out and scowling at some dead weeds growing at the edge of the crumbling asphalt. "Damned things," she said, then caught sight of Kristi. "Oh. Hello. I heard you fixed those locks yourself." She was already shaking her head and reaching inside for a wide-brimmed hat to add to her outfit of brown corduroy slacks, a pink flannel shirt, and a beige cardigan sweater with the sleeves pushed up to her elbows. "I told you Hiram would handle it."

"I couldn't get hold of him in time."

She plopped the hat upon her head, covering her curly salt and pepper hair. "Well, then, I'll need a set of keys to your unit, and if you think you can take the expense of changing the locks off your rent, then you can think—"

"I'll see that you get a set," Kristi said, irritated with the money-grubbing landlady. "I heard that Tara Atwater lived in my apartment."

The older woman reacted and Kristi knew she'd hit a nerve. "Tara? The girl who ran out without paying her last month's rent? That's right, she lived upstairs."

"And she's missing."

"All I know is that she took off on me without paying."

"Or was taken. Some people think she was abducted."

"That girl?" Irene snorted derisively. "No way. She was a partier and a runaround. My guess is she took a notion to take off and did."

"And no one's seen her since."

"Probably because she was messed up with drugs." Irene squinted at Kristi. "I know the press gets worked up when girls drop out of college, making something out of nothing. The police don't seem to think there's foul play. Those girls who went missing? They've done it before. Their families aren't even concerned and I can vouch for that as far as the Atwater girl goes. I called her mother, and the woman could barely talk to me.

Complained of working two jobs with two younger kids to support. As for the dad, now there's a lost cause. Been in and out of jail. The last I heard he was still serving time. No one wants to ante up the back rent."

"You're saying no one really cares about Tara."

Irene lifted a scrawny shoulder, the pink and brown plaid of her shirt shifting in the sunlight. "She was a party girl. Always with the boys." She clucked her tongue, then leaned down and picked out one of the weeds daring to grow in the cracks of the parking lot. "That spells trouble to me."

"Do you know the names of the boys she dated?"

"I keep my nose out of my tenants' business."

That, Kristi knew, was a bald-faced lie. Irene Calloway had already told Kristi enough that suggested she loved to gossip, so, Kristi figured, it was only a matter of buttering her up or trading information to learn everything the landlady knew.

"Who collected her things? Someone had to pick up her stuff if she just left it."

"Not yet they haven't! And I'm charging 'em rent, too. Space ain't cheap, even storage compartments."

"You boxed her things up?"

"Me? Nah." She shook her head. "That's a job for the manager."

*Hiram. The do-nothing. Great.*

Kristi left the old lady muttering to herself as she yanked a few more weeds from the parking lot. Irene Calloway's take on things always had a negative spin on it.

Jaywalking across the street, Kristi headed to Adam's Hall, the vine-clad building that was home to the English Department, where her writing class with Dr. Preston was located.

As she reached the steps of Adam's Hall, her cell phone jangled with a special tune reserved for her father.

Of course.

"Hey," she said, making her voice sound cheery, even though she was a little bugged that he'd called. Had there been a day he hadn't checked in, making up some excuse to talk to her? Well . . . maybe a couple, but for the most part, Rick Bentz had phoned daily, inventing some lame excuse to talk to her.

"Thought I'd call because you said something about wanting your bike and I thought I could run it up to you this weekend."

"Give it up, Dad. You're making an excuse to check in with me," she said, squinting as she glanced back across the grassy area separating Adam's Hall from the religious center. The chapel spire rose above the branches of the surrounding live oaks and the brick face of the abbot's lodge, which was attached to a cloister, all part of the old monastery that was located on the premises.

Her father laughed and Kristi couldn't help but smile. "Old habits, you know," he said.

"Yeah, I do, and I would like the bike, but don't make a special trip up here. I'll get it my next trip down."

"And put it in the Honda?"

"I've got a bike rack. . . ." Staring at the chapel, she saw two figures emerge: one, a priest, not Father Tony, but the other guy; and two, Ariel O'Toole. So just how many hours did Ariel spend in the chapel or with the priest? Was she having an affair with the guy? Applying to become a nun? Confessing a myriad of sins?

"Look, Dad, I've got to run. We'll talk later . . . or text me, okay? Bye."

She clicked off and watched as Father Mathias, ever brooding, hurried into the chapel and Ariel, head down, walked rapidly in Kristi's direction. Once again, Kristi saw her in shades of gray. Despite the sunlight, a coldness swept through Kristi's bloodstream. She swallowed hard and knew she couldn't confront the girl head on. Ariel would think she was a nutcase, for sure.

No, Kristi would have to be sneakier about it. She dashed up the remaining steps and slipped into the hallway, then waited until she spied the glass doors open again and a group of five or six students pass through. Ariel lagged a little behind them but didn't look up or notice Kristi as she turned down the corridor to Dr. Preston's classroom.

Kristi followed and as soon as the door to the classroom closed behind Ariel, she went inside. Ariel found an empty desk and Kristi snagged one nearby. She didn't catch the other girl's attention, just waited and pretended interest in Dr. Preston as he began to lecture on the importance of perspective and clarity in writing.

"So let's talk about last week's assignment," Preston was saying. He dropped his chalk in favor of a stack of printed papers. "The assignment was to write two pages about your darkest fear . . . right? Most of you used description very well, but, let's see—" He flipped through the pages until he came to the one he sought. "Mr. Calloway had an interesting take on the subject. He writes: 'This is supposed to be a creative writing class and I cannot write creatively when forced to write upon a specific subject. My creativity—and that word is in quotes—is stifled.' " Preston looked up and focused on Hiram Calloway, who stared defiantly back at him. "Well, that's an interesting way to get out of an assignment." He glanced to the rest of the class, his gaze touching lightly on Kristi's before moving on. "However I would have been more impressed had Mr. Calloway said something like, 'I feel chained to my desk, forced to write a paper I loathe.' He might have gotten an A for that response; as it is, he'll have to settle for a B as the paper, or lack thereof, was original." He smiled then, white teeth against suntanned skin, blond hair gleaming under the lights. "Now, I'd like to read something more traditional and worthy of the A she received. This paper is written by Miss Kwan and I would say she has a good understanding of writing viscerally and descriptively."

Kristi glanced at Mai, who lifted her chin a notch as Preston began to read.

"'I fear the devil. Yes, Satan. Lucifer. Evil incarnate. Why? Because I think he, or she, if you so believe, lurks in all of us, at least, if I'm honest, he lives in me, deep in the nether regions of my soul. I struggle to keep him trapped and locked away for fear of what he, and I, as his vessel, might do. I cannot imagine the pain and suffering he might inflict should he be unleashed.'"

Preston grinned at Mai, almost as if he knew her intimately. What was *that* all about? "That was just the first paragraph and yet we feel the writer's battle, her fear, her worry about her own psychosis. For in that one paragraph we see that she still has the upper hand. She talks not of the devil breaking free but of her unleashing him. She still has control, albeit a very tenuous hold on Satan and her sanity." He nodded as if agreeing with himself, his blond hair catching the light of the fluorescent bulbs humming over his head. "Well done, Miss Kwan. She received the only A because she was the only one of you who made me believe she was indeed writing from her heart."

Mai smiled self-consciously, blushed, then looked down at her desk, as if she were slightly embarrassed, but Kristi wasn't buying it. She knew her neighbor better than to believe the humility act. But the subject matter of Mai's fears gave her pause.

Satan in her soul? Not spiders or snakes or dark places or airplanes, or falling from bridges or marrying the wrong person, but the devil lurking in her soul? Where did *that* come from?

"Jesus," Kristi whispered, and caught a quick, non-approving glance from Ariel. "I just meant that was pretty creepy." Frowning, Ariel gave a little shrug.

Her attempt at becoming Ariel's friend was not going well. At this rate it would take eons for Kristi to gain her trust, and she felt as if she were running out of time. Why did she even care? Because Ariel was Lucretia's friend? So what? And the gray-faced thing, maybe it was all a figment of her imagination.

Leaning back in her desk chair, Kristi forced her full attention to the lecture. Finally, after Preston tossed the chalk a few times, returned their papers and gave the next assignment, Kristi gathered her belongings and walked out of the building, one step behind Ariel. The day was still warmer than usual but the sunlight was now filtered by high, thin clouds, causing dappled shadows on the ground.

Kristi figured she'd blown her chance at cozying up to the girl. No surprise there. Kristi had never been able to fake a friendship or hide her true feelings. She couldn't count how many times she'd been told she wore her heart on her sleeve. It just wasn't in her to fake it, so she decided to just flat-out ask Ariel what was going on. "Hey, Ariel," she called.

Hearing Kristi's voice, Ariel stopped dead in her tracks. "What?" she asked, and pointedly checked her watch.

"Are you okay?"

"What do you mean?" She started walking again, a little faster. Obviously wanting to get away.

"You seem preoccupied." Kristi kept up with her, stride for stride and tried not to think that she had to get to work in less than half an hour.

Ariel hazarded a quick glance at Kristi. "You don't even know me."

"I can tell that something's bothering you."

"And you're here to help?" She shot Kristi a bewildered look, and in that instant Kristi decided to confide in her.

"Look, I know this sounds weird, but . . . I . . . have

this thing, okay? Call it ESP, or whatever, but I've had it ever since I was in the hospital and nearly died. The deal is that I . . . can kinda see into the future. Not always, but sometimes, and I can see if someone's in danger."

Ariel folded her arms, shrinking into her oversized hoodie. "Either you're crazy or this is some kind of weird joke."

"I'm serious."

"What are you saying? That I'm in trouble?"

"Danger. Possibly life-threatening," Kristi answered earnestly.

"Oh. My. God. You are nuts! Leave me alone."

"It's just that sometimes, when I see you, there's no color in your skin. It's like you're in a black and white movie."

Ariel shuddered despite her bravado. She backed away from Kristi, her eyes searching around as if for help. "Leave me alone. Don't ever talk to me again. You must be on something. Or you're a head-case. This isn't funny, you know." Kristi took a step forward and Ariel looked ready to scream. "Get away from me. Now!"

"I'm just concerned."

Ariel snorted, putting more distance between them. "You'd be the first," she muttered fiercely as she hesitated at the gate of Wagner House. Her face was so washed out she looked half dead already. "Stay away from me! You hear? Don't ever come near me again or I'll call the police and have a restraining order slapped on you."

Before Kristi could say anything more, Trudie and Grace rounded a corner not far from the library. Ariel saw them and began to wave frantically, like a panicked, drowning woman hoping for a lifeline. Without another word, she met up with her friends and walked through the open gates. They all headed up the steps to the old stone manor. As Kristi understood it, Wagner House had been the home of the original settler of this tract of land. Now it was a museum.

Grace pulled one of the double doors open and the three girls stepped inside. Ariel turned to slip Kristi a final look, her face wan and shadowed. Though they were only yards away from each other, Kristi felt as if there were oceans of distance between them. The thick wooden door shut behind the trio with a distinct thud.

Kristi hesitated. Obviously the girl didn't want her help. And who was to say that Ariel was caught in some dire, fatal situation? Sure, the elderly woman on the bus had died, but so what? Her father was still alive, wasn't he? True, the glimpses she'd caught of the ghostly Rick Bentz had been fleeting and spotty, sometimes not being apparent for months, but he didn't seem on the brink of death.

The knot in her stomach said otherwise, but she wanted desperately to believe she was mistaken about him—that she was wrong about all her visions. However, in the case of Ariel O'Toole, the ghostly appearance was steady. Every time Kristi caught sight of her she was washed out, pale and gray. Ariel had needed to be warned, but Kristi already knew she'd made a mistake in confiding in her. Now Ariel thought she was deranged and should be in a mental hospital, or that she'd been playing a cruel joke on her. Worse yet, the secret Kristi had kept for all the past months was no longer hers alone. That wasn't good. She shouldn't have blurted out the truth, but what other choice had she had?

She glanced up at the mullioned windows of Wagner House and thought she saw Ariel's image, shattered and misshapen, by the beveled panes of glass. Even so, she appeared a ghost.

# CHAPTER II

Officer Esperanza in Missing Persons wasn't happy. A big bosomed woman, she leaned on the other side of the counter separating the work space from the reception area and glared at Portia. She didn't like Portia Laurent or anyone else questioning her authority, and it showed in the tightness of her lips and the flare of her nostrils. Portia pressed her lips together waiting for the explosion. Pushing sixty, her hair dyed a Lucille Ball red, Lacey Esperanza was not known for her restraint. Smart, sassy, and sometimes downright ornery, she took her job beyond seriously. Waaay beyond.

"I'm gonna tell you exactly what I tell anyone who calls from the press, Detective, and that is to take it up with the goddamned FBI. They have the resources, the manpower, and the GD know-how to deal with this," she said in a gravelly voice. "They've been notified and are running their own investigation or lack thereof. The way I see it and we all agree here, there is no case. Yes, the girls disappeared from All Saints. Missing? Phooey! Murdered? Then where the hell are the bodies? I don't know about you, but I got a butt-load of work to do on cases where people are actually"—she made air quotes with her fire-engine red fingernails—"missing. You know, where family members or friends are calling and looking for someone." She leaned close enough so that Portia could smell the scent of stale cigarette smoke mingling with her perfume. "What's wrong over there at All Saints that they can't keep track of their students, huh? LSU is what? Five or six times the size of All Saints and they seem to keep track of theirs."

Which was exactly the point. What was it about the smaller college that caused it to lose some of its coeds? Portia didn't say it to Esperanza, but she believed there was a predator at large and his hunting ground was the campus of All Saints College. She'd checked. Lacey was right. Louisiana State, located only thirty minutes from the campus of All Saints, hadn't reported any missing students. Nor had Our Lady of the Lake, or Southern University, or the community college, or any of the bible colleges or even the beauty schools. Just All Saints.

So far.

Until this monster that Portia believed was stalking the small college broadened his hunting ground. Dear God, she hoped she was wrong.

"Let me tell you," Lacey rambled on, "I get nearly a hundred e-mails a day and that's after the spam has been filtered out. Double that many come in over a weekend. I'm pretty damned busy. Let the Feds figure it out. However"—she turned her palms toward the acoustic tiles of the ceiling—"if you want to look in the files, be my guest. I guess it says something about the Homicide Department if you have time on your hands to go rootin' through our files."

Lacey turned to a coworker sitting at a nearby desk so clean it looked as if no one actually worked there. Not a photo, dying plant, or name plate on the desk. The in-basket was as empty as the out. "Mary Alice, if Detective Laurent wants anything, you see that she gets it, y'hear. Me, it's time for my break."

Lacey scraped her pack of cigarettes from the top of

her cluttered desk, then rained a saccharine smile on Portia as she opened the top of the long counter that served as a gate. Squeezing her way through, she walked briskly between the scattered desks to the staircase leading to the front entrance of the station.

Mary Alice, a thin girl with stringy mouse brown hair, looked up at Portia with huge hazel eyes. "I apologize, Detective. Lacey, she's got herself a passel of trouble at home what with that daughter of hers. Nearly forty years old and the woman can't seem to hold down a job or get her act together. Sheeeeit, she's got three kids of her own, for God's sake, and that oldest one, Lacey's grandson, he's already got hisself into trouble with meth. Nasty stuff, that."

Portia couldn't agree more. "That's too bad."

"Praise the Lord and amen to that!" The small woman pushed on the edge of her desk and rolled her chair backward far enough so that she could stand, showing off her slight figure, slim skirt, and high heels. "So, tell me again, what is it exactly I can get for you?"

Portia slid the list of names across the counter. "Everything you've got on these girls."

"The fearsome foursome," Mary Alice said as she eyed Portia's handwritten note. "Most of this is on the computer. Don't you have your own files?"

*And then some.* "Nothing official," Portia hedged. "I've looked over what's on the computer but, if you don't mind, I'd like to see the actual files."

"Makes me no never mind long as Lacey's okay with it. Just give me a sec." High heels clicking, Mary Alice walked to a bank of file cabinets and started searching through the folders. In a matter of minutes, she had slapped the pathetically thin files on the counter and Portia signed them out. Portia carried the few documents back to her cubicle and decided she'd copy everything within the files just so she'd be ready.

She prayed she was misguided, but all her instincts told her it was only a matter of time before one of the girls' bodies showed up.

When it did, and there was an actual homicide case to be solved, she'd be ready.

*Two classes down, too many more to go,* Jay thought as he drove north on Friday night. With Bruno by his side, nose to the crack in the window, and Springsteen blasting through the stereo, he hauled some new plumbing fixtures and tiles toward Baton Rouge. Even in the darkness as he squinted into the headlights of cars heading toward New Orleans, he noticed more evidence of Katrina that had yet to be cleared: uprooted, long-dead trees, piles of rotting boards alongside homes being restored by the most stalwart and determined of Louisianans.

So far he'd settled into his new routine. He enjoyed the challenge of renovating his cousins' house and had found teaching exhilarating. Except, of course, for dealing with Kristi. After the first night when she'd run him down to clear the air between them, they hadn't spoken. She hadn't asked a question in class, nor had he singled her out to answer one he'd thrown at the students. She'd sat at the back of the room, taking notes, watching him, her expression fixed and bland. Icily cool and disinterested.

Definitely un-Kristi.

The fact that she tried so hard to look studious and unanimated made him smile. Obviously, by her attempt at detachment, she was having as hard a time dealing with him as he was with her.

*Well, fine,* he thought, flipping on his wipers for a second, just to scrape off the thick mist that was settling with the night.

Kristi deserved a little discomfort. As much as she'd served up to him. Jesus, in the past two weeks he'd had three dreams involving her. One hot as hell, their naked bodies covered in sweat as they made love in a bed that was floating down a swift, dark river. In the second dream he'd watched as she'd taken off with a faceless man, looping her arm through his as they walked into a chapel with bells chiming, and in the third, she was missing. He kept catching glimpses of her, only to watch as she vanished into a rising mist. That nightmare had tormented him just last night, and he'd woken to a pounding heart, dark fear pumping through his bloodstream.

"Gonna be a long term," he advised the dog as he signaled to leave the highway. Up ahead the lights of the city cut through the fog.

His cell phone rang. Bruno let out a soft woof as Jay managed to turn off the radio, answering without looking at the digital display.

"McKnight."

"Hi."

Well, speak of the devil. Jay's jaw hardened. He'd recognize the sound of Kristi Bentz's voice anywhere.

"It's me, Kristi," she said, and then added, "Kristi Bentz." As if he didn't already know.

"You memorized the number." The wipers skated noisily over the windshield and he switched them off, driving for half a second with his thigh.

"Yes, I guess I did," she said tightly.

His right hand gripped the wheel again and he braced himself. "Need something?"

"Your help."

"With an assignment?"

She only hesitated a heartbeat, but it was enough to warn him. "Yeah."

God, she was a liar. "Lay it on me."

Angling his truck off the main road at the outskirts

of the city, he followed what was becoming a well-worn route to his cousins' house.

"I can't. Not over the phone. It's too complicated and I'm already late for work. It, uh, it took me a long time to screw up the courage to call you."

Now that was probably the first bit of truth in the conversation. He didn't respond.

"I thought that maybe . . . maybe we could meet," she said.

"Meet? Like in my office?"

"I was thinking somewhere else."

Jay was watching the road, spying a kid on a motorized scooter who, as he passed, zipped out of a driveway to speed across the road behind him. "Jesus!" he muttered.

"Wow . . . I'll take that as a no."

"I wasn't talking to you. I'm driving and a kid nearly hit me." He slowed for a stop sign. "Where?"

"I don't know. Maybe the Watering Hole."

"For a drink?"

"Sure. I'll buy."

He stepped on the gas and drove to the next corner, where he turned down the street to his part-time bunga-low. "You mean, like a date?" he asked, knowing she'd probably see red.

"It's just a damned beer, Jay."

"A beer and a favor," he reminded her. "You want me to help you with something."

"Call it whatever you want," she said, a tinge of exas-peration in her voice. "How about tonight? Around nine? I'll meet you there. It's not far from where I work."

He knew he was asking for trouble just seeing her again. Big trouble. The kind he didn't need. Just having her in his class caused him to have nightmares. Any-thing more intimate was bound to spell trouble.

He hesitated.

Who was he kidding? He couldn't resist. Never could, when it involved Kristi. "Nine it is," he said, and as the words spilled out of his mouth he was already giving himself a hard mental shake. *Idiot! Lamebrain!*

"Good. I'll see you then." She hung up and he drove into the driveway with the cell phone still clasped in his hand. What the hell could she possibly want from him? He slammed the truck into park and sat behind the wheel. "Whatever it is," he said to the dog, "it's not gonna be good."

Kristi untied her dirty apron, dropped it into the hamper near the back door of the restaurant where she worked, snagged her pack from a hook, then headed toward the restroom. Inside the cramped room she stripped off her grimy skirt and blouse, then stepped out of the black flats she wore on the job. With a spritz of perfume in lieu of a shower, she glanced at her reflection in the mirror, groaned, and pulled on her jeans and a long-sleeved T. In one motion she yanked the band holding her ponytail to the back of her head and shook her hair loose. Half a second later, she laced up her running shoes and stuffed her dirty clothes into her backpack. She was late, as usual.

It was already nine and she didn't want to stand Jay up. She was bugged that she had to ask for his help, but she'd been butting her head against the wall when it came to getting more information on the missing girls. Kristi needed someone with connections, though asking her father for help was out of the question. But Jay was on campus, available in Baton Rouge part of the week, and since he was a professor he had access to records at All Saints. Her six hours a week working for the registrar weren't enough to open the locked doors and filing cabinets she wanted to search. Nor had she been given a password to the most private and sensitive information stored in the school's database.

So, she was forced to turn to someone on staff.

She'd thought about Lucretia and discarded the notion; her former roommate wasn't the most trustworthy or helpful person on the planet.

So she had to find a way to persuade Jay to get involved.

If she could have come up with another person who had access to the kind of information she needed, she never would have called Jay—at least she *hoped* she wouldn't have. She'd come to terms with suffering through his class for a few weeks, but this was different. It put her in closer contact to him.

*Maybe that's what you were angling for.*

"Oh, shut up," she said to that persistent and irritating voice in her head. She did *not* want to be close to Jay. Not now. Not ever. This was just a necessity, a means to an end.

"Date my ass," she muttered, leaving the restroom and yanking her jacket from a peg.

With a wave to Ezma, she was out the back door of the restaurant, where two of the line cooks were smoking in the blue illumination from the security lights. The night was cool, a mist sliding through the parked cars in the lot and clinging to the drooping branches of the single tree.

Kristi took off at a jog for the Watering Hole. The student hangout would be crowded enough so that it wouldn't feel intimate, yet there were spots in the connecting rooms that were quieter than the open space around the sports bar. There was a chance Jay might be seen with her, but she figured it didn't matter. Who would care?

Barely breaking a sweat, she made it to the hangout only eight minutes late. Shouldering open the door, she slid inside. With a quick perusal of the semidark, crowded interior, she zeroed in on Jay seated at the bar, nursing a drink, staring up at a television screen where some football game was being played. He was facing away from her, but she recognized his shaggy brown hair, wide shoulders stretching the back of a gray sweatshirt, and jeans she'd seen him wear in class, the battered, sun-bleached ones with a tear at the top of a back pocket. The stool beside him was empty, but he'd claimed it by resting the sole of his beat-up Adidas running shoe upon one of the cross-rails, as if he were saving her a seat.

Fat chance. She knew he hadn't wanted to come. She'd heard the hesitation in his voice.

But then, Kristi couldn't blame him. It had taken her half a week to work up to calling him, and the only reason she had was that she was desperate and needed help. His help.

She took in a deep breath as she wended her way between the tables and knots of patrons talking, laughing, flirting, and drinking. Glasses clinked, beer sloshed, ice cubes rattled, and the smell of smoke hung in the air despite all the efforts of a wheezing air-filtering system. The televisions were muted but music wafting from speakers mounted high on the walls competed with the noise of the crowd.

Jay kicked out the stool just as she reached him, as if he'd sensed her presence.

"Nice trick," she said, and he lifted his glass toward the bar and the mirror behind it, where her reflection stared back at her.

She slid onto the stool. "And for a second I thought maybe you were clairvoyant."

One side of his mouth twitched upward. "If I was, then I'd know what the hell it is you want from me, now, wouldn't I?"

"I guess you would." To the bartender wiping up a spill, she said, "I'll have a beer . . . light. Whatever you've got on tap."

"Coors?" the bartender asked, tossing his wet rag into a bin under the bar.

"Yeah. Fine." Forcing a smile she didn't feel, she met Jay's brutal gaze. "Bet you were surprised that I called."

"Nothing you do surprises me anymore."

The bartender set a frosted glass in front of her and she placed her ID and several bills on the bar.

"That's a tip," Jay said to the man behind the bar. "Put her drink on my tab." To Kristi, he added, "Come on, let's talk in the dart room where it's a little quieter. Then you can tell me what this is all about."

"And beat you at a game."

"In your dreams, darlin'," he said, and her stupid heart did a silly little flip. She wasn't falling for his charms. No way, no how. There was a reason she'd broken up with him all those years ago and that hadn't changed. Worse yet, he was wearing a three-day's growth of beard, the kind of pseudo-chic look that she detested. Of course it just made him look cowboy-rugged. Crap. The least he could do was look bad.

She grabbed her beer and again serpentined through the tables and crowd to a booth where a busboy was busily picking up near-empty glasses and platters bearing the remnants of onion rings, french fries, and small pools of ketchup. With a nod from the busboy, Kristi slid into one side of the booth while Jay sat opposite her.

Once the table had been swabbed down and they were alone again, Kristi decided to cut through all the uncomfortable small talk. "I need your help because you're on staff here and have access to files I can't see."

"Okay . . ." he said skeptically.

"I'm looking into the disappearance of the four girls who went missing from All Saints," she said, and before he could protest she launched into an explanation about her concerns, Lucretia's worries, the lack of anyone seemingly interested in what happened to the coeds, and the fact that they could have all met with foul play.

Arms crossed over his chest, Jay leaned against the

wooden backrest and stared at her with his damnable gold-colored eyes as she laid it out to him.

"Don't you think this is a matter for the police?" he asked.

"You *are* the police."

"I work in the crime lab."

"And you have access to all records."

He leaned forward, elbows propped on the table. "There is a little matter of jurisdiction, Kristi, not to mention protocol and the fact that no one but you and maybe a few hungry rogue reporters think a crime has been committed."

"So what if we're wrong? At least we tried. Right now, we're just sitting around not doing anything because no one else gave a damn about these girls."

"There's no 'we.' This is your idea."

But he still hadn't said no or argued that he wouldn't help her. He took a long swallow from his beer and stared at her. The wheels were turning in his mind; she could almost see them. And the one thing that she'd admired but had also disliked about Jay was that he was a bona fide do-gooder. A regular Dudley Do-Right when it came to matters of the law.

"Doesn't matter whose idea it is, we need to check it out," she insisted.

"Maybe you should contact the local police."

"I've tried. Gotten nowhere."

"That should tell you something."

"Just that no one gives a damn!" She half rose from her chair. She was reminded just how maddening Jay could be.

"If the locals aren't interested, you could consider talking to your dad," he suggested.

"I considered it and threw the idea in file thirteen. He's already freaked about me being up here. He knows about the missing girls and he's damned sure I'll be the next."

"He could be right, what with you poking around and all."

"Only if there is a psycho on the loose. If not, I'm in no danger. If so, then we've got to do something."

"By making yourself a damned target?"

"If need be."

"For Christ's sake, Kristi, didn't you learn your lesson the last time, or the time before that?" he demanded, his lips thinning in frustration. When she didn't answer, he snorted and said, "Apparently not."

"So are you gonna help me or am I gonna have to go this alone?"

"You're not going to guilt me into this." He cocked that damned broken eyebrow and drained his glass.

"How'd that happen anyway?" she asked, motioning to the little scar.

"I pissed a woman off."

"*Really* pissed her off. And she beat you up?"

"Hurled a ring at me."

So that's what had happened to the engagement she'd heard about. "At least she was passionate."

"Maybe a little too passionate."

"Didn't think that was possible."

One side of his mouth lifted into a knowing half grin. "Passion can run hot and cold, Kris," he said. "When one person can't get what he or she wants, that passion can turn into brutal frustration and anger. I figured I was better off without a woman who would tell me she loved me one second and try to kill me the next." His gaze touched hers. "I think that's all you need to know about my love life. So, spell it out. What do you want me to do? Copy all the personnel files, grade reports, loan applications, social security numbers of the girls?"

"That would be great."

"And illegal. Forget it."

"Okay, okay, so just look through the information and let me know if you see anything that looks suspi-

cious, anything that links the girls besides their choice
of classes and the fact that their families gave new
meaning to the word dysfunctional. You're a cop."

"And I could lose my job."

"I'm asking you to do a little research, not break the
law."

His lips compressed as a waitress came by and asked
if they wanted another round. Jay nodded and Kristi
said, "Sure," then drank half her beer while still waiting
for an answer. Finally she said, "If you find anything,
we'll go straight to the police. Or the campus security
and leave it to them."

"You'd do that?" he asked, skepticism tingeing his
words. "Just hand over everything you've got?"

"Of course."

He snorted in disbelief.

"Come on, Jay, I'll play you a game of darts. If I win,
you'll look through the records."

"And if I win?" he asked.

"You won't."

"So sure of yourself?" he asked, his eyebrows slamming together. "No dice. I want to know what the stakes
are if I win."

The waitress came back with the new round, scooped
up Jay's empty and left Kristi with a beer and a half in
front of her. "Okay, *Professor,* if you win, then you
name it."

"That's pretty cocky."

"Just confident." She finished the first beer and stood.
One dartboard wasn't being used. She walked over to it
and plucked one set of darts from their holder.

He slid out of his side of the booth and said conver-
sationally, "I'll expect you to pay up when I win and,
trust me, you're not going to like what I want as pay-
back."

She felt a little thrill sizzle through her blood, ignored it, and concentrated on winning. She didn't like

the stakes at all. God only knew what he would want from her.

But it didn't matter.

She wasn't about to lose this match.

# CHAPTER 12

As he sat in the driver's seat of his truck, the engine cooling and ticking in the parking lot of Kristi's apartment building, Jay decided he was a moron.

A bona fide, dyed-in-the-wool moron.

Kristi was gathering her bag together and reaching for the door handle. He'd lost at darts to her. Not once, but the best of two out of three, then three out of five. He'd only won one of their matches and he suspected that she'd intentionally mis-thrown so that his bruised masculinity wouldn't be completely destroyed. Though that wasn't really Kristi's way. For as long as he'd known her, she'd been a competitor to the nth degree. Throwing a match just wasn't her style.

He could have blamed it on the beer, but he'd only drunk three over the course of as many hours. She'd kept up with him and showed not one sign of having been affected at all by whatever alcohol existed in light beer.

So he'd lost the damned bet, but she'd agreed, albeit reluctantly, that he could take her home. So here they were in the parking lot of her apartment building, which was really an old three-storied clapboard house that showed influences of Greek Revival architecture with its massive white columns and wide portico. However, even in the poor light cast from a security lamp, he could see that the building had lost much of its original luster. Far from its once grand beauty, the old home was now cut into individual units, the massive front porch and veranda above now converted into walkways between the apartments.

A shame, he knew, but kept his mouth shut.

Kristi cast a glance in his direction. "Come on up," she suggested, opening the passenger door and stepping out of his truck. "I'm on the third floor."

*Big mistake,* he thought. *No, make that impossibly huge mistake.* And yet his hand was on the door handle as she slammed the passenger door shut. He stepped outside, pocketed his keys, and mentally chided himself for agreeing to this.

He comforted himself by thinking it might be a good idea to look around and ensure that she was safe. But that was just an excuse; he was rationalizing and he knew it. The truth of the matter was that he wanted to spend more time with her and, it seemed, she did with him.

He followed her past a row of overgrown crepe myrtles and some shrubs that looked like sassafras. Under the portico, on the far end of the building beneath the porch light, a single guy was seated in a plastic chair smoking, the tip of his cigarette glowing in the night. He turned to watch them head up the steps but didn't say a word.

Kristi was already on the stairs and Jay followed.

*Don't trust her. Sure, she might have grown up in the last nine years or so, but what was it Grandma used to say? "A leopard doesn't change his spots overnight." Or in this case nearly a decade.*

She led him up two flights to the third floor, and with her a step or two ahead of him, he couldn't help but notice the way her jeans hugged her.

*Holy Christ, she had a tight little ass.*

He remembered all too well and hated himself for it.

*Damn it all to hell.*

He dragged his gaze away, tore his attention from her to the apartment building. On the third floor they reached a single unit tucked under the gables of the once-massive home. Thankfully, his gaze was centered higher now, over her crown as she unlocked the door. It appeared that the uppermost story housed only one unit whereas the lower two floors had been cut into two or three units. There was less square footage up here as the roof angle was sharp, and he guessed that the third floor might have originally been servants' quarters.

From the landing at Kristi's door, he was able to gaze across the small backyard of the apartment house, then over the massive stone wall surrounding All Saints. He could make out the tops of trees and the bell tower and steeply angled roof of the church. Other buildings, illuminated by watery street lamps, were visible through the trees. He recognized the portico of the library and a turret of Wagner House.

The lock clicked and Kristi shouldered open the door. "Come on in," she said, stepping over the threshold. "It's not much, but for the next year or two, if I can stomach dealing with the Calloways, it's home."

Still thinking this was a major mistake, he entered her apartment and closed the door behind him.

Kristi dropped her backpack onto a battered couch, stripped off her jacket, and hung it on a hook near the door. "Isn't this place kinda funky-cool?" she asked with obvious pride. The hardwood floors were beaten and scratched, full of character. A fireplace with painted peeling bricks dominated one wall and peekaboo windows peered from dormers. The kitchen was barely a counter with holes cut into it for a sink and stove. There was a smell of age to the building that the candles and incense she'd scattered around the rooms couldn't hide. Kristi's home looked like it needed the kind of facelift he was giving his cousins' bungalow, but she seemed to love it.

"Definitely funky. I'm not sure about the cool part."

Amusement glimmered in her eyes. "And what would you know about cool?"

"Touché, Miss Bentz." He smiled. She had a way of putting him into his place. "Cool is something I'm not into."

"Well . . ." She'd already dismissed the topic and was on to the purpose of why she'd invited him up. "Here's what I've got so far," she said, pointing to a table covered with papers, pictures, notes, and her laptop. A chipped cup held pens and a small bowl contained paper clips, tacks, pushpins, and a roll of tape. On the wall she'd tacked up posterboard that included pictures of the four missing girls. Beneath the photographs, she'd listed personal information that included physical and personality traits, family members, friends and boyfriends, employment information and schedules, addresses for the past five or six years, classes taken, and various other information in the form of notes that looked like she'd printed them off her computer.

"Do you give this much attention to your studies?" he asked, noting the colored overlining on some of the information.

Kristi snorted. "Want a beer—? Oh, wait, I don't know that I have any. Damn." She walked to the kitchen alcove and peered into a narrow, short, obviously barren refrigerator. "Sorry. Didn't know I'd have company. All I've got is a hard lemonade. We could split it."

"I'm okay," he said as she extracted the drink, slamming the refrigerator door shut with her hip. She opened the bottle, poured it into two glasses, and found a bag of microwave popcorn in a cupboard. "I missed dinner," she explained, placing the bag onto the rotating platter.

She set the timer, switched the microwave on, and handed him a glass of lemonade that he didn't really want. Her shoulder brushed just above his elbow as she studied the intricate charts she'd created. He smelled a hint of perfume over the lingering scent of smoke from the bar. She took a swallow and said, "I've assigned each of the missing girls a color—for example, Dionne, the first girl that we know went missing, is in yellow." All of Dionne's information had been highlighted by a neon yellow marker. "Then there's Tara, who, incidentally lived here—"

He jerked his gaze away from the charts to stare at her. "Here? In this apartment?" he asked, even though he saw the address listed in her information. He couldn't believe it.

She was nodding, her gaze turned to his. "This very unit."

"Are you kidding?" But he could see she was serious. Dead serious. "Jesus." She had all of his attention now and he didn't like what he was hearing. One of the girls who'd disappeared had lived in this very studio? What kind of weird twist of fate was that? He studied Tara's chart as if it were the key to salvation. He held up a hand. "She lived here right before she disappeared? Did you know that when you moved in?"

"No, it was just a strange coincidence." She set her drink on a side table, then reached onto the desk, grabbed a rubber band and twisted her hair onto her head before snapping the band in place.

Her hair was a messy knot, her neck long, and she looked damned good. He took a swallow from his own glass.

"I don't like this." He felt an uncomfortable anxiety creep through him as the kernels began to pop and the smell of hot butter filled the room. "If the girls were really abducted—"

"They had to have been." She nodded. Certain.

"And you're *living* here."

"Hey, I didn't know, okay?" She gave him a hard

look as the muted sound of corn popping increased. "But it doesn't matter anyway. I've changed the lock on the door and fixed the broken latches on the windows. I'm as safe here as anywhere. Maybe more so. If someone is really behind their"—she motioned to the pictures on the charts as the corn popped wildly—"disappearances, and I believe someone is, then he won't show up here again. Lightning doesn't strike twice in the same spot."

Jay shook his head. "We're not talking about some freak of nature."

"Aren't we?" she asked, her voice suddenly low.

Her tone arrested him. "What do you mean?"

She picked her words carefully. "I think whoever's behind the girls' disappearances is into something really dark. Evil."

"Evil?" he repeated.

She nodded and he saw her shiver. "I think we're dealing with something so vile and inherently depraved that it might not even be human."

"What are you saying, Kris?"

"I've been doing a lot of research. On vampires."

Jay's breath expelled on a laugh. "Okay. You had me going there."

"I'm dead serious."

"Oh, come on. You don't believe in all that pop-culture-fiction-romantic—"

"There's nothing romantic about this," she cut in. "And do I believe in vampires? Of course not. But some people do, and you know what? If a person believes something is true, then it is. At least for him or her."

"So whoever's behind the girls' disappearances believes in vampires. Is that what you're saying?"

"I can hear you laughing inside."

"I'm not. Honest."

"What I'm saying is: this guy believes in vampires, or maybe he believes *he's* a vampire. I don't know. But

a person like that, Jay? Someone deluded or obsessed . . .
They're dangerous. This guy is dangerous."

A whisper of something slid over Jay's skin. Fear?
Premonition? "Maybe you've let your imagination
carry you away," he said, but could hear the uncertainty
in his own voice.

Kristi simply shook her head.

"Just listen to me, Lucretia," he said angrily from his
end of the wireless connection. "I know that you're concerned. Hell, I even know that you've been trying to sort
all this out, wrestling with your conscience, but you can't
have it both ways. You either trust me or you don't."

"I trust you," she said, her heart thumping with dread
as she imagined his handsome face, remembered their
first kiss, a gentle, tender meeting of lips that had promised so much more. They'd been standing on the back
porch of Wagner House, in the dusk while rain poured
from the dark heavens. Some people claimed the house
was haunted; she thought of it as magical. The only light
had been the strands of tiny Christmas lights strung
over the building. Each bulb seemed a miniature candle,
glowing softly in the December night. She remembered
the smell of the rain on his skin, the tingle of her nerves
as he'd brushed his mouth over hers so tenderly.

She'd ached to give herself to him and he'd sensed it.

Hours later, in her room, they'd made love, over and
over again, and she'd felt a blending of her soul to his.

And now he was ending it?

"I don't understand," she said weakly, and they both
knew it was a lie.

"If I can't have absolute faith—"

"You mean power, right?" she said, finding some of
her old spunk. "And obedience. Blind obedience."

"Faith," he said in a soft voice that reminded her of

his breath whispering over her ears, his lips working magic on her naked body. How he could make her sweat and tingle all at once . . .

How willingly she'd lain beneath him, staring in wonder at the power of his body as he raised himself on his elbows and kissed her nipples. She'd watched as their bodies had moved, his cock sliding in and out of her.

Sometimes he'd stop for a heartbeat, pull out and flip her over, only to take her from behind more forcefully. Often he would nip at her, biting a bit, leaving the sheerest of impressions upon her neck, or breast or buttocks, and she'd spend the week being reminded of their long, sensual session.

"I said I trust you."

"But I can't trust you. That's the thing. We both know what you did, Lucretia. How you betrayed me. I know you were confused. Frightened. But you should have come to me instead of going outside the circle."

"Please."

"It's over." The words rang in her ear. Hard. Final.

"No, I'm sorry, I should have—"

"There are lots of things you should have done. Could have done, but it's too late. You know it."

"No! I can't believe—"

"That's right, you *can't* and therein lies the problem. I hope that you know what you experienced is sacred and as such it's never to be talked about. Can you keep your tongue? Can you?"

"Yes!"

"There is a chance then, a slim one, but a chance that you will be forgiven."

Her heart did a stupid little flip. She thought he might be lying again, tantalizing her in order to keep her from going to the police or campus security.

"But if you say a word, then I can't keep you safe."

"You're threatening me?"

"I'm warning you."

*Dear God.* Tears welled in her eyes, clogged her throat. Misery surrounded her heart. She couldn't give him up.

"I love you."

He paused a minute, the silence heavy, then said, "I know."

The phone went dead. She stared at it a minute, the pent-up tears sliding down her cheeks, falling onto her chest. This was wrong, so wrong. She loved him. LOVED him. "No," she wailed softly, feeling as if someone had ripped out her very soul. She was hollow inside without his love. Empty. A useless vessel.

She was sobbing now, hiccuping even as she tried all sorts of mental panaceas.

*There are other men.*

"But not like him," she said aloud, "not like him." She wrapped her arms around her knees and rocked herself, cradling her body. She tried not to dwell on the realization that she would never kiss him again, never touch him, never make love to him, but the thought was always at the back of her mind. Through her tears she gazed across the thick pile of her carpet to the corner that housed her desk.

On top of the desk she saw her computer, a few pictures, not of him—he wouldn't stand for it—but of two of her friends. Beside the framed photographs was a potted Christmas cactus still in bloom and a cup that held pencils, pens, and a pair of scissors. Sharp scissors.

She bit her lip. Did she have the nerve to end it all?

*He's not worth it.*

"Yes, he is." She could sacrifice herself, show him just how much she loved him, spill her own damned blood!

If only she had trusted him blindly, if only she was like the others, if only . . . if only she hadn't drawn Kristi Bentz into this. He would still love her. Still caress her. Still tell her she was beautiful.

She squeezed her eyes shut and fell to the floor, where she curled into a fetal position. Again she rocked herself on the thick carpet, but it was no use. When she opened her eyes again, she was focused on the scissors. Twin snipping blades that could easily slice through her skin and open a vein or an artery.

The irony didn't escape her.

Had she been willing to trade her jeweled cross for a vial of her own blood, she wouldn't now be contemplating suicide and dying for her love.


The microwave dinged loudly. A few kernels kept popping, sounding like gunfire. Jay had been silent, processing for long minutes, as had Kristi.

"You've worried me," he finally said. "I think I should leave Bruno with you."

Kristi managed a half laugh. She'd wanted him to hear her, believe her, but she didn't need another damn savior. Her father was enough. "Mrs. Calloway would *love* that monster in here. I can't have pets." She walked to the microwave and gingerly removed the plump, slightly burned bag.

He glanced pointedly over to the water and food dishes on the floor near the refrigerator. "Looks like you already do."

She opened the bag and steam escaped in a buttery cloud. "Houdini is a stray. He doesn't live here, really." She noticed the skepticism in his expression and added, "I don't have a litter box. So the answer is a big N-O to the dog, but thanks, just the same."

"Then I'll stay."

She sucked in a quick breath. "Uh . . ." Her eyes met his again. "I don't think that would be such a hot idea. And what would be a worse one is if you had any thoughts, any thoughts at all, of explaining this to my dad."

"He might be able to help."

"Not yet," she insisted, pouring the popped corn and blackened unpopped kernels into a bowl. "Later."

Rubbing the back of his neck, Jay looked out the window toward the campus. Just then he heard the sound of the chapel bells tolling off the hour through one slightly open window.

Midnight.

The witching hour.

"On top of everything else, I don't like the fact that you're living in Tara Atwater's apartment. That's too co-incidental to me."

She carried the bowl to the desk and shoved aside her paper clip cup to make room for it. "I found the apartment over the Internet. I called and rented it before I even knew Tara had lived here, or that I was going to get so involved." She plucked a few popped kernels from the bowl and plopped them into her mouth, hold-ing the bowl toward Jay, silently inviting him to join in. He took a small handful. "At the time I didn't even know Tara Atwater's name, or that she was one of the missing coeds. I mean, I'd vaguely heard about them, of course. My dad had brought up the fact that some of the students might have disappeared, and there was a bit about them on the news, not a lot, or not a lot that I was aware of. At the time, I thought it was all conjecture. No one knew for certain they'd been abducted. I mean, no one still does. The fact that I ended up with one of the apartments is probably because most people already had their leases set for the school year. I signed up for January classes, so I was looking in December, when there weren't a lot of apartments available."

"You sound as if you're trying to convince yourself."

She smiled faintly. "Okay . . . it's a little freaky, yeah. But if you think about it logically, it really is just a coincidence."

"Uh-huh. And then you *just happen* to end up living here in Tara Atwater's apartment and then you *just hap-*

*pen* to assign yourself the duty of becoming Nancy Drew in The Case of the Missing Coeds?"

"I was interested anyway and then Lucretia asked for my help."

"Lucretia? Lucretia . . . ." He frowned, thinking back to place the name. "Didn't you have a roommate you hated named—"

"Yep. She's one and the same." Kristi explained about running into Lucretia, how she was worried about the missing girls but was afraid to say anything because she'd just been hired by members of the administration who were taking the stance that nothing was wrong. "I told Lucretia I'd look into it," she finished.

"I still don't like you living here alone." It felt to Jay like everything was slipping a little, "off" in a way he couldn't define.

"It's just an apartment. Sorry, the dog can't stay. Neither can you. End of story." She motioned to her charts again, then pointed to the poster dedicated to Tara Atwater. "Back to the colors. Tara's in pink, Monique is green, and Rylee is in blue. You can see that I've listed places, people, and things that they might have in common, then connected them. The connections show two or three or four colors."

He took in all the information. The overlapping data, where the colored lines converged, aside from a few stray friends or places, was the missing girls' class schedules. Every one of them had been English majors and they all had taken classes from a handful of professors here at the university.

Kristi said, "These girls didn't have a lot of friends and their family life was negligible. I tried to reach the parents and pretty much came up with nothing. They had the attitude of 'no news is good news.' All the girls had been in some kind of trouble. Drugs or alcohol or boyfriend problems, and their families gave up on them."

"What about girlfriends? You know, the BFF thing on all text messages?"

"If any of them had a Best Friend Forever, I have yet to locate her. Even Lucretia wouldn't cop to being close to any of them." Kristi frowned, puzzled, little lines forming between her eyebrows. "I've tried to call Lucretia a couple of times since then, and she hasn't called back."

"Why?"

"That's the million-dollar question," Kristi said, picking up a pen and twirling it in her fingers as she thought. "It's almost as if she felt like she had to do *some*thing, so she told me about it and that was the end of it."

"She passed the ball. Got rid of feeling guilty for thinking something was wrong, and then put it on you."

"Or she regrets even mentioning it to me."

Kristi had set the bowl back on the desk and now Jay absently reached for it. "So these girls were basically loners. Or, at least alone in the world."

"I've talked to people in their classes and some coworkers, and what they said over and over again was, 'I didn't really know her,' or 'she was pretty closed off,' or 'she kept to herself,' that sort of thing."

Jay studied her charts again, focusing on the areas where the lines met and intertwined. He pointed to the class schedules. "Each of them took writing from Preston, Shakespeare from Emmerson, journalism from Senegal, and The Influence of Vampyrism from Grotto?" He felt a chill slide through him. "Christ, Kristi, this is *your* schedule."

"I know."

"You know?"

She shrugged. "It's really not that odd. Or unique. The college curriculum is set up through computers, right? Block scheduling. Depending upon your major. So these aren't the only students who had this curriculum, not by a long shot. And there are some variables. For example, Tara took forensics from your predecessor, Dr. Monroe, and both Monique and Rylee took a literature class from Dr. Croft, the head of the English Department, just before they went missing. Oh, and here . . ." She pointed to Dionne's schedule and tapped the notation. "Dionne took religion from Father Tony and Introduction to Criminal Justice from Professor Hollister along with the other classes."

"Heavy schedule."

"She was fast-tracking, trying to graduate early, I think. The term she went missing she had a load of six classes, eighteen credit-hours. And she worked part-time at a local pizza parlor. Here's a kicker, too. All of the girls, without exception, participated in Father Mathias's morality plays, again associated with the English Department."

"Morality plays?"

"I know. Kind of out there, isn't it? Like something out of the Dark Ages. I haven't really figured them out yet, but I heard a couple of girls in the class on vampirism talking about the first one of the term being Sunday night, so I thought I'd check it out. Don't suppose you want to come?"

"You want me to?"

Did he make it sound like a date? Probably, because Kristi backtracked fast. "No, I'll go alone. It'll be better. People might notice you."

"Maybe I should go."

"Nope. I mean it, Jay. This is my deal."

"I don't like this," he muttered. If she was right, there was a psycho on the loose, abducting women from the campus; if she was wrong, *something* was driving the girls away. Four missing coeds within less than two years on a campus this size was more than unusual, more than suspicious. "I can't believe the university isn't all over this."

"The administration is trying to sweep it under the rug. Admissions are already down and they don't want any more bad press. I brought it up with the dean of students and was shuffled right out of her office. Told I was imagining things and treated as if I had the plague."

"But the liability—"

"Only if you recognize it. They're into the 'see no evil, hear no evil, speak no evil' mode. Therefore the evil doesn't exist."

"My ass." He stared at the charts and shook his head. "You have to take this to the police."

"Oh, yeah, right. Think about it." She finished her drink. "Let's say I stroll into the Baton Rouge Police Station. Who do I talk to?" she asked with a lift of her shoulders. "Probably the Missing Persons Department, right? Maybe I'll have these charts with me. And then I'll say . . . what? That I'm the hotshot New Orleans detective Rick Bentz's daughter and you'd better pay attention to me? Even if I don't bring him up, they'll put two and two together and get all pissy about jurisdiction and protocol."

A thin black cat slid through the partially open window over the sink.

"If I did anything so ludicrous, I'd be thrown out on my ear and my dad would be called on to the carpet. No thanks."

She had a point.

"Hey, Houdini," she said as the cat shot off the counter and under the couch. "Getting friendly, aren't ya?" she joked as the cat peered suspiciously from the shadows.

Jay wasn't about to allow the subject to be changed. "The authorities need to know what you've found. Maybe you could phone your father and explain—"

"Oh, sure. He'd yank me out of here so fast my head would spin."

"He couldn't do that. You're an adult."

She glared at him as if he were insane. "Oh, right. You tell him that! He'd either assign me a damned bodyguard or come and stake out this apartment himself. No, informing Detective Bentz is out of the question. I *am* an adult and we're going to do this my way."

"Whatever *this* is."

"Right." She suddenly smiled at him, sensing his capitulation even though he'd been certain he'd given nothing away.

God, she was beautiful. He tried not to notice, but there it was as she stared at him with those damnable eyes. For half a second he felt a swell of heat rise in his veins, desire tinged with memories of holding her gasping, perspiring body next to his. The back of his throat turned dry and he looked away, jabbed his hands deep into the front pockets of his pants. He set his jaw in an effort to tamp down his stupid urges. Here she was talking about abductions, the potential murder of four students, and he was still responding to her.

Which was just plain ludicrous. "I think I'd better shove off," he said.

"But you'll help me?"

"As long as you don't ask me to break any laws."

"Okay, I promise," she said, then blushed and looked as if she was about to bite her tongue.

She didn't have to say why. He remembered her repeating just those words nearly a decade ago when he'd slid a tiny ring upon her finger.

"Good," he said quickly, as if he didn't remember. No reason to dig up the past. Hell, they'd just been kids. "See ya in class." And then he left, not even glancing over his shoulder.

Yep, he thought as he descended the stairs, he'd been right. Where Kristi Bentz was concerned he was a bona fide moron.

# CHAPTER 13

For the most part, the chat rooms were a bust.

After Jay left, Kristi spent over an hour instant messaging different screen names and joining chats online, some of which were disturbing, others which were silly and just plain inane. She figured those were probably filled with kids just messing around on their computers when they were supposed to be sleeping. However one room, dedicated to blood in literature, as opposed to shape-shifters, werewolves, or vampires in the campiest and most twenty-first century of meanings, intrigued her. For the most part she lurked, watching the conversation between several of the participants. Whereas some of the chat rooms talked up the *Buffy* television series to death and another focused on the *Blade* movies, this one dealt with vampires in literature, and for a minute Kristi thought Dr. Dominic Grotto himself might be leading the discussion. There was a little talk about Count Dracula, the work of Bram Stoker, questions about Elizabeth of Bathory, the countess who bathed in the blood of her subjects, and even Vlad III, the Impaler, also known as Vlad Dracula, whom the discussion suggested was the inspiration for Bram Stoker in creating the character of Count Dracula. Some talk centered around Transylvania and Romania and fact versus fiction, and questions abounded about the drinking of blood.

But all in all, in this particular chat room, the participants seemed interested in more than trying to score some shock value; they seemed sincere in their quests, whatever they were.

Kristi poured herself a glass of Diet Coke, then made notes on everyone who partook of the chat and what their particular bend was. Or at least she kept track of the screen names they used, all of which, it seemed, included some reference to the subject. Since she wanted to blend into the group, she had signed in with the screen name of ABneg1984, though her own blood type was O positive and she wasn't born in 1984. She used a couple of blind aliases to hide her true identity and asked a question or two every five minutes, just to keep the other users from thinking she was spying on them.

Which, of course, was the whole point of her being online at this ungodly hour.

It was a bit of a juggling act as she kept several screens open at the same time. They each were dedicated to a different live chat room, and, at first, she had a little trouble keeping up with all the conversations. Soon, however, she was getting the hang of it and clicked out of a few that seemed off topic. What she needed were other people online from Baton Rouge or at least Louisiana. There was just no way to tell by the screen names and as far as she could tell the chatters could be from anywhere in the known universe.

It was like looking for the proverbial needle in the haystack, even though she tried to narrow down the rooms by mentioning Louisiana.

Finally, in the intellectual-sounding room, there was mention of All Saints Campus and vampirism.

"Bingo," Kristi whispered as if she were afraid the other chatters could actually hear her. Fortunately, her laptop mic and camera were disabled. She couldn't believe her good luck. Someone by the name of Dracoola lived nearby. Or at least had connections to the school.

She lurked. Waiting. Tried to read between the lines, even going so far as visualizing the different characters, many of whom supplied their own icons. Blood drops, snarling fangs, and flying bats seemed to be the favorites. People came and went, but some of the chatters seemed in for the night. One was JustO, who eventually mentioned Dr. Grotto's class.

Kristi felt a tingle of anticipation. Things were coming closer to home. "Now you're talkin'."

Several people responded, all agreeing. Kristi quickly scribbled down the screen names for Dracoola, JustO, Carnivore18, Sxyvmp21, Deathmaster7, and Dmin8trxxx. "Sheesh," Kristi said to the cat, who stopped short, skittery, halfway to his bowl. "Who *are* these people?" Houdini pressed himself to the wall, all muscles tense.

Kristi tried to think of a way to bring up the missing girls, but the conversation wasn't segueing in that direction and she wanted to buddy up to the weirdos who spent their nights virtually talking to strangers about blood and vampires and otherworldly beings. She let the others guide the conversation, all the while trying to find out something, some little hint about vampire cults on campus, or some connection to the women who had gone missing. One of the latecomers to the conversation had a screen name of DrDoNoGood and there was something about his questions, something a little bit familiar, that disturbed her.

Did she know this guy?

Or was it a woman?

A medical doctor? Wannabe? PhD? A James Bond/Ian Fleming fanatic as his name might be a play on words for *Dr. No*?

He asked another question and she froze. She'd seen

that very question before in her study notes for her class with Dr. Grotto.

Could DrDoNoGood be a cybernet alias for Dr. Dominic Grotto?

Her mind raced. What was the meaning of his name? Or was she just jumping to conclusions in the dead of night? Or . . .

Her pulse jumped as she read only the capital letters in the screen name. DDNG or DrDNG.

Didn't Grotto's middle name begin with N? Or, again, was she forcing a connection? Making something out of nothing? Hadn't she seen Grotto's name somewhere? From something she'd gotten from the school?

With her attention split between the computer screen and the bookshelves over her desk, she located the course handbook for the college. It was beat-up and dog-eared, but she flipped it open to the section on the staff of All Saints College. "Come on, come on," she murmured, barely managing to stay on top of the conversation discussing the ritual of drinking blood and the sexuality inherent in the act.

"Yuck." She shuddered. "No thanks." Flipping the pages, she finally saw Dr. Grotto's picture. Damn, he was good-looking. Piercing eyes, strong chin, high forehead, and dark hair. Underneath his photo she read: Dominic Nicolai Grotto, PhD.

Could it be?

DrDoNoGood and Dr. Dominic Nicolai, one and the same?

She couldn't prove it, but she felt a rush, the same gut instinct her father experienced when he would figure out a clue in some homicidal maniac's twisted game.

"Like father, like daughter," she told herself as she asked a simple question about the class.

She wondered if there was a way to uncover his identity, some way to flush him out. Maybe she could pander to his vanity, complain about him as a teacher and see what happened.

Still reading the conversation, now about cultural mores and human blood, she pulled out her class notes. Maybe if she quoted him, she'd get a response . . . and if she said something about him being more an actor than an intellectual, more into theatrics than literature, she was certain he'd be unable to pass that up. She pulled up another screen in the program on which she kept her notes, but before she could come up with a significant question, he logged off.

"What! No!" she cried, and quickly reopened the other chat room screens, hoping he'd show up somewhere else. But he wasn't anywhere she could find. If he'd entered another cyber chat, it was one she hadn't located. "Of all the bad luck!" She tossed the school catalogue aside and was about to close out the windows for the chat rooms when she saw a strange question in the room so recently vacated by DrDoNoGood.

Deathmaster7 asked: Do you wear a vial?

Kristi froze.

Three people responded with a yes while one, Carnivore18, answered with a question mark. Obviously Carnie didn't get it either. One person didn't respond and two typed in *no.* Kristi decided to go with the flow and responded *yes.*

Carnivore18 created a line of question marks. He clearly felt out of it.

"Join the club," Kristi said, and wondered how she should prod the conversation along. But she remembered something—hadn't Lucretia mentioned that some of the girls in the "cult" and Dr. Grotto's class wore vials of their own blood?

Deathmaster7 asked: Whose?

Kristi stared at the screen, her pulse leaping at the

thought that she might have just stumbled onto the connection she needed to find out more about the vampire cult that was supposedly on campus. But she had to be careful, not answer too quickly. What if she were wrong? What if Lucretia had given her bad information? Fingers poised over the keyboard, she waited.

The only one who responded was JustO: Mine. Who else's?

Kristi grinned. "How about that."

None of the other chatters was responding but Kristi wanted to keep this alive. Following JustO's lead she typed: My own.

The other vial wearers were strangely silent until they, too, answered along the lines of JustO. Were they reticent to tell the truth, or like Kristi, liars with their own agendas?

For the first time since logging on, she sensed she was getting somewhere and could barely contain herself. She bit her lip so hard she nearly drew blood as she thought. Kristi was certain JustO was cyber-texting about blood. So who was she or he? How, if at all, was he or she connected to the cult? Kristi tried to imagine who JustO was. Someone in Dr. Grotto's class? Someone she saw every time she stepped into the classroom? Was his or her name, like Kristi's, for the purpose of this chat room all about blood? Was JustO's blood type O?

Kristi felt a rush of adrenaline and could barely sit still. She felt certain this person was female, though she couldn't quite put her finger on why. She just had some sense of it. Almost like a memory.

Could it be that JustO really did wear a vial of her own . . . Oh, God! It hit Kristi then. She did know who this person was! She was sure of it. Hadn't she heard of a student at All Saints who went by one initial. Just "O"?

Kristi's own father had mentioned the girl. He'd interviewed "O" while investigating a homicide a couple of years earlier. It had been one of the cases that had been linked to Our Lady of Virtues, the abandoned mental hospital located a few miles outside of New Orleans. One of the victims of that particular nutcase had been a student here, at All Saints.

Detectives Bentz and Montoya had driven to Baton Rouge, where they'd interviewed students, family, and staff. One of them had been a girl who had worn a vial of her own blood around her neck.

Feeling almost dizzy with the connection, Kristi stretched her arms over her head, hearing her spine pop, but still she kept her gaze fastened to the conversation on her monitor. Her mind spun backward as she remembered the conversation that had taken place in her father's living room. She hadn't been living with him then, but she'd been visiting. Olivia hadn't been home, but Bentz and Montoya had been discussing the case and Montoya mentioned something about the "weird Goth girl" wearing her own blood. She hadn't wanted to be called Ophelia, her given name. She'd told the detectives to call her "O" or "Just O".

There *was* a girl named Ophelia in Grotto's class, a sullen, quiet girl who always sat at the back of the room. Kristi hadn't actually met her face to face, hadn't been close enough to notice if she wore a chain around her neck and a tiny vial of her own blood.

But that was about to change.

Even though the idea of anyone taking the time to draw blood, seal it in a tiny bottle, then wear it . . . Jesus, that was really out of the boundaries of normal.

The screen flickered and JustO logged out of the chat room.

Kristi felt a sense of disappointment. She knew she was on the verge of something important, though she wasn't certain what. She glanced at the clock on the com-

puter screen and groaned. It was nearly two and she had
an early morning class. Besides, she really needed to
think about what she'd learned online. Process it. It was
probably just as well that JustO had left the conversation, which seemed to be rapidly going downhill. Even
Carnivore18 gave up the ghost and logged off.

Her eyes burning from lack of sleep and staring at
the monitor, Kristi closed out all of the open screens
and thought about how she would approach O, the quiet
girl, how she would get her to admit that she was JustO.
If the vial were visible, that might start the conversation, but Kristi would have to pretend to be someone
else because ABneg1984 had bragged about wearing her
own blood and Kristi couldn't fake it. If the people
wearing the vials were part of a cult, there was probably
a certain vial they used, maybe a certain necklace on
which it hung, some sort of conformity that would
make it immediately evident if she came up with a fake.
Maybe the vials were a certain shape, or etched, or dark
glass or . . . Oh, she couldn't think about it now.

Yawning, she stretched again and envied the cat, who
was already back in his hideaway.

She wasn't certain of the significance of what she'd
just discovered, but it sure looked like it had a lot to do
with Dr. Grotto's vampyrism class. Maybe the cult Lucretia had mentioned was a subject of the class.

"I don't know what the hell is going on, but I'm definitely getting closer to something . . . something that's
going to make one helluva book," she said aloud as she
switched off the computer and watched the screen turn
black.

Why in the world would anyone wear a vial of their
own blood? And what, if anything, did it have to do
with the girls who had vanished?

She walked to the window overlooking the campus.

Somewhere out there, was a predator, someone preying on students who took a particular combination of

courses. "So who are you, you sick bastard?" she whispered. "Just who the hell are you?"

It was hours after midnight and Vlad felt an insatiable hunger, a craving he could no longer fight. The need to kill thundered through his brain as he drove ever closer to New Orleans, the tires of his van singing along the pavement, the traffic at this late hour thin and spotty.

All the better.

It was wrong to hunt tonight.

Dangerous.

He could easily make a mistake.

And then who could he blame?

Only himself.

This he knew. Yet Vlad could wait no longer. He knew there was a protocol, a reason to wait for the killing.

And yet, he found it impossible to tamp down his urge, and for that, he had the "lessers," the women who would suffice physically if not intellectually.

And there were issues to deal with. A naysayer who had to be quieted, a guilty conscience that had to be silenced or all would be lost, and he couldn't allow that.

His head began to throb.

He was empty. Hungry. Yearned for the thrill of the kill.

Could no longer hold back.

And he rationalized that this, tonight's kill, would be a sacrifice to her, the one to whom he was forever linked, the one to whom he was fated.

And perhaps this unplanned killing of another lesser would throw the police off, send those who suspected on a wrong path in a different city.

*Don't do this. If you succumb to temptation, if you kill, you could be exposed, your mask stripped from your face.*

His hand began to tremble as he considered turning around, resisting the urge that was a living breathing thing within him, a need so fierce he was its slave.

A willing slave.

He swallowed hard and felt the emptiness within. His hand steadied on the steering wheel as he saw the bright lights of New Orleans washing up against the night sky in the distance.

There was no turning back.

He knew the one he wanted . . . the perfect woman. Her skin was near translucent, her neck a long, welcoming arch, her body firm and ripe. His skin flushed, his own flesh heating at the thought of taking her.

Alive . . . oh, she needed to be alive, to know that theirs would be a hard, night-long union of passion and lust where she could satisfy his every need. And then she would give him the ultimate gift of her lifeblood.

Oh, how he would take her tonight.

He felt a throb of anticipation heat his veins at the thought and savored what he would do to her. Before. And after.

From deep in his throat came a soft growl of anticipation. Of need. He heard his own blood pumping through his veins, felt his pulse jump in expectation of the night ahead.

He closed his eyes for the barest of seconds, felt his erection hard and strong and straining. Which was good. Necessary. He needed the edge, the relentless resolution, the sheer testosterone-driven will that kept him sharp, cunning, and ruthless.

He caught a glimpse of his reflection in the rearview mirror and smiled at his transformation. His disguise was complete. No one would recognize him. Eagerly, he took the off-ramp he wanted, then wound through the city, driving carefully, under the speed limit on the empty streets. He knew where to park, where to wait.

He'd planned this one for a long time, knowing that at some point he would give in to his needs and search for a lesser one who would satisfy him for the next few days. Until the next.

The street on which he parked was nearly deserted, in a section of the city where the hurricane's wrath had been mighty. There were a few parked cars, some abandoned and tagged, a few others occupying stretches of the battered street. He rolled down the driver's window and breathed deep of the cool winter air. Even here, in a desolate section of the city, the Louisiana night felt alive. He heard the sound of insects buzzing, the whirr of bat wings in flight, and he smelled them all, a rat scurrying into a sewer hole, a raccoon searching the street for garbage, a snake slithering up the side of a tree.

Far off was the muffled sound of traffic on the freeway. Every so often headlights cut through the night and a car rolled past.

His nostrils flared and he drank it all in, his eyes easily adjusting to the dark. Lust was his constant companion. It had been since he'd been eleven or twelve, maybe younger. . . .

He leaned back against the cushions of the driver's seat, his hands tapping on the steering wheel. There were several lessers he wanted, those whose lives would be given without the elaborate rituals of the entitled, ones he'd earmarked for just the purpose of the letting of their blood. This one, the woman he would sacrifice tonight, would not be missed for several days. In that she was perfect.

He knew she would come. He'd watched her before, had met her several times, here in New Orleans. She was beautiful, her body toned, but she had no interest in improving her mind. And that was her mistake. Her soul could not be elevated. She was not royal, only a servant.

*As are you,* that nagging voice in his head chided. *Are you the master? Of course not! You gave your free will over long ago and here you are, adhering to rules that you find restraining. Whether you admit it or not, there is a chain around your neck, one that is always kept taut.*

He closed his mind to such arguments, knew they were blasphemy. He saw her then, walking alone, the friend who was sometimes with her missing. Good. She strode briskly in her high heels, her footsteps sharp and hard. Determined. Trademarks of a strong woman.

A dancer.

Who called herself Bodiluscious, but whose real name was Karen Lee Williams.

Wearing a short miniskirt, crop top, and jean jacket, she walked alone on this desolate street, heels clicking on the pavement. She probably knew better than to walk this way, but it was the quickest, straightest shot to her small house.

And a perfect place to become lost.

He waited until she was nearly a block away and then he slipped noiselessly from his vehicle. There were no lights, no alarms, just a soft little click of the door.

Though it was dark, with his eyes he zeroed in on her. He walked swiftly, hiding in the shadows, keeping near the empty buildings. Hard to believe any woman was stupid enough to take a shortcut and walk home after a night of writhing around a pole for money. Money used to support a habit instead of her child.

She deserved to die.

And she was lucky he was here to save her from her lowly existence.

He'd heard her complaints about her life, the unfairness of what fate had cast her, but she hadn't wanted to change. It was all just idle chatter, used to garner his sympathy.

Smiling to himself, he followed her, then took a shortcut through a few vacant lots where, with his heightened vision, he could avoid the rubble, rats, and scavenging dogs.

Tonight, he thought, his blood singing through his veins, he'd release her from her misery.


Karen was edgy. Nervous.

And sick of the mess that was her life.

It had been a bad night, she decided as she clipped her way home on high heels that were beginning to hurt. She was walking through a part of the Big Easy where she'd once felt safe but now was a little nervous. But she had no choice: this route was the quickest way since her car had broken down a few weeks ago and she couldn't afford a cab.

Besides, she needed a little time to breathe some fresh air and think. Get away from the throbbing music, hooting customers, and smell of stale beer and cigarettes. The club had gone downhill, too. The night was a little chilly, but the further she got from Bourbon Street, the quieter and calmer it seemed. She even imagined she could smell the river, which was probably just her imagination.

She had danced until eleven, when she'd been forced off the stage by Big Al's latest "find," a girl who wasn't a day over sixteen unless Karen missed her guess. But the girl, Baby Jayne, with Kewpie doll makeup, long blond pigtails that nearly swiped her tight little ass, see-through baby-doll outfit, and boobs that would make Dolly Parton envious, had all the customers streaming in for the after-midnight show. Even though she was awkward with the damned pole. Karen had watched a lot of the younger woman's act, spent time lurking near the door, observing Baby Jayne's pornographic moves.

There was no seduction in her dance, no allure, just the obvious.

Now, it was late.

Nearly three in the damned morning.

It just wasn't fair.

To think that at thirty, she, Bodiluscious, had been demoted. Her tips a few years back had been incredible—on some nights she'd made enough to pay her rent and buy a bit of nose candy—but now, after the storm had nearly wiped out the town and Baby Jayne had strolled into the club, Karen was lucky to have enough money to pay the bills each month. Which was probably good. If she had extra money, it tended to find her nasal passages. She'd been clean for over two months and she intended to stay that way. She was gonna put her life together. Hell, she couldn't dance forever.

She kept angling toward her little house, which had miraculously suffered only minor damage in the storm. For that, she'd been thankful.

She cut across the street and felt as if someone were watching her, which was ridiculous. For God's sake, that was her career, to have men ogling her, the more the better. She *knew* what that felt like.

*Click, click, click.* Her footsteps kept right on hitting what was left of the sidewalk. And she kept her eyes ahead of her, afraid to make a misstep on the cracked concrete and end up turning her ankle. What then? Her career would definitely be over.

Maybe it was time to patch things up with her mother and kid, move back to San Antonio. At least that way she could see her daughter more than once or twice a month. She smiled to herself when she thought of Darcy; now that girl would go far. At ten she was already at the top of her fourth-grade class and the piece of art she'd made for Karen last Christmas was incredible. The kid was a genius even if she had a no-account father doing time for possession, and a mother who danced on a stage, making love to a metal pole six nights a week.

A car rolled slowly down the street and Karen just kept walking. New Orleans had become dangerous, and if the press were to be believed, the crime rate sky-high. But she was careful. Never headed out alone without her small pistol tucked beneath her jacket. If anyone tried to mess with her, she'd be ready.

The car passed without incident, but she still felt edgy. Something wasn't right. Something more than Baby Jayne stompin' all over Bodiluscious's turf.

The feeling that she was being observed, maybe even followed, hung with her. She hazarded another quick glance over her shoulder and saw nothing . . . or did she? Was there someone just out of her line of vision?

Her skin crawled and a spurt of adrenaline shot through her, spurring her on. She was nearly running in the damned shoes now.

*Don't go crazy. You're letting your imagination run wild.*

But she opened the flap of her purse, where she could grab her pistol, cell phone, or canister of mace in one quick movement. She looked over her shoulder again, and saw no one.

Good. She was only three blocks from home now, approaching a safer area where the flood damage had been minimal and cleaned, the streetlights working, at least a quarter of the homes occupied, another quarter nearly cleaned and renovated.

*Hurry, hurry, hurry!*

She was walking so fast she was nearly breathless, and that was something she prided herself on: how fit and strong she kept herself with the dancing. She made it into the pool of light cast by the first strong street lamp along her route and she drew in a calming breath.

She looked behind herself once more, then realized, standing in the circle of light, she was an easy, visible target.

*You're almost home, girl. Just keep walking. Fast.*

She saw her house on the corner, then cursed herself for forgetting to turn on even one light. She hated walking into a dark house, but at least she was home.

She raced up the new walk and newly fixed front steps, her key in her hand. On the porch, she opened the still-squeaking screen door, then unlocked the dead bolt and shouldered open the new, heavy front door.

Inside, the smell of fresh paint assailed her as she flipped the dead bolt and reached for the light. The house was silent. Strangely silent. No hum of the refrigerator. No whisper of the air from the fans. She flipped the switch.

Nothing happened.

The entry hall light remained dark.

*Scraaaape.*

The sound of a shoe against the floor?

Oh, Jesus, was someone inside?

Her heart fluttered wildly with fear as she flipped several switches. No lights. She fumbled into her purse for her pistol with one hand, while the other scrabbled on the door for the dead bolt.

A hand clamped over hers.

Harsh.

Strong.

Brutal.

It crushed her fingers and she started to scream, only to have another hand cover her mouth.

Oh, God, no! She squirmed wildly. Writhed. Bit the leather covering her lips. Kicked at his legs, but his grip only tightened.

"Slow down, Karen Lee," he said in a voice that was as seductive as it was frightening.

He knew who she was? This wasn't random? She fought harder.

"There's nothing you can do," he assured her. "Nowhere you can go."

*That's where you're wrong, cocksucker,* she thought as her fingers brushed the cool nickel of the pistol. She grabbed the gun, yanked it out of the purse, heard the bag hit the ground with a soft thud. She drew her hand up, ready to blow this jerkwad to hell when she caught a glimpse, just a hint, of the guy's face and she nearly dropped the gun.

Red eyes glared at her, fuckin' *red* eyes from deep in the folds of some black hood.

A face black as night with ghoulish features and purplish lips was inches from hers. *The face of evil,* she thought wildly.

Oh, God! She nearly peed.

Hot breath washed over her.

Holy shit.

She struggled. Fought. Even though she was shaking from head to foot. Fumbling with the safety, she tried to think clearly. All she had to do was swing the gun around, over her shoulder, and fire.

But from the corner of her eye, she saw the thing, this fiend from hell, draw back those awful lips and expose a nasty array of sharp white teeth.

Sweet Jesus!

She had the safety off.

Immediately, she swung her arm upward.

Teeth slashed.

Blood spurted.

Pain screamed up her arm.

She squeezed the trigger.

*Blam!* The gun fired.

Blasted next to her ear.

The smell of cordite filled the air.

But her attacker held on, twisting back her arm so that she was helpless, her legs no longer able to kick. Her shoulder wrenched, throbbing in pain.

Oh, dear God, she'd missed hitting him. And the pain . . . excruciating. Blinding. *Help me, Lord, help me fight him off!*

She arched her back, still fighting, still hoping for a chance to get one good kick to his shins or his damned crotch. But he was heavy and strong. All sinew and muscle and determination.

Agony tore through her.

Her legs buckled.

In the darkness she saw the floor rushing up at her and now could only hope that somewhere, someone had heard the shot.

*Bam!* Her head cracked against the new hardwood.

She nearly passed out from the pain.

He fell atop her and shifted his hands. Before she could scream his fingers were on her throat pressing harder and harder as he straddled her. Alarmed by the red eyes glinting with malice, she fought back, her hands flailing at him, scraping at the leather on his body. If he was going to kill her, by God, she wasn't going to make it easy.

But her lungs were burning, shrieking for air, and the hands on her throat were tightening so that her eyes felt as if they might pop right out of her head.

She kicked and writhed frantically.

Her lungs were bursting with the pressure.

Blackness seeped into the edges of her vision.

*No! No! No!*

She tried to scream and failed, couldn't even drag in a breath.

Oh, God, oh . . . God . . .

Her legs stopped moving.

Her arms were leaden.

The burning in her lungs was pure agony.

*Let me die, God, please. End this torture!*

He leaned down and in the fog that was overcoming her she saw his fangs. White. Shining. Needle-sharp.

She knew what was to come.

A quick puncture. A quick sharp nip of pain as his hands relaxed and she dragged air into her windpipe in a wet hiss.

But it was too late.

She knew she was going to die.

# CHAPTER 14

"If you want to keep them for the full day, they're due back tomorrow at"—the clerk in the camouflage T and dusty jeans looked at the clock hanging over the door of the Rent-It-All store—"nine-thirty-six, but I'll give y'all till ten." Winking at Kristi, he offered her a gap-toothed smile that showed flecks of tobacco. She tried not to notice.

"Kind of you," she said, trying not to sound too sarcastic. He was, after all, just a kid.

About eighteen years old, "Randy" as the name pinned to his shirt claimed, was gangly and fighting a case of raging acne, but still tried to flirt with her. Kristi smiled back. At least he'd helped her locate the right kind of bolt cutters she needed in this dusty warehouse full of equipment and would be do-it-yourselfers. "That'll be thirty bucks."

"Really?"

"Yes, ma'am. Them things ain't cheap."

*Talk about highway robbery. Sure they were the expensive ones, but really, how much could they cost brand new?* "Great," she said with an undertone of sarcasm.

"So what did ya do?" Randy asked, adjusting his trucker's hat and trying a little too hard to be friendly. "Forget your locker combination?"

*Yeah, that's me, just a dumb woman with a bad memory.* "Something like that," she said, then handed him two twenties, waited for her change, and declined his help in carrying out the long-handled tool. "Thanks, I got it," she said, slipping the ten into her wallet and the strap of her purse over her shoulder.

"Now, if them there cutters don't work fer ya, y'know, because y'all are a woman and they're meant for a man, then you might want to rent a hacksaw or a sawzall." He nodded, as if agreeing with himself. "That'd do the trick."

"I'll keep that in mind," she said, silently bristling. It wasn't as if she were some tiny little frail stupid thing, for God's sake, but she kept her sharp tongue in check as she hauled the bolt cutters outside. At eighteen, she'd hadn't exactly been an Einstein either, and there was just no reason to get into it with the clerk.

She'd considered asking Jay to help her with her new project. She suspected he might own a pair of bolt cutters which could have saved her the thirty bucks, but she wanted to limit his involvement. First of all, he was misinterpreting her interest in him. He seemed to think she was angling to date him and that was *not* what she'd intended. So it was a good thing to keep him at a distance. He'd ask too many questions and what she was doing was bordering on illegal. As it was, he'd be in plenty of hot water if he was caught getting the information she wanted from the school and police records. If he even did that much for her. She wasn't certain that he'd cross that line and so she hadn't shared everything Lucretia had told her about vampires and cults. It was hard enough to get Jay on board without getting into the surreal, goth stuff.

Besides, she told herself as her running shoes crunched in the gravel of the Rent-It-All parking lot littered with battered pickups and a couple of monster trucks, some things were for her to do by herself. And breaking into the storage unit holding Tara Atwater's personal things was one, despite what Randy, the eighteen-year-old expert, thought. She slid behind the wheel and started the car. Dust had settled over the windshield and the interior of the car was warm, the sun visible through high, thick clouds. Kristi found a pair of sunglasses in her glove box and slid them onto her nose. She backed out of her parking space, trying and failing to avoid potholes in the dirty gravel. She passed a jacked-up truck covered in mud, where a man lit a cigarette as he packed a chainsaw in the back.

"Idiot," she muttered under her breath, then eased her Honda onto the side road and headed for the freeway that cut north from this section of low-slung, commercial buildings on the southeast part of town toward the All Saints campus.

Her plan was only partially formed, but she was rolling with it. Having Tara's things tucked away in the basement of the house she was renting was a godsend. She'd turn everything over to the police for evidence, of course, but until they were interested, she figured whatever was in the storage unit was fair game. She'd already found out the type and make of the combination lock Irene Calloway had used to secure Tara's things, then had spent two hours going to three different hardware stores before she'd found a lock that appeared the same.

Now she was ready.

A huge Suburban passed her covered in LSU stickers. *A tiger fan,* she thought with a faint smile. Kristi considered Louisiana State with its huge student body in Baton Rouge. Wouldn't a larger campus make for a wider, less-noticeable hunting ground? Why girls at All Saints?

*Because whoever is doing this is comfortable there. He's either a student, a member of the faculty, or an alumni. LSU or another campus is unfamiliar. Whoever is doing this is intrinsically connected to the college, knows how to get around, has hiding places, blends in.*

She felt a little frisson of fear slide down her spine. She was convinced that there was a monster stalking the ivy-clad brick buildings of All Saints, a psycho who had, so far, gotten away with his horrendous deeds.

"Not for long, bastard," she said, and glanced down at the speedometer. She was flying, driving nearly twenty miles over the posted limit. She eased off the throttle and glanced in her rearview mirror, certain she would see flashing red and blue lights, but no highway trooper was following her. This time, she'd gotten lucky. Good. She couldn't afford a ticket.

She took the exit closest to the campus and wound through the side streets, then parked in her usual spot near the staircase leading to her unit. Rather than head upstairs, she found the door leading to the basement laundry and storage facilities and unlocked it with one of the original keys she'd gotten from Irene Calloway. The stairs leading downward were dark and creaky, the walls made of ancient cement, the few windows small and grimy and shrouded with cobwebs, their thin threads littered with the drained, brittle carcasses of dead insects.

"Lovely," she said as she turned a precarious corner. Three steps later she was in the bowels of the building. At least the basement was dry. There were stains on the walls indicating that water had at one time or another seeped through old cracks, and areas where an attempt had been made to patch the damage with little or no success.

On one wall two washers were already churning, and one of the dryers was spinning and heating, something inside its drum clanging with each rotation. Kristi didn't dare try to break into the storage cage now, when someone might catch her. She didn't want to explain herself.

She planned to wait until the middle of the night and bring down a couple of boxes, though the thought of being here in the dark, with only a few sparse overhead lights, was nerve-wracking.

She left the basement, climbed up to her apartment and grabbed her laptop. She had a few hours before her shift started at the diner, so she planned to work at the local coffee spot where she could connect wirelessly to the Internet and listen to the buzz of conversation. She'd already figured out that Bayou Coffee, on the far side of the campus near Wagner House, was the most popular with the All Saints students. She slid her computer into her backpack, snapped her hair into a top knot, and pulled on a baseball cap, then took off.

From her door to the coffee shop's took twenty minutes and, as luck would have it, two Asian students were leaving a small table near the window. Kristi snagged it, dropping her backpack onto one of the wooden seats, then stood in line to order a vanilla latte and a raspberry scone. As an espresso machine shrieked and steam rose over the groups of patrons, Kristi waited for her drink and surveyed the crowd. She recognized a few kids either from class or just running into them in the student union, library, or walking across campus.

Thankfully, no one turned gray before her eyes.

She was just picking up her order when the door opened and a tall, leggy girl with straight brown hair that fell halfway down her back walked inside. She looked familiar and Kristi placed her as someone in her classes who usually sat near Ariel O'Toole. The girl studied the tables as if searching for someone.

"Hey," Kristi said as she passed the girl. God, what was her name. Zinnia? Zahara? Something with a Z . . .

"Oh, hi," the girl looked like she was having trouble placing Kristi.

"Zena, right? You're a friend of Ariel's?"

"Oh . . . yeah?"

"I'm Kristi, you're in a couple of my classes. Grotto's vampyrism and Preston's writing."

"Huh . . . " Zena said without a hint of enthusiasm, and Kristi could tell that the girl still wasn't connecting the dots, which may have been just as well.

"Have you seen Lucretia?"

"Stevens? Oh, uh, not since last week, I think. I've been kinda busy getting ready for the play."

"You're in the drama department," Kristi guessed, and the girl visibly brightened.

"Yeah."

"With Father Mathias?"

"Uh-huh. I'm not really into the morality play thing, but hey, it's a start. He promised me if I did well, I would be considered for something deeper. I think they're doing Tennessee Williams in the spring. *A Streetcar Named Desire* maybe, and I'd love to play Blanche DuBois."

"Who wouldn't?" Kristi said, though she had no interest in anything remotely to do with acting or being on stage. "So what's with the morality plays?"

"I don't know," she said with a lift of one shoulder as she eyed the oversized menu of coffee drinks suspended over the baristas' heads. "Just Father's thing, I guess." She stepped up to the counter and ordered a chai-tea latte and a muffin.

Kristi could tell Zena wasn't interested in more conversation, so she walked back to her table and opened her computer. With one eye on the screen and the other on Zena, she picked at her scone.

Before Zena's order was up, the door opened and Trudie arrived. Her round face was red and she seemed breathless as she spied Zena. She hurried up behind her and gave her own order. Within five minutes the two friends had scoped out the busy shop and were hovering near a booth being vacated by two young mothers and their babies. One infant was contentedly sucking on a

pacifier while the other one was making noises that indicated he was winding up for an out-and-out wail. His
mother was working feverishly to strap him into his
stroller and get him outside. Her friend, with the calmer
boy, wasn't as frantic, but the minute the women had
wheeled their tiny charges away from the table, Trudie
and Zena nabbed it and sat down.

Kristi strained to hear part of their conversation, but
only picked up a few words. She made out "Glanzer." As
in Father Mathias Glanzer. And "morality." Probably the
play. Zena was all about the play. And then she thought
she heard the word "sisters." But nothing more.

Kristi decided she was lousy at eavesdropping and
was about to leave when Lucretia, wearing a long black
coat and five-inch heeled boots, swept through the side
door. Already a tall woman, she was now well over six
feet. Kristi considered confronting her ex-roommate.
After all Lucretia had asked for her help, then had been
avoiding her. But Kristi decided she'd wait and see what
happened. Maybe Lucretia was meeting someone here.
Her lover, or boyfriend, or fiancé or whatever? Or
maybe she was just grabbing a cup of coffee on the run.
Whatever the reason, Lucretia, never particularly
cheery to begin with, was looking perturbed and frustrated, her features bordering on haggard. As she stood
in line, she ran a hand through her curly hair and stared
up at the menu as if she'd never read it before. Or as if
she were lost in thought, a million miles away.

Kristi lowered her head to her laptop. Still wearing
her baseball cap, her face partially hidden by the computer screen, she thought she might avoid being de-
tected.

No such luck.

Just then Lucretia glanced away from the menu, zeroing in on Kristi. "You!" Lucretia gave up her position
in line to stalk across the tiled floor, nearly knocking

over the cart holding a display of Christmas mugs and coffees that were marked down to half price. The cups with Santa and Frosty on them wobbled and Lucretia righted them in time. "Are you following me?" Lucretia demanded.

"What? No. I've been here for half an hour."

"You're sure?" Lucretia asked, glancing over at Trudie and Zena who, engrossed in their own conversation, hadn't yet noticed her.

"Pretty sure," Kristi said dryly, more than a little annoyed. "I have called though. Left you two messages."

"I know, I know. I—I've been busy. Look—" She placed her hands on the table in front of Kristi's computer and leaned closer. "I made a mistake." Her voice was a sharp, nearly inaudible whisper. "About those girls."

"You mean Tara and—"

"Yes, yes!" she said emphatically. Her throat moved, as if she were swallowing hard. "I should never have told you about . . . about everything. I was wrong. Okay? I'm sure that all of the missing students will turn up eventually. When they want to. After all, they were all known runaways."

"But you said that you knew them, they were your friends—"

"Not my friends," she bit back. "I said I knew of them. And now I'm telling you I was wrong. So . . . just forget it. I made a mistake. You lived with a cop for a father. You know how they are. If there was really something criminal going on, the police would be all over it, so just drop it, okay? And . . . don't call me anymore."

"Are you all right?" Kristi asked.

Lucretia blinked. "Of course. Why?"

"You look pale."

"Oh, God." Lucretia gulped and stared at Kristi as if she'd seen a ghost. "So, what? Are you going to tell me

I'm in danger? Like Ariel? She told me, y'know. Thinks you're a flippin' head case. What the hell is that all about?"

Inwardly, Kristi cringed. She knew she should have never confided in Ariel, figured it would come back to bite her. "Obviously, you and Ariel are close."

"She knows you were my roommate, for Pete's sake. I introduced you, remember? And then you act all weird. As if she's in black and white."

"Sometimes, I . . ." Oh, what was the use? How could she explain that there were times when people appeared colorless, as if they were drained of blood.

Drained of blood . . .

Kristi's heart thudded uncomfortably as she made the connection to the vampire cult. But that wasn't certain . . . no, the woman on the bus who had died hadn't been in Grotto's class. "It's just a strange thing that I see."

"Strange like a psycho, so stop it, okay? And leave me the hell alone. Face it, Kristi, you're odd. Maybe it's because of everything you've been through, but you're definitely out of step."

"You asked me to look into this," Kristi reminded her, her voice and temper rising. The older couple at a nearby table glared at them.

"You're causing a scene," Lucretia hissed. "God, I'm sorry I dragged you into this."

"Into what?"

"Nothing!"

Lucretia rolled her eyes and reached up to push her hair from her face. As she did, her sleeve slid and Kristi got a glimpse of gauze taped over Lucretia's left wrist.

"What happened?" Kristi asked, indicating the bandage.

Lucretia turned chalk white. Her hand fell to her side. "I had a little accident. No big deal. I . . . oh, hell, I'm kind of a klutz in the kitchen," she said, and it was obviously a lie. "But I'm okay. Really. And that's not the point. What I'm asking, no, *telling* you to do, is forget we ever talked before about . . . you know."

"The cult—"

"I was wrong, damn it!" Lucretia blurted out. "And now I want you to back off."

"You said that already, but . . ." Kristi trailed off. She was talking to dead air as Lucretia had already swung around and was hastening to the booth with Trudie and Zena. Trudie made a big deal of sliding over as Lucretia talked with them for a minute or two, before taking her place in line again.

Kristi wasn't sure what to think. She knew Lucretia had been ducking her. That much had been obvious, but to pretend that their conversation basically hadn't happened? After talking about missing, possibly abducted, coeds and vampires and cults? What was that all about? And the bandage. Kristi would have thought it was no big deal, but Lucretia's reaction said otherwise.

Had someone warned Lucretia off?

The hairs on the back of Kristi's arms raised.

*Someone found out she talked to you and they're threatening her. And someone's following her, scaring her spitless. Even hurting her. That's why she's hiding a bandage.*

Kristi glanced at the table where Lucretia now sat with the other girls and caught her ex-roommate staring at her. Lucretia's face was drawn and white, her lips pursed, and she looked worried as hell. She met Kristi's eyes for the briefest of seconds, then looked away. As she did, her face turned the color of cold ashes.

Kristi's heart nearly stopped. What the hell was that all about?

*Maybe it's nothing,* she quickly assured herself. *You've been seeing a lot of this, haven't you? No one has died . . . yet.*

She swallowed hard.

Lucretia's color returned. As if it had never washed away.

*Jesus, Mary, and Joseph, Kristi. Maybe you* are *the freak!*

She thought about the conversation with Lucretia, how her ex-roommate had wanted her to forget everything they'd discussed before. Why?

*Someone got to her.*

Kristi folded her computer closed and packed up. She left the coffee shop without meeting Lucretia's eyes again, but she'd be damned if she was going to back off. If anything, she was more committed than ever to finding out what had happened to Dionne, Monique, Tara, and Rylee.

It was only when she'd unlocked the car and slid inside that she realized what else was off about Lucretia. Not only did she look worried as hell, not only had she tried to convince Kristi to back off, but she was no longer wearing the ring on her left hand, the one she'd been so coy about. Kristi had looked at her hands as she'd leaned over the table and they'd been bare. Even the nail polish missing, her fingernails bitten down.

*Have you been following me?*

Lucretia's accusation echoed through Kristi's mind.

*Not yet,* Kristi thought, *but maybe that's not such a bad idea.*

"I already told you, I don't know which professor Lucretia Stevens is dating," Ezma said as she tossed her apron into the bin for dirty clothes. "Maybe it was just a rumor."

"So who told you?" Kristi wasn't about to be derailed. It was nearly eleven P.M. and both she and Ezma were getting ready to leave.

"I don't know . . . oh, wait . . . it was someone from school, I think, a professor." She snapped her fingers to

jog her memory. "Oh, who was it?" Her face was drawn
into a deep knot of concentration. "Oh, Lord . . . Oh, I
got it!" She looked up, her eyes bright. "I was waiting
tables right here, and I overheard two women gossiping.
Let's see, it was Dr. Croft, the head of the English Department, and, oh, hell, who was she sitting with that
day?" She rubbed her chin. "I think it was the journalism instructor. The new one."

"Professor Senegal?"

"That's who it was, but I couldn't hear much. They
kept their voices low, especially when I was anywhere
nearby. I was kinda surprised. I mean people gossip, of
course, but Dr. Croft's the head of a department and this
is a pretty public place. Oh, well . . ." She lifted her
shoulders, then smoothed out the bills she'd gotten for
tips, counting them and leaving some for the busboys.

Kristi did the same, handing the girl who had cleared
the tables a percentage of her tips. She and Ezma
walked out of the restaurant together. The night was
clear and cool, the air crisp as Kristi climbed into her
Honda and Ezma slid onto the seat of her moped and
strapped on her helmet. A few seconds later, the motor
bike was humming out of the lot.

Kristi started the car. Though she usually walked to
work, today she'd been late, so she'd driven the short
distance. Before she put the Honda in gcar she tried
calling Dr. Grotto again and was immediately asked to
leave a message on his voice mail. Kristi didn't bother—
the guy already had two from her. Obviously he wasn't
picking up his calls or he was singling her out and ignoring her. Nah, that didn't make sense.

She drummed her fingers on the wheel and decided
if she didn't hear from him by Monday she'd have to do
a sit-in at his office, force him to talk to her. There were
also the Internet chat rooms. Maybe she could test the
waters with DrDoNoGood, if he showed up. Flirt with
him, pander to his ego. So far she hadn't turned on the

video cam on her computer, preferring anonymity, but maybe it was the only way to reach him. She could buy a cheap wig, colored contacts or glasses. She had to do something to get the creepy professor to start a conversation with her.

Shoving the hatchback into drive, she nosed out of the parking lot. Gunning the engine, she drove ten miles over the speed limit on the way home. She was anxious to gain access to the storage unit containing Tara Atwater's things.

Maybe she would finally learn something about the missing girl.

She parked in a hurry, running up the steps to her apartment. Inside, she quickly stripped off her work clothes and tossed them into her laundry bag. She also threw in two packets of detergent, the bolt cutters, and a flashlight, then stepped into jeans and a sweater. After slipping on a pair of tennis shoes, she started on her mission.

She was nervous as a cat, her stomach knotted as she descended two flights before unlocking the door to the basement and snapping on the wimpy lights.

At night the cavernous room below the building was even more formidable, the nooks and crevices more shadowy and dark. None of the washing machines were agitating, nor the dryers heating and spinning.

Good.

Carefully, certain someone would walk down the dark stairs at any second, Kristi removed the bolt cutters and set them on the floor near the wire storage bins, then she sorted her clothes quickly and started two of the washers.

As the machines began to fill, she grabbed the bolt cutters and studied the bins. They were each clearly marked and locked, one for each unit and two extras. One of the extra bins held gardening supplies and tools, obviously used for the apartment house, the other was filled with boxes. Kristi shined her flashlight through the mesh and saw Tara Atwater's name scrawled across them, along with a date of November 13, over a month after the girl had been deemed missing.

"Good enough," she said, and went to work.

Unfortunately Randy of the I-Man, You-Woman caveman mentality had been right. Using the bolt cutters proved difficult. She could get the blades over the shackle, the metal piece that attached the lock to the door, but then she didn't have the strength to make the damned cutters snip through.

Which ticked her off.

"Come on," she said, and tried again, pushing the handles together so hard that her arms ached, pain screaming down them, the muscles trembling with the pressure. "Wuss," she muttered under her breath as the washers continued to fill, water rushing into the tubs.

Again she put all her strength behind it.

Again she failed, only managing to score the shackle with the cutters. "They must be dull," she told herself, and twisted the cutters around, so that they were pressed against the side of the steel door. Setting her feet on the concrete floor she shoved against one handle with all of her weight, wedging the other into the door. Straining . . . straining . . . sweating . . . eyes squeezed . . . jaw set . . .

*Click!*

*Oh, God, was that someone at the door?*

*Damn!*

*What idiot would be doing their laundry this late at night?*

*Just you.*

Her heart, already pounding, soared into overdrive. Adrenaline shot through her bloodstream. With a grunt she shoved harder just as she heard the key turn and the upstairs door creak open over the changing of gears in the washers, then footsteps. Heavy tread descending.

*No!*

With all her strength she gave one final shove.
*Snap!*
The shackle broke.

Kristi didn't check to see if it was cut through. She shoved the bolt cutters into her laundry bag and, sweating, though the temperature in the basement couldn't have been over sixty, she bent over the dryer and opened the door as if checking on her wash.

Except someone else's wash was already there. Still very wet.

Criminy! She hadn't thought to check to see if there were clothes in the dryer. "Hell," she muttered, straightening just as a huge shape hovered at the bottom of the stairs. Her insides turned to water. Dear God, could this be the abductor? Is this how the psycho found his victims, alone in a dark basement? Had Tara been down here when . . .

She was about to reach for the bolt cutters to use as a weapon when Hiram stepped beneath the weak light of one of the overhanging bulbs.

She let out her breath and snapped back to the problem at hand. Would he notice the broken lock? "Hey, are those yours?" she asked, pointing at the dryer, then opening the door of the second one. It too was filled with wet clothes.

"Yeah." Hiram was dressed in flannel pajama bottoms that hung low on his hips and a hooded gray sweatshirt, his hands in the single front pocket of the hoody. On his feet were huge slippers that barely covered what had to be size thirteen or fourteens.

"Didn't you turn the dryers on?" she demanded.

"Yeah."

"When?"

"I dunno. Couple of hours ago." He was getting defensive, his lips, behind his scraggly beard, folding in on themselves.

"Well, your clothes are still wringing wet."

"I used 'low' so my jeans wouldn't shrink," he said as if it were she who was the imbecile who didn't know a thing about laundry protocol or procedure.

"Well, you've got about thirty minutes before the washers are finished with their cycles and when they are, I'm going to need both dryers."

"Too bad, you'll just have to wait." He made a big deal of checking the sodden clothes. Like he really cared. From the looks of his outfit, this might have been the first time he'd used the laundry facilities since Christmas.

Hiram hit the start button again, the timer set for twenty minutes, the temperature once again on "low."

She said, "That's not going to work."

He snorted, turned, and faced the storage cages.

Holy crap! Her heart was trip-hammering like mad.

What would she say when he accused her? Could she lie? From the corner of her eye she saw her laundry bag, the outline of the bolt cutters visible. She kicked the washer. The resulting clang rang throughout the basement.

Hiram spun as if a top on a string.

"Damned thing," she said, shaking her head.

"What was that noise?"

"I don't know but it's been doing it ever since I loaded it."

"The washer? Which one?"

She pointed to the one she'd kicked. "Every couple of minutes or so it does that banging noise. Can't be good. You're the super or the manager or whatever, maybe you could fix it."

"It didn't do it for me."

"How do you know? Were you down here?" she asked, and saw by his eyes that he hadn't been. Good. Her lie was safe. "Maybe you should get your toolbox."

He nodded and edged toward the stairs. "Yeah, I will, but after you're done with the washer, you, uh, might put a note on it that no one is to use it until I, um, get it fixed."

"Good idea," she said, and let out her breath as he, hands in the front pocket of his hoodie, started to climb the staircase. Every step seemed to groan in protest with his weight.

She waited until she heard the door at the top of the stairs open and close, then she didn't waste a second. She pulled the lock off the security cage, flung open the door, and started opening the boxes within. Clothes, CDs, candles, pictures in frames, books, and various personal items. Too much to fit into the laundry bag in one trip and she didn't dare carry the boxes upstairs. As quickly as possible, she grabbed up some small items, intending to come back for the rest later.

Then she took off the lock and replaced it with the one she'd purchased earlier today, the one with a combination she knew. It clicked into place. Until someone came down here and tried to get into the storage unit, no one would be the wiser.

# CHAPTER 15

Kristi, damn her tight little ass and sassy in-your-face attitude, had gotten to him.

No two ways about it, Jay thought, disgusted with himself.

Maybe Gayle had been right all along.

Maybe he'd never gotten over Kristi Bentz.

"Fool," he muttered as he sat in his desk chair in the lab in New Orleans. Ever since leaving her apartment last night, he'd been thinking about her, worried that she was getting into something dangerous. So he'd had to do something.

Instead of tearing out the old bathtub and starting to fix the plumbing at Aunt Colleen's house, Jay had rolled out of bed at the crack of dawn Saturday and, with Bruno at his side in the pickup, had driven like a bat out of hell back to his house in New Orleans. Once he'd dropped the dog off, he'd driven to the crime lab and the computer at his desk, where he'd sifted through all of the police databases he could, accessing information on the missing coeds.

And he hadn't stopped there.

Over the course of the day, he'd called a couple of friends who worked for the Baton Rouge Police, a sheriff for the parish of East Baton Rouge, and even an old college buddy who was working for the Louisiana State

Police. If they were off duty, he then tracked them down by their cell phones, interrupting their days. He figured it didn't matter. He was going to get to the bottom of Kristi's obsession come hell or high water.

*Because she's yours,* his mind taunted. *You've been obsessed with that woman from the first time you set eyes on her, and if you think you're doing this for any reason other than to score points with her, guess again.*

His jaw tightened and he pushed the thought aside. Besides, it wasn't true. He would have checked into any of his students' concerns. Maybe not with quite so much fervor, or he might have passed the information along to the proper authorities and then stepped back, but he would have taken some action.

*Face it, McKnight, you're pussy-whipped.*

He refused to listen to the voice as he worked in his office, which was not much more than a closet with a window, but it had a computer terminal and access to all of the police databases. "All I need is here," he said aloud, though it was a lie. What he'd like was a beer. Instead, he settled for a semi-chilled can of iced tea from the vending machine and snacked on peanut butter cups and red licorice.

At least it was quiet here, the weekend shift busy in other areas of the building, away from his small office.

Everyone he'd phoned was willing to talk to him and all agreed to call him back if they found any information on the four girls, but so far no one had offered up anything he didn't already know.

To a one, the police officers believed Dionne Harmon, Monique DesCartes, Tara Atwater, and most recently Rylee Ames were troubled girls who had just taken off. If their credit or debit cards hadn't been used, it was surmised that they'd found a different money source. Probably dealing drugs or prostituting themselves for cash. Maybe gambling? Mooching off some low-life friends?

The only glimmer of hope Jay received was from his friend Raymond "Sonny" Crawley, with whom he'd gone to college and who now worked in the Homicide Department at Baton Rouge.

"Jeeeezus, McKnight," Sonny had said when he'd answered his cell phone. "What happened? You been talkin' to Laurent or somethin'? That's the trouble with that damned woman, she won't let this thing go, I'm tellin' ya. No bodies. No crime scene, but she seems to think the girls were abducted or killed or God only knows what. Trust me, we got all the work up here we need without creatin' any more, but she's not convinced. Pissin' everyone off."

"Who's Laurent?" Jay asked, scribbling a note to himself as he stared at the computer screen with the picture of Rylee Ames, the girl who was supposed to have been in his class this term.

"Portia Laurent's a junior detective with the department who has a bug up her butt about those girls. Hell, we all want to find them, but sheeeit, there just isn't a case. Not yet. But you know how those newbies are. They tend to get fired up about any little thing. Not that I'm makin' light of the situation, but there just isn't much we can do about it until we come up with a body, murder weapon, suspect, or witness. So why the hell are you interested?"

"Just curious," Jay hedged. He'd already decided to keep Kristi's name out of it, unless he determined that she was in any kind of danger. The fact that she lived at the address of one of the missing girls bothered him. "I work up there, part-time, teach a class on forensics, and there's been a lot of talk about what happened to the girls."

"Don't I know it?" Sonny agreed. "Every time it's a slow news day around here, I get some reporter nosin' around, tryin' to stir up trouble, make news if there isn't any. Take that Belinda Del Ray from WMTA . . . what a pain in the ass she is. Good-lookin', I'll grant you that. And she uses it, let me tell you. But she's like a damned pitbull with a bone, don't ya know? Won't take no for an answer and keeps pokin' around even when we try to steer her to the PIO. But she's not interested in the official statement from the Public Information Officer, no siree, not Belinda. She wants more than we're willing to give. As far as the department's concerned: no bodies, no case. But some reporters don't know how to butt out."

"Just doing their jobs," Jay said, playing devil's advocate. He was ambivalent about the press. A necessary evil. Often useful. Sometimes a real pain. Especially the aggressive reporters hungry to make a name for themselves.

"Humph," Sonny snorted. "Obviously you haven't dealt with too many reporters."

This was going nowhere. "So tell me about Detective Laurent. Why isn't she buying the company line?"

"Fuck, I don't know what the hell Laurent thinks. You'd have to ask her. Oh, hell, I got another call comin' in."

He clicked off and Jay stared at the notepad on his desk. Portia Laurent. He definitely wanted to hear what she had to say. He circled her name, tore off the sheet, stuffed it into a pocket of his jeans, and settled in to work.

By the end of the day, chewing on his last brittle rope of red licorice, he didn't know a whole helluva lot more than he had last night. Just enough, though, that he was starting to believe that Kristi was onto something. As for the whole vampire thing, he was surprised how many people bought into it. Not only books, movies, television, online gaming, but there was an entire Internet culture, linked, he was certain, to real people.

A cult?

Maybe.

Centered at All Saints?

He hoped to hell not.

He thought about all the missing girls and Dr. Grotto's class. He'd heard from a few members of the staff he'd met about the guy's theatrical way of presenting the class, the fake fangs and contacts that covered his irises and made his eyes appear flat and black. Without a soul. Inhuman. But no one was worried about it. It was drama. Flair. And the students loved it. The fact that he was taller than most with thick dark hair and penetrating eyes didn't hurt the image either.

Jay rubbed the back of his neck and rotated his head to relieve the tension, all the while staring at the computer screen, where the face of Rylee Ames met his gaze. Young. Beautiful. Vibrant. At least in the head shot. But obviously messed up.

Runaway? Or abduction? Possible murder victim . . . ?

Had she been a part of some private cult?

Was Grotto into it? Hell, if so, he was flaunting his part, wasn't he? Really out in the open with this vampire crap. How stupid would that be, to point a finger at himself? Or was it Grotto's ego? Did he really think he was invincible? If so, the intense teacher wouldn't be the first. Jay chewed hard on the tasteless candy, then tossed the wrapper into his trash can, all the while thinking about his colleague at the school. Maybe it was time for a background check on Grotto, a deeper check than the university had made. For that matter, what about some of the other professors and department heads? Or members of the administration? From what he knew about cults, they crossed all sorts of social barriers. He had the resources, he decided, and there was no reason not to use them. All he had to do was cross reference names and addresses. Some of the information would be public, other private. He'd go as far as he could without breaking the law.

*And then what?*

*What if you need to dig deeper?*

"Hell," he muttered. He would damned well cross that slippery bridge when he came to it.

His cell phone vibrated in his pocket.

Shifting on his chair, Jay retrieved the phone and saw Gayle's home phone number flash onto his screen. Inwardly groaning, he considered not answering, but knew that was only postponing the inevitable.

He had tried to be kind.

It hadn't worked.

The woman wasn't taking the hint.

"Hey," he answered, hating the upbeat sound of his voice. It sounded as phony as his feelings.

"How are you?" Her voice too was sunny, a little breathless.

"Busy."

"Always." She sighed and he imagined her face turning petulant. God, how had he ever thought it was cute? "I suppose you're in Baton Rouge and don't have time for a drink or anything?"

"Afraid not, Gayle."

"I could head up that way."

He didn't tell her he was in New Orleans. He didn't intend to spend the night here, anyway, and he definitely didn't intend to spend it with Gayle. "I'm working."

"Well," she said, and he imagined her walking across the plush carpet of her home, probably standing at the floor-to-ceiling windows to stare out at the night. The suggestion wasn't unexpected. "You won't be working all the damned night, now will you? I could stay over. . . ."

If it wasn't so damned sad, it would be funny. Gayle, living in the lap of luxury, spending the night in Aunt Colleen's torn-up bungalow without any hot water or much else.

"Conditions are rustic. I sleep in a sleeping bag on a cot, Gayle."

"Cozy," she said, deliberately misreading what he

meant. "I could get a hotel. You could stay in something a little less primitive for a night."

"I don't think so." He leaned back in his desk chair again, his weight making it squeak in protest as he placed a foot on his desk. He thought of Kristi, the difference between the two women, and the fact that he'd never really felt the same way about Gayle. Not even close. Gayle had been right about that, her feminine instincts honed.

"You're avoiding me," she said with a little pout in her voice.

Jay steeled himself. There was just no way to sugarcoat this. "I can't make time for you right now."

He heard her swift intake of breath. "Wow. I guess I didn't expect that. I thought we were going to be friends."

Outside the door of his office, he heard footsteps and soft conversation as two colleagues passed. Further away a phone rang.

"I think we have a different opinion on just what being friends is."

She charged, "You don't want me to come up there."

"It wouldn't be a good idea." There was a pause. He didn't really know how to do this without hurting her, then decided he had to be cruel to be kind. "Gayle, I don't think we should see each other again. Not even as friends."

"Why're you doing this?" she cried, appalled.

"We both agreed it's over."

"Your idea. Not mine!"

"You weren't happy."

"I could be."

"Oh hell, Gayle. It would never have worked. We both know it."

"*You* wouldn't let it."

"I'm not going to fight about it."

"You bastard," she said, her voice switching tones.

"It's Kristi Bentz again, isn't it? I knew it. That's why you went up there in the first place. Because she was going to school up there—surprised I know that?"

No, he wasn't. That was the problem. "It's over, Gayle."

"For the love of God, Jay, will you never learn?" Her voice rose and once again he heard someone walk past his door as the phone momentarily cut out, heralding an incoming call.

"I gotta go. Another call."

"You're seeing her! Goddamn it, Jay, I was right, wasn't I? The least you could do is admit it. You're still in love with her!"

"Good-bye, Gayle," he said, and clicked off, but her accusation rang through his head, echoing and sharp: *You're still in love with her.*

"Damned straight," he said to himself. Okay, there it was. He was still fascinated as all get-out with Kristi. More than ever. "Shit."

He clicked to the other call. "Hello?"

"McKnight?" Rick Bentz's voice caught him off guard.

"Yeah."

"I need a favor." No beating around the bush with Bentz.

"What?"

"Kristi needs her bike. If I run it up there she'll accuse me of butting into her personal life. I know you're teaching a class at All Saints and that you've got a truck. Maybe you could run it up to her."

Sometimes fate had a funny sense of humor, Jay thought. "Sure." He considered confiding in the detective; after all, Bentz was Kristi's father and she seemed poised to get herself into trouble. Thinking of her, he held his tongue. For the moment.

They made arrangements for Jay to pick up Kristi's fifteen-speed at the station later in the day and Jay didn't mention anything about the fact that Kristi was his stu-

dent, that she'd confided in him, that she was digging
into vampire cults, or that Jay intended to see more of
her.

He hung up and wondered if he'd made the right
choice. What would he tell Bentz if Kristi got herself
into real trouble? Danger? What if she ended up abducted? How would he feel then?

He swore under his breath. Kristi would kill him if
she found out he confided in her father and that would
be the final straw. They would never reconcile.

"Shit." So that's where all this was going. What a
mess! He clicked off the computer and got to his feet.
Maybe it was time to head back to Baton Rouge.


Nothing!

Kristi didn't find one damned thing in Tara's belongings that helped her figure out what had happened to the
girl.

"Damn it all to hell." Rocking back on her heels,
Kristi studied Tara's things, all of which were strewn
over the tarp she'd laid across the floor. If she'd hoped
the jewelry box had contained a necklace with a vial of
blood attached to it, she'd been sorely disappointed. If
she'd thought she'd find a treasure map leading to a secret meeting place of a vampire cult, she'd been wrong
there, too.

"There has to be something here," she said out loud.
"Just find it."

But the obvious items were missing: computer, purse,
cell phone and/or BlackBerry. There was no secret diary.
No love letters. No address book or phone Rolodex. In
the boxes of clothes, she had found a backpack that
she'd unzipped, searched, and even turned upside down.
One of the straps had been broken, but there was nothing inside except an empty pack of cigarettes, two sticks
of gum, a half-full box of breath mints, couple of re-

ceipts from a local quickie mart, a squashed tampon, and a rubber band.

She felt a little like Geraldo Rivera when he'd opened up what was supposed to be Al Capone's vault on live national TV in the eighties, expecting to find all kinds of treasures or evidence against the gangster only to find the area empty except for debris. Which is just what Kristi had—nothing but debris from a missing girl.

After almost being discovered by Hiram, she'd made three trips downstairs with her laundry bag, hauling up Tara's things bit by bit, then searching through the pockets of her pants and jackets, looking for anything that might be a clue. But nothing came to light.

"My father would be disappointed," she said to the cat as he stared at her from an upper shelf on the bookcase flanking one side of the fireplace. "What am I missing?" She sifted through the piles of jeans, khakis, and shorts, then the sweaters, T-shirts, and jackets one more time.

Nothing.

Disappointment crawled through her. "Maybe I'm just not cut out for this," she muttered while the cat watched her box up Tara's things. Either Tara had taken everything of value with her when she left, or her abductor had. Kristi folded her own laundry, whipped out a paper for Dr. Preston's writing class, and kept nodding off in bed while reading the latest assignment from the tome of Shakespearean plays.

"Tomorrow," she confided in Houdini as he hopped onto the bed and lay in the far corner, still ready to jump for cover should she startle him. Theirs was a growing, but extremely tentative, relationship. Bit by bit Houdini was edging closer, almost letting her pet him upon occasion, though his ears were often pinned back. Whenever she reached down he leaned away from her. She'd only managed to brush her fingertips along the tips of his fur.

Not too far from the way she and Jay reacted to each other, she thought. Wary. Suspicious. Interested but frightened. God, why did she always seem to return to Jay? He was her professor and he'd agreed to help her figure out what had happened to the four girls, but that was it. There was absolutely nothing romantic or sexual in their relationship. And that's the way it had to stay.

"Right, Houdini?" she asked.

The cat gazed at her, unblinking.


Father Mathias Glanzer paced through the church, past the glass votives holding candles that had burned low. His footsteps sounded hollow along the floor-boards of the nave. At the altar, before the huge suspended crucifix, he genuflected, made the sign of the cross, and sent up a small prayer for guidance as the image of Jesus stared down at him.

In anger?

Or compassion?

His clasped hands were clammy, his body beneath his robes covered in a nervous, self-loathing sweat. He'd been a priest for nearly fifteen years and still he sought guidance, still he doubted. His faith wavered, though he would deny it to anyone who asked.

But God knew.

As did he, himself. "Forgive me," he whispered, and though he knew he should stay and pray for hours, he found no solace in prayer, no comfort in seeking God's counsel. Straightening, he left the church, the door to the nave shutting behind him with a soft, definitive thud.

Outside, the night promised rain. Clouds were thick, the moon and stars blocked from a storm that was pushing inland. The January wind was cold, with a harsh bite as it blew through his soul.

He'd come to All Saints thinking he could start over, reaffirm his vows, make changes in the college. In himself. Find God again.

Just as in a marriage when spouses become too comfortable and take each other for granted, lose interest or vitality, so had he accepted his faith as pure and important and all-knowing. He'd become prideful. Vain. Seeking his own glory over that of God.

And, of course, as high as he'd climbed, as far as his blind ambition had taken him, it had abandoned him. Now he was falling, tumbling into a darkness so bleak, he feared there was no return. Moving to All Saints hadn't been a blessing, but a curse.

He wanted to blame Dr. Grotto, or Father Anthony, or Natalie Croft with her damned vision for the English Department. He'd gone so far as to harbor feelings of injustice at the school administration with so many laypeople on the board, including the descendants of Ludwig Wagner, the man who had given the original plot to the archdiocese to build the school, but, in truth, all of his railing against the fates and those with whom he worked was foolhardy. The person who was at fault was himself. He thought of those who had gone before him, pure men who had tortured themselves in horsehair or with flails, who knelt for days upon cold stones, who fasted until they fainted . . . he would never test himself as they had.

For years he'd told himself those penances were for the weak and addled, that he was above them. Now he knew differently. They were for the strong, and only cowards like himself—weak, mortal men—would run from God's challenges.

*You can never outrun yourself, Mathias, now, can you? And even if you could, the Father would see your*

*pathetic efforts. He looks deep into your soul and wit-*
*nesses the wretched darkness within.*

*He knows of your sins.*

The chapel bells tolled, their deep dulcet tones reverberating in his brain, echoing in his heart. They should
have uplifted him, but their deep resonance only served
to remind him of how much he'd lost, how much he'd so
willingly, almost eagerly, cast away.

Swallowing hard, Father Mathias made the sign of
the cross over his vestments yet again as he strode
through the wet grass. He would go to his apartment,
drink a little brandy, and try to come up with a plan, an
escape.

*Coward! You can never break free. You are con-*
*demned to hell by your own hand. You are Judas.*

From the corner of his eye, he saw a movement, the
slightest shiver of the shrubbery flanking the galilee,
the porch at the west end of the church.

Father Mathias felt his heart shudder. He told himself not to be so frightened, the movement was probably
caused by a cat out on a nightly hunt, or an opossum
hiding beneath the branches or . . . Oh, God.

He froze.

A dark figure rose from its crouching position beneath the narrow tracery windows. "Father Mathias," it
whispered hoarsely as it drew near.

Mathias was struck by fear as dark as Lucifer's soul.

"What is it, my son?"

The being, for that's how he thought of it, was large,
a man in a costume, or something otherworldly? Male?
Or an Amazon woman? Or sexless? Its features were
hidden in the dark recesses of a thick cowl, its eyes
seeming to glow bloodred.

Mathias trembled, cold as death.

White teeth flashed in the darkness. Lips dark, as if
stained with blood, warned, "Do not betray us. I see it in

your eyes, feel it in your expression, smell the fear within you." The lips curled as if in disgust and for a millisecond he imagined he saw fangs within that shadowy evil countenance. "If there is a whisper of treason, the barest breath of your disloyalty, you will be blamed. And, I assure you, you will be punished."

Before Mathias could raise his arms to hold his crucifix in the demon's face, it lunged, grabbing hold of his wrist in a painful grip. Hot breath scorched his skin.

"No!" he cried.

Too late.

Cloth ripped.

Lips curled back.

Fangs clamped down hard.

"Aaaah!"

Pain screamed through his arm as the fiend's teeth sliced into his flesh. "God in heaven no!" Mathias cried, horror tearing through his body.

The demon wrenched on his wrist and he screamed out again. "Please, don't!"

"Shhh!" The creature raised its dark head and blood—the priest's blood—dripped from its horrid lips. "Be gone," it hissed, spraying Mathias with his own lifeblood, a forked tongue visible through those blood-smeared incisors.

*Holy Father, what kind of beast from hell was this?*

Stricken, the priest fell to his knees, scrabbling for his rosary, sending up prayer after prayer in his terror-riddled, near-paralyzed state. What had he gotten himself into? *What?*

He heard voices. From the other side of the church. Dear God, he couldn't be found like this . . . had no explanation. The fiend turned and ran, sweeping almost silently across an expanse of lawn, then into the darkness.

Mathias crumpled into a heap. Tears tracked from

his eyes. Tears of fear. Tears of remorse. Tears of a broken, faithless man.

"Our Father," he started to mumble, but the words stuck in his throat. His tongue was thick and awkward, his repentance too little, too late. He'd gone too far. Crossed a burning threshold from which there was no return. Prayer wouldn't help. Confession, the ultimate cleanser of all sins, was no longer his salvation.

The truth of the matter was that he, like so many before him, had sold his very soul to the devil.

And Satan wanted his due.

# CHAPTER 16

Boomer Moss had hunted gators all his life. Sometimes he'd done it all legal with a tag, in season, and sometimes, like tonight, not. He figured alligators were mean sumbitches who deserved to die, and if he could make a few bucks off their hides, their heads, and their meat, all the better. He was doin' the world a big fat favor by takin' the motherfuckers out, one slithery life at a time.

The fact that there was a season for the huntin' and tags to be purchased and forms to be sent into the government really got his balls in an itch. His family had been hunting the swamps, ponds, lakes, and canals around New Orleans for over two hundred years. The government had no business, no damned business tellin' him what to do.

Besides, huntin' in the swamps in the dark was a rush like none other. Boomer had a few beers stashed in a cooler as he trolled the black waters and passed the ghostly, skeletonlike trunks and roots of the cypress trees. He had his snares set, but you could never tell when you might come across a gator in the water, dormant season or not.

Sometimes he'd kill himself a raccoon or an opossum or a snake if he could catch one. He figured these

swamps belonged to him. Here he ruled, and the bounty
of the boggy land was his for the taking. He didn't want
to mess with any tags—hell, no. And he knew a raccoon
or skunk was better bait than the cow guts sanctioned
by the state.

Again, the government should have better things to
worry about. Christ! Using the beam of a heavy-duty
flashlight, Boomer scoured the water, hoping to see
eyes emerge from the darkness, just over the inky
water's surface. The gators were sluggish this time of
year, most dormant, but not impossible to find.

He had his traps set and come morning he expected
to have at least one of the fuckers, maybe as many as
five or six if he got lucky. For now, he'd troll, check the
bait he had strung up a couple of feet above the water,
hoping to lure a gator into propelling himself to leap up
and snag himself on the hook.

He saw their eyes in the darkness, realized they not
only saw him, but sensed him, as they did any movement in the water. Big dang toothed lizards. He heard a
splash, saw one slide into the water not far from a nest
where the grass had been beaten down, noticed the
mound of mud and grass that indicated where the eggs
had been laid.

"Come on, Mama," he said in a cooing voice. "You
all come over here to Daddy." He waited, searching, his
twenty-two pistol in his hand. But the she-gator hid in
the shadows, away from the beam of his light, and he
moved on, slowly, one hand on the tiller, the sounds of
the night filling his ears: the whirr of bats' wings, the
hoot of an owl, the croak of bullfrogs, the hum of a few
insects over the rumble of the boat's small outboard
motor. Every now and again he heard a splash, a fish
jumping or a gator sliding into the still water.

He spent long hours trolling, not getting close enough
to shoot a damned gator and haul him into the boat, but

scouting out the swamp. Through the hours, he downed a six-pack of Lone Star and two of Mindy Jo's fried oyster po'boy sandwiches.

Finally, as the night waned, he checked his snares. The first was empty, the bait stripped clean.

"Shit," he said, steering his boat further to the next trap, and there, hanging partially in the air, was a gator. Eight feet if he was an inch. "Hallelujah, brother," Boomer said, moving close enough that he could raise his pistol to the critter's small brain. He fired, the sound a sharp report. Had to make sure the reptile was good and dead before cuttin' him down. Boomer sure as hell didn't want any four-hundred-pound gator thrashing around in the boat. It was tricky enough dealing with a dead one.

He prodded at the gator with an oar, then certain the big reptile was indeed dead, carefully lowered the massive carcass into the bottom of the boat. The bull alligator was a prime specimen, not many scars on his hide. He'd fetch a damned good price. Feeling as if the night wasn't a complete waste, Boomer checked his other snares, found the bait still hanging over the water without any gators attached. Might as well leave the traps baited for now. He could still get lucky.

He turned the boat back toward the dock where his truck was parked. He didn't bother with gutting his prize, just wrapped the gator in a wet tarp, winched him into the truck bed, and drove back to the house, a small single-wide set on concrete blocks deep in the woods.

Boomer felt good. He'd go home, shower, then wake his wife and screw the devil out of her, just as he always did after a successful hunting trip. He could hardly wait, his hands clenched over the steering wheel as the old Chevy bounced and shimmied through the potholes in the gravel lane leading to the house.

Mindy Jo never complained about being waked for the sex, no siree. She was probably at home now, waiting for him, her cunt already wet. She loved it when the old testosterone was flowin' fast and hot after the thrill of a hunt. He'd spend hours in the big old bed they shared, pushin' her to the brink over and over again, rutting over her like a damned stallion.

She'd get so turned on she'd even let him slap her buttocks in the process. Man, she loved that!

At the house, he parked in the garage, put some ice over the tarp, then went inside. He decided to forget about the shower and see what she'd think if he smelled of the hunt . . . he'd done that a time or two and this morning it seemed like a damned good idea, so he stripped out of his hunting clothes, left the camouflage shirt and pants in a pile in the kitchen in front of the new washer and dryer, then walked into the bedroom.

King of the realm.

It was dark, the black-out curtains drawn, and it smelled of cigarette smoke and the damned cats she insisted on keeping around the place.

"Honey, izzat you all?" she mumbled, her face buried in the pillow.

"Oh, yeah," he said, "it's me, all right, and I'm horny as hell. Caught myself one helluva bull gator."

"Oh."

He touched her thigh with a finger and she rolled away, making a disturbed, bothered sound. He didn't buy it. Kneeling on the mattress beside her, his dick rock hard, he touched her again. "Did you hear me? He's a big un." He slipped his hand around her body, touching her breast.

"Oh, Boomer. Not now. Leave me alone."

"No way, baby," he said, and she sighed, already waking. Maybe he'd get lucky. Maybe she'd suck him off.

"Ooh, God, you stink." She rolled over and faced him, her mouth only inches from his cock. "Didn't you shower?"

"Nah!"

"Oh, God, Boomer. Go clean up!"

But he'd already leaned down to kiss her and he took one of her small, soft hands and placed it on his penis. "I can't wait, baby. You're just so damned beautiful."

"And you're a lyin' son of a bitch. It's too dark in here to see anything."

"I see you in my head, honey."

"What a bunch of crap," she said, but her fingers were already flexing around him and as he came to her, she opened her mouth, kissing him with a fever that was always with her in the morning. More and more it seemed that at night she was just too tired for sex and slapped him away, but she woke up horny in the morning and that was fine with him.

He rolled atop her and decided since he'd been up all night as it was, he wasn't going to spend too much time getting her to come. No siree. He would work fast and hard, touch all her hot spots right off the bat and once he'd felt her start to move against him, going into that low moan of hers, he would finish the job. But, he'd rushed things. Misjudged her reaction. She was a little tight this morning, not fully awake or into it like she usually was, and by the time he'd got her slicked up inside, he couldn't wait and came in a rush, before she was ready, flopping down on her just like the dead gator.

Which really pissed her off.

"You big oaf," she declared, pushing him to the side of the bed. "What the hell do ya think ye're doin?"

"It's all right, baby, I'll take care of you."

"Forget it. I'm not in the mood." He tried kissing her roughly and she pushed him away. "Stop it, Boomer. You got your damned rocks off, now just leave me alone." She rolled to the side of the bed and scraped her fingers across the nightstand, feeling for her cigarettes. One of her stupid cats walked across his pillow, its tail brushing his nose and reminding him that they were never alone, not with all the goddamned felines crawling through the house.

Boomer closed his eyes and figured he'd sleep for a few hours. The gator was safe, iced up as it was. He heard the click of a lighter, then smelled burning tobacco as she inhaled. Tired as he was, he fell asleep and only opened an eye when he felt her stir nearly six hours later. He wanted to sleep longer—hell, he deserved it—but he had to check on the gator and make sure it was still cool and besides, the damned banty roosters that belonged to Jed Stomp, his stupid-ass neighbor, were crowing up a high-pitched raucous that could wake the dead.

A bit of a headache nagged at him as he climbed out of bed. He gave Mindy Jo's naked, round little butt a playful slap and headed back to the kitchen, where he pulled on his hunting clothes again.

The sun was high in the winter sky, the day promising to have a little heat for January. A crow sat on the peak of the roof, eyeing him and emitting irritating caws.

"Oh, shut up," he grumbled, wishing he had his twenty-two. Damn noisy thing.

In the carport, he opened the bed of the truck, then worked to slide the gator and the tarp out onto the gravel of the driveway. The crow's caws were echoed by a jay who'd come to squawk. To add to the noise, he heard the damn squeal of the coffee grinder from inside the house. Mindy Jo was up and going through her ritual of grinding coffee, which he thought was a big bother when you could buy a can of Folgers for less money at the Piggly Wiggly.

Ignoring the morning cacophony, Boomer grabbed his sharpest knife and went to cuttin' on the gator. It was hard work, but he was already counting the dollar signs in his head and thinking that he'd go check the other traps later. Maybe he'd gotten lucky. Just about finished with the messy job, he heard the screen door creak open, then slam shut.

Mindy Jo, wrapped in some silky Asian robe, pink slippers, and faux ostrich feathers, walked onto the screened-in porch. She held a steaming cup of coffee in one hand and a lit cigarette in the other. Three of those miserable cats wound around her leg. The gray tom, with no tail and only one eye, had the nerve to glare at him. God, he hated that stupid lynx.

"He is a big un," she said, not stepping off the porch as she eyed the alligator's carcass. "Just get one?" She took a drag from her cigarette and tipped back her head to let out a stream of smoke from one side of her mouth.

"Fer now. I'll check the traps again later this morning." He was sweating, working hard as he eviscerated the animal. "And he ain't too scarred. Skin's good. The hide'll fetch a good price."

"Nice," she said, drawing hard on her cigarette. The banty rooster started up again. Mindy Jo ignored the screeching. "Ya want grits and bacon?"

"Yeah."

"Eggs?"

"'Course . . . hey . . . what the hell?" He saw something that just looked wrong. He'd gutted a helluva lot of alligators in his lifetime and never had he seen one of 'em's stomach look so oddly shaped. "What the fuck you been feedin' on, big fella?"

"Don't you dare open up his guts here!" Mindy Jo screeched.

Too late. Boomer's curiosity had already gotten the better of him. He slit the stomach wide and the inside, smelling of stomach acid and dead fish, opened up.

Boomer jumped back. "Holy shit!" He nearly threw up at the sight.

"What?" Mindy Jo asked.

"I think we're in trouble," he said, wondering how

the hell he was going to explain the obviously poached alligator and already trying on several lies to save his own skin. But Boomer did have a conscience. "Big trouble." How could he explain this? "Call the sheriff."

"The sheriff?" Mindy Jo's slippers clipped down the two steps and along the brick path toward him.

"Do as I say. This gator ain't been snackin' on Fig Newtons, that's fer sure."

The clicking stopped and her shadow passed over him and onto the open belly of the dead reptile. "Lord, Jesus!" she whispered, her eyes bugging at the smelly contents of the gator's gut. Amongst the crayfish, frogs, turtles, and fish lay an arm, a very human female arm and hand, painted fingernails and all.

*Stroke, stroke, stroke.*
Kristi cut through the water of the pool cleanly, breathing easily, feeling her muscles begin to strain. She'd been at it over half an hour, was going for forty minutes.

The smell of chlorine was everywhere and there was mist on the windows of the college's pool house, but aside from an older guy several lanes over, she had the water to herself.

She hadn't swum in over a month and it felt great. Energizing. Cleared her mind.
*Stroke.*
She thought of Jay and had to admit she liked seeing him again. But just as a friend . . .
*Stroke.*
She hadn't found anything in Tara Atwater's personal items, but she'd look again. There *had* to be some evidence about her disappearance in the same damned apartment in which she'd lived.
*Stroke.*
Ariel and Kristi's father were still very much alive.

So her black and white vision thing might just be a physical thing, not some kind of special ESP or visions of the future.

*Stroke.*

There were no such things as vampires. And she was going to talk to Professor Grotto and see what he had to say for himself. Then, perhaps, the police.

*Stroke.*

Maybe she should call Jay. . . . No way. She needed his help, yes, but that was it. She was *not* trying to start something up with him again.

*Stroke.*

*Liar! There's something about him that gets you. Damn!*

She couldn't think about Jay McKnight as a man. That part of their relationship was long over. Still . . . she found the way he pushed his hair from his eyes endearing, the boyish hint of a smile in the corner of his mouth fascinating, and the way his eyes darkened with humor or interest compelling. Dear God, she was a mess when it came to that man.

She told herself that she didn't want him before and she couldn't want him now. The whole forbidden fruit thing? Totally overrated. Yet she was thinking about him in ways she shouldn't, and that really ticked her off.

Reaching the edge of the pool, she glanced up at the clock. Forty-three minutes. Long enough. She was breathing hard as she pushed her hands on the side and pulled herself up to the concrete pad. What was it about Jay that got to her? Grabbing her towel from a hook near the locker room, she dried herself vigorously. Needed to rub Jay out of her life.

She glanced over the water's aquamarine surface and realized the old man who had been swimming laps when she'd dived into the pool had already left. She was alone in the pool house with the steamy windows. Outside it seemed as if night were descending, late afternoon shadows creeping through the windows.

She suddenly sensed that someone was watching her through the glass, someone she couldn't see. Her body shivered convulsively. Chiding herself for her fear, she dabbed at her face.

*Don't overreact. All your research on the missing girls is getting to you.*

Inside the women's locker room, she tore off her wet swimsuit, showered, and changed into jeans and a sweatshirt. As she left the building, once again she wished she had her bike instead of having to walk across campus. It wasn't as if she were alone; plenty of students were on the walkways heading to a late class or the library or their dorms. A lot of the people she passed were in groups or listening to iPods or talking on cell phones. Nothing was out of the ordinary, except that she caught a glimpse of a tall, blond girl she'd seen in some of her classes, and the girl's skin changed in front of her eyes, the color leeching from her skin.

This was nuts!

Hadn't Kristi just convinced herself that the whole gray pasty look was just some trick of her mind? Ariel was still alive. Her father was still walking the earth, chasing bad guys for the New Orleans PD. This black/ white thing was a figment of her imagination, *her* problem. Still . . .

Kristi kept on following the pale girl who was striding at record speed past the chapel. She nearly had to jog to keep her in sight and was worried that she was leaving All Saints, heading to a parking lot off campus.

"Damn," she said, wondering what she'd say to the blonde, if and when she finally caught up with her. *Are you feeling okay? Man, you sure look pale. Do you need a study partner for Dr. Grotto's class?* "Lame, lame, and lame," she muttered under her breath as the girl reached the gate of Wagner House, walked inside, and hurried up the steps.

But the museum was closed.

Kristi hesitated. The blonde—what was her name, Maren or Marie? Something like that—had entered without a problem.

After a moment Kristi strode through the front gate as if she'd intended to head into Wagner House all along, and flew up the steps. Though a sign on the door said CLOSED and listed the hours of operation, she tried the latch and the glass-paned door swung open. Huh, she thought, crossing the threshold and stepping inside. The latch clicked softly behind her and she was alone. In the supposedly haunted house. With no sign of the blonde.

The foyer, decorated with an antique table and a plaque giving a short history of the house, was empty. A single Tiffany lamp glowing in shades of amber and blue threw a bit of illumination into the deepest shadows of the room.

From the entrance, stairs led to the upper floors, and a parlor room was to the right. It, too, was lit by a single lamp, the rest of the room in shadow. Antiques and period pieces were placed around a patterned rug and a marble-inlayed fireplace, and mullioned windows flanked a floor-to-ceiling bookcase stuffed with leather-bound, ancient-looking volumes.

This house, she knew, had belonged to Ludwig Wagner, the first settler of the area, a rice or cotton baron who had left his estate and part of his fortune not only to his children, but also to the Catholic church for the purpose of building All Saints College. Several of his descendants were still on the board and played active politics with the school. But the house had been preserved, used for formal parties and opened on some afternoons as a museum. The velvet ropes, which forced people who viewed the house to file through the rooms without disturbing anything, were still in place.

Marcia or Marcy, or whatever, wasn't anywhere to be seen as Kristi crossed to the foot of the stairs. The house was silent. She heard nothing. But the slight scent of perfume still lingered. Kristi thought about calling out, but dismissed it.

A few days ago Ariel and her friends had walked into this grand old manor. Kristi hadn't thought much of it at the time; the museum had been open. But now . . .

She turned into the dining room where a long table covered by a runner and candelabra gleamed in the semidark. A built-in hutch in deep mahogany filled a wall, and an arched doorway led to a kitchen that had been roped off. Kristi stepped over the velvet barrier and, reaching into her purse, pulled out her keys and the minuscule penlight on the ring. The beam was small but intense and helped her find her way. She looked around the antiquated room that still housed a wood-burning stove along with a newer gas range. A butter churn stood in one corner and the back door led to a huge porch. Kristi stared out the window but didn't open the door for fear some alarm might go off.

She listened hard, hoping to hear some noise, but the house was deathly quiet. No sound of air movement. No hum of a refrigerator or tick of a clock. All she could hear were the faint sounds of her own heartbeat and footsteps, the latter muffled by her running shoes.

So where had the blonde gone?

Was she meeting someone?

Was this where she worked?

A place of refuge?

Outside, night had fallen, darkness caressing the windows, the few pools of light cast by the well-placed lamps giving off no warmth. The house felt cold and still, devoid of warmth.

*As if it has no soul.*

Oh, God, please, she silently chastised herself. Now she was starting to fall into the trap of everything she'd been reading from Shakespeare's bloody tragedies that her biker of a teacher, Dr. Emmerson, had assigned. Those plays with their guilt and ghosts were bad enough, but then there were the bloodlusting creatures in Grotto's class. She thought about Grotto, tall, dark, handsome, and brooding, with eyes that seemed to see into a person's mind.

*All an act*, she reminded herself. *Theatrics.*

She continued on, past the pantry door and another that was locked, leading, she supposed, to a cupboard or a set of stairs that accessed the basement. She eased around the back side of the staircase, past a wall laden with hooks for coats, to the front of the house again without making a sound. Once again she was at the foot of the darkened, roped-off staircase. She stared upward into the gloom. No lights burning up there.

Did she dare?

She hesitated, then mentally called herself a wimp. The blonde—Marnie, that was her name—was somewhere inside.

Quickly, before she changed her mind, she stepped over the fading velvet rope and started up the wide staircase. She made little noise as a faded floral runner muffled her steps, her tiny bluish penlight beam guiding her.

At the landing, the dark figure of a man stood in the corner.

*Oh, God!*

She gasped, her fingers reaching into her bag for her mace.

She was about to flee when she realized the "man" was unmoving and she shined the penlight at him only to realize he wasn't a man at all, but a suit of armor standing guard near the landing's window.

Kristi set her jaw and counted to ten.

Stiffening her spine, she dashed up the remaining risers to the second floor, where she expected to see a long hallway with a row of closed doors that opened to bedrooms. Instead the head of the stairs widened to a library area complete with narrow, tall bookcases and a reading nook that housed chairs and a window seat. Across from the bookcases was a baby grand piano, sheet music open above the keys, a silent metronome sitting atop the gleaming wood.

Kristi moved past the piano and bookcases. Further ahead was a hallway that led into a suite of rooms: his and hers bedrooms separated by a lavish bath that had obviously been added long after the house was originally built. A canopied bed decorated in floral prints and pillows sat before a fireplace with hand-painted tile in one room, while the other was filled with heavier masculine furniture, a hunting rifle hung above the mantel of a massive stone fireplace.

Lots of antiques.

But no blonde.

For a second Kristi wondered if the girl had dashed in the front of the house, zipped through the main floor, and left through the kitchen.

Maybe she'd made a mistake.

There was a chance searching through this house was just a big waste of time.

And yet . . .

She reached the staircase again, shining her penlight up the risers to the third floor. "In for a penny, in for a pound," she said, and began ascending. The steps were narrower as they wound to the upper floor. At the top was the expected hallway with doors on either side.

The hairs on the back of her neck raised as she remembered searching through the intricate, soulless corridors of the abandoned mental hospital, Our Lady of Virtues, outside New Orleans, and the psycho she'd met

within. The memory gave her pause. Wagner House was
far different from the old asylum, but poking around in
the massive old structure reminded her all too well of the
events leading up to her hospital stay and her resulting
condition.

Holding on to her courage, Kristi placed a hand on
the first doorknob and opened the door slowly. It
squawked on ancient hinges.

*Great. Announce to anyone hiding within that you're
here.*

The room was decorated as a child's bedroom. A
small white bed was pushed into a corner and a rocking
horse with fading paint and hemp mane and tail was
placed near the window . . . and it was moving slightly.

Forward and back on its rockers.

As if a ghost child were riding it.

Kristi nearly dropped her penlight.

In this still house where the air was motionless and
dead, the horse was rocking.

It slowed to a stop but Kristi's heartbeat was rollick-
ing.

The closet door was shut. She licked her lips. Did she
dare open it?

What if . . . ?

Holding her penlight shoulder high, she placed her
other hand on the handle and yanked hard.

The door swung back.

Revealing a dark, empty space with pegs and a rod,
but nothing else. No killer or abductor of women ready
to spring out at her, no vampire snarling and showing
slick white fangs dripping with blood, no damned ghost
child whispering "help me."

Kristi nearly sank from relief. The power of atmosphere. Wow.

Then she noticed the other door, a glass door separating this room from the next. She walked through and
found another room, another girl's room with a small

bed and a table on which a Victorian dollhouse sat, showing off miniature rooms decorated in intricate detail.

She retraced her steps to the hall. The other two rooms were similar, another bedroom with a larger bed and a small wheelchair parked near the iron bedstead, which was covered with stuffed animals, and a fourth decorated as if a boy, interested in boats and fishing, had last resided within. A game of jacks was spread upon a table near an old slingshot.

But, again, no blonde with ashen features fleeing the campus.

Kristi walked to the window and stared out at the night. From this viewpoint, she saw across the quad in the center of the campus and past a few other buildings. Through the trees, she spied the far wall. Beyond that, a roof line was partially visible, illuminated by a street lamp. Dormers peaked from the gables and a light illuminated the room. It was too far to see clearly into the room, but . . .

Her heart clutched.

Was it *her* apartment?

She squinted, her heart drumming at the thought that someone standing here could stare straight into . . .

A shadow passed in front of the window.

Of *her* apartment.

*Inside?*

Was someone *inside* her home?

Anger and fear burned through her and she turned quickly, intent on charging back to her place and confronting whoever was searching her rooms.

*And what if he's got a weapon? What then? Girls have disappeared, you know.*

And whoever was in the apartment might even now be going over her notes, logging on to the Internet through her computer, sorting through her belongings, searching Tara's things. . . .

She started toward the stairs when she heard something. A steady noise. Footsteps?

So she wasn't alone after all.

Quietly, she hurried down to the second level, where the steady ticking became louder and she realized it was too perfect to have been caused by footsteps. At the landing she saw the metronome clicking off the beats of some unheard musical piece.

Kristi's blood ran cold.

Someone had set it rocking. Someone knew she was here and was toying with her.

*Someone or something.*

Her fingers tightened over the canister of mace and she shined her small beam into the darkest corners and crevices of the landing, but she appeared to be alone.

She didn't believe in ghosts or vampires, but she did think that someone else was inside the house. Marnie, the blonde, messing with her mind? Nah. No reason. So who else?

She heard the front door open and close and she pressed herself into the shadows of the second floor hallway, her pulse thumping. She heard hushed voices—female voices—and footsteps, more than one. What the hell was going on? Her penlight was tucked under her arm and she gently clicked it off. Carefully, she edged near the railing, looking down to the foot of the stairs, but she saw no one, just heard them pass through the foyer and, she thought, the hallway that led to the back of the house.

On stealthy footsteps she eased her way back to the first floor. She was still gripping her little canister of mace in clenched fingers as she moved to the back of the house and the kitchen, keeping close to the wall.

Empty.

The women had disappeared.

Kristi entered the kitchen and stopped, ears straining, but she heard nothing. She peered through the windows, but saw nothing outside. The answer was the locked door to the basement; it had to be. She tried the handle. It didn't budge. So the girls who came here had a key.

To what?

She thought of Lucretia's talk of a cult. Could this be the meeting place, an old manor complete with gargoyles and a haunted history? Could the cult meet here? Her heart raced, perspiration ran down her back, and she gripped the damned mace as if it were the very essence of life.

Leaning close to the door panels, she closed her eyes and strained to hear anything, but the house was again silent as a tomb. She tried the door again. Nothing. She shined her light over the kitchen looking for a key—anything—that might open the dead bolt, but found nothing.

And she couldn't wait here any longer.

Not if she wanted to catch the person who had broken into her place.

Holding her can of mace in one hand and her phone in the other, she slipped out of Wagner House and started running across the campus, adrenaline spurring her, unaware of the eyes that were following her every move.

*Run, Kristi, run.*
*You'll never get away.*

Vlad watched her flee across campus and he smiled to himself. He'd known she was in the house, had sensed her presence, seen her from his hiding spot outside on the overhang of the portico. She was a brave one. A little foolhardy, but athletic, strong, and smart.

One of the elite.

It was only a matter of time before she joined with the others, and though her sacrifice wouldn't be as willing, it would be complete. So much more satisfying than those thrill seekers who came to him eagerly. Pathetically. They were searching for something only he could give them, a feeling of family and unity, a chance to no longer be alone.

They didn't completely understand, of course. Couldn't know what would ultimately be expected of them. But it didn't matter. Eventually they gave.

As Kristi would.

He stared after her until she reached the far side of the quad, then he slipped inside the window and started down the stairs. Tonight was the choosing. Later would be the giving.

He only hoped that the bloodletting would be adequate. . . .

But of course it wouldn't.

It never was.

The need was insatiable.

# CHAPTER 17

Kristi hit the speed dial button on her phone as she hurried across the street. She hated to be one of those women who always turned to a man, but damn it, she needed a back up and Jay was the only person she'd confided in. Armed with the mace in one hand and her phone in the other, she reached the rear entrance of her apartment house and paused near the hedge of crepe myrtle by the stairs. The phone rang one time. Twice. "Come on, come on," she whispered just as Jay picked up.

"Hey."

"I've got a kind of a situation," she whispered without any preamble. "I think someone might be in my apartment."

"Are you there now?" he asked urgently.

"I'm outside. I saw a shadow in the window."

"Human?" Jay asked, but he'd relaxed a bit upon hearing she wasn't in the unit.

"I think so."

"I'm on my way. Don't go in without me."

Suddenly she felt foolish, as if she'd let the night get to her. She was probably overreacting. "Maybe I made a mistake. I don't know."

"I can be there in five. Just wait."

"Jay—"

"I said I'd be there," he said tersely. "Wait for me."

She heard a door open above her, so she hung up, switching the phone to silent. Hiding at the base of the stairs, she stayed in the shadows, waiting for whoever was inside her apartment to appear. There was enough light at the base of the stairs to be able to catch his image on her cell phone, or so she hoped. Then she could follow him on foot or in her car and figure out just who he was and what he wanted. If he had a car, she'd get the license plate number; if he was on foot, she'd tail him.

Why would anyone break in to her apartment?

*Maybe because it belonged to Tara Atwater.*

Yeah, but that was months ago. Why now? And how? The locks had just been changed.

Nerves strung tight, Kristi waited on the balls of her feet, ready to match wits and weapons with whoever it was.

*But if he had a gun . . . ?*

Footsteps descended and she counted off the steps . . . ten, eleven, twelve . . .

And then a pause.

At the second story.

Crap! He must've seen her. She hugged the building, straining to hear, squinting up at the staircase where a bulb glowed in the ceiling of each level. *Come on you bastard,* she thought. The footsteps resumed, but they were light and quick, farther away. Not descending.

*What?*

Oh, damn! He'd slipped off the stairs at the second level and was moving along the wide portico of the building to the far staircase, the one located near the crosswalk that led to All Saints. She was off in a shot, springing from the shadows just as a pickup screeched into the parking lot, bright beams of headlights flooding the front of the apartment house.

Jay!

He was out of the truck in a second, his face taut and drawn. "What happened?"

"He's getting away!" She heard whoever it was clamor down the stairs at the far end of the building, vault over the railing, then run across the street. "That way!" She only got a quick glimpse of a figure in black before he ducked behind the large house and disappeared.

There was a squeal of breaks, an angry honk of a horn, and a man's shout: "What the fuck kind of idiot are you!" the driver shouted.

"Who is it?" Jay demanded, catching up to her as she ran.

"Don't know." She crammed her cell phone and her can of mace into the pocket of her sweatshirt. Her bag flopped at her side as she sprinted, her feet pounding the cement and uneven asphalt. Damn it, she was going to catch the creep!

Running easily alongside her, Jay whistled sharply, and from the open window of the truck's cab, Bruno sprang, landing on the pockmarked pavement with a soft woof. Kristi and Jay rounded the building together as the angry driver's car, a red Nissan, disappeared at the next light, veering toward the freeway.

The street in front of the campus was suddenly empty.

"No!" Kristi cried as she dashed across the two lanes and the sidewalk before shooting through the main gate of the college. *Damn, damn, damn!* He couldn't get away.

Once past the tall columns, she ran to the edge of the live oaks skirting the brick wall and stopped short. Breathing hard, she scanned the tree-lined walkways and grassy spaces between the buildings, the very pathway she'd just raced across. Jay slowed to a stop beside her, breathing deeply, his eyes scanning the area. Lamps illuminated the pathways, but shadows and shrubbery flanked the old halls and newer buildings. The mist had begun to rise again and there were many murky hiding places. Groups of students as well as those walking alone were heading through the quad, scattered about the walkways and hurrying up the steps into the wide entrances. Kristi looked from the library to the student union but saw no one fleeing into the darkness.

"On your right!" a woman's voice yelled over the sound of changing gears as a bike whizzed past, the rider hunched over her handlebars.

Bruno let out a low growl.

Kristi's heart sank as she studied the grounds.

No one seemed out of place. She didn't see a dark figure darting through the trees or dashing up the steps of one of the tall, vine-clad buildings that comprised the small campus of All Saints. "Damn . . . damn . . . *damn*!" Lurking in the distance, at the far end of the quad and tucked behind some willow trees was the massive dark structure of Wagner House. Lamplight from the lower floor was barely visible.

"Did you see him?" Jay asked tensely. "What did he look like?"

She was glad for his presence as he stood near her, his gaze scraping every visible inch of this section of the quad. "No . . . he was just a shadow in the window and the blur of a dark figure when I was closer." She motioned toward Jay's dog. "Can Bruno find him?" The dog, hearing his name, turned his eyes to Jay, waiting for direction. "Isn't he part bloodhound?"

"And part blind. But he has a great nose. Maybe if the guy left something at the scene, in your apartment, or something he might have dropped along the way, but Bruno's not trained." Jay eyed one knot of students then the next, studying anyone walking alone.

It was useless.

Kristi knew it.

The intruder had vanished.

At least for the moment.

She let out a long sigh and tried to tamp down her anger; her frustration. "I guess we lost him."

"Looks like." Eyebrows slammed together as he squinted at a trio of girls walking through the library doors. Jay asked, "So what happened? How'd he get in?"

Kristi shook her head.

He gave her a long look and said, "Okay. Let's go see what he took."

"Oh, God . . ." She didn't want to think that her computer might be missing, or any of her things. She had her wallet, her cell phone, and all of her ID, but everything else, including her meticulous notes on the abductions, her small amount of jewelry—thankfully mostly costume stuff—and pictures of her father as well as her mother . . . oh, God, if he took those . . . "I don't want to think about it." Jay would insist she call the police and then she would have to explain about Tara Atwater's things—assuming they were still in the apartment—and her theory that something of value within them might connect her to the other missing girls, or their kidnapper.

Then there was the issue of her father. Mentally she groaned. Despite the fact that she was an adult, there was just no way Rick Bentz wouldn't learn about what she was doing. There would be hell to pay.

Squaring her shoulders, Kristi walked back to her apartment with Jay and Bruno. She braced herself for the battle that was to come. It wasn't as if she hadn't taken on Rick Bentz in the past. She would just have to do it again. Sooner or later he'd figure out that he couldn't tell her what to do, right?

But he could sure make life damn miserable in the meantime.

At her third-story unit, the door was shut, the dead bolt in place.

"The intruder has a key?" Jay asked, as there was no way to unlock the door without one. "That narrows the field of suspects a bit."

"Quite a bit," she said, thinking of Irene and Hiram Calloway, the only people beside herself who possessed a key. But why would either of them be nosing around her place?

With emotions ranging from anger to dread, Kristi unlocked the door and stepped inside.

"Stay," Jay ordered Bruno; then to Kristi, "Don't touch anything."

"I know." If they had to call the police for the break-in, the crime scene couldn't be disturbed.

But the apartment was dark. Still. She hit the light switch and overhead illumination flooded the studio.

Everything was just as she'd left it. Her computer was on the desk, her posters tacked to the wall, Tara's things strewn on the tarp on the floor. All of her pictures were where she'd left them, nothing outwardly disturbed. And no lamps had been lit; the only illumination came from the light on the old stove, the one she used as a night-light, the one that had allowed her to see the intruder. It seemed that her small apartment was the same as when she'd left it.

Except that someone had been inside. She'd seen him. The thought made her skin crawl. Who was it? What did he want?

"This doesn't make any sense," she said.

"Why?"

She stepped into the room and studied the contents more carefully. "Nothing's disturbed."

"You're sure?"

"I . . . yeah, I think so." Her gaze scraped the mantel, bookcases, tables, and bed, before landing in the kitchen, which, dishes in the sink, was also exactly as she'd left it.

"But someone was in here?" he asked.

"Yes! . . . I think so." She thought back. "Of course they were. I saw him in the stove light. When I got here, I heard him on the third landing of the staircase, then he descended a flight to the second floor where the porch runs across the face of the building to the stairs on the far end. I don't know if he saw me or what, but he got scared and didn't come down the only staircase leading from my door. Instead he took off on the second-level porch." She walked to the sink, grabbed a cup from the counter, and drew some water from the tap. "Whoever it was *had* to be up here." She took a long swallow of the tepid water.

"But not necessarily inside."

"No, no, I'm sure I saw . . ." She was going to say she was certain that she'd seen someone inside her apartment, but was she? She looked through the window over the kitchen sink and stared into the night, but it was too dark to see the outline of Wagner House over the wall and through the trees. As there were no lights turned on in the upper floors of the manor house turned museum, she couldn't decipher the building's silhouette, let alone that third-story window where she had been standing when she'd seen someone in her unit.

Wagner House was so far away.

And it had been dark.

For the first time since spying someone in the window, she doubted what she'd seen.

"Well?"

"I . . . I don't know. I *think* someone was in here."

He glanced down at the tarp covering the floor and all of the items placed so carefully on the plastic surface. "What's this?"

"A long story," she said, not certain she wanted to share it. Nervously, she grabbed a long-handled lighter and lit a few candles in the apartment. Then, deciding candle glow might be too intimate, she turned on all the table lamps.

Jay whistled to the dog and made Bruno lie on the floor. Then he closed the door and sat, straddling one padded arm of the single chair in the room. "Well, Kris, you're in luck. I just happen to have all night."

The crime lab techs had already arrived and Bonita Washington, one of the smartest women Bentz knew, was barking out orders, making certain no one disturbed "her" scene. "I mean it," she was saying, "you all wear booties and you don't touch anything or you don't get it. That goes double for you," she said, her green eyes narrowing on Bentz's partner, Reuben Montoya. African American and proud of it, Washington was a few pounds overweight and all business. "You signed in?" she asked Bentz.

He nodded as he followed her into the small frame house that had been recently renovated. Just inside the door, he stopped and looked around. Furniture had been kicked back, there were scuff marks on the floor, and in the living room a dark stain, most likely blood.

"We checked," Bonita said, nodding. "It's blood all right."

"But no body?"

"Nuh-uh."

One of the criminalists was taking pictures, another dusting for fingerprints. The story was that the police had taken a call from Aldo "Big Al" Cordini, owner of one of the strip joints in the Quarter. One of his dancers, Karen Lee Williams aka Bodiluscious, hadn't shown up for work for a couple of nights and he'd sent someone to her house to check on her. No one had answered the door and her car, which she'd told the owner of the club was inoperable, was still in her garage.

The blood on the floor wasn't enough to suspect a homicide but the fact that Karen Lee hadn't shown up in any of the local hospitals or clinics added to the fear that she'd been killed. *Or abducted,* Bentz thought, his mind returning to the missing coeds at All Saints in Baton Rouge.

Not that whatever happened to Karen Lee had anything to do with the missing girls—there was nothing to link them—but because of his daughter, his mind naturally went there. The coeds at All Saints had disappeared without a trace. Karen Lee obviously went down fighting.

They looked over the scene and started talking to the few neighbors who had returned to their homes in this storm-devastated part of the city. No one had seen anything unusual. All Montoya and Bentz learned was that Karen Lee was a single mom with a kid tucked away with Karen's mother somewhere in west Texas. The child, a daughter, was nine or ten, or thereabouts, and named Darcy. No one knew of any friends or family nearby, any boyfriends past or present. No one knew what had happened to the kid's father, as Karen Lee had never talked about him.

"So we've got a big zero," Montoya said as they returned to Bentz's car. "Not even a body."

"Maybe she's alive."

Montoya snorted, climbed into the passenger side, and shook his head. "I wouldn't bet on it. She might not have been dead when the bastard hauled her out of here, but I'm thinking he's killed her by now."

"We could get lucky," Bentz said as he started the car and rolled into traffic. They'd drive down to the club, figure out who had seen Karen last, and find out who'd been in the bar that night. Chances were that her killer had been watching and waiting, maybe followed her home.

"Luck's for fools," Montoya said, and reached for his nonexistent pack of cigarettes before he remembered he'd given up the habit.

"Like I said, we could get lucky."

\* \* \*

Jay leaned forward in his chair and said, "So what you're telling me is that you broke the law by opening the storage unit, then compromised evidence in a potential abduction or murder case, then trespassed in the Wagner House chasing after some 'blonde' that you thought might be part of this vampire cult. Then, though you didn't find the blonde, you heard voices and then looked out the window, saw someone in your apartment, and came streaking back to confront him." Jay's disapproval wasn't hard to miss.

"Someone was here," Kristi insisted. "And so what if I was breaking a law or two? I'm trying to find out what happened to those girls, damn it. And come on, Jay. You're not entirely innocent, are you? You dug through government records, right?" Kristi was having none of this blame-game BS. She was seated in her desk chair and rubbing the tension from the back of her neck.

"I didn't put my life in jeopardy."

"Just your career. Okay, Jay, let's just get down to it. Someone was in my apartment and I want to know who. And why." She glanced at the computer where she, while explaining everything to Jay, had logged on to a couple of chat rooms. A few familiar names had come and gone. Deathmaster7 was cruising the rooms and JustO had lurked for a while but hadn't joined any conversations.

"Who do you think would break in?" He checked the window she'd left open for the cat, but that would require roof access.

She'd told him that Hiram and Irene were the only ones who possessed keys, so she shrugged and said, "Who else could it be but Hiram and Irene?"

"We'll start with them. Meanwhile, I'm staying here." His long legs were stretched in front of him, Bruno lying on the rug wedged between the daybed and the chair.

"I don't think that's such a hot idea."

"Gonna kick me out?" he asked, a dark eyebrow cocking, damned near daring her to try.

"Jay—"

"That's Professor McKnight to you." She gave him a look that caused him to smile. "Kris, I'm not budging, so let's find some place that delivers all-night Thai or Chinese or Italian food, then call it a night. Either that, or you can come back to my aunt's house that I'm renovating and we can share a sleeping bag."

She stared at him incredulously. "Are you joking?"

"You think someone broke in to your apartment," he reminded her, reaching for his cell phone. "So what is it going to be? Pad Thai? General Tsao's chicken? Mushroom and sausage pizza?"

"I can't do mushrooms."

One side of his mouth lifted. "I know."

Kristi felt a traitorous glow of warmth that he remembered her aversion to mushrooms, which ticked her off to no end. "I guess . . . pizza . . ."

"What kind?"

"I don't know."

He got up from the chair. "Figure it out while I go get your bike."

"My—bike?"

"Your dad asked me to bring it up. Knew you needed it and didn't want to show up here and be accused of invading your privacy or being overly protective or whatever. It's none of my business what goes on between you two, but, yeah, I did bring the bike. It could get stolen in the truck. I'll bring it inside."

"Great." Kristi's tone reflected her ambivalence.

"How about a combination, sans mushrooms?" Jay was already messing around with his cell phone, searching for a restaurant. As he headed outside, she could hear him ordering. A few moments later he returned with the bike. He slammed the door behind him, and Houdini, who had been hiding beneath the bed, finally made himself known by growling low at Bruno. The dog, still coiled into a sleeping position, barely raised his head.

"Another voice heard from," Jay remarked as he propped the bike against the wall near the bathroom door.

Houdini wasn't finished. Hissing, showing off his teeth, his back arching, he suddenly shot across the room, a black streak hurtling himself onto the daybed. Then he sprang to the mantel and from there picked his way to the bookcase.

"Is that cat always in a bad mood?" Jay asked.

"Yes."

Bruno couldn't have cared less. He let out a sigh and let his chin fall into his outstretched front legs.

Houdini suddenly scurried across the shelf, sending a picture of Kristi tumbling to the floor, where the frame shattered and the glass broke. Frightened out of his mind, he sprang from the shelf, flew across the floor, hopped effortlessly onto the counter, slipped through the partially open window, and was gone.

"Friendly," Jay observed dryly.

"He's getting better."

"Uh-huh."

"He is." She picked up the broken pieces and tried to prop them up on the shelf, which was several feet above her head.

"Let me help you."

"I can get it."

"If you had a ladder." He was already walking up behind her, plucking the picture from her fingers, placing it on the shelf.

Kristi was determined to ignore the length of his body, pressing up against her back, the smell of him—a little cologne, a little musk—mingling in the air. He was just too damned close.

Jay hesitated a bit too long for comfort and she

thought he was feeling it, too, that hint of electricity in the air between them, the awareness of the opposite sex in such close proximity. She wondered if he, like she, was thinking how she'd broken up with him, thought him too young, too familiar, too hometown while now . . . Oh, Lord, she was *not* going to remember how he'd once made her feel, how she'd looked forward to kissing him, to touching him, to feeling his weight atop her. . . .

He pressed closer and she noticed the wall of his chest against her back, the stretch of his arm over her head.

"What's this?" he asked and broke the spell.

"What?"

He was fingering the shelf of the bookcase, which was higher than his head. "I don't know . . . wait . . . hell . . . here, take this." Standing on his toes, he placed the picture into her hand again and, as if he had been totally unaware of the charged air between them, said, "Move to the side." As she got out of his way, he reached upward as high as he could.

"What is it?"

"I think there's something up here, like a little niche in the back of the bookcase where it meets the shelf. I think there's something in it. . . ." He was straining. "Now, if I can just get my finger in there. . . . What the hell?" He pulled his hand back and rocked back on his feet. From his fingers dangled an intricate gold chain. Hanging from the chain was a small glass vial filled with dark reddish liquid. It glittered and swung in the soft light.

"Oh, God," Kristi said, her stomach turning. She knew without a doubt that she was staring at an ampoule of Tara Atwater's blood.

Vlad slipped through the long hallway, the tunnel that connected the abandoned basement lab to another

building, another forgotten chamber deep in the heart
of the campus, a room few knew of. This secret place
was carved out of the ground by Ludwig Wagner centuries before as a place for his own private trysts. Marble lined the walls of the subterranean spa, where warm
water was piped from an underground spring to the
massive tub in the center of the room. Candles had been
lit. There was no electricity down here.

She lay in the middle of the tub, the water lapping
over her perfect body, the sound of drips from ancient
pipes the only noise over a soft gentle rush of air within
an old ventilation shaft.

*Elizabeth.*

Flawless white skin was visible in the ripples, round,
rose-colored nipples sometimes breached the ever-
moving water, only to pucker with the cold. A dark
thatch of curls was stark against the alabaster white of
her slim, long thighs. No tan lines were visible, no age
spots dared darken her perfect complexion. Her hair,
black as night, was caught with a bloodred clip and held
atop her head.

Though her eyes were closed, he knew that she was
aware of him. It was always so. Always had been. Theirs
was a bond that started early in life only to grow and
strengthen with time.

She'd known of his fascination with her even as a
child. She had molded him into what he'd become. The
process had been long, taken years, and yet, he suspected that Elizabeth had seen his weakness the first
time she'd laid eyes upon him and had understood his
needs. Though she'd been a child of seven, and he only
five, she'd set about weaving her web upon him and he'd
wanted her so desperately—still wanted her—he'd done
everything she'd suggested.

Willingly.

Eagerly.

His IQ brushed genius.

Hers was higher.

A fact he never forgot.

Nor would she let him.

She allowed him his infidelities, encouraged him, even sometimes watched him, but she knew, they both knew, that he was hers. Forever bound to do her bidding. He hid little from her, but tonight he would have to tread lightly. He would not let it be known that Mathias, the weakling priest, was balking. He would not mention that Lucretia, the slut, was having second thoughts and confiding in Kristi Bentz, the cop's daughter, who now claimed she could see danger before it was apparent, that she witnessed it in the color of their skin, as if the blood had drained from their bodies.

Prophetic?

He wondered . . . if she looked in a mirror, would she see her own pale image staring back at her?

But for now, he would forget.

For now, he would concentrate on Elizabeth.

Her eyelids raised just a fraction, enough that he saw reflections of the candles in the exposed slits but not enough that he could read any emotion that might betray her feelings. The room was cold, only a piece or two of furniture pushed into the corners, a small bed, a kerosene lamp upon a table, a few books, always the latest books about her namesake, stacked neatly on the table, mirrors abounding. He saw his own reflection in the looking glasses, refracted images that caught his every move.

"I thought you'd come tonight," she said.

Was there any doubt?

Without a word, he walked to the raised tub and sat upon the marble ledge. The scents of lilac and magnolia rose with the steam from the warm, clear water. She let him touch her, allowed his fingers to slide up the length of one thigh, but when he tried to explore further, to enter her most private of spaces, she snapped her legs shut and brushed his hand away. "Ah-ah-ah," she said in that throaty voice he found so wickedly intriguing. "Not yet." But he knew that she was as ready as he was, that her blood ran hot and wild within her.

"Not yet," she insisted, as if to convince herself that it was not yet time, a time she dictated. "You brought more, didn't you? From your hunt?"

He stared at her. Surprised at her nearly ESP like qualities.

"You think I don't know about the stripper?" Sighing, she clucked her tongue.

"You set the rules," he reminded her, surprised that she had read his mind, had known whom he'd taken.

Her face drew into a little pout. "But a stripper? Really?" She wrinkled her nose. "I don't think so. No." She touched her pointed chin with one wet hand. "I know we are getting low, that we need a refill, but a stripper? Remember, this is an intellectual, as well as a physical experience."

That, he doubted. She could rationalize all she wanted, come up with lofty excuses, even reasons, but he'd faced the truth: they both enjoyed the search, the hunt, the kill. It was simple. She was into torture more than he; he was into pure, primal, sexual pleasure. Hurting and wounding wasn't necessary for him. Her sadism wasn't infectious; he had no real use for it unless it heightened his sexual experience. He got his thrills in the lovemaking and the death.

He wanted to argue that "Blood is blood," but knew better, so he held his tongue as she deliberated, obviously tempted.

"Use what's left of the others," she finally said.

"Then we'll be out. You'll have to wait for your next fix."

"You think this is a drug, that I'm an addict?" A smile curved her perfect lips and it was all he could do to restrain himself from taking her now, before they went through their ritual. But he would wait.

"Do I think you're an addict?" he asked. "Absolutely."

She didn't disagree, just cocked her head, exposing the long length of her neck, the curve of her throat. "Maybe so, but I don't want my addiction to be tainted, now, do I? Bad blood? I think not. I'll wait." She was toying with him now, amused that he was challenging her. "What is it they say? 'Patience is a virtue'?"

"I think it's 'All good things come to he who waits.'"

She corrected, "Or she who waits."

"Or she."

"For now, though, there is no waiting. The moon has risen, the timing's right."

"Agreed." He knew what he had to do and what was to come. His heart beat a little faster as he reached for the knob on the top of the tub, the one attached to an iced cooler that he so diligently kept filled. After priming the pump, he twisted the tap. It squeaked a bit as he opened the valve slowly and saw her expectation in the pulse at her neck and her white, glistening teeth sinking into her lower lip.

Slowly, in an uncoiling ribbon, the blood began to flow. Ice cold and thick, it spread its dark stain into the clear water, a plume of thinning red that dissipated and curled.

When the first drip of the dark liquid caressed her skin, she sucked in her breath, her abdomen shrinking, her eyes closing with the ecstasy, for she believed, like the woman whose name she had taken, that cleansing with the blood of other younger, more vital women would elongate her life, keep her skin clear and flawless, and renew her vitality.

A bloody fountain of youth.

Was she mad?

Or a visionary?

He didn't care which. Either way, she gave him a purpose to hunt, to kill, and he could convince himself that the thrill he felt while taking a life was for the ultimate good. For her. And as for madness, had he not questioned his own sanity at times? Did he not struggle with reality and fantasy? But then, he knew, the line between madness and genius was thin and frail.

He was, without question, her dedicated disciple.

Her tongue flicked upon her lips as the water chilled.

Soon she would be ready. She was already letting out those soft, sexy moans that were his signal. His nostrils widened and he drank in the scent of the aromatic water, the blood, and his own rising lust in this dark cavern.

Soon she would invite him into the tub. Her legs were opening and she was beginning to draw in quick little breaths.

Soon he'd fuck the living hell right out of her.

He reached for his belt and let his pants fall to his ankles. Kicking them aside, he unbuttoned his shirt, his eyes never leaving her. His erection was thick, his need running hot through his veins, the water over her body now murky and red. He stepped inside and lowered himself against her, expecting her to welcome him, for her nails to dig deep into the muscles of his back.

Instead she tipped her head upward so that she could breathe against his ear. "The next one," she said hoarsely. "When you take the next one, I want to go with you. And it won't be some aging pole dancer who works for dollars stuffed into her thong! It has to be someone smarter, cleverer, more vital. Not someone whose life has already been drained from her. I should never have agreed to your 'lessers.' If they are indeed less, I don't want them."

"There are only so many I can take from the school," he protested.

Her beautiful features twisted into a sneer. "Do I have to do *everything* myself?"

"Of course not."

But she wasn't dissuaded. "I will come out with you; I will see that she's worthy."

"You've already helped me pick them," he reminded her. Elizabeth, too, had sorted through the pictures of the students at All Saints.

"I should never have agreed to the lessers." She was seated upright now, glaring at him as the bloody water drained over her exposed skin, running in red rivulets from her shoulders, over her breasts, to the dark pool surrounding her.

Oh, how he longed to lap up that tangy sweetness.

But she wasn't in the mood. "Don't you get it?" Elizabeth demanded, hands rising from the scarlet depths. "That's why this isn't working, why my skin hasn't improved. The blood of those whores is tainted, lacking life."

"They weren't whores."

"Then where did you find them?"

His jaw tightened but he bit back a sharp retort, not allowing her to bait him about his previous life, one that she knew intimately. Only she knew his real identity, only she could ruin him.

Only she could make him complete.

"Of course you can come," he said.

"I wasn't asking! It's not your decision. Remember that!" Mollified, she settled into the bloody water again.

This was new. She'd never ventured out for a kill. But then she was always evolving, never content to let things stagnate or become routine. And truth be told, he was a little concerned about the girl who would next give up her life. Once she'd been so avid and zealous about being a part of their inner circle. He'd approached her and she'd leapt at the chance to belong, to connect with someone. Now, however, he sensed she was nervous. Wary. Unsure.

He might have to change his routine a bit to ensure her compliance. Elizabeth wouldn't like that. It would be best if he acted alone.

"You're certain about this, that you want to be a part of it?" he asked again, and Elizabeth smiled cruelly up at him, her eyes in this half-light dark and unreadable.

"Of course." Her red lips twitched a bit as the now warm, bloody water swirled around her. "I thought you understood. The next time, I intend to watch. Not just the mating, but the surrendering of her soul. The sacrifice."

# CHAPTER 18

"Christ Almighty!" Jay stared at the tiny vial and shook his head. "What in God's name is this?"

"It's Tara Atwater's blood," Kristi said with conviction. She eyed the angling bit of glass as if it were a precious, though cursed stone, and her stomach curdled as she thought about how or why the blood within it had been extracted. "I'd bet my life on it."

"Then we have to take it to the police." He transferred the delicate chain carefully from his hand to hers. "And you have to own up to what you've found out."

"There's still no proof of murder."

"I know, but it's a police matter." He rubbed at the beard stubble on his jaw and wondered what the hell they'd stumbled onto. "You think this is what whoever was in your apartment was looking for?"

"Maybe. They didn't take anything."

"Then the place will have to be dusted for prints."

"Can't you do it? You're the police. You work with the crime lab."

"Not if you want to nail the bastard, whoever the hell he is. We've got to do this by the book."

She sighed. "They'll take my notes. Confiscate my computer. Check me out."

"Probably. I called a friend in the Baton Rouge PD. He gave me the name of a detective I think will help us. Portia Laurent. Seems as if she's taken an interest in the missing girls and thinks they might have come to bad ends."

"Finally. Someone who doesn't believe the cock and bull about all of them being runaways. Now if I could give her something more . . . then maybe they'd work with me."

The doorbell suddenly pealed and both Kristi and Jay reacted. "I'll get it," he said. Through the peephole, Jay spied a teenager with long hair, bad skin, and a nervous tic causing him to wink. He was carrying a flat box in an insulated pack.

"Pizza's here," the kid called.

Jay looked at Kristi and they both laughed. He opened the door, paid for the pizza, tipped the kid, then threw the dead bolt. Meanwhile, Kristi was careful with the vial, placing it in a plastic sandwich bag and carefully setting it on a cotton towel in the kitchen. It creeped her out, thinking it held Tara's blood, but she didn't want Jay to see how she felt.

"Before we call the cops, I'm backing up all of my files," Kristi told him around a piece of pizza, her eyes inadvertently straying to the vial. She was having a certain amount of trouble swallowing. "Not only for my homework and personal stuff, but for everything about the case."

Jay nodded, wondering if they were sitting in the middle of a crime scene. The box of pizza was placed between them on the daybed while Bruno watched their every bite, hoping for any spillage. He, at least, was unaffected by the discovery of the necklace and vial.

"So why was the vial hidden?" Kristi asked, dropping the remains of her slice back into the box. "Or, was it just forgotten?"

"Hidden. The necklace was pushed into a crack near the wall."

"Why hide it? Some of the girls who have them—and as far as I know, it's just girls—wear them openly."

"You think Tara hid it herself?"

"Who else?" Kristi asked. She wiped her fingers on the paper napkins that came with the pizza, then pushed herself upright and walked to the desk. Once there, she began transferring information to a small pocket-sized jump drive. She chewed on her bottom lip as she worked. "If we're going to the police and Detective Laurent, then I guess we'll have to call Dad." She made a face at the thought. "He'll have a fit, of course, but at least he'll make sure none of my stuff is ruined or lost."

"You're willing to suffer through his lectures?" Jay asked, closing the pizza box and disappointing Bruno.

"It's not as if I'm not used to it."

"In the meantime, as I said, I'll camp out here."

"You don't have to."

"I do." He was positive.

"But—"

"Admit it, Kris, you want me to stay."

"Oh, please." His arrogance knew no bounds, even though he was partially right.

He wasn't intimidated. "You still want me."

She made a strangled sound. "Y'know, I'm fine. It's better if you just go." Snagging her jump drive from the computer, she capped it with more force than necessary and stuffed it in a small pocket in her purse.

He shrugged, making no move to leave.

"I can't believe you said that," she added.

"You're still thinking about it."

"Jay, so help me . . ." She cut herself off as she walked to a closet, where she found a sleeping bag that had seen better days and a tattered throw pillow with the stuffing exposed, compliments of Hairy S., Kristi's stepmother's scrappy little dog. Jay watched her with a knowing air that really chapped her hide. She should just toss him out. But he was right in one regard, damn him: she didn't really want to be alone.

But she did not *want* him.

"If you're staying, you've got the chair. You can use the coffee table for an ottoman." She tossed him the pillow and sleeping bag, then stopped for a moment, regarding him seriously.

"What?"

"Just to be clear. I need one more week before I tell Dad or Portia Laurent what's up. By then, I should have more information for the police, but if we go to them with what we know now, my hands will be tied. To Detective Laurent and the Baton Rouge PD, I'll just be Rick Bentz's daughter playing amateur detective. To Dad, I'll be risking my neck again and he'll freak."

"He should."

"I need some time," she stressed.

"I can't give you any, Kris."

"Sure you can. It'll ultimately make the case stronger."

"You don't know that."

"Yes, I do. It's you who has doubts."

"We should both have doubts," Jay retorted. "There's a lot we don't know. We're just surmising, Kris. Let the police handle it."

"I'm only asking for a week. No one seems to have cared about these girls all this time. One . . . week." Crossing the room, she walked up to him, only stopping when the toes of her shoes touched his.

Jay tried not to be affected but he smelled some kind of soap mingled with sweat on her skin. Her flesh was so near to his, and in this light her hair was shot with streaks of red. It was a potent combination. Craning her neck to look up at him, Kristi offered the faintest of smiles, that little, sexy grin that always cracked his armor.

"Please, Jay, it's important. You can keep the vial and all of Tara's things, if it makes you feel better. But give me a few more days, one lousy week."

"And then you'll cease and desist?"

"Then I'll take a back seat to the cops."

Oh sure. Like that was her style.

"It could be dangerous."

"I won't do anything stupid."

That, he didn't believe. "Kris—"

"Come on," she begged.

He felt it then, that little twinge of desire when he looked into her wide eyes, watching her pupils, dark and large, as they pleaded with him. Damn the woman. She *knew* what she was doing to him. His gut tightened and deep inside the wanting began, a light tattoo beating inside his skull, a wave of heat expanding within his chest. Desire grew as he caught a glimpse of the slope of her cheekbones, the intelligence in her gaze, the quirk of her lips.

"You're trying to seduce me into this," he stated flatly, trying to keep a rein on his emotions.

"That's just plain insulting."

"Is it?"

"Yes! When did you become an egomaniac?" she demanded. Her green eyes snapping fire, she looked as if she might slap him. But she wouldn't. "If you remember, I was the one who broke up with you, right? It wasn't the other way around."

"Biggest mistake of your life," he assured her calmly.

"The biggest mistake of *my* life was getting involved with you again!" she blurted. The minute the words crossed her tongue, she regretted them, wished she could call them back. He was staring down at her as if he could actually read her mind, the big oaf. Oh, hell!

What was it about Jay that drove her nuts? "I've changed my mind. Just go."

"No."

"GO!"

"You want me to stay, you're just too thickheaded to admit it."

"You make me crazy!"

"Good."

Talking to him, trying to reason with him, only made things worse. Somehow he'd gotten the upper hand. She'd *given* him the upper hand. And now he was smiling that damnable boyish grin that she found so stupidly irresistible. One side of his mouth lifted and in that second she knew he was going to kiss her. Oh, God, she couldn't let that happen.

Never.

She warned, "Don't even think about—"

Too late. In an instant he'd dropped the blanket and pillow and had yanked her hard against him. His lips slanted over hers in a kiss that sucked the breath from her lungs and left her bones feeling weak.

Which was just damned ridiculous!

And that warm tingle that slid through her bloodstream?

Totally out of line!

Totally!

Yet she didn't pull away when his tongue pressed against her teeth and she heard a soft, almost eager moan escape her own throat. *Oh, for the love of God. Stop this, Kristi, stop it now!*

His hands splayed over her back, pulling her even closer, and she began to be lost in the moment, in the desire that swept through her. She finally found the strength to push him away.

"Bad form, McKnight," she said, stepping back, aware her chest was rising up and down more rapidly than normal, her voice disgustingly breathy. "You're my professor."

He laughed aloud. "And you're of age. Try again."

"We have a history, Jay. And it's not good."

"It's not bad." He wasn't giving an inch as he stood glaring down at her, his amber eyes dark with desire, his lips thin and hard.

"Stay back . . . I'll think of something."

"Your excuses are getting weaker."

"Jay—"

"What?" His mouth was coming close to hers again.

"You're deluded," she said, pulling back sharply. "That's what you are, McKnight. Blind-ass dumb and deluded. And even if I was interested in you—which I'm not—but if I was, I wouldn't be stupid enough to get involved with you again. Especially now. Didn't I already tell you this? You know it as much as I do. We've got too much to do. And come on." She mustered up a disgusted glare. "There might be a little something there, between us, okay. But it's nothing."

"It's something," he argued.

"Nothing." She picked up the forgotten bedding and tossed it to him again, pointing to the chair. Then she turned to Bruno and pointed to the rug. "As for you, you sleep there." He cocked his head and thumped his tail, but didn't move.

Jay whistled. "Here, boy," he said, and Bruno ambled to the rug. "The boss has spoken."

Kristi ignored the jab. "The way I see it, we don't have much time. I figure whoever was here earlier was looking for the vial. I bet he's not giving up. I bet he's going to strike again and soon."

"And maybe you're his next target." Jay's tone had changed from playful to serious. "That could be the reason he was here earlier."

"No."

"Let's hope not." He patted the dog's head absently, then walked to the bike and rolled it in front of the door. He propped the frame against the jamb and lever, ensuring that it would fall over and crash loudly should anyone try to enter. Once the bike was balanced to his satisfaction, Jay turned and looked at the ceiling, as if searching for divine intervention. Shaking his head, he said, "I should have my head examined, but you win." His eyes returned to hers, their amber irises steady with determination. "Okay, we'll play it your way. I won't call the police. For now. You've got one week and not a second more."

Could she go through with it?

Ariel looked around her small apartment and wondered what the hell she'd gotten herself into. Sure, she'd needed friends and the rush of being in some exclusive, secret cult. She'd even loved all the vampire stuff that went along with it.

She'd never felt so alive as when she'd allowed "the master" to bite into her neck, to let some of the blood flow out and to collect those drops into a vial.

The ritual had been exciting, the feeling of belonging, of doing something dark and sensual and out of the norm, seductive. To have been chosen had been heady and she finally, for the first time in her life, felt like she was someone, that she belonged, that she was even better than a lot of her peers.

Now, she had doubts.

Tomorrow night there was another meeting, one scheduled after the morality play, and she was nervous. Though she didn't really know who was a part of their secret group, a few girls had dropped hints and she realized that Trudie and Grace and probably Zena were all members of the elite few. There were others, she knew, but had no idea who they were.

She felt more than one frisson of fear slide down her spine. Because, damn it, she sensed that some of those girls who were missing, the ones the press brought up every now and again, had been part of their inner circle. Though she couldn't be certain . . . who could? The ritual was so bizarre, so . . . dark . . . But the girls were definitely missing. And during the ceremony, she'd heard their names . . . he'd called them each sister and used their names.

Had they been willing members of their group?

*Of course they were! Don't be an idiot. They're gone because of what they got themselves into, what you, yourself so eagerly embraced. They're either dead or—*

"No!" she said aloud to the four walls of the tiny walk-up where she lived alone. "No, no, no!" He wouldn't betray them so. Those other girls, Tara and Monique and Dionne . . . they probably left because they'd been scared after the vampire ritual, that was it. The same with Rylee, the last girl reported missing. Ariel remembered her as kind of shallow, always worried, truly a lost soul.

Could they really all be dead?

Her heart turned stone-cold as she stared at the tiny room she'd called home for over a year, noticed the cheap faux-designer touches she'd bought to try and make the apartment appear homey, the worn, broken-down furniture that had come with the place, the few pictures of a family who really didn't care about her scattered on the tables and plastic yellow bookcase she'd put together herself.

Scratching at her throat, her nerves stretched as tight as ever, she looked up at the picture of Jesus she had mounted on the wall near the window. She'd once been so religious, so convinced of her own piety, and now . . . oh, Father . . . now . . . she was lost . . .

Ariel swallowed hard.

Then there was that Bentz girl. Daughter of a cop. Nosing around. Who claimed she'd seen danger in the color of Ariel's skin or some such crap! What did that mean?

Her skin crawled as she thought perhaps she might be the next one who disappeared, that something was going to happen to her. . . .

"No way." She crossed to her minifridge and pulled a bottle of vodka from the freezer. Uncapping it, she lifted the mouth to her lips and took a long swig. She just needed to calm down. She was getting rattled.

Kristi Bentz had done this to her. What a freak. Wiping the back of her hand over her lips, Ariel caught sight of her reflection in the mirror. Her skin *was* pale, her fingers tight over the neck of the cold bottle, her eyes round with fear.

Maybe she should just run.

Like the others.

How long would it take to pack a bag and disappear? It wasn't as if she hadn't done it before.

*Leave now, tonight. Before you change your mind. Hop a bus and get the hell out of here.*

Could she just not show up?

She walked to the closet and reached to the upper shelf for her big backpack, the one she camped with, the one that could hold almost all of her pitiful belongings. She was dragging it down when her cell phone rang.

Her heart sank as she plucked the phone from her purse, read the screen, and realized that he was calling.

*As if he'd known.*

Her heart knocked wildly at the thought of hearing his voice, of knowing that he cared, that he loved her. . . .

She didn't answer, let the call go to voice mail, and within minutes she heard his steps on the stairs and a rap of his knuckles on the tarnished panels.

"Ariel," he said, his voice low, melodic, and insistent. "Open the door."

Shivering, water surrounding her, Kristi tried to swim. She was in the middle of a pool, in a building that was dark as night. A few candles had been placed on the tile rim and their little flames flickered and threatened to die in this cavern.

Where the hell was she?

Gasping, feeling as if she'd been treading water for hours, she glanced around. Was she alone? She looked downward, toward the bottom of the pool, but it was deep and dark, and though she saw no one in the Stygian depths, she felt his presence. As surely as if he were breathing against her skin.

*Swim, Kristi, for God's sake get the hell out of here!*

She kicked hard, took a big gulp of the stagnant air, and began stroking. Hard. Toward the nearest edge. She didn't understand why, but deep in her heart she knew that something, someone evil, was hiding in the water, skulking in the shadows, where a fine mist rose toward a ceiling she couldn't see.

*Don't think about it, just get the hell out of here. You're a strong swimmer, you are.*

*Stroke! Stroke! Stroke!*

She forced herself to cut through the water, her legs to kick, but her limbs felt leaden and no matter how hard she tried, she got no closer to the edge. Either it was shrinking away from her or she was just treading water.

*Come on, try harder.* Gritting her teeth, she threw herself into her struggles and as she reached over her head to pull herself through the water, the tips of her fingers touched something, got wound in something fibrous, like thread. She tried to pull her hand away, but whatever it was came with it.

There in the dark, nose to nose with her, was a severed head. Tara Atwater's eyes were open and blank in her bluish face, and from her neck a thick stream of blood invaded the water.

Kristi screamed and tried to disentangle her fingers. Panic constricted her heart. Fear propelled her to swim, dragging the damned head only to bump into something that rose from the bottom of the murky depth.

Another head! Even in the weak light she saw the blond hair as the head bobbed and turned, facing her, Rylee's wide eyes open and staring. Damning.

Kristi shrieked, stroking away, with Tara's head still caught in her fingers. But as she shot ahead her crown crashed into something hard. She turned to see Dionne's face staring at her, blood flowing from her neck, her eyes wide and dead.

No!

Dionne's eyes blinked and she looked down as if in warning. Then Kristi knew, though she couldn't see the bottom, that evil lurked in the murky depths.

*Swim! Get away!* Her mind screamed.

She turned again and saw another disembodied head. Not Monique's as she'd expected. The ashen face that floated on the surface was Ariel's.

*God, oh, God, get me out of here!*

Panicked, she started flailing, trying to scream, trying to get away. But the harder she struggled to reach the gleaming tile, the further away it appeared.

Her lungs burned, her body was heavy. She knew she was about to drown. In this pool of bloody severed heads, she would die.

Before she had a chance to tell Jay that she loved him, before she saw her father one last time.

She tried to scream, but her throat was thick and she was being pulled down, deeper and deeper, the water becoming dark.

*Oh, God, help me.*

Panic gripped her.

She flailed, trying to surface.

She gasped.

And then she noticed the water was turning red, a deep scarlet color. . . .

"Kristi!" a deep male voice said, and she felt his hand upon her ankle, pulling her further down. Into the bloody depths!

"Kris! Hey!"

Her eyes flew open and she found Jay, dressed only in boxer shorts, leaning over her. She was on her day-bed, in her nearly dark apartment, and he was shaking her out of sleep.

"Jay," she whispered tremulously, the effects of the dream so real she was certain her skin was damp. She threw her arms around him.

"It's okay. Nightmare's over," he whispered, pulling her close and holding her tight, but she knew in her heart, it wasn't. Whatever evil had invaded her mind was very real and existed deep in the soul of the campus.

Shivering, trying to talk herself out of the fear that still enveloped her, she clung to him and, for a second, took solace in the pure strength of him.

He kissed her temple and she blinked back tears of relief. She knew that if he hadn't been here, if she'd been alone, she would have woken up and dealt with the stupid nightmare on her own, but still, it felt so good to sink against him, to accept his strength.

"You all right?"

"Yeah." That was probably a lie; she was far from okay, but now that the nightmare had receded a bit and she was conscious, she wasn't going to fall apart on him either.

"Wanna tell me about it?"

"I don't want to think about it. Not now." She let out a long breath and stared at him in the thin, bluish illumination coming from the stove. The room was secure, smelling of lingering garlic and tomato sauce from the pizza and jasmine from the scented candles no longer lit. The vial lay on the counter. "I'll tell you about it later. Maybe in the morning."

"Good." He was sitting on the bed, still holding her, but when he moved to get more comfortable, somehow his mouth was only a breath away from hers.

Anticipation slid through her blood.

His scent filled her head, and her body responded to his nearness in traitorous ways. Her limbs turned to wax and she just needed, wanted, him to lie down with her. She struggled with the thought of pushing him aside, but she no longer had the strength or the heart. He'd accused her of wanting him and she'd told him he was crazy, but, of course, he'd been spot on. And now, she wanted him more than ever.

His eyes found hers in the darkness. Whatever he saw gave her away completely. "Kris—" he whispered.

She turned her face to him and he kissed her. Tenderly at first, as if anticipating her rejection.

But she couldn't turn away.

Here in the sanctity of her apartment with the evils of the night locked outside, she kissed him back, opening her mouth, feeling his tongue glide between her teeth, sensing him shift so that one of his big hands splayed against the dip in her spine, just above her buttocks.

Memories of making love to him years before poured over her as she tasted him. Salty. Familiar. Sexy. So male. How had she ever thought he wasn't good enough? That he wasn't intellectual enough? That he wasn't man enough?

Stupid, stupid, girl.

Her heart was pounding, not from fear now, but desire. Her limbs, which had been so heavy in the nightmare, were strong. Anxiously she embraced him, drawing him closer to her. Her skin, which had seemed so wet from the dream's red-stained water, was damp again. And hot. With the warm perspiration and excitement of physical need.

He shifted, his body poised above hers, one hand stroking a strand of hair from her face. She watched as he swallowed, his Adam's apple working as he tried to contain himself, and she felt the stiffness of his erection against the juncture of her legs. Hard, thick and straining. Separated only by a thin barrier of cotton.

"Kris," he whispered again, and in the half light she saw the desire in his eyes, the darkness of his pupils. "I don't want to—"

"Sure you do."

"I mean—"

"You want me," she said, throwing back the words that he'd taunted her with earlier in the evening.

With a groan he started to roll off her, but she grabbed his arms, held him fast.

"It's four in the morning, Kristi. I'm not in the mood for word games."

"What are you in the mood for?"

"Don't do this," he said.

"Do what?"

"You know."

"Yes."

He warned, "This is dangerous."

"No, Jay, it's not," she said, and lifted her head to kiss him hard on the lips. He didn't respond, but she felt the heat in him, sensed the tenuous hold he had on his emotions.

"You told me earlier that it wouldn't work and now,

after what I would assume was a very disturbing nightmare, you want to make love?"

"I won't think less of you in the morning. I promise."

He half laughed. "Goddamn it, woman, I missed you." Before she could respond, he kissed her again and this time there was no turning back. She skimmed his boxers off his buttocks and he nearly tore her pajamas from her body.

Her arms wrapped around his neck as they wrestled on the small bed, their limbs straining and entwining.

As they had years before.

It seemed so natural as the old bed creaked and the dog, resting on the rug, snored softly.

Kristi kissed Jay feverishly, warm sensations rushing through her veins, her skin heating as he caressed her. Her breath came short and fast. He kissed her lips, her throat, the hollow between her breasts. His thumbs circled her nipples and deep inside the wanting heated in a liquid spiral and she thought only of making love with him until dawn, maybe later. . . .

Her fingers traced the sinewy muscles of his shoulders and she felt the scrape of springy hair against her smooth flesh as he breathed across her breasts only to take a nipple in his teeth.

She arched and he kissed the tight bud, his tongue teasing her flesh, her body aching with need. The sound that came from her throat was breathy and primal. Blood rushed through her veins in heated spurts.

Lower he descended and her heartbeat quickened as he parted her legs fuller and lifted her up, his hands on her buttocks. Her own fingers clenched in the bedsheets and her back arched.

How long had it been since she'd loved him? How many years had she wasted? She cried out as he kissed and laved her, creating a need so hot she began to writhe, wanting more, aching for all of him.

"Jay," she whispered, her voice cracking. "Jay—oh, oh, God."

"Right here, darlin'." And his warm breath reached the deepest part of her before he lifted her further off the bed, adjusting her legs over his shoulders.

She bit her lip rather than beg for him to come to her and then as she looked at him, he grinned wickedly in the night, pulling her hips downward as he met her. In one slow thrust, he entered her.

She gasped, feeling her eyes round, her heart pound so hard she thought it might burst. He withdrew, and she cried out, only to have him push into her.

"Oh, God."

Again he thrust and again, his fingers dug into her flesh, his body straining with each hard thrust.

And she met him eagerly, her mind spinning, her eyes open as she watched him moving so easily, pleasuring her while still holding back. Her throat tightened, her entire body heating as he came to her, faster and faster until she could barely breathe, couldn't think. Though it was dark, she saw him, felt him, smelled the pure musk of him.

Faster and faster, he pushed into her, pulled her against him, and her legs wrapped around his neck as she gave more of herself to him, felt his hand, along with his erection, touching intimate parts of her, sending jolt after jolt through her nerves.

*More,* she thought wildly, *more!*

*Faster! Faster!*

She grabbed hold of his arms and arched her back as the first wave jolted through her and the images in her mind flashed behind her eyes. She saw Jay's face now, the younger, roguish smile, and ropey muscles, and . . . and . . . and . . . She convulsed then, her body jerking as Jay cried out and collapsed upon her.

He bucked several times as she gasped for breath,

clinging to him, wrapped in the scent of sex and musk and candles that had burned low.

She kissed him then, on the shoulder, and tasted the salt of his sweat. Turning, he pressed his lips against her neck and then nipped at her with his teeth.

"Hey!"

He laughed, tousling her hair. "Just messin' with ya."

"Dangerous," she said, still struggling for breath as he rolled to the side. "You don't know what I was dreaming about."

"Oh, right, sorry." But he laughed again and she rolled her eyes. "Are you going to throw me back to the chair?"

"No . . . though you might deserve it, you creep."

"That's Professor Creep to you."

She groaned. "I forgot how corny you could be."

"And sexy and manly and—"

She snagged the pillow from behind her head and hit him with it.

"Don't test me," he warned.

She arched a brow. "Yeah? What're ya going to do about it?"

"You want to see?"

"I figure you're all talk, no action."

"Oh, hell." He rolled over again, pressing his body hard against hers. "Then I guess I'll just have to show you, won't I?" He kissed her hard and she felt her so recently banked fires start to ignite again.

She was smiling and feeling safe and secure for the first time since she'd moved to Baton Rouge. "Sure you can handle it, Professor Creep?"

For an answer he kissed her again, then lifting his head, deftly turned her onto her stomach and stuffed the pillow she'd flung at him under her hips. Lying atop her, he leaned forward so that his breath ruffled the hair over her ear. "Watch me," he whispered wickedly, and Kristi buried her face in the bed and giggled until his slow, sensual movements earned an equally slow, sensual response from deep inside her, and she found herself gasping and begging and urging him to love her more . . . more . . . more. . . .

# CHAPTER 19

*Rap! Rap! Rap!*

Kristi groaned as she rolled over and stared at the clock. Nine-thirty in the morning . . . Sunday morning. Who would be beating on her door? And why? She wanted to pull a pillow over her head when she realized she wasn't alone. Jay was wedged in tight against her.

Images of a night of lovemaking slipped easily through her mind and she smiled to herself.

*Rap! Rap!*

Whoever it was, was insistent. *Go away,* she thought, cozily snuggled against Jay, then jolted awake thinking the person outside the door could be her father.

Bruno gave off a soft, disgruntled woof.

Jay lifted his head. "What's going on?" He glanced at the clock and blinked.

"You look like hell," she said, noting his puffy eyes and hair stuck at all angles.

"You're beautiful."

"Oh, yeah, right."

The rapping continued and before Kristi could stop him, Jay rolled off the small daybed and yanked on his boxers.

"Don't answer that!" she warned, her mind clearing, her eyes feeling as if they had sand in the sockets. She didn't want anyone to see her half-naked professor answering her door. "Don't!"

But Jay wasn't listening. He looked through the peephole and started moving the bike.

"Who is it?" Kristi scrambled into her pajamas. What was wrong with him? "Jay . . . oh, damn . . . don't!"

Ignoring her, he unlocked the door just as she pulled the bottoms over her naked body. Her underwear was in the middle of the floor. She swore under her breath as she shimmied into the very unsexy T-shirt with All Saints emblazoned across it.

A rush of cold air entered the room, but nothing else. He stood, blocking the entrance with Bruno nosing past him, wagging his tail. Through the slit of space left between his waist and the doorjamb Kristi caught a glimpse of a red T-shirt and khaki-colored pants.

"Is there something I can do for you?" he asked.

"Oh, uh, I was looking for Kristi . . . Kristi Bentz," a female voice asked. *Mai Kwan.* Kristi made a face. *Great. Her snoopy neighbor. On the prowl again.*

Kristi rolled off the daybed, hearing it squeak, tossed the covers over what was a mess of sheets and blankets, then kicked her bikini undies into a corner. Pushing her hair from her eyes, she came up behind Jay.

"You're Dr. McKnight," Mai said, extending her hand at that moment. "Mai Kwan, I'm a neighbor. I live on the second floor."

Jesus! She was introducing herself to Jay? Now what?

"Professor. No PhD, at least not yet."

"Hi!" Kristi tried to sound bright and cheery though she felt anything but chipper. She stepped around Jay, but Mai's eyes didn't so much as flicker in her direction.

She was zeroed in on Jay. "And you work in the crime lab, right?"

How did Mai know that?

"Yeah."

"I didn't know you two . . ." She motioned her hand back and forth, then finally looked at Kristi again. "I mean . . . I didn't know you knew each other."

"We went to the same high school," Jay said.

*Too much information.*

"Was that why you stopped by or was there something else you wanted?" Kristi asked, wondering how to shut Jay up. To her horror he draped an arm over her shoulders. Damn him, he was enjoying this. She shot him a look she hoped would send him the message.

"I was just thinking you might want to go out for a run or get a cup of coffee or something," Mai said. "But I see you're busy, that you've got company, so . . . maybe some other time."

Was it Kristi's imagination or did Mai actually look slyly at Jay when she made the last offer? "It wouldn't have worked this time anyway, I've got a ton of homework and then my shift at work starts in a few hours," Kristi said. Why was she explaining herself? What she did was no business of Mai's. Kristi only hoped to God that Jay wouldn't be polite enough, or stupid enough, to invite the other girl in.

Jay suddenly snapped his fingers. "Mai Kwan. You called me a couple of days ago, right? About a piece for the school newspaper?"

Kristi stared at Mai with new eyes and Mai lifted her chin just a fraction, as if she knew the wheels were turning in Kristi's mind. "Yeah, I did. I'm doing a story on criminology. I'd like to interview you, get some of your credentials and background, then tie it all in to what you're teaching here at All Saints. How what you discuss in the classroom could be applied to real police work. In the field kind of stuff. I was hoping for an interview with you, then maybe with a local detective, maybe even Kristi's dad since he's pretty famous and has helped with some cases on the campus."

Kristi inwardly groaned. No wonder Mai had been buddying up to her. So much for true friendship.

Jay nodded. "I think I can help you."

Mai smiled brightly at him and said, "Anytime. You name it."

So Kristi was supposed to believe that Mai had just stumbled onto Jay here? Or had she seen his truck, watched him come in with Kristi last night, and decided to force an encounter this morning?

"I'll have to check my schedule and get back to you," Jay said. "I still have your number on my voice mail."

"Oh. Sure." Mai couldn't hide her disappointment as her gaze slid to Bruno. "Your dog?" she asked Jay.

"Uh-huh."

"He's cute." She lowered herself to one knee and scratched Bruno behind his big floppy ears.

Jay said, "Don't tell him that. He thinks he looks fierce."

Mai laughed and Kristi wondered if she'd ever take the hint and leave. "Okay, well . . . look, I'll catch up with you later, Kristi." Then she flashed a girlish smile at Jay. "Nice to meet you, *Professor* McKnight."

Kristi said, "See ya," as she pulled the door shut. She then gazed disgustedly at man and dog. "I distinctly remember telling you not to answer."

"Embarrassed of me?"

"No . . . yes . . . Oh, I don't know," she admitted. "Look, I just don't want it spread around campus that I sleep with my professors, okay?" She pushed her hair out of her eyes.

He nodded, but she could tell he wasn't taking her seriously. "Your secret is safe with me."

"It's not you I'm worried about," she pointed out, padding into the kitchen and opening the cupboard, though she knew she was out of coffee. "And admit it, you got off on opening the door."

"Bristly this morning, aren't we?"

" 'We' had a short night. Remember?"

He came up behind her and circled her waist with his arms. "Vividly. And it was a great night," he reminded her, his breath ruffling her hair.

She thought about kissing him, about falling back onto the unmade bed, but she really didn't have a lot of time. "There are just some things about Mai that bug me. She asks too many questions, wants to know all about my personal life, and then she doesn't cop to what she really wants. Now, at least, I kind of understand why: she's all about Dad being an ace detective."

"Kind of?"

"Who knows if she's telling the truth? I just don't trust her."

His hands fell away. "You don't trust anyone."

His remark cut harder than it should have. She slammed the cupboard door shut and turned to face him. "Oh, God . . . I'm becoming my father!"

"Isn't being a detective what you're trying to do here? All the"—he made air quotes with his fingers—" 'investigating' about the missing girls. I'm no psychologist, but it seems to me you're trying to prove something to dear old Dad."

"I trust people, though, okay? I'm not . . . like him."

"Not much," Jay said, his smile quick.

She narrowed her eyes at him. And she was still irritated with Mai, sure there was more to the story than just some interview for the school paper.

Jay wisely let the subject drop and opened the refrigerator door. Bruno was at his side in an instant. "Sorry, Buddy, not much in here."

"I keep meaning to go to the store, but it's a low priority."

"We won't starve," he assured her, and managed to pull out what remained of the pizza, three cold slices wrapped in wrinkled foil. "Breakfast."

"No way."

"You got coffee?"

"No. I'm out. I've got one tea bag and a couple of bottles of beer, but that's it."

"Too early for beer. Even for me. And no thanks on the tea. You want a slice?" He opened the aluminum foil and offered up the congealed pizza.

She took one look at the brown hamburger, with its hint of white fat all stuck together, over withered olives and onions and thick tomato sauce, and her stomach turned. "It's all yours. I think I'll grab something at the restaurant. They've got a breakfast sandwich called a MacDuff, which is kind of a rip-off of a McDonald's Egg McMuffin. Maybe I'll try it." She glanced at the clock as he, still only in his boxers, rested a hip against the counter and chewed the cold pizza without bothering to heat it in the microwave. Bruno, ever vigilant, sat at his feet, eyes on the prize, tail sweeping the floor whenever Jay looked down at him.

Kristi shuddered and turned away. This hanging out in her apartment was a little awkward. And already one person had found out they were lovers. In the past, while she and Jay had dated, they'd never lived together, so this morning was a little difficult to handle. She didn't really know how this relationship, if that's what you'd call it, might or might not develop.

"I'm going to shower. I've got a lot of things to do today, which, unfortunately includes work."

He nodded. "Me, too. At the house." He brushed his hands together and Bruno sniffed for crumbs on the floor. "Then I have to answer some e-mails and grade some papers, including yours."

"Be kind."

"After last night I'll be harder on you than anyone just so no one can claim I'm biased."

"Don't get crazy. And no one's going to know about this, remember?" she reminded him, though she doubted Mai would keep her mouth shut.

"I'm free for dinner."

She gave him a look. "Are you asking me out on a date?"

"My turn." He crumpled the tin foil and tossed it into the trash, then located a paper towel to wipe the grease from his fingers. "You've been doing all the asking lately."

"The other night, when I smoked you at darts, that was *not* a date."

"Right." His eyes, no longer puffy from sleep, glittered a deep amber at her obvious irritation. "So I'll meet you back here. When do you get off work?"

"Two-thirty or three, I've got lunch today. Depends on the crowd or lack of it. But then I've got to finish a couple of assignments, and I want to go online and check out the chat rooms later."

"So call me and we'll hook up." He walked into the living area, grabbing his jeans off the floor as he passed them.

And just like that they were a couple? She wondered at the wisdom of rekindling their romance, but decided, for the moment, to go with it. "Okay."

"I want to see what goes on in the chat rooms as well. And Wagner House."

"Yeah, me, too."

He scrounged on the floor for his clothes, then shook out his shirt. She dragged her gaze from his bare legs, all sinewy muscle, taut skin, and curling dark hair as he stepped into his Levis. Just seeing him dress did strange things to her insides, and the simple fact that he seemed oblivious to his effect on her made him more fascinating. God, what was wrong with her? Surreptitiously she watched as he threw his shirt over his head, stuck his arms through, and stretched slightly, lengthening the flat of his abdomen as he pulled the shirt over his shoulders.

*Lord in heaven, he looked good. Too good.*

She turned away as his head came through the neck

of his shirt. "I thought you promised to tell me about that nightmare," he said, patting his pockets and making his keys jangle. Once assured they were where he wanted them, he reached for his shoes. "Remember it?"

"Yeah." She felt as if the temperature in the room dropped ten degrees when she recalled the bloody pool riddled with severed heads of the missing girls. "Oh, yeah."

"Want to talk about it?"

She shook her head. "Not now . . . maybe later."

He was putting on a shoe but stopped and looked at her, concern etched on his face. "That bad?"

"Pretty bad."

His frown deepened as he wiggled one foot into a shoe, then laced it up. "Want me to come to the diner with you?"

She shook her head vehemently. "I'm fine. Really." She just didn't want to go there, not now. "I'll tell you about the nightmare later, okay?"

"You're sure?"

"Absolutely."

"If you say so." He finished with the other shoe, then said to the dog, "Ready to go?"

Bruno emitted an excited woof and turned circles at the door.

"I'll take that as a 'yes.' " He winked at Kristi. "So I'll see ya later."

She was nodding, expecting him to cruise out the door any second. But he surprised her. He crossed the few feet separating them and grabbed her so quickly she gasped. "Hey—"

"Didn't think you'd get rid of me that fast, did you?"

"What?"

He kissed her. Hard. His mouth melding over hers, his arms holding her fast against him, his tongue slipping between her teeth. Memories of the night before washed through her brain. It would be so easy to tumble back into bed. . . . She wound her arms around his neck as he broke off the kiss and touched his forehead to hers. "Don't forget me."

"You're already just a memory," she teased.

He laughed. "Remember to be careful." Before she could answer, he released her, and with the dog at his heels walked out of the apartment.

She heard his steps, light and quick, as he descended the staircase. She closed the door, locked it, then, shaking off all thoughts of making love to him, of getting involved with him, of falling in love with him again, she pulled off her oversized T-shirt. She had too much to do to think about the complications of a relationship with Jay McKnight. . . .

Oh, Lord, a relationship? What the devil was she thinking? And the fact that her mind even skimmed the thought of falling in love with him . . . well, that was just plain nuts. Dropping her T-shirt onto the floor, she stepped out of her pajama bottoms when she felt it again . . . that silly little notion that she was being watched.

She shivered. There was no one in the apartment and the window shades were drawn. No one could see her. No one.

And yet she sensed hidden eyes, watching her every move.

"Guilt, for sleeping with Jay," she told herself, but she yanked the bathroom door closed and locked it.

She turned on the faucet, adjusted the spray, and waited for the water to heat. Stepping into the small glass cubicle, she pushed all thoughts of some unseen voyeur out of her head and took one of the shortest showers of her life.

Aunt Colleen's house could wait, Jay thought as he drove to the cottage to drop off the building materials he had stored in the back of his truck.

It was threatening rain again, the sky gloomy, the defrost mechanism on his truck struggling with the condensation that had collected overnight. As it was early Sunday morning, traffic was thin, a little heavier by the churches.

As far as Jay was concerned his battling cousins, Janice and Leah, could bloody well cool their jets as well. Oh, they'd probably start pushing him again, especially Leah with Kitt, her do-nothing of a husband. Kitt spent his time getting high and jamming with a garage band and dreaming of becoming a rock star. Kitt saw his dead mother-in-law's cottage as a gold mine and a way to prolong his status as an out-of-work musician. Jay understood that his cousins needed to sell the place and Jay intended to keep up with the renovations, but right now, he had more important things to consider.

Uppermost on the list?

Kristi Bentz's safety.

Leah's damned granite countertops and stainless steel appliances were a far-off second.

As soon as he unloaded the pickup and cleaned up, he intended to return to her apartment and go over it carefully with his evidence collection kit, though what he expected to find eluded him. It had been months since Tara Atwater had lived in the unit, and there was no indication that it had ever been a crime scene. But if a prowler had broken in, there was a chance he'd left a fingerprint or latent shoe print or hair or something . . . maybe.

Jay didn't know what to believe. The place had seemed undisturbed.

But the studio apartment had belonged to Tara Atwater and she was definitely missing.

"So we'll just see what we shall see," he said to the dog as the clouds grew darker. He stopped for a traffic light and waited for a woman jogger pushing a baby carriage in front of her as she crossed in front of him.

When the light changed, he beat out a minivan filled with teenagers. Once ahead of the van, he switched lanes, feeling a sense of urgency he couldn't quite shake.

Later today he planned to install yet another new lock on the door, one that Irene Calloway, her grandson, or anyone else they thought needed a key, wouldn't have. He also considered installing a camera for the front porch. Afterward he would double-check on the staff of All Saints, particularly Dr. Dominic Grotto. Jay had already retrieved some information, but it was spotty at best and he wanted to do a deeper background check on the instructors who had taught the missing students. Jay also was going to take the official tour of Wagner House while Kristi was working. Something had been going on there last night, long after the museum doors were supposed to have been locked, something that frightened the bejeezus out of Kristi, who didn't scare easily.

He turned a corner just as a beagle puppy dashed into the street. Jay jammed on his brakes. Bruno fell against the dash. "Christ!" A sedan coming the other way skidded to a stop.

A tall, thin man in his twenties, running with a leash wound in one hand, sprinted between the cars, yelling as he chased after the wayward dog.

"You okay, buddy?" Jay asked Bruno, his heart beating overtime.

Bruno climbed into the passenger seat again and barked at the disappearing pup while Jay drove the few blocks to the bungalow. At the house, Bruno pressed his nose closer to the glass and wagged his tail.

"You think this is home?" Jay asked, and parked in front of the dilapidated cottage with its sagging porch and overgrown yard. "Nah!"

But then what was? His sterile place in New Orleans?

That wasn't any better.

Truth to tell, since Katrina, Jay had been restless,

feeling as if he didn't truly belong anywhere any longer. His renovated apartment had suddenly seemed small and confining, and when he'd stayed with Gayle in those months they'd dated, he'd felt as if he hadn't belonged at all, always concerned about wearing his shoes in the house or spilling coffee . . . no, her house had been too perfect, everything in its place except for Jay. He'd been the one thing Gayle had chosen that hadn't fit into her home or her life.

Then there was Kristi's studio, where he could pop a beer, eat cold pizza on a Sunday morning, or leave his jeans crumpled on the floor.

"So what?" he said aloud.

Kristi Bentz's apartment was no more the answer to his need for a permanent home than this cottage that belonged to his cousins.

Not liking the path his mind was determined to take, he climbed out of his truck. Bruno sprang to the ground, ready to lift his leg and mark every scraggly shrub and pine tree leading to the front door. Jay unloaded the truck bed, taking out the bags of cement, light fixtures, and cans of primer and paint. He hauled everything inside, then fed the dog, and headed to the shower.

His thoughts turned to Kristi and their night of lovemaking. After all of his warnings to himself, all the mental admonitions, he'd fallen into the same old trap and had ended up in her bed. Just where he'd really wanted to be. And damn it, as a scientist he didn't believe in a lot of romantic nonsense. Sex, after all, was sex. Some better than others. But he hadn't really bought into the emotional connection of it. At some level he'd even hoped that after tumbling into bed with Kristi and spending hours making love, he would somehow, miraculously, be cured of her.

Of course he'd been wrong.

Seriously wrong.

With Kristi, there was more to it than pure sexual

gratification. Always had been. In fact, if he were honest with himself, he'd admit his fascination with her
was worse than ever. "Good goin', Romeo," he muttered,
yanking off his clothes and stepping into the shower of
the Day-Glo green bathroom. He couldn't help but wish
she was with him, that he could wash her body with
soap, feel his hands slide down her slick skin, kiss her
breasts while water cascaded over them both, and lift
her up, feel her legs wrap around him and . . .

Oh hell. He was giving himself a hard-on just thinking about it. He scrubbed quickly, turned the spigots to
cold and braced himself as his erection softened.
Within minutes, he toweled off, then pulled on clean
jeans and a long-sleeved T-shirt from his duffel bag.
Socks and shoes followed, and he grabbed his notebook
computer and was out the door again, calling to Bruno,
who was lying in the overgrown yard beneath a live
oak, where a squirrel had taken up residence on a
bough just out of reach.

"Give it up," Jay advised his dog as the squirrel, tail
flickering, scolded noisily. "Let's go."

On cool days, he took the old hound with him everywhere. Bruno was content to wait in the car while Jay
ran errands. As long as the temperature allowed, Jay figured it was better than having the dog cooped up in the
semi-gutted bungalow for hours at a time.

He pulled out of the driveway and onto the street.
Next stop: the hardware store followed by Wagner House,
which would be open in the afternoon. He thought he
might even stop by the diner for lunch, see Kristi in action.

She would hate it.

And he would love it.


Kristi didn't have much time, but on the bike she
zipped across campus, cutting between pedestrians, jog-

gers, and skateboarders to Wagner House. Today in the gloomy daylight the house appeared less sinister, the sharp peaked roof, beveled glass windows, gargoyle downspouts all just part of the architectural style of a bygone era.

Before leaving her apartment, Kristi had taken the time to pull up a list of students in the school, locating Marnie Gage on the roster. Marnie's picture had flashed onto the screen along with her short bio indicating that she had graduated from Grant High School in Portland, Oregon, and was an English major working on a minor in theater.

Again, the English Department, Kristi had thought. It didn't take a PhD to figure out that the girl probably was or had been in the same block of classes as Kristi and the missing coeds were. Kristi was starting to believe the entire department was somehow involved in this underground vampire cult or whatever it was.

"That's ridiculous," she told herself.

But was it?

Her skin crawled, and she sensed again that someone was watching her. Someone hidden. Someone evil.

She felt a chill, a cold gust of wind brush against the back of her neck. As the clouds overhead threatened rain, she propped her bike against the wrought-iron fence and tried the gate. It was locked. Of course. No matter how hard she pushed on it, or fiddled with the clasp, it didn't budge, and the hours of operation posted on the gate indicated the museum wouldn't be open until two this afternoon. Supposedly the museum closed at five-thirty PM.

*But it had opened last night.*

Kristi had damned well been inside. Along with Marnie Gage and at least one other person, maybe more. Had they been in the basement, down the locked staircase? Was it the meeting of the cult Lucretia had mentioned, then denied?

"Weird, weird, weird," she told herself. Staring through the wrought iron bars of the fence, she studied the old foundation but could only see the tops of basement windows, dark and opaque. Probably used for storage. Not secret meetings where blood was let and vampires revered.

But the blond girl, Marnie Gage, had gone inside, and someone had been following her throughout the upstairs rooms. Could Marnie have doubled back and gotten behind her? But why? Was this place somehow connected to the missing girls, the damned cult that Lucretia now disavowed?

In that second she felt cold as death. Hadn't she seen Ariel hanging around here? Then Marnie? Both whose faces had turned the color of death. That left Lucretia. Kristi didn't know of any connection she had with the old house, but she was willing to bet her life that her ex-roommate was somehow involved with this old, dark edifice.

*So how does Dad fit in?*

Kristi curled her fingers around the bars of the fence. As far as she knew Rick Bentz had nothing to do with Wagner House or anything else concerning All Saints College. He'd solved a couple of crimes connected to the campus, and sure, his only daughter was enrolled here, again, but that was it. Her vision of his gray pallor didn't seem connected.

So, maybe her visions had nothing to do with premonitions of death, and everything to do with something wrong in her own mind, something that had just slipped out of gear after she'd been attacked.

So many questions.

And no answers.

"The museum is closed until later this afternoon."

She nearly jumped out of her skin.

"Two o'clock," Father Mathias said, glancing to the sky as the wind picked up. "Wagner House opens then."

"I know, but I have to get to work and I . . ." She thought fast. "Well, I think I lost my sunglasses here. They're prescription."

"I'll check the lost and found." He unlocked the gate and as he did, the sleeve of his cassock fell away, exposing part of his arm and a bandage.

"What happened?" she asked automatically. He pulled back his keys and the sleeve covered his arm again.

"Nothing. An accident. From yard work," he said quickly. "Electric hedge clippers. Guess I'll wait for the gardener next time. Come back after two when the docent is here. If I find your glasses, or she does, you can pick them up then."

"But I need them for work. I'll come with you."

"Really, child," he said, "I can't allow it. Two o'clock isn't that far away. I'm just stopping by for a second myself." He slipped through the door and up the steps as the gate swung shut. On impulse she stopped it from latching with her foot and waited until Father Mathias disappeared within.

As soon as she heard the door of the mansion close behind him, she swept into the fenced yard and walked quickly around the perimeter of the house. What she expected to find, she didn't know, but she peered through the basement windows just the same, spying nothing in the darkness, feeling like a fool.

At the back porch, she considered walking up the steps and trying the door when she heard a voice inside. A woman's voice. "I told you to take care of it," she said. "Don't make it my problem!"

The other voice was muted, farther away. Male.

Father Mathias Glanzer's?

Or someone else's?

Kristi strained to listen as the first drops of rain started to fall, but she couldn't hear what the man was saying, only the woman's sharp, quick response. "The whole thing backfired, I know, but you should be able to handle it. The sooner the better. Before the police get involved. Do you know what would happen then? *Do you?*"

Again the male voice.

Arguing?

Explaining?

Coming up with excuses?

Kristi's heart was pounding, her nerves strung tight. She was about to risk it and climb up the steps when she felt it again—that eerie sensation that she was being watched. Slowly she dragged her gaze up the side of the building, past the kitchen and second floor to a window high above, shadowed by heavy eaves. Her blood ran cold as she saw a face . . . a girl's face . . . white as death, taut with fear.

Ariel O'Toole?

Or someone else. The image was too blurry.

Kristi blinked and she was gone, the window empty.

# CHAPTER 20

"Sunday morning, not even noon, and how did I know that you'd be here?" Del Vernon asked as, holding a manila envelope, he rested a hip against Portia Laurent's desk at the station.

"Are you insinuating I don't have a life?"

He lifted a shoulder. "Nah. Just that you're a workaholic."

"It takes one to know one." She leaned back in her chair and stared up at him. Lord, he was a handsome man. Eyes as dark as midnight, long straight nose, a shaved head that seemed flawless, and a mouthful of white straight teeth.

"Possibly."

"So what brings you in here? It *is* Sunday morning."

"Thought you might want to see this." He handed her the envelope. "I think you might just have your body."

"My body?"

"Well, part of one anyway."

She opened the flap and slid out an eight-by-ten photograph. "Sweet Jesus," she said as she stared at the picture of what appeared to be a slightly decomposed arm. Female arm. Left hand. Polished fingernails.

"Where did you find this?"

"In the stomach of an illegally caught alligator. We're lucky the hunter, a yahoo named Boomer Moss, had the smarts to turn it in. We're searching that part of the swamp where the gator was caught, but don't have a whole lot of expectations. The animal could have moved from one spot to the next, the body drifted down there. . . . From the looks of it, we're guessing the arm was in the water less than a week, but the ME isn't certain, at least not yet."

Portia was rapidly getting up to speed. She'd come into the department on a Sunday to catch up on paperwork, which she instantly shelved. "So you think it's one of the girls from All Saints? That our perp captures them, keeps them alive, then finally kills them and gets rid of the bodies," she said, feeling vindicated, excited, and sick inside all at once. She, too, had held out hope that the girls had run off, left town, hoping to disappear, but as she stared at the picture of the severed arm, she knew better. She could only pray that if the scenario she'd just outlined was the truth, some of the missing coeds were still alive.

Tortured, maybe.

Traumatized, certainly.

But alive.

Del frowned, his jaw set and hard. "We don't have many answers yet. There's a chance this doesn't belong to any of the girls from All Saints."

She snorted. Her gut told her this belonged to Tara, Monique, or Rylee. The only missing coed excluded was Dionne, because of her race. The arm in the photo belonged to a white girl. A girl who liked plum-colored fingernail polish.

"If he doesn't keep them alive, then why wouldn't the arm show more signs of decomposure?"

"Don't know, but it doesn't look like he cut the limbs. It's ripped and bitten, consistent with the alligator's jaw."

Her stomach clenched. None of the scenes running through her mind were good.

"The ME thinks the gator did it. But there wasn't any more of the body in his digestive system. We checked."

"So what finally convinced you that this arm belongs to one of the girls from All Saints?"

"Missing persons says no other white girl has been reported missing recently, at least not up here; New Orleans has a few. I've already checked with the local hospitals and no one's shown up missing an arm, from an accident with a hungry gator or otherwise. But here's something odd: the first thing the ME noticed was that there was no blood in the arm."

"Maybe it drained out when it was severed."

"Uh-uh. ME says the severing occurred post mortem."

"Drained in the gator's stomach? Degraded by the time in the water or with stomach acid?"

"The ME's double-checking," Del said, but he sounded doubtful.

"What about distinguishing marks?" Portia said. "Monique had a broken finger, left index, an old softball injury. If the fingers are intact that should show, and Tara, I think, had an arm tattoo." Portia scooted her chair closer to the computer monitor and her fingers flew over the keyboard as she pulled up her files on the missing girls. A second later, she was reading the information she'd gathered on Tara Atwater. "Yeah, here it is, a broken heart, but damn, the tattoo is on her right arm."

"What about the others?"

"I'm looking." Portia had already started searching all of the notes and documents she'd collected. "You'd think there would be something," she said, anxious for a clue, any clue as to the girl's identity. "I assume you've fingerprinted it." She hitched her chin toward the picture of the severed arm.

"Tried. But even if we get a decent print, there's a chance the girls weren't fingerprinted."

"A few of them had records, were busted for drugs. . . ."

Yeah, here we go . . . Dionne and Monique both were hauled in and charged after they were juveniles. Dionne has a love tattoo on her back with a hummingbird and flowers. Surely one of the girls had a distinguishing mark on the left hand. . . ." But there was nothing obvious in her data.

"I thought I told you to leave this case alone," Del Vernon said as she closed one of her files.

"It's a good thing for both of us I ignored you."

He actually flashed a smile. Del Vernon of the ever-grim, studious countenance and tight butt, rained a quick but sexy grin on her for a second. "It's never a good idea to ignore me. This time, you were right and I was wrong. You might want to mark this date with red letters because I seriously doubt it'll ever happen again."

Uh-huh, Portia thought, as she watched him saunter away.


Ariel? Was it really Ariel's face she'd seen, looking so scared. And what was she doing inside Wagner House?

Putting her own misgivings aside, Kristi hurried up the steps at the back of Wagner House and tried the door. It clicked open under her hand. It wasn't locked. Amazed, she stepped inside the darkened kitchen and her heart began to pound. She saw the door to the basement and knew this was her chance. No one knew she was inside.

Yet.

Tiptoeing quietly to the basement door, she reached for the knob.

Too late. The door swung open in front of her. She snatched her hand back as Father Mathias stepped into the kitchen.

"Oh!" he whispered, startled. Then, focusing on Kristi, he scowled harshly. "You again. Didn't I just tell you the museum wasn't open?"

"Yes, but my glasses—"

"I've already looked in the lost and found. They weren't there." Obviously irritated, he closed the door tightly shut behind him. "Now, really, you have to leave."

"Father?" A female voice. The same voice she'd heard through the window. "What's going on?" Wrapped in a black coat trimmed in dark fur, a tall regal-looking woman strode swiftly into the kitchen. Deep-set eyes glared down an aquiline nose. "Who are you?" she asked, then before Kristi could answer, followed up with, "And what are you doing here?"

"She claims she lost her glasses on the last tour."

One of the woman's eyebrows lifted in superior disbelief. "When?"

Kristi had the lie ready. "Last weekend. I came by with friends."

"Really?" Her smirk revealed her skepticism. "Well, the staff will certainly look for them. Come back when the docent is on duty."

"I really need them for work." Kristi stood her ground. "Today."

"Yes, yes, so you said, but I told you the house is closed," Father Mathias insisted.

"So you're not the docent?" Kristi ventured. She didn't like this woman, with her perfect complexion and officious attitude, but she wanted to know more about her.

"Of course not," the woman said. "That's Marilyn Katcher!"

Kristi pushed. "So why are you here? For a place that's closed to visitors, there seems to be a lot of people running around."

"I'm Georgia Clovis," she bit out. "Georgia *Wagner* Clovis." She said it as if it were supposed to mean something to Kristi.

Mathias, like a puppet on a string, said quickly, "Mrs. Clovis is a descendant of Ludwig Wagner and—"

"Direct descendant," she corrected frostily, her red lips turned down at the corners.

"Direct descendant of the man who so graciously donated this house and property to the archdiocese to establish the university."

Kristi gave Georgia a bland "So what?" look.

"Mrs. Clovis, along with her brother and sister, still sit on the board of Wagner House. Very important to All Saints. Now, if you'll come back when Mrs. Katcher is here . . ."

"Someone's upstairs," Kristi said, just to gauge their reaction. She'd come this far, might as well go for broke. She didn't think she would get another chance and she wasn't frightened of either of these two people. Father Mathias was often brooding, but he seemed like a weak man. Georgia Clovis, tall, slim, her dark hair twisted onto her head, tried her best to be intimidating—and wasn't half bad at it—but Kristi wasn't about to be cowed.

"No one else is in the house," Georgia said through her teeth. "Not that it's any business of yours."

"I saw someone in the window. That's why I came inside. It was a girl, er, woman, and she looked scared out of her mind."

"Impossible." She shook her head, but the perfect facade cracked just a bit. "You imagined it."

"I didn't."

"A play of light," Mathias put in, shooting a look at Georgia.

"One way to find out." Without waiting for any kind of permission, Kristi headed through the dining room and up the stairs.

"Wait a minute. You can't go up there!" Georgia called after her, high heels clicking across the hardwood floors. "Wait!" To the priest, she added shrilly, "What does she think she's doing?"

Kristi didn't waste any time. She raced to the third

floor and once there, dashed to the door of the room that overlooked the backyard, the one where she was certain she'd seen Ariel, or someone, standing near the watery panes of glass.

Father Mathias's heavier tread was climbing the stairs. "Miss . . . please . . . you aren't allowed . . ."

Kristi twisted the knob and the door swung open to an empty room. The one that held the Victorian dollhouse. No one was inside, but the dollhouse, which had been closed, was now open, the perfectly furnished rooms on display.

"Hello?" Kristi called, her voice disturbing dust motes but nothing else. She checked the closet, just to be sure.

Empty.

But near the window overlooking the back porch hung a black cloak with a white bag above it, both facing the window . . . as it had the night before when she'd searched the house.

Had she been mistaken?

Thought she'd seen a face when it was just this cloak and bag?

"Satisfied?" Georgia demanded, entering with Father Mathias on her heels, her pale skin flushed from the exertion of the rapid climb. "No one hiding in the corners? No 'scared out of her mind' girl?" She was shaking her head. "I know the stories that run rampant about the house and yes, in the early 1930s a person was killed here, the murder never solved. I also know about the group of 'Goth' kids who hang out around here, fascinated by the architecture and history of the house, but it really is just a museum, filled with very personal and valuable artifacts. Therefore we can't have anyone, including *you*, running wildly through it. If you really did lose your glasses, which I suspect is a total fabrication, please return when Mrs. Katcher is on duty and she can help you."

"Last night, a girl walked into the house," Kristi insisted. "I saw her. Followed her. She came inside and . . . disappeared. Maybe . . . into the basement?"

"*Another* girl? Or the same scared one?"

"Different."

Georgia snorted contemptuously. "The basement? Why?"

"I thought you could tell me."

"It's only used for storage."

Father Mathias hovered in the doorway, almost as if he were afraid to enter. "I was just in the basement and it's not empty," he said to Georgia. "I found evidence of rats. I think we should call an exterminator, but other than old furniture and crates, boxes, there's nothing downstairs." Reaching into a deep pocket within his alb, he found a handkerchief and dabbed at his forehead.

"Yes, call someone to take care of the problem." Georgia was dismissive. "As for you . . ." She glared at Kristi. "Who are you?"

Kristi thought about lying but it was too easily checked. "Kristi Bentz. I'm a student here."

"Well, Kristi, if you really did come into the house last night, you were trespassing," Georgia said, her lips pursed at the corners. "If we find anything missing, believe me, we'll contact the police and your name will come up."

"Don't you have security cameras?" Kristi asked. "You know, with all your valuable things, I'd guess you'd have some kind of security system in place. Check the tape."

"Until now, we haven't had to have one," Father Mathias said coolly.

Georgia sniffed. "Obviously it's something we need discuss at the next board meeting. Now, Miss Bentz, it's time you left."

"I'll escort you outside," the priest offered. "I'm already running late. It's past time to get ready for mass."

There wasn't any point in arguing and Kristi, too, needed to leave.

As Father Mathias ushered her out, including opening the door for her, Georgia Clovis followed, her coat billowing around her as she headed toward a sleek black Mercedes.

Kristi had thought about mentioning Marnie Gage's name but had decided to keep it to herself for the time being. Maybe she could talk to Marnie. Not interrogate her, but cozy up to her, befriend her, although so far the plan of permeating what appeared to be the inner circle of the vampire "cult" hadn't worked. Not only Ariel, but now Lucretia, was avoiding her like the plague.

The chapel bells chimed, breaking into her thoughts, as the priest hurried down the steps to unlock the gate and hold it open. "Be careful," he said under his breath, so low she almost didn't hear the words. "God be with you."

She turned, but he was already hurrying toward the church and she didn't have any time to chase after him. Strapping on her helmet, Kristi swung onto her bike, picking up speed and clicking through the gears as the cold rain began to fall more steadily, bouncing on the pavement and running beneath the collar of her jacket. Father Mathias's warning echoed in her mind as she headed for the diner. Her tires hummed across the cement and brick walkways, cutting through puddles beginning to form. She skirted the library, then sped across a parking lot before catching a main street and riding the six blocks to the back lot of the restaurant.

What was the priest trying to tell her? Obviously to back off. But there was more, she knew, secrets he wasn't about to share.

Her heart was beating like crazy as she swung off the

bike and locked it against a post. Tearing off her helmet and wiping the rain from her face, she headed inside— and straight into the heart of chaos. The Bard's Board was filled with the brunch crowd, people standing and waiting for tables, the line cooks working like mad, the wait staff searching for orders and hurrying through tables, the bus people clearing tables as soon as they were vacated.

One of the ovens had given up the ghost the night before and one of the fry cooks, who considered himself a handyman, was trying to fix it. He was on his knees, head inside, his big size-thirteen feet sticking in the small galley so that everyone had to step over him.

Kristi whipped on her apron, washed her hands, and grabbed her notepad. She didn't have time to think about what had happened at Wagner House.

"Thank God you're here!" Ezma breezed by with a tray of water glasses. "The new people can't keep up."

"I thought I was one of the new people."

"I'm talking about Frick and Frack," Ezma said under her breath. "They're useless." She slid a glance at two waiters. One, Frick, was a tall thin boy who looked no older than sixteen and was really named Finn. Frack was a girl somewhere around twenty with rosy cheeks, springy brown curls, and curves she didn't bother to conceal. Her real name was Francesca, but it didn't seem to fit. Even during this mad rush, Frick-Finn was taking time to flirt with her and Frack-Francesca was eating it up, ignoring her tables.

Kristi scanned the specials. "This is it?" she asked, noting that some of the more popular items, shrimp crepes, crab cakes, and crawfish etouffee had been erased from the chalkboard, the faint outline of their Shakespearean names still visible.

"With the oven on the fritz we're down to a lot of the stuff that was made earlier or can be sauteed. Push the jambalaya and catfish fritters."

"Okay."

"Can I get a clean table?" the harried hostess asked of the kitchen staff. She was standing a few steps from the front desk and door where patrons were clustered, waiting. "What about thirteen? Or eleven? I've got people who've been waiting out front for a half hour!"

"I'm on it." Miguel, one of the busboys, hurried past and was picking up dirty plates, glasses, and flatware before Kristi finished tying her apron.

Francesca looked up, spied Kristi, and immediately went into complaint mode. "It's about time you showed up," she chastised, breaking up her tête-à-tête with Finn. "It's been a nightmare this morning, let me tell you," she said, as Finn, with a quick look over his shoulder, turned back to the tables in his section of the restaurant.

Francesca's cheeks were flushed as she untied her apron, further showing the area of her blouse where the fabric gapped, offering a peek at her lacy bra and cleavage. "People with kids, and I mean *young* kids, babies, and the tips have been miserable. Just awful. I should have stayed home and called in sick." She stuffed her dirty apron in the laundry basket and reached for her jacket.

*Waa, waa, waa,* Kristi thought, wondering if the lousy tips had anything to do with the girl's obvious lack of interest in her job.

Unfortunately Ezma and Francesca's evaluation of the situation was spot on. With one oven disabled and a cook out of commission as he tried to fix it, the finished orders were slow to reach the window where the waiters were to pick them up.

Worse yet, in Kristi's section, she saw familiar faces. Dr. Croft, the head of the English Department, had just been seated along with Dr. Emmerson, her Shakespeare 201 instructor with the biker dude persona. Today, though, he'd shaved, his usual T-shirt given up in favor of a gray sweater, his hair still a carefully planned mess. The third member of the group was Dr. Hollister, Jay's boss, head of the fledgling Criminal Justice Department.

*A toxic trio,* Kristi thought as she greeted them, handed out menus, and smiling, rattled off the specials that still remained. ". . . and if you're interested in jambalaya, I hear it's wonderful today."

"Is it hot?" Dr. Emmerson asked, his eyebrows lifting, almost flirting. "Spicy?"

"No more than usual, but yes, I think it's got a little kick to it."

"Just the way I like it."

"Down boy," Natalie Croft said, her lips twitching a bit.

*Yuck,* Kristi thought. But at least it drove out all thoughts that she was way behind in his class, and she had several assignments that she hadn't yet read.

"Can I get you anything to drink?"

"Mmm. I'll have sweet tea," Dr. Croft said. She was a tall woman, with porcelain skin, dark hair, with just the beginnings of crows feet showing in the corners of her eyes. Her nose was patrician, her demeanor a little standoffish.

"Coffee for me," Dr. Hollister said, slipping a pair of rimless reading glasses onto her nose as she studied the menu, tucking a wayward strand of black hair behind her ear.

"Yeah, me too, the coffee. Black." Dr. Emmerson looked up at her and a spark of recognition touched his face. "You're a student of mine, aren't you?"

Kristi nodded. That was the trouble with this damned job, located as it was, so close to campus.

He snapped his fingers. "Shakespeare, right? Two-o-one?"

"That's right."

Kristi didn't want to get into a discussion here in the middle of rush hour at the restaurant, but she didn't have to worry as Dr. Hollister inadvertently came to the rescue. "Oh, I'd like cream with my coffee. No, make it skim milk, is that possible?" She gazed questioningly at Kristi over the tops of the half-glasses perched on her nose.

"Not a problem. I'll be right back with it."

"Miss!" a petulant man's voice called from a table in the next section. "We've been waiting here for ten minutes and would like to order. Can you help us?"

Kristi nodded. "I'll get your server."

"Can't you just take the order?" he asked, checking his watch. He was seated with a grumpy-looking heavy-set woman and two preteen kids who were already beginning to fiddle and slap at each other.

"Stop that!" the woman said sharply.

The older kid ignored her and stuck his tongue out at his sister. She shrieked as if he'd slapped her.

"Oh, for God's sake, Marge, control them, will you?" the man insisted as Kristi flipped the page of her note-pad.

"Sure, I can take your order," Kristi said to stem the tide of pandemonium that was about to erupt amongst this happy little family. "What would you like?"

"Strawberry waffles!" the girl yelled. "With whipped cream."

"It has a different name. It's called—" her mother said.

"That's okay, I've got it." Kristi managed a smile as she hurriedly finished taking the order. In the kitchen Finn was nursing a cola and looking as if he'd just run a marathon. "No time to rest," she warned him, tearing off the page for his table. "Take care of this. Table seven. And you'd better not mess around. The natives are getting restless."

"What's that supposed to mean?"

"Figure it out!" She slapped the order into his hand, tried to ignore his I-didn't-do-nuthin' expression, and grabbed the plate of drinks for her table, even remembering the small pitcher of nonfat milk. After depositing the drinks at Dr. Croft's table, she took their food orders, then stopped by several other tables as well, including a surprise birthday party for an elderly woman with a walker who had trouble understanding the Shakespearean lingo her equally old, but spry, husband found so amusing. Somehow the cook-cum-electrician got the oven working again and with him on the line, orders came up faster and tables could be turned. Even Frick-Finn, after a scolding, pulled his act together.

All the while she worked, Kristi felt as if the professors in the diner were watching her. She passed by their table several times and heard snatches of conversation.

". . . might have to make a few changes . . ." Natalie Croft said as she bit into her beignet and wiped the extra honey from the corner of her mouth.

A few minutes later, she was still speaking. ". . . well, I know, but it was Father Tony's idea. Trying to make the school more interesting and Grotto's a natural. I don't know why Anthony's so insistent that we continue with the courses, but it is popular. . . ." She lowered her voice as Kristi stopped by to refill the coffee cups.

The conversation caught Kristi's interest but she couldn't eavesdrop as her tables, though clustered near each other, were filled with noisy patrons needing service. However as she carried out trays of plated food, refilled glasses and tallied up bills, she noticed that the three professors were deep in discussion, serious and unsmiling. They declined dessert, gave her a reasonable tip, and left as the crowd finally began to thin.

She was about to close out her section when Jay strolled into the restaurant, big as life. He spoke with the hostess and landed one of the small two-person tables in her part of the restaurant.

Kristi propped one fist against her hip. "You're kidding, right?"

"Didn't get much to eat at your place," he said with a wink.

"Neither did I." She'd been so busy she hadn't noticed how hungry she was, but now that things had slowed down, her stomach rumbled.

"So what do you suggest?"

"That you wait for me outside and take me somewhere *else* for lunch."

"Better yet, we'll order from the to-go menu and take it back to your place. There's something I want to show you."

"Give me fifteen minutes to close out the section," she said as he scraped back his chair, catching the evil eye from the hostess who had seated him specifically where he'd requested.

Kristi finished up in no time, untied her apron, tossed it into the laundry hamper, and waved good-bye to Ezma, who was pulling a double shift. A few minutes later, getting soaked by the rain, she steered her bike to Jay's pickup, tossed it into the back, and pushed Bruno out of the way as she climbed inside. The cab was already filled with the spicy scent of tomatoes, garlic, and seafood. "Don't tell me, the hostess suggested the jambalaya."

"Sounded good." Jay backed out of his parking space while Bruno shifted on her lap and they headed to her apartment.

*Just like a married couple,* she thought idly while the windshield wipers battled the rain. *The husband comes and picks up his wife after work.*

"I was late for my shift today," she said as the radio played some country song, "because I stopped by Wagner House." She gave him a quick, abbreviated version of what had happened and Jay listened quietly as he drove the short distance to Kristi's place. When she'd finished, ending with Father Mathias's warning, his expression was sober. "Maybe it's time we went to the police."

"With what? Some kind of warning about me not trespassing? I don't think either Georgia Clovis—oh, excuse me, Georgia *Wagner* Clovis—and Father Mathias Glanzer are any big threats."

"I've met Georgia," he said. "I wouldn't underestimate her."

"You met her?"

"At one of the faculty/administration meet and greets. She was there, along with her sister and brother." He glanced at Kristi. "As far as I could tell, there's no love lost between the Wagner heirs. They avoided each other all night. Georgia seems like the alpha dog of the group."

"Is that your way of calling her a bitch?"

One side of his mouth twitched. "The rest of the clan wasn't all that much better. Her brother, Calvin, looked uncomfortable as hell, as if he were at the get-together under duress, and the younger sister, Napoli, kept to herself, but I had the distinct feeling she didn't miss much. An odd group. All hung up on being 'Wagners' like the name held the same weight as Rockefeller or Kennedy."

"Like them, did you?" she teased.

"They were a laugh riot."

She grinned and scratched Bruno behind his ears. "So what are your plans for the rest of the day?"

"I have to work this afternoon. Grade some papers."

She groaned, knowing hers would be among them. "Give me an A plus, would ya? I could use one."

"I told you I'm grading you the hardest."

"Hmmm. What can I do . . . to change your mind?"

His lips curved and he pretended to think hard for a minute. "I'll take sex."

"Sex for an A plus?"

"No. I'll just take sex."

Kristi made a strangled sound. "I'm not that easy, Professor McKnight. You might want to call Mai Kwan. She was all about you this morning. I think she's got a crush."

"A 'crush,'" he repeated thoughtfully. "How about you . . . Student Bentz?"

"Nah."

"You're a bad liar. You've got a major crush on me."

"A complete fabrication."

He grinned like a dope and she had to look away, her heart tripping over itself with stupid joy. All too fast she knew she was falling in love with Jay, something she'd sworn to herself she would never do. And damn it, he knew it. She saw it in the smug smile that settled over his sexy, in-serious-need-of-a-shave jaw. Damn him to hell and back.

Adjusting the wipers to a quicker pace, he said, "So, I thought I'd work from your place."

Kristi smiled faintly. The thought of being cooped up with him for the rest of the afternoon with rain beating on the eaves, maybe a fire in the grate, sounded like heaven. She needed a break, needed to quit thinking about missing girls and vampires and vials of blood. "Sounds good."

"Yeah, I think I'll look very studious, very professor-ish on camera."

"On camera?"

"Yeah, film," he said enigmatically, obviously enjoying her consternation as he turned a corner and the apartment house came into view.

"You want me to, what? Take a movie of you? I don't have a video camera and even if I did, I really don't have time—"

"Not you."

"What're you talking about?"

The truck bumped its way into the parking lot and Jay pulled into an open space by her car, then cut the engine. "You'll see," he said, and suddenly there wasn't a trace of laughter in his eyes. "Come on up."

"I'm getting a bad feeling about this."

"You should. But whatever you do, just act natural

when we're inside, don't ask any questions." He handed her the sack of food as she opened her door and Bruno hopped to the ground. "Take this. I'll get the bike."

"What's going on?"

"Nothin' good."

He was right behind her as they climbed the stairs and she unlocked the door to her unit. Inside, everything appeared just the way she'd left it. He parked her bike near the door as she dropped the bag and her backpack onto the coffee table. "Are you going to tell me why the hell you've been acting so weird?"

"I just couldn't wait to get you home," he said, pulling her close. In her ear, he whispered, "Play along." Then said in a normal voice, "Didn't I loan you a textbook, you know, the one on DNA analysis?"

"What book?" she asked, but he was already looking at the bookcase near the fireplace.

"The one you promised you'd bring back, oh . . . I think I see it." He smiled and slapped her playfully on the butt, then headed to the other side of the room.

Wondering what the hell he was up to, Kristi did as he asked, opening the bags, removing the cartons, and locating spoons and napkins. From the corner of her eye, she watched Jay walk to the very corner of the room, hoist himself onto the bottom half of the bookcase and prop some of her books up against the fireplace.

"Here we go," he said while she scooped the jambalaya onto their plates. He shoved several books closer to the fireplace, then wiggled a brick loose from its place to expose what appeared to be a black box, the size of a cell phone or pager.

She started to say something but caught him shaking his head. What the hell had he found?

Tara's cell phone?

Then why all the secrecy?

A pager?

Pocket recorder?

Her blood froze in her veins. Had someone been recording her conversations? She thought back to all the conversations she'd had, one-sided on the phone, or . . . Oh, no, last night with Jay . . . !

"I guess you don't have it," he said, replacing the brick and hopping to the floor. "I'll get it later. Let's eat. . . . Hey, how about some music? You have a radio?"

"My iPod player."

"Good." He found the player, clipped in the iPod, and turned the volume up loud enough to cover any of their conversation. Stomach in knots, shock giving way to anger, she sat on the edge of the daybed, and he pulled the big chair up to the opposite side of the coffee table, his back to the fireplace.

"You've been bugged," he said, hunched over the spicy seafood and rice dish, his voice barely audible over the music. "That little black box is a camera."

She nearly dropped her fork. Someone had been *watching* her, was trying to see her even now? As she studied, or watched television or slept or . . . Jesus, Mary, and Joseph, she looked up at Jay and wanted to fall through the floor.

"State of the art," he said.

She wanted to die a thousand deaths as she thought that all last night, while she and Jay were making love, someone might have been watching. Recording their every touch or kiss. Getting off while they were in the middle of what she'd thought was a private, intimate night.

She thought she might be sick.

Jay nodded as if he could read her thoughts. "Even though we didn't know about it, you and I just made our first sex tape. How's that for dirty pool?"

# CHAPTER 21

Oh. My. God.

Kristi couldn't believe her ears. Someone was actually using a hidden video to tape her? The contents of her stomach curdled. "This is insane!" she sputtered, keeping her voice low just in case Jay wasn't pulling her leg.

"Laugh like I just said something funny," he instructed, tucking in a forkful of jambalaya.

While her home was being bugged, she was supposed to act as if she were amused? But Jay, she could see, was serious. She managed a weak, stupid laugh, but her heart wasn't in it. Kristi had seen a lot in her twenty-seven years. Her father was a homicide detective and all her life she'd been exposed to his cases. Some more than others. Then there was the fact that her life had been threatened more than once and she'd almost died recently, but never had she felt so coldly violated, so maliciously *used* as at this moment in time.

"Someone's been watching me?" she whispered, anger burning through her.

"Uh-huh, and, unless I miss my guess, they might have done the same to Tara Atwater as well."

She wanted to kill the bastard behind the camera. For the love of God, what had he seen? Pictures of the last few days flipped through her brain: She saw herself walking naked from the bathroom to the bedroom, or exercising, dancing like a ninny when a great song came on her iPod, studying at her desk. Then, of course, last night when she was lost in the throes of passion, moaning, crying out, begging for more while she and Jay lay entwined and sweating on the bed. To think some twisted voyeur watched as they made love! Her skin crawled, then flushed hot with embarrassment. "Who?" she demanded.

"That's what I intend to find out," he said, and she had to strain to hear him over the music. "It's a remote camera. I don't know how much range it has, but the receiver could be anywhere. I made sure I put a book over the lens, so I'm banking that whoever it is will try to get back in here and move things so that his view isn't compromised. I checked around and I think that there's only one camera."

"What?" She withered inside. "You thought there could be more?"

"Of course there could, but they're not cheap. Someone would have to be pretty intent on spying. I thought maybe the bathroom, but it looks clean."

"This is outrageous." She wanted to leave. Pick up everything that belonged to her and get the hell out.

"I couldn't chance taking out the batteries without jostling the camera and letting whoever it is who's watching us know we're on to him."

"So what're we going to do?"

"Wait," he said, and that only infuriated her. She wanted action. Now. To get back at the spying bastard and quick. "Two can play at this game." He was scooping up his jambalaya so calmly she wanted to scream. His plate was almost empty.

"I'm not great at waiting or pretending."

"I know. But all you have to do is just act natural."

"Oh, right." Like that would happen.

"Or we could go to the police." His voice was still

hushed while the music played loudly and he'd stopped eating long enough to stare at her and evaluate her reaction. "It wouldn't be a bad idea to let the pros handle this now, and don't—" he said, cutting her off before she began, "suggest that I am a pro. We both know that I'm bending the rules as it is. The smart thing to do would be to call the police, and have them dust for prints as we hand them the vial of blood. Yeah, they might seal this place off and confiscate all of your stuff, but you've backed up the computer."

"You said something about waiting. And 'two playing at this game.' What's that mean?"

He grinned and she felt a little better. The gleam in his eye told her he'd considered the options. "Let's step outside." Loudly, he said, "Okay, Bruno, I get it, you need to do your business. Come on." He whistled sharply and headed for the door with the dog and Kristi on his heels. Stepping onto the porch, he looked up to the rafters of the overhang. Following his gaze with her own, she squinted and saw what he meant. Tucked between the spider webs and old wasp's nests, mounted over the door just above the porch light, was a tiny black box much like the one that was mounted in the bookcase near the fireplace.

"I decided that if he comes back, we'll get his mug on video."

"That's your camera? Where do you view it?"

"My place, actually Aunt Colleen's. We'll go there and wait tonight. So you might want to bring your computer and sleeping bag. Deluxe accommodations, it's not."

"As long as we nail the bastard."

"And just in case we don't get a clear picture, I've got another camera mounted over the window in the kitchen, looking straight at the fireplace. When he turns to leave, we'll get him."

"You've been busy," she said admiringly.

"Thanks."

"He has to be someone who has access . . . probably Hiram?" She thought of Irene Calloway's big grandson. He really didn't seem to have the brainpower to pull off something like this. And Irene? Would she really spy on her tenants?

"He's at the top of my list, but I'm going to do some checking. I got the name and model number of the camera. Like I said, state of the art, so I'm going to find out who bought one in the last eighteen months or so."

"By using your connections with the police?"

"See, you are a bright girl," he teased, obviously not concerned that their little lovemaking session might turn up on YouTube or MySpace or God-only-knew what video-sharing site on the Internet. Someone who recognized her could even send it to her father's e-mail account.

She winced at the thought.

"Relax," Jay said, as if reading her thoughts. "The lights were out last night. I don't think it's an infrared camera."

"Oh, God." She hadn't thought of *that*. Nor did she want to consider that whoever this techno-geek might be, he could be sophisticated enough to enhance the video imagery.

Things were rapidly going from bad to worse.

Jay reached for the door. "So, let's both go inside and let him know that you won't be around tonight, give him plenty of opportunity."

They reentered and Kristi glanced toward the camera, still blocked by her books. They both made a big fuss about the dog and returned to their spots. Jay turned off the music and they talked about everything and nothing, then made plans to go to "his place" without giving out any specifics. She packed her things, including her computer, sleeping bag, the necklace with the vial they found, the bike, and a change of clothes.

Since she intended to attend Father Mathias's morality play and Jay had a dinner meeting with the head of his department, they took separate cars through the rain to the address Jay had written on a business card and slipped to her, thus avoiding anyone overhearing where they would be staying. It was also important that she take her car so that her own personal voyeur would realize the Honda wasn't parked in its usual spot, and he would feel safer and hopefully take the opportunity to break inside and reposition his equipment.

The thought of him skulking around her place, maybe searching through her drawers and touching her underwear, made her shiver. Who was the guy?

She thought about the sicko who got off watching her, as she followed Jay's truck through the rain-washed streets. Had the pervert watched Tara? Had he learned her routine and plotted her abduction, all with the help of his little camera? Did he have tapes of the other missing girls? Did he keep those tapes for his personal use, his twisted enjoyment, or, worse yet, had he made them public, placed them on the Internet?

If he was into this depraved videotaping, could it be even worse? Could he have films of the girls' abductions? Their abuse? Even their murders?

Dear God, she hoped not. Her fingers tightened over the steering wheel as she attempted to rein in her imagination. "Don't borrow trouble," she warned herself.

And besides, she had no basis for these runaway thoughts. If the missing girls had shown up on the Internet, wouldn't someone at the college have seen them by now? Recognized them? Surely the police and campus security had searched the World Wide Web.

Taillights flashed ahead.

Jay's truck stopped at the light.

Lost in her reverie, Kristi had to slam on her brakes. Her Honda skidded, tires squealing. Antilock brakes grabbed, released, grabbed again. She braced herself, ready for the impact and shriek of twisting metal.

Her hatchback's nose stopped less than an inch from the Toyota's bumper.

"Oh, God." She let out her breath, then gasped at the screech of tires behind her. Glancing fearfully in the rearview mirror, she helplessly watched a big van shimmy and slide, narrowly avoiding smashing into her.

Kristi exhaled slowly, her heart pounding. Jay, his silhouette visible to her, looked up. She lifted her hands, palms upward, to acknowledge that she'd been an idiot. She hoped the guy in the van who had barely missed hitting her witnessed her silent apology as well.

"Concentrate," she told herself as rain pummeled the windshield and the wipers struggled to keep up. She had to pay better attention. The roads were slick with rain, the clouds dark and close, the day gloomy and winter-dark.

The stoplight switched to green. Jay eased into the intersection and Kristi followed carefully. She tried her best to keep her mind on the surrounding traffic and road ahead, but the truth of the matter was that her thoughts were elsewhere. Someone had broken into and wired her apartment. Watched her. Videotaped her. Her skin crawled as she imagined him getting off on watching her undress, or sleep or shower or make love to Jay.

"Bastard," she muttered as she drove through the city, her wipers struggling with the rain. "You'll get yours," she added, following Jay onto a side street. The car behind her, only visible as headlights through the rain, made the turn as well.

It was the same dark van that had nearly slammed into her.

Right?

Another turn.

The vehicle lagged behind.

But eventually the headlights swung in behind her.

As if he were tailing her.

Which was ludicrous. Her imagination really was running wild.

Nonetheless, Kristi's heart clutched. Every nerve in her body tightened. She told herself to let it go, but she couldn't drag her gaze from the rearview mirror.

Was the guy in the van—if it was still the van, she wasn't completely sure—was he the same person who had run the surveillance operation on her apartment?

Jay turned onto a final lane, a cul-de-sac, the street sign nearly shouting out the address that he'd written on the back of his business card, the one lying on the passenger seat.

She shot by. Barely braking.

The vehicle behind her stayed with her, didn't peel off to follow Jay. "Who the hell are you?" she thought, and made certain all her doors were locked. She angled through the side streets of the neighborhood until she recognized one as being a major arterial. Turning left onto the two-way street, she checked her rearview mirror.

Sure enough, the big rig followed.

But it was more cautious now, blending into the increasing traffic. Her phone began to ring, but she ignored it. She had to concentrate. A half mile later, making certain the dark van was boxed between a Taurus and a Jeep, Kristi saw the light ahead turn amber.

Perfect.

Heart thudding, fingers clenched around the steering wheel in a death grip, she trod on the accelerator, reaching the intersection just as the light changed. It turned a blazing red just as she sped through.

The rest of the traffic stopped.

"You son of a bitch! Just keep coming!" she yelled jubilantly. Her cell phone started ringing again but she couldn't get it. She had to concentrate, keep moving.

She blew past the first side street, and turned a quick corner at the second one, just as she noticed the stoplight, where the van was held up, changing again.

Damn!

He might try to cut her off. She took another right, spied a church parking lot and slid inside, killing her running lights and cutting a three-sixty in the empty lot, so that she was faced out, her foot off the brake, the car idling and partially blocked from view by an overgrown laurel hedge.

Sure enough, the van sped past, the driver, a dark blur.

Turning on her lights, she edged into the street. She saw the van turn the corner she'd taken less than three minutes earlier. "Bastard." If she could get close enough to spy the numbers on his license plate, then she could have her father or Jay check with the DMV and nail the jerk.

For the first time since she'd started this investigation she felt as if she might be getting somewhere. She reached the corner and turned the wheel sharply, throwing up a sheet of water as her tires hit a puddle. The van was two blocks up and moving slowly, brake lights intermittently glowing red as he searched for her.

She stepped on the gas, her heartbeat thudding. What if he stopped? He would recognize her car. "Too bad." She speed-dialed Jay as she closed the distance.

"What happened to you?" he demanded.

"Someone was following us . . . or me."

"Jesus, Kris, where the hell are you? Are you okay?" She heard an edge of panic in his voice. "I'm coming—"

"No, I gave him the slip and now I'm following him."

"I'm calling nine-one-one."

"Just hang on the line."

"I'm on my way. Where the hell are you?"

"Don't know . . . somewhere off the ten . . . not far from University Lake."

"That far south? Holy shit!" She heard keys rattling and he was breathless as if he were running. Then a door slammed. "Tell me the next cross street."

"Hang on! Oh, no . . . He's heading for the freeway."

"Let it go."

"Can't do it." She tossed the phone onto the seat and hit the accelerator as a sports car, roaring around a corner, cut in front of her. "Idiot!" she screamed, hitting the brakes and feeling the car shimmy beneath her. "You son of a bitch!"

The driver, oblivious, cut around another car and Kristi gunned her Honda onto the ramp for the freeway, but she knew before she merged that the chase was over.

The bastard had disappeared.

She picked up the phone. "You still there?" she asked, already searching for the next exit.

"What the hell happened?"

"Nothing, he lost me. I'm on my way back."

"For the love of God, Kris. Don't—"

"I said I'm on my way back. I'll be at your aunt's house in twenty minutes."

"You scared the bloody hell out of me," he admitted, and she heard it in his voice, how worried he'd been. Which made her feel warm inside. She knew she was falling in love with him. Oh, hell, maybe a tiny part of her had never stopped loving him, but she hadn't been convinced that the feeling was mutual. Until now. "You know, Kris, this is starting to get dangerous. Maybe we should rethink going to the police."

She imagined her father's reaction, the fight that would ensue. She eased onto the exit ramp. "How about we wait until we see who thinks he's the next Spielberg," she said. "Once we catch him on tape, we'll have something more concrete."

"And then?"

"And then we'll discuss it. Come on, Jay," she cajoled, as she headed north on River Road, past the old state Capitol building, a Gothic castle-shaped edifice that loomed on a bluff above the slowly moving Mississippi River. "You promised me a week."

"My mistake."

"The first of many," she teased, feeling better. "I'll see ya in a few." She hung up before he could argue, or before she let it slip that she was going to set her own little trap. Tonight.

At Father Mathias's morality play.

She only hoped her plan would work.

"So far, we've got ourselves a big potful o' nothing!" Ray Crawley snorted in disgust and cast an "I-told-you-so" look at Portia Laurent.

A detective for the Baton Rouge Police Department, Crawley was a big, bulky bear of a man who stood six-four and fought the beginnings of a beer gut. He had huge hands and a nasty disposition when he was angry, and now, standing in the rain, he was well past angry and doing sixty toward infuriated. Shoulders hunched, he smoked a cigarette and stared at the swamp where boats with divers and bright lights were searching the water through a relentless downpour.

It was getting dark, the gloom of the day seeping into Portia's skin, the shadows in the boggy wetlands growing longer as she stood clustered with Del Vernon and Crawley, who called himself "Sonny," and a hunter by the name of Boomer Moss.

Wearing the raincoat and boots she always kept in her car, Portia huddled under an umbrella. Her boots sinking in the mud, she thought she would just about kill for a cigarette, but decided against bumming one from Crawley, who was just looking for an excuse to round on someone.

"You sure this is where you caught the gator?" Sonny asked with obvious skepticism, rain sliding off the bill of his police department cap. The area had been searched by boat, on foot, and when possible, by divers. With no luck.

But Moss, the poacher, was adamant this was the area in which he'd bagged the bull alligator. That prime gator that the cops had confiscated and trucked off to their crime lab.

"Right through them there trees," Boomer Moss insisted, pointing toward a stand of ghostly white cypress, their roots twisting and visible above ground and the black water.

"We looked there." Crawley drew hard on his cigarette.

"I'm tellin' ya, that's where I got him." Moss's voice elevated an octave in agitation. Dressed head-to-toe in camouflage, he jabbed a finger at the nearest cypress. Even in the gathering darkness, with the cold winter air sitting heavy in the swamp, Portia saw that Boomer was sweating, drips drizzling from beneath his hunting cap and down a cheek stretched over a wad of tobacco. Obviously, he didn't like dealing with the police.

But then, nobody did.

Portia watched a boat slide noiselessly over the water as a diver, shaking his head, surfaced. It had been that way for hours.

"I just hope to hell you're not bullshitting me," Crawley said as he stubbed out his cigarette and it hissed against the wet weeds.

"Why would I even bother to come in?" Moss asked.

"You knew you'd be in trouble. So maybe you were

just showing off. Proud of the arm . . . maybe you're involved."

"Well, if I was, I'd have to be a real dumb-ass, now
wouldn't I? I came to you guys cuz I thought it was the
right thing to do. My civic duty, or whatever ya want to
call it. The arm was in that gator's gut, and I figured you
all would want it. But I don't know where it came from
before it ended up in that gator's stomach."

He was mad now and he spat a stream of tobacco
juice to the ground. "I done what I had to. Can I go now?"

"Not just yet," Crawley said, obviously enjoying the
poacher's discomfiture. That was the trouble with
Sonny Crawley, Portia thought, he had a mean streak.
But it looked like the hunt would be fruitless, at least
for today.

Whatever secrets were hidden deep in this swamp
would remain submerged, concealed beneath the murky
water for at least another night.

# CHAPTER 22

Hours later, Kristi drove back to campus.
She didn't like lying.

As a teenager lies had slipped over her tongue easily,
but now, ten years later, she had more trouble hiding the
truth.

She'd had to lie to Jay.

She'd gotten to his house and explained about the
van and he'd wrapped his arms around her and held her
as if he never wanted to let her go. "You stupid, stupid
girl," he said into her hair.

"I'm not taking that as a compliment," she responded.

"It wasn't meant to be one. Who knows who that guy
was? What he's capable of? Oh, for the love of God. . . ."
He'd kissed her hard then, his lips hungry, eager, his
hair wet from the rain. She'd wound her arms around
his neck and returned the ardor of his kiss. "Jesus, you
scared me," he said. "I was afraid—"

"Shh." She hadn't wanted to hear his fears. Had only
wanted to be reassured by his strength.

He hadn't disappointed. With his hands firmly splayed
over her back, his legs had pressed against hers, and
silently, still kissing her, he began walking forward, strong
thighs pushing against hers and forcing her backward.
They'd tugged at each other's clothes, yanking them off,

breathing hard, as he guided her through an open doorway and into a bedroom painted a hideous color of blue.
Her calves encountered something hard and Jay pulled
her down so that they tumbled together onto a small cot
with a sleeping bag and single pillow.

She hadn't cared.

She'd only wanted to lose herself in him.

Their lovemaking had been fast and anxious, lips
touching and tasting hungrily, fingers skimming hot,
fevered skin, desire fueled by anxiety.

Release had come quickly.

They'd collapsed together, spent, sweating, their heart-
beats pounding in tandem on the skinny little cot.

Kristi had hated that she needed to lie. Had put it off
and put it off, not wanting the afternoon with Jay to end.

"This is ridiculous," she said, pushing her hair out of
her face and staring into his slumberous amber eyes.

He laughed. "And I was going to say it was magical . . .
wondrous . . . incredible . . . and—"

"And you're full of it, McKnight." Then she kissed
him and rolled off the cot to pull on her clothes.

He'd been pretty damned adamant about going to the
police again, and she'd had to talk fast and hard to convince him to wait. She hadn't been completely truthful,
at least as far as her plans were concerned. She hadn't
been able to be.

She'd waited until he was distracted with grading papers and watching the computer screens that showed
the porch and interior of her apartment, compliments of
his surveillance cameras. She pretended to be absorbed
as well, double-checking the chat rooms, though it was
far too early for any of her newfound Internet "friends"
to appear. Then while Jay was in his study, she retrieved
the chain with the vial of what she presumed was Tara
Atwater's blood. Tonight, at the play, she planned to wear
the weird necklace. See what kind of reactions she got.

Jay had already tried to lift a latent fingerprint from the tiny vial, but the glass had been clean, so Kristi wasn't disturbing any evidence—as long as the vial filled with the dark red liquid was intact.

It was slightly horrific, but so what?

So was the camera in her apartment.

So was being followed by a dark van.

If she wanted to break into the inner circle of this cult, she'd better work fast.

The vial of blood had been a godsend.

*Or the work of the devil.*

So she'd escaped without Jay noticing she'd taken the vial and here she was, driving toward campus, checking her rearview mirror for looming dark vans. Had it been navy blue? Black? Charcoal gray? She didn't know. She hadn't gotten a clear view of the plates, but had thought they weren't from out of state. The windows had seemed tinted but she didn't know the make. Maybe a Ford. Or a Chevy. Something domestic.

So much for her incredible powers of observation.

The defroster in her Honda had decided to malfunction and was giving her fits. She had to keep the window down in order to see through her windshield to the wet, shiny streets. It was already dark with clouds completely blocking the rapidly setting sun, rain drizzling from the sky, and night coming fast.

Thankfully, traffic was thin and sparse on a Sunday evening and there was a chill in the air that reminded her that it was the dead of winter.

Jay had left for his meeting as Kristi headed to Father Mathias's morality play, yet another rendition of *Everyman*, though Jay had made a last protest.

"I don't like you going to the play alone," he'd said seriously as she was getting ready to leave. "I can cancel with Hollister. She just wants to discuss how the class is coming along, I think. Compare it to how Dr. Monroe handled it. But it's not a big deal, I can reschedule."

"I don't think it would be good if we're seen together."

"Someone already has," he remarked. "And took a video."

"Don't remind me." She'd grimaced. "Besides, Hollister is head of your department."

"I don't have to see her today. Besides, I've talked with Dr. Monroe a couple of times since I took over and I've got her notes to work with. I'm pretty much sticking to her curriculum. If she comes back next term, she'll be good to go."

"Is she returning?" Kristi asked.

"Don't know. Depends on the relocation of her mother. She's having trouble finding the right place for her."

"So you don't have any idea if you're going to be teaching next term?"

"Not yet. Though maybe you could convince me to take the job if it's offered."

He waggled his brows lasciviously and she laughed as she headed out.

It was dark now, her headlights catching all the raindrops falling in silver streaks to the pavement. She was halfway to All Saints when her cell phone rang. She expected it to be Jay, once again warning her to be careful.

"Hello?" she said, turning into the parking lot of her apartment building.

"Kristi Bentz?" a deep voice asked as she pulled into a spot a few over from hers because some jerk had taken hers with his jacked-up pickup and oversized tires. Before she could respond, he said, "This is Dr. Grotto. First, I want to apologize for not getting back to you sooner. I did get your message." His voice was so smooth, the same tenor as when he taught, and in her mind's eye she saw him, the tall man with black hair and dark eyes, his strong jaw dark with beard shadow. She forgot being angry that she had to park a few steps further from the stairs. "You mentioned you'd like a meeting and now my schedule has cleared a bit. So how about tomorrow afternoon? Say . . . four? I have some time then."

Kristi did some quick mental calculations. She was scheduled to work the dinner shift, but she figured she could find someone to cover an extra hour for her. She wasn't going to blow this. "Sure," she said lightly, as if she had nothing more to ask him about than a particularly tough assignment. She thought about the dark van and wondered if Grotto might have been the driver. "I'll be at your office at four."

"I'll see you then."

He clicked off as Kristi cut the Honda's engine. She couldn't wait to talk face-to-face with Grotto; after all he was the last person thought to have seen Dionne Harmon alive.

After double-checking the parking lot to make certain no one was lurking between the cars or behind the hedge of crepe myrtle, she nervously headed into her unit. As far as she could tell everything was just as they'd left it. She didn't think anyone had been inside.

She felt the urge to stick her tongue out at Jay's camera, or do a little strip tease for him as a joke, but refrained. Just in case there was another camera they hadn't found. All she managed was a wink at the camera over the sink.

Houdini came out from his hiding spot under the bed. "I wondered when you'd show your face again," she said. "Did that big dog scare you? Trust me, Bruno wouldn't hurt a flea." She slid a hand over the cat's back and he quivered and tried to slink away from her touch. He wasn't as quick to disappear, however, so she poured cat food into his bowl and watched with some amusement as he sniffed disdainfully at it. "Hey, don't forget your roots," she said to him. "Beggars can't be choosers."

The cat stared at her as if she were a complete moron before hopping onto the counter and slipping through the open window. "No good deed goes unpunished," she called after him, then, in the bathroom, did a quick change into black pants and turtleneck. She threw on a jacket and grabbed her purse, complete with her cell phone and canister of mace, and was out the door.

The weather had let up a bit, though her defroster was still making visibility difficult. She had to use her hand to clear a spot in the windshield, but she saw no dark, malicious van idling in the alleys. Still, she was on alert as she took her car the short distance to campus, another means to make it appear that she wasn't home tonight, though "inviting" the pervert into her home bothered her a little.

What little daylight there was quickly faded as Kristi parked behind Wagner House. The museum was set to close in ten minutes, but she wanted to check the place one more time.

The gate was unlocked and the front door swung open without a creak. Kristi stepped inside, where a gas fire was burning cheerily. Lights, with their colored Tiffany-style shades, glowed like jewels. Victorian settees, carved mahogany tables and club chairs were clustered in groupings, the dining table set with crystal and silver, as if a dinner party were planned for later in the evening.

Three fiftyish women were oohing and aahing over the furniture and knickknacks while a younger couple with a baby who was strapped to the father in some kind of sling were strolling through the lower rooms.

"Hello." A slim woman, with an easy smile and streaked hair that swung to her chin, greeted Kristi. She was wearing a long skirt, boots, and a cowl-necked sweater. Her name tag read: Marilyn Katcher. "I'm Marilyn, the docent, and I was about to give a little tour of the house before we close. Would you like to join the others?"

Kristi looked around at all the expectant faces. "That would be great."

After that, she followed along and listened as the docent, with more enthusiasm than Kristi would have believed possible, walked the small group through the lower floors, explaining the history of the family, making a big deal of old Ludwig Wagner and his heirs, telling how he'd donated this portion of his vast holdings around the Baton Rouge area to the church for the express purpose of starting a college. She led the way upward to the bedrooms, explaining about the children who had resided within and how the current Ludwig descendants had spent much of their own fortunes restoring the house to the way it had been when Ludwig and his children, including his wheelchair-bound daughter, had lived here. Some of the pieces were authentic, others used to add to the feel of the home, not all necessarily period-true.

Once they were downstairs again Mrs. Katcher checked her watch and attempted to usher everyone out. But Kristi hung back and asked about the basement.

"It was used by the staff, originally, of course, and I think it had some connecting tunnel or other way to access the carriage house, which is right next door and now houses the drama department. There was also egress to the stables and barns, but all of those passageways were deemed unsafe years ago, condemned by the parish, so they've been sealed. Today the basement is used for storage." She held open the front door. "To be honest, I've never set foot downstairs. I don't think anyone ever goes down there."

*Father Mathias does,* Kristi thought. The priest and Georgia Clovis already knew Kristi had seen him appear through the basement door, and the fact that there were tunnels, condemned or not, beneath the building intrigued her. What if they still existed? What if Marnie Gage had gone downstairs and used them? But why?

Marilyn Katcher was nothing if not on a schedule. She managed to herd everyone outside and lock the gate behind them at five-thirty on the dot.

The wind had kicked up as they headed into the dark that had descended while they were inside. A shimmer of rain flashed by Kristi, and vapor lights glowed an eerie blue as she made her way to the student union. In the cafeteria-style restaurant she looked for some of the familiar faces in her English block of classes, but she didn't see Trudie, Grace, Zena, or Ariel. She remembered then that Zena had said something about being cast in Father Mathias's morality play.

Maybe she'd see the girl on stage.

She drank a decaf cappuccino and tried to call Lucretia again. After all, her ex-roommate was the one who'd originally mentioned the "cult" before her abrupt turnabout. But, as with everyone these days, it seemed her call was sent directly to voice mail.

Kristi didn't leave a message. Lucretia was avoiding her.

Powering down her phone, Kristi headed toward the auditorium. If she got there a little early, maybe she could poke around a bit. All of the missing girls had attended Father Mathias's morality plays, so there had to be a connection between them and the vampire cult, right?

It was as good a place to find answers as anywhere else.

Deep in her underground spa, standing naked in front of a tall mirror, Elizabeth surveyed herself carefully.

She was irritated.

Antsy.

Obviously in need of more.

*More what?* her mind taunted, for she disdained saying that she needed blood, the blood of others.

It made her feel weak, or like an addict, and that wasn't the case at all. She was strong. Powerful. Vital. But, truth to tell, she did crave more. . . .

She wanted to feel that rush of rejuvenation again. But it was not to be, for the mirror highlighted every flaw, even the faintest. Located in the same area as her bath, it was lit by a few soft lights on a dimmer switch, which she could ramp up should she need to examine any imperfection in her skin.

On a purely intellectual level, she couldn't believe that blood of younger women would actually retard aging or revitalize her skin, but then again, hadn't she noticed the changes to her own body?

With a critical eye, she surveyed herself in the mirror, searching for the telltale signs of age: wrinkles around her lips; crinkling at the corners of her eyes; the beginning of a crease at the base of her neck; the sagging of her abdomen despite a regimen of crunches, sit-ups, weight lifting, and cardio workouts. There was a thin line between being fit and slim and just plain skinny. But none of her bones showed where they shouldn't. Her musculature was perfect and her skin still creamy and taut, her nipples tight and dark. No strands of gray dared shoot through her lustrous black hair.

Yet.

But age, she knew, was a relentless enemy and though she'd used all kinds of creams along with her private regimen, she hadn't gone so far as to seriously consider liposuction or dermabrasion or a laser peel.

For the moment, she'd refrained from doing anything so radical.

She hadn't needed to.

Because her remedy was working. Now, studying her flawless, age-spot-free skin minutely, she found it near perfect. Youthful. Vanity caused her to smile. She hadn't been born beautiful; in fact, she remembered her mother saying she'd been an "ugly" baby, her head misshapen, her eyes too large, her hair patchy, her body frail. But she'd blossomed from an awkward tot and gawky girl into a teenager who had made boys and men twist their stupid necks as she'd strolled by.

It was that feeling, that rush from the power of her beauty, that she refused to relinquish. And so she'd done her research and realized despite her genes, and the help of products, age would try to destroy her. Her eyes would sag and grow puffy and dark, her skin would lose its elasticity, her breasts would droop, and flabby little pockets would try to appear.

Except she had a way to fight back.

Her secret method, she thought, twisting in the mirror and looking over her shoulder at her reflection. Her buttocks were still tight and firm, her waist small. And, from the pictures she'd seen, she looked amazingly like her stunning namesake. Actually, she decided with a tilt of her head, she was even more beautiful.

She'd known about her ancestor, Elizabeth of Bathory, for as long as she could remember and had been fascinated with the countess, but only recently, when she'd realized that her age was beginning to show, had she assumed Elizabeth's name and regimen.

The story was, loosely, that Elizabeth, obviously a bit of a nutcase, had worried about losing her legendary beauty. Also, the countess enjoyed torturing and tormenting others, and one day, slapped a servant so hard that the maiden's blood spilled onto her arm. Elizabeth had been even more outraged and raving until she noticed that the area of her skin the blood had stained appeared more youthful and beautiful than the surrounding flesh. From that day forward, Elizabeth found ways of ever more increasing cruelty to drain the blood of others for her own personal use.

Now, obviously, the woman had been deranged. Mental case with a capital M. Sadist to the nth degree.

All that royal inbreeding.

No wonder.

Of course many of the stories or legends about the "blood countess" hadn't been proven, including the bathing in blood. That she had committed atrocities on dozens of young girls was not in dispute, however, and she was eventually tried and convicted of murder and sent to live walled into her castle. Those who had assisted her weren't so lucky.

But it was the legend, the folklore surrounding the baths drawn from the blood of peasant girls and her eventual nobility that intrigued this new Elizabeth.

Even if the legends had been embellished with the passing of decades, and despite the fact that some of the more bizarre cruelties ascribed to Elizabeth had no foundation in historical fact, the theory about the blood of younger women wasn't just intriguing, it seemed to have merit.

Hadn't she, herself, proven its validity?

Now, staring into the mirror, Elizabeth arched her neck, surveying every inch of her body as she slowly rotated in the light.

Hadn't the first traces of cottage-cheese-like bumps beneath the skin of her thighs, the barest breath of cellulite, disappeared with her first blood-infused baths? And that little suggestion of spider web veins, near the back of her right knee? Hadn't they faded after the first bath?

Of course they had. Now, the back of her knee was silken and smooth, not even the tiniest line of her veins visible.

She was so convinced of the rejuvenation of her skin, the restorative powers of the blood, she'd almost agreed to dip into a pool injected with some of the blood of Vlad's lessers.

But no!

She watched her reflection visibly cringe at the

thought. It was one thing to cover her body in the blood of smart, young girls. Elizabeth didn't kid herself into thinking they were "virgins" or "pure" or any of that rot, but at least they hadn't pole danced for ogling, drooling, fat-assed men. Or, so she told herself. What, actually, did she know of those she'd helped Vlad choose?

Just that they were intelligent, seeking higher education. Something that escaped Vlad.

She grimaced.

Vlad.

Or so he insisted on being called, though, of course she knew his true identity.

He'd given himself the name of Vlad the Impaler, though he had enough names already. But, fine, if he wanted to be Vlad, she'd go along with it. She had taken Elizabeth's name, assumed her identity, so he, too, had felt compelled to become someone else.

Always a follower, was Vlad.

But she needed him, just as the original Countess Elizabeth had required the help of others who had been as sadistic as she.

Twisting her dark hair onto her head, she admired her profile, then adjusted a few curls to fall loosely at her nape, to play into *his* fantasy.

That was the difference between them. She was a practical woman who was only trying to extend her life and her beauty, to keep turning heads and feeling vital. And yes, there was a little sadism involved, but all for a purpose.

Vlad, on the other hand, was into the sensual feel of the killing, the bloodletting, the sex of it all.

Which was fine.

She could get as turned on as anyone, she supposed, frowning a bit as one tendril refused to curl seductively. She caught a glimpse of herself and forced her face muscles to relax. She didn't need to test her own theory and start new lines from forming, marring her perfectly smooth brow. So far, the blood was working, although Vlad had intimated the blood supply was running low.

What kind of a moron allowed that to happen?

He was afraid, that was it. Balking at ramping up the killings of the good ones, always talking of his "lessers." For the love of God, he just didn't get it. But then he couldn't. As intelligent as he was supposed to be, honestly, sometimes Elizabeth wondered. But he was her partner and devoted and she could twist him around her perfect little finger. All he asked was to have sex with the women before and after death. Yes, it was a tad odd, but as long as he pumped the blood from their bodies, so be it. And he adored her. Was faithful in his heart and head, if not his dick.

Who cared?

The only thing she needed to ensure herself was that there would be enough. And so she'd suggested that she accompany him on the next killing. Because he was getting nervous. Jumpy. Concerned that the police would take notice. It was a problem, but the answer was obvious: take more than one. Kill several at once. Then start hunting somewhere else. Somewhere less obvious.

But always hunt for smart, supple, clever women who were young enough to still have vitality. And never a mother, like that last lesser Vlad had tried to palm off on her. Come on! Didn't he know that childbirth robbed a woman of her vitality? That once a mother had given her lifeblood to another, a babe in the womb, and then bled for days or weeks afterward, she was never the same?

Elizabeth finally managed to force the wayward tendril of dark hair into place. Gazing raptly at her own reflection, she decided it was time to tell him. She reached for her cell phone to convey the happy news. Tonight she not only wanted to watch him kill. Tonight she would help and ensure that there would be more than one victim.

Several coeds' images came to mind.

The clearest belonged to Kristi Bentz.

# CHAPTER 23

Jay was just walking out the door for the meeting with Dr. Hollister and wondering how to cut it short when his cell phone chirped.

Sonny Crawley's name appeared on the small screen.

"What's up?" Jay asked, hauling his briefcase and laptop outside, where the rain was beating on the overhang of the porch and dripping over the edge of the sagging gutters.

"I thought you'd like a heads-up about those missing girls."

Every nerve in Jay's body tightened. "You found something?"

"Maybe, maybe not, but I thought you'd like to know."

Bruno slipped through the door and Jay pulled it shut. Together they dashed across the wet yard. "Tell me."

"Well, it all started with a poacher findin' a damned woman's arm in a gator's belly, and we're thinkin' it might belong to one of those missing coeds, but we haven't been able to find the rest of the body."

Sonny recounted the whole story as Jay loaded his things and Bruno into the cab of his truck. He slid behind the wheel without turning on the ignition, staring out the windshield as he learned the poacher had called the Sheriff's Department, which had taken the alligator with its stomach contents to the morgue, that tests were being run on the severed female arm, and the police were trying like hell to get fingerprints from the partially decomposed and consumed limb. Search teams were still looking for the body or bodies and the theory was that this arm could have belonged to one of the missing girls. So far, they'd had no luck.

"One of the oddest things about it was that there was no blood in that arm. Not a drop," Sonny confided. "You'd think there would be something. You cut off a finger, ya got blood. You cut off a guy's dick, ya got blood. I'm no doctor, no sir, but I figure there should be some blood in those veins and arteries."

*You and me both,* Jay thought, finally starting the engine of his truck, his mind turning to all the talk of vampires. "So the arm is at the morgue, and the other evidence, like anything under the fingernails, chips of the polish, for instance—that's at the lab?"

"Yeah. You might want to call Laurent. She knows more about this than I do."

"I will, but in the meantime, I need a favor."

"Another one?"

"I'll buy you a beer."

"You bet your ass, you will."

"I'll buy you a six-pack," Jay amended, hearing Sonny's affront.

"Shoot."

"Can you check if anyone who works at All Saints owns a dark-colored van?"

"Anyone at the college?"

"I'll e-mail you a list of names."

"You can't check this out yourself?"

"I need this yesterday. I was hoping you could help me out. And I'll need to see if any of them has a criminal record. A deep probe."

"Might take a while."

"Put a rush on it, we're looking at a half-rack."

He laughed hard, a smoker's laugh that ended in a coughing fit. "For that much beer, I'll do it. Let you know what I find. Probably tomorrow on the DMV records, the other as soon as I get the info."

"Thanks."

"And I want real beer, you hear me? None of that lite shit."

"Real beer," Jay promised.

"Gotta go. Another call comin' in and it is Sunday night. You know, I do have a life." Crawley clicked off and Jay let his mind catalogue this new information.

A chill slid through his soul. A severed arm with no blood. None whatsoever. Had it been drained and digested by the alligator, or had something else happened to it, something unworldly? As a man of science he didn't believe for a second that there were vampires walking this earth, but if Kristi was right, there was a cult nearby with true believers and who knew what they were up to.

Of course, the severed arm might belong to someone other than the girls missing from All Saints.

But he doubted it.

Sliding the truck into gear, he dialed Kristi to give her the news, but her phone went directly to voice mail. "Hey, it's me. Give me a call," he said, then hung up, a feeling of restlessness overtaking him. He should never have let her out of his sight. Things were happening too fast. He needed to tell Crawley or Laurent or someone what the hell was going on at All Saints.

Kristi would be pissed, but so what?

He ground his teeth together. He should have blown off his meeting with Hollister and gone with Kristi to the damned play. But it was too late now.

Glancing at his phone, he willed it to ring. "Come on, Kris. Call," he said. But the phone remained silent, and as he drove toward the college his restlessness and worry only increased.

\* \* \*

   In the women's room at the student union, Kristi slid
the gold necklace around her neck and wondered if she
was making the worst mistake of her life. Beneath the
harsh fluorescent bulbs the little vial gleamed, its dark
contents looking nearly black.

   It felt strange.

   Outré.

   Almost evil.

   With a sound of annoyance she stuffed the necklace
beneath her sweater so that the tiny glass pressed against
her skin. It felt cold, surprisingly so, for its small size.

   Adding a bit of gloss to her lips, she walked purposely toward the far side of campus, where she joined
a crowd of students and faculty members heading to the
brick building housing the English Department and a
small auditorium not far from Wagner House. Lights
glowed around the south entrance and a white sign
painted with black letters proclaimed "Play tonight:
*Everyman.*"

   *The quintessential morality play,* Kristi thought as
she spied the girl named Ophelia who called herself
"O" and also wore a vial of her own blood.

   Perfect.

   O was trying to buy a ticket from a girl seated behind
a long table. Some kind of medieval-sounding pipe
music filled the antechamber, and the ticket taker,
dressed all in black, seemed to have trouble making
both change and eye contact. Her black hair, scraped
back and showing light brown roots, was in stark contrast to the thick white makeup covering her face.

   "The play's already sold out?" O demanded, glaring
down at the girl in charge of the till.

   "Yes . . . I mean, I don't know. . . . Just a second."

   "This is required for my class!" O wasn't about to be
put off. "I have to get inside."

   "I know! Everyone's saying the same thing." The

flustered girl caught sight of Father Mathias, who was hovering near the curtained entry to the theater. Clad in a black cassock that was probably all the rage for clerics in the 1400s, he pulled at one sleeve, the one covering a bit of barely visible bandage.

"Father Mathias? Could you help me a second, please?"

"What is it, Angel?" he asked, and Kristi wondered if Angel was really the girl's name. Or did it have something to do with the play? Or, worse yet, was it Father Mathias's own pet name for the flustered girl?

"Do you know how many seats we have left?"

"A few more," he said softly. Patiently. Despite the girl's discomfiture. "We're setting up some extra folding chairs." He eyed the gathering crowd. "I was afraid of this," he said under his breath. Then, in a louder voice announced, "Thank you all for attending. Unfortunately the crowd is greater than we anticipated."

There was a jostling behind Kristi, and one guy said, "Are you kiddin' me?"

"The auditorium has a maximum seating capacity according to the fire marshall and we're at capacity."

"What?" A girl behind Kristi was beside herself. "I'm supposed to write a paper on this production!"

"Hey, what's the deal?" another shouted.

Father Mathias lifted his hands and lowered them as he said, "Please, everyone, accept my apologies. We can only sell ten more seats tonight, but we're planning a repeat performance tomorrow, or possibly Friday, whenever the auditorium is available again and the actors are able to perform, so you'll be able to see the play."

"Tomorrow? What the fu—?"

"I work Monday nights," another voice protested.

"This is bullshit," an angry boy said.

"Please, please." Father Mathias was adamant. "I'm sure we can work something out. We're recording, and if you can't see the live performance, it will be available in the drama department. The next performance will be posted on the campus Web site as soon as I can get things organized. Thank you, all!"

He slipped away then, leaving the hapless Angel to handle the unhappy throng. O managed to get a ticket and Kristi, too, was one of the last lucky attendees who, for five bucks, received a thin, slick playbill and entrance ticket. She walked into a small anteroom where a person actually went through the contents of her purse, as if she were attending a rock concert and bringing in contraband. "We ask that you leave your cell phone with us," the attendant said.

"Why?"

"The problems, you wouldn't believe." She handed Kristi a colored claim ticket and a pen.

"It's already turned off."

"It's the rules. You have to leave it. Write down your name and a land-line or e-mail address where you can be reached, just in case there's a mix-up."

Kristi did not like giving up the phone, but she didn't have much of a choice if she wanted to get inside. She filled out the information, kept one half of the claim ticket and, surprised that her canister of mace wasn't confiscated, grabbed her purse and hurried inside, where the temperature seemed to rise twenty degrees. People were jam-packed into the rows of auditorium chairs, but she managed to find a folding chair angled into a side aisle and next to O, who was already positioning her purse near her feet, her eyes fixed on the stage. Faded velvet curtains, once a deep maroon color, were drawn shut, and overhead there were minimal lights trained on the stage. The auditorium held about fifty people at capacity—tonight closer to sixty-five. The heater was working overtime and the damned Renaissance music permeated everything, loud over the whisper and crush of the crowd.

A thirty-something man sitting in front of Kristi had

splashed on too much aftershave, possibly to cover the scent of marijuana that clung to him. The Old Spice trick hadn't worked; it had only made the cloying odor more noticeable.

Feedback screamed through the auditorium for a second, then suddenly all was quiet. Kristi looked around and saw familiar faces, people who were also in her English block. Near the back of the room Hiram Calloway was studiously reading his program. He was alone, it appeared, and she wondered if he'd sold her out, given someone a key to her place, or if he was the one who had been videotaping her unit. She flushed at the thought and shot daggers at him with her eyes. As if he felt her gaze, he glanced up, caught sight of her, then buried his nose quickly in his playbill again.

She remembered chasing the guy she'd seen at her apartment and Hiram just didn't seem right. He was a little doughy, like an ex-football player gone to seed, and she was an athlete, had always been fast. If she hadn't been a swimmer, she'd probably have been a track star, so surely she could have caught him as she chased him into the night.

*Adrenaline could have spurred him on. Fear of getting caught.* If so, it was a wonder he didn't have a heart attack. Or, maybe it hadn't been him at all. But the only other person with the key was Irene Calloway, and she was close to using a cane. Surely Kristi could have run her to ground.

Then *who?*

She stared at Hiram, who didn't dare send a glance her way. *Loser,* Kristi thought, and let her gaze drift around the room. She spied Grace near the front of the room. But no Lucretia. No Ariel. She checked her program, thinking Ariel might be in the play, but Ariel was neither listed as a performer nor anyone who worked behind the scenes. A nod was given to Dr. Croft, as head of the English Department, and to Father Mathias, of course, along with Dr. Grotto, who was listed as "an advisor," whatever the hell that meant. Zena Regent, the next Meryl Streep, was listed as playing the part of Good Deeds, while Robert Manning, an African-American student who was in a few of Kristi's classes, was the lead. Gertrude Sykes was listed as Death. And at the bottom of the back page mention was given to Mai Kwan, who had designed the playbill and helped with "advertising and press releases."

Mai had never mentioned that she was connected to the drama department, but then Kristi had never asked too much about her classes or outside interests. Kristi knew little about the girl other than that she was nosy, a journalism student, had been acquainted with Tara Atwater, and dreaded doing laundry in the basement.

Now, Mai, too, was connected to the drama department and therefore Father Mathias and his obsession with morality plays . . . the plays all the missing girls had attended.

The houselights blinked, and then, within a few minutes, went down altogether. In the ensuing hush, a spotlight appeared and Father Mathias began the introduction.

Kristi had never seen the play before but had read it, or part of it, in high school. The gist of it was that Everyman, symbolizing all men and women on earth, was too caught up in worldly goods and had lost his soul. When called upon by Death, Everyman had nothing. He confronts other characters including Good Deeds, Knowledge, Confession, and more in his quest to take someone with him to the afterlife.

What interested Kristi was not so much the play itself, but the actors who represented the roles. She recognized Lucretia's friend Trudie, listed as Gertrude in the playbill, as Death. Zena, of course, was emoting all over the stage, and some of the other characters looked familiar, as if she'd seen them in class but couldn't quite put a finger on their names. One of the characters, Angel, was indeed played, albeit unconvincingly, by the girl who had sold tickets. The audience was also filled with students in some of Kristi's English classes, and she thought for a fleeting moment that she caught a glimpse of Georgia Clovis lurking in the alcove of a side exit.

What would she be doing here?

Kristi's eyes narrowed on other attendees. A number of her teachers had shown up as well, a regular Who's Who of the English Department. Dr. Natalie Croft, head of the department, was seated next to both a man Kristi didn't recognize and Dr. Preston, who still looked as if he were ready to catch the next big wave. He, in turn, was seated next to Professor Senegal, Kristi's journalism instructor.

Didn't these people have lives?

Or was this a command performance?

In the dark, she pulled on the chain around her neck, lifting it upward so that the vial was now on the outside of her sweater. It was still partially hidden by her jacket, but when the houselights went up, she planned to talk to a few people and see if anyone commented or noticed. The play went on, with only minimal flubbing of lines, and the guy in front of her who reeked of musk and weed started to snore. His head was bent forward and the woman next to him jabbed him in the side.

He snorted himself awake, sounding like a ripsaw, and the woman shushed him but good.

Kristi sat on the edge of her seat. Nervously she waited, and when at last the play was over and the cast had come out for a group bow, she was ready. As the applause died down and the lights went up, she stepped around the snorer and caught up with O as she filed out.

"You're O, right?" Kristi said, as if she'd just seen her that second. "I think we have a class together."

O rolled one bored eye at her. "Which one?"

"Maybe    Shakespeare . . . or . . . Grotto's    vampire class."

"Yeah. Well, maybe."

"I'm looking for a study partner."

"I'm not."

"Do you know anyone who is?"

O turned to face Kristi as they reached the doorway to the anteroom. "Do I look like a fuckin' counselor?" she demanded. Then her gaze landed on the vial at Kristi's neck. "What the hell are you doing?" she said, blanching. "Hide that thing."

"Why?"

"Why?" O repeated. Her eyes narrowed. "You are part of . . ." At that moment Father Mathias began heading their way and O widened her eyes in silent appeal.

Kristi quickly tucked the vial under her shirt again.

"Enjoy tonight's performance?" the priest asked.

"Immensely," O said, though it was an obvious act.

"Good, good!"

"Father Mathias, congratulations!" Natalie Croft made her way through the crowd. She was beaming at the priest. "Job well done," she said, though Kristi disagreed. No one in the cast of tonight's performance was going to make any Academy Award thank you speeches anytime soon, or probably in Dr. Croft's lifetime.

"*Everyman* is my favorite of all the morality plays, though I'm looking forward to exploring others as well as the mysteries and miracles. I hope you return. Oh, and for those of you who want another viewing, we'll be adding another performance tomorrow night. Thank you."

Father Mathias exited the back of the theater as the houselights went up and everyone began picking up their belongings. O was out the door in a flash and Kristi tried to follow her, but got caught in the crush and held up retrieving her cell phone, which was, as promised, ready and waiting for her. She handed another attendant, a girl who had played Knowledge in the play, her claim ticket and was given her phone without any eye contact. Kristi then made her way out the door and into the night, hoping for a glimpse of O. But the girl was gone. As were the others she'd recognized in the audience.

*Great,* she thought, slinging the strap of her purse over her shoulder. All the girls who had been abducted had attended Father Mathias's plays, so she'd hoped she'd find some connection, but she was at a loss. Standing in the dark, buffeted by the cold wind, she watched as other attendees left the theater, some heading to the parking lot, others toward the heart of campus. The professors who had shown up had all left, beelining out of the theater as if they couldn't escape fast enough.

The few stragglers who'd stopped to talk or smoke or just hang out weren't people she knew. So what about the people in the play? Didn't she suspect they might all somehow be connected?

*Face it,* she thought, discouraged, *you should leave being a detective to your father.*

On the way back to her car, she walked past Wagner House. Dark, angular and looming, it looked even more forbidding at night, with only the faintest of light coming from the windows. She checked the gate again, and of course it was locked. Then she noticed a flicker, just the tiniest bit of light, coming from a basement window.

Was she imagining it?

When she looked again, the glimmer of light was gone.

Had it been a reflection? A figment of her imagination?

*Flash!*

She saw another bluish light through the dirty glass. It too disappeared quickly.

*Storage area, my ass,* she thought. Who would be

sorting through old crates at night? And why had Father Mathias been down there the other day? He really hadn't explained himself, except to say that he'd seen evidence of rats, but maybe that was just an excuse to make her stay away. Well, it damned well wasn't working. She'd been beaten and chained, dealt with snarling, vicious dogs, demented psychos, lost her mother and her biological father, and nearly died. A few rats were nothing.

Skirting the building, she tested the back gate and found it locked as well. *Screw it.* She was going inside. Climbing the wrought iron fence was a simple matter and she knew there were no cameras. Hadn't Georgia Clovis admitted as much?

Though the fence itself was comprised of black wrought iron spikes, the top of the gate was decorated in scrollwork. Kristi pulled herself to the top of it and vaulted over, landing in a crouch on the inside brick walk. Glancing around to make sure she wasn't noticed, she hurried up the steps of the porch and tried the back door.

Locked solid.

*Damn.* She'd never had any luck with the credit card trick that seemed to work so effectively in the movies, and she had nothing with which to pick a lock.

So now what?

A window?

She tried all of the windows on the porch but they didn't budge, nor could she reach any from the ground. Maybe she could somehow squeeze through a basement window? She walked around the huge Gothic house, but not one window she reached, nor the front door, would budge. Unless she came back with a crowbar, she was effectively locked out.

And the flickering lights she'd seen?

Flashlights?

Candles?

Penlights?

The illumination had disappeared. The basement was now dark as a tomb.

Disappointed, Kristi climbed back over the gate and walked to her car. As she did, she felt those unseen eyes watching her every move. A bit of wind stirred, causing the wet leaves on the ground to lift and brittle branches of live oak to rattle.

As she reached her car she thought she heard a voice . . . a soft voice, the barest of whispers quietly crying.

She stopped short.

"Help me," it called.

Kristi spun, searching the shadows. "Is someone there?" she responded, looking across the parking lot to the house. She strained to listen but heard nothing over the sough of the wind.

*All in your head,* she told herself, but she waited again, listening, skin prickling, feeling as if her every move were being scrutinized. Measured. Second-guessed.

"Is anyone there?" she tried again, rotating slowly, her heart hammering in dread, her fingers unzipping her purse and closing over her canister of mace. "Hello?"

Nothing.

Just the drip of rain from the downspouts as the chapel bells began to peel the hours. Goose bumps rose on her skin and she glanced up to the roof of Wagner House. Was someone in an upper window staring down at her? A dark figure in the shadows, or was she truly imagining it all? She half expected some deranged creatures with bloody fangs to swoop down on her. The vial at her neck felt like it weighed a hundred pounds.

"Get over yourself," she admonished once she was in the car. She reached for her phone, turned it on, and listened to two messages. One from Jay insisting she call him, the other from her dad, who tried his best to sound like he was just checking in, but there was an underly-

ing gravity to his voice that couldn't be missed. ". . . so
call me when you can," he said as he signed off.

"Will do, Dad," she said, putting the car into gear and
glancing once more toward Wagner House.


Vlad watched from the bell tower of the church
chapel. Kristi Bentz was becoming a big problem.

Elizabeth was right.

It was time to leave, before they got caught. There
were other hunting grounds, but they would take some
time to establish, so it would be necessary to sacrifice
more than one tonight and again tomorrow. Then they
would stop for a while. Make the blood last.

The taillights of the Honda faded in the distance and
he licked his lips at the thought of Kristi Bentz and her
long, supple neck. He imagined sinking his teeth into
her as well as doing all sorts of things to her body.

So Elizabeth wanted to watch.

Who better to start with than the girl who was trying
so desperately to unmask them? Wouldn't there be
sweet irony in Elizabeth viewing it all?

Yes, he decided, there was a poetry, a symmetry to it.

As if the taking of Kristi Bentz's life had been preor-
dained.

But he was getting ahead of himself.

First, there were others to attend to. Beautiful girls
who had already pledged their souls.

Tonight, one would be taken.

Tomorrow, if all went as planned, there would be two.

Their images came to mind and he felt a hot lust run
through him. He imagined their surrender.

But first, tonight, one was waiting. . . .


Ariel was groggy, couldn't lift her head, and she was
cold, so damned cold. The room was dark, but some-

how familiar, as if she'd dreamed it. And she was naked as she lay upon a couch of some kind, the pile soft against her bare skin.

*You know what's happening.*

*You suspected this, didn't you?*

*Why were you so desperate for friends?*

Dazed, she sensed a change in the atmosphere and knew she wasn't alone. She was on a stage of some kind, it seemed, a raised platform, and she felt as if dozens of eyes were watching her, though she saw no one.

She tried to say something, but her mouth wouldn't form words, her vocal cords seemed paralyzed, just as her body was. Fear screamed through her and she tried like hell to move, to roll off the couch, to do anything.

She'd only wanted friends, had gone out for a few drinks, ordered the "Blood Martini," which had seemed fine . . . at first, and she hadn't really bought into the whole thing, but she'd been intrigued and her newfound friends had assured her the "drinking of the blood" was all part of the ritual, all part of the fun, all part of this whole funky vampire craze.

But now she was sick with fear and the rising mist that slowly seeped through the floor gave her the creeps.

What was going on?

Where was she?

How had she gotten here, in this dark, cavernlike room?

Who, dear God, who were the people she felt watching her, their eyes caressing her?

Men?

Women?

Both?

Oh, Lord, what were they going to do to her?

She heard a footstep and tried to twist her neck, but failed.

Another footstep.

Her blood ran cold through her veins.

*Help me,* she silently prayed. *Please God, help me.*

Frantically she tried to see who was approaching. One person or more?

"Sister Ariel," a male voice intoned.

*Sister?* Why would he call her that? She did remember foggily some mention of an initiation rite . . . that must be what this was. But why did she have to be naked and God, oh, God, why couldn't she move?

She recognized his voice, didn't she?

"Sister Ariel comes to us willingly."

*Who is "us"? And no, no I didn't come willingly.*

More steady footsteps, and though he was at her back, though she couldn't see him, she felt his presence. He touched the spot behind her ear and she wanted to recoil, but couldn't. There was something dangerous and frightening, but also seductive, in his touch.

His finger grazed the back of her neck and a thrill slid through her even though she was revolted. Her heart was pounding loudly inside her head and a red glow had turned the stage, if that's what it was, to a dark scarlet mist.

It crossed her mind that she might be dreaming, or tripping out on some drug, but deep in her heart she knew this was real. He touched her intimately, leaning closer, breathing across her skin, brushing a nipple with one hand.

Her body responded though she willed it not to. She still could not see him, could not twist to stare into his face. "Sister Ariel joins us willingly tonight to make the final, ultimate sacrifice."

*No . . . this can't be right.* Ariel struggled inwardly, but her body wouldn't, couldn't, move.

"Our sister. A virgin."

*For the love of God, what was this? She wasn't a virgin. . . . This was nuts, just plain crazy.*

She struggled wildly, not one muscle moving, and felt his hand begin to stroke her. "Now, Sister Ariel, it's time," he said, bending close, so close that his hot breath slid over the bare skin of her neck and she felt herself tingle. With anticipation? Or terror?

*No! No, no, no!*

His lips brushed against her skin.

"You know who I am," he whispered, and she did. Oh, Lord, she knew who he was and there had been times when she'd fantasized about him. But not like this . . . not with . . . with an audience. Not when fear and seduction were mixed, when she was unable to move, to speak.

There was just the hint of a smile in his voice when he said, "Don't be afraid."

But she was. Oh, God, she was afraid.

He bent his head to her and she felt a white hot prick, like a needle into her neck. Her heart fluttered wildly. She tried to cry out but only a moan left her lips.

His mouth held fast to her.

The blood began to flow, even and warm.

Oh, yes. She was afraid.

She was paralyzed, consumed, stricken with fear.

*God, help me. . . .*

# CHAPTER 24

Kristi decided to stop at her apartment for a change of clothes. Once again, it seemed as if nothing inside had been disturbed. Maybe they'd scared the voyeur off. "Good riddance," she said to the empty room as Houdini, who had been perched on top of the bookcase, dropped down and looked as if he wanted to do figure eights between her ankles. He wanted to trust her but hadn't quite made that leap of faith yet.

"I'll be back tomorrow," she promised him, then headed out the door and drove to Jay's aunt's mess of a cottage.

Jay was just getting out of his truck when she pulled into the cracked drive, and Bruno was already marking every bit of shrubbery on the way to the front door. Jay grabbed her and kissed her hard enough to make her mind spin.

"Miss me?" she asked when he finally released her and she could catch her breath.

"A little."

"A lot," she teased.

"I'm just glad you're here," he said seriously, wrapping an arm around her shoulder and shepherding them both around a dripping gutter as they made their way onto the front porch.

Once inside, they checked the taped feed from her

apartment but there was nothing other than the cat coming and going.

"You think he's ever going to show?"

"In time," Jay said grimly.

Kristi changed into her pajamas, carefully removing the vial from around her neck, feeling faintly guilty about not telling Jay she'd worn it. When she returned to the living room, Jay was building a fire from wood scraps. Eager flames snapped and popped, the scent of wood smoke permeated the rooms, and Jay then cracked a bottle of red wine. They drank out of paper cups and sat propped up against worn furniture covered with sheetrock dust. "Home sweet home." An ironic twinkle sparked in his eyes.

"I saw Hiram at the play tonight," she said, staring into her cup. "It was all I could do not to go up to him and accuse him of being a pervert."

"He would just deny it."

"I know, but if not him, then he gave my key to someone. Or maybe Irene did."

"Yeah, like the cable guy or phone repairman, or a plumber. We don't know who this guy is."

"It hasn't been that long since I changed the locks."

"We'll get him," Jay predicted. "Just be patient."

"You mean, *more* patient."

He smiled but didn't argue. A damned good idea. Kristi knew that patience wasn't her long suit, but lately, what little patience she possessed had been stretched thin. It seemed as if she were forever waiting, biding her time, hoping for a break.

"You know, I can't stay here while you're in New Orleans," Kristi said. "I have to go back to my apartment."

Jay vehemently shook his head. "How would that make you feel, knowing his camera's still there? That he could come for it at any time? It's not safe. Don't worry, I'll drive back after I get off work. Commute."

"After ten-hour days?"

"It's not that far."

"Yeah, it is."

"We're talking four nights a week."

"I can take care of myself," she assured him, growing slightly testy. It was one thing to have him be concerned for her safety, quite another to have him try to bully himself into her life. Overprotect her. She'd been down that road.

"I'm coming back and that's that, but I do have to go to the crime lab," he admitted, then proceeded to tell her about everything he'd learned from Sonny Crawley before she could offer further protest.

Kristi listened, flabbergasted, as he spelled out what he knew from the discovery of the female arm and hand in the gator's belly, to the search of the swamp where the reptile had been found. She didn't interrupt when he explained how the police were trying to ID the person to whom the arm had belonged, and that he'd asked his friend in the department to search through DMV and criminal records.

"—so they're looking for more evidence, more bodies," Jay wrapped up as he took a long swallow from his cup. "It turns out that one of the detectives, Portia Laurent, has suspected all along that the girls who are missing from All Saints were abducted. They just didn't have any evidence to prove it."

"But now they might," Kristi said. She was still processing and almost missed it when he changed directions and asked her about the morality play. Slightly distracted, she told him about the events of her night, carefully skirting any mention of the vial because she knew he would demand it back, and she had every intention of wearing it to her meeting with Dr. Grotto the next day.

She finished with her less than productive snooping around Wagner House and her belief that she'd heard someone call for help.

"I'm not crazy about you meeting Dr. Vampire," he said, pouring them each a little more wine. "And don't go back to your apartment again."

Kristi ignored that. "What's Grotto gonna do to me? I'll be at his office in the English Department."

Jay's eyes had turned dark as he stared into the fire. "But he's involved in the girls' disappearances; I can feel it. You seeing him, it just doesn't feel right." He rubbed his chin and shook his head. "And what about whoever was crying 'help me' outside Wagner House?"

"I said I *thought* I heard it, but it could have been a cat mewing or . . . I don't know, something else. The wind was blowing, it was raining, and I was maybe imagining things."

"You're not one to imagine things," he pointed out, and she decided it was time to set him straight.

"What if I told you I could predict death by just looking at someone?"

"You have some psychic power I'm not aware of?"

"You could say that."

He smiled lazily and stretched out in front of the fire, his head propped on one hand, his drink in the other, his gaze fastened on hers. "Lay it on me."

And so she did, explaining about her dreams where her father died and the way she saw people in black and white before, she assumed, they were to die. When she was finished, she took another long swallow from her cup and noticed that his smile had faded.

"I'm waiting for the punch line."

"There isn't one," Kristi assured him.

"You're serious."

"Mmm-hmmm."

"But your father, and Lucretia and Ariel, they're still alive."

"Yes, I know, but there was the one woman on the bus."

"An *elderly* woman."

"I'm just telling you what's going on. Whenever it

happens, I feel cold inside. Like death is cutting through my soul," she said, her voice lowering a bit, feeling more and more foolish as she tried to explain. "I know it sounds nuts. But it's as if evil itself were looking through my eyes."

"Kris—"

"I know, I know. I sound like a psycho myself, that I need years of therapy, but it didn't happen until after the accident."

"You told your father this?"

"As paranoid as he is about me? No way. I thought about confiding in his wife, Olivia, because she has, er, *had*, this psychic thing going on, but then she'd feel obliged to tell Dad, and so the only one I told was Ariel." She sighed. "Who knows how many people she blabbed to."

"No one will believe her. They'll just think you're loco."

"Perfect," she said. "Do you think I'm loco?"

Jay hesitated long enough to raise Kristi's temper, but then he held up a hand and said, "I think something's going on with you. This—phenomenon—the gray pallor vision—could be something physical."

"A sight problem? A brain problem?"

He shrugged. "All I know is I really don't think you should meet with Grotto. Or at least wait for me to go with you."

Kristi would have liked to have an all-out argument about her "ability," but maybe it was enough that she'd at least told him. For the moment anyway. She negated his suggestion about Grotto with, "That would blow everything."

"I can be outside his office. Nearby. You have your phone on, put it on mute, so he doesn't hear anything, and I'll listen in. If anything goes wrong, you let me know, and I'll burst through the door like John effin' Rambo."

"Okay," she said. Fortunately she didn't have to work.

Flirty Francesca had agreed to take Kristi's shift at the restaurant. "Wait at the library until you hear me talking to him, just so you know we're in his office and he won't see you, then once I'm inside, you can come into the English Department. Closer. Afterward we can go to the student union and talk, then to your class."

"Sounds good."

"Do we need a code word in case I get into trouble with Grotto?"

"How about 'Help' or 'Jay, get the hell in here'!"

"Those'll work," she said, almost laughing. "I'm only mildly crazy, you know," she added.

"I know."

She looked into his handsome face and wondered what had taken her so long to get to this point. To trust him. Love him.

She almost told him about the vial, but decided she'd keep that bit of information to herself at least for one more night. Until she'd seen Grotto's reaction.


Portia was putting on her coat, ready to call it a day, when Detective Crawley, reeking of cigarette smoke and in need of a shave, showed up at her cubicle. She'd never much liked the man, but couldn't fault him on his skills as a detective. He was just a little rough around the edges, which seemed to work for him, at least on the job.

"You all get a call from Jay McKnight?" he asked. It was after five and Crawley was already wearing his rain jacket, a battered briefcase in one hand, a printout in the other.

"No."

"He's with the crime lab, teaches a night class at All Saints. A friend of mine from way back. I gave him your name."

"Because?"

"He's got an interest in those girls that went missing.

Seems to think they're more than just runaways, like you. Thought you might want to talk to him. Compare notes. He also asked me to look up some info on some of the teachers who work at the college."

"What kind of info?"

"Vehicle ownership, specifically he's lookin' for a dark van, if anyone who works at the college owns or has access to one. With Louisiana plates. Probably domestic and full sized, I think, not a mini. Claims someone was following Kristi Bentz. She's a student there, and Rick Bentz of the New Orleans PD's daughter."

"What's her involvement?"

"I think she's playing amateur detective."

"Just what we need," she grumbled. "And how is McKnight involved?"

"He's her professor. Friend."

"More?"

"Probably."

"Great," she said, thinking the Bentz girl was more likely than not in the way.

"McKnight also wants background checks on some of the professors and staff who work at the college."

She lifted her eyebrows. "He thinks one of his colleagues is involved?"

"I got the info from DMV, but thought you might want to work on the staff as I've got a few days off while my ex is in the hospital—knee replacement. I've got the boys. I'll be back on Friday." He handed her a sheet of paper with a list of names and another with five vehicles, potential matches. He gave her a quick rundown of what had happened to Jay and Kristi Bentz.

Portia couldn't help the first tingle of excitement that ran through her blood. For over a year she'd sensed there was more going on than students at All Saints becoming runaways. Now, at least, someone seemed to agree with her.

"I'll be checkin' in with ya," Crawley said, poking a

finger at her nose. "And don't screw it up, okay? I got a half-rack riding on this."

"Do I get some of that?"

One side of his mouth lifted. "Connect the dots and I'll buy you a real drink. What do you drink? Cosmopolitan? Daiquiri?"

"Martini straight up. Three olives."

"A woman after my own heart."

"Just what I wanna hear," she said, already taking off her coat and settling in for what was bound to be a long, but promising night.

Elizabeth rarely visited.

It was an unwritten rule: he would go to her. Always.

The last time she'd shown up in his private quarters was over a year earlier, but now she was pacing along the edge of the pool, light from the underwater fixture giving the water a bright aquamarine glow, the reflection casting shifting bluish shadows on her pale, flawless skin. Dressed in a long black coat and boots, she walked from one end of the room to the other.

Vlad finished doing his laps, refusing to interrupt his routine, even for her, then hoisted himself from the pool.

"Something's wrong," he said, naked and dripping, allowing the cool air to caress his skin. He'd hoped to spend some time in the freezer with Ariel and Karen Lee, aka Bodiluscious, after his workout, but obviously he would have to change his plans.

"We have to work faster," Elizabeth said, glaring at him as if whatever was wrong was his fault. "We agreed to collect more and it has to be soon."

"What happened?"

"Other than the arm being discovered?" she sneered. "I have sources in the police department. That was careless, Vlad. When you dispose of the . . . corpses, you need to take them *far* away. Out of the parish. Out of the state." She whirled on him, her anger visible in the snap of her eyes, the flare of her nostrils. "For God's sake, what's wrong with the damned Gulf of Mexico? They could be used to feed the sharks . . . never found. People fall off boats and are *never* located again."

As if it were that easy to dispose of a body.

"The gator incident was unfortunate."

"And stupid! What're the chances of the rest of the body showing up? Or the other ones?" She was shaking and it was all he could do not to put his hands on her and try to calm her, but he knew from past experience that touching her now, while she was dressed, not in her murky bath, would infuriate her further.

"They can't link the arm to us."

She stared at him as if he were a cretin. "Do you even watch TV? What"—she made air quotes—" 'they' can do is very sophisticated. Maybe not *CSI* sophisticated and certainly not so quickly, but sophisticated nonetheless. With enough time, oh, yes, they can link that damned limb to whichever girl it belonged to and eventually to us!" Scratching her long neck thoughtfully, Elizabeth, ever restless, kept up her pacing, then stopped short as she caught her reflection in one of the mirrors he'd placed in the room. Her fingers curled in on themselves until she realized what she was doing, that she might mar her skin with her scratching. Momentarily distracted, obsessed with her image, she also took in several deep breaths and made her face a calm mask once again. The lines of consternation and frustration between her brows and around the corners of her eyes smoothed, and the expression of seething fury disappeared.

"We have to step things up. Immediately." She said, more evenly, "You know what to do. We've planned for this day, I just wish it hadn't happened so soon." Sighing, she shook her head, her dark hair sliding across her shoulders. "This Friday," she said with a note of wistfulness. "It will be our last performance here."

"And then?"

She arched a perfect brow. "We start over, of course. We just need to get enough blood to last until we settle somewhere else." She seemed to have chased away her anger with thoughts of a new future, a new place, new young, supple bodies. "But for now, we must concentrate."

She crossed the cavernous room to his desk alcove and saw that he'd already strewn campus ID pictures across the top, photographs of those he thought most worthy. Leaning one hip against the desktop, she quickly slid aside those she deigned not pretty enough, or supple enough, or fresh enough. She hesitated over a few and clucked her tongue at opportunities missed.

In the end three pictures remained. "These are the ones," she said, and he stared down at the beautiful girls in the pictures. Each was a younger, more vibrant version of Elizabeth.

The center photograph was of Kristi Bentz.

"Three will be difficult."

"Then you'll just have to hone your skills, won't you?" She smiled at him, a careful, poised grin that showed few lines. "If you can't get them all, at least be certain you get the Bentz girl."

All too gladly, he thought.

"And remember, these"—she swirled a finger over the photographs—"are just the ones we need for their blood. There are others who have to be disposed of as well."

Of course he knew what she was talking about: the clean up. Getting rid of those who could ruin them. That thought was more than pleasant. He couldn't wait to get rid of them. They'd been pains in the neck from the get-go.

They deserved to die.

Had been asking for it.

Vlad, with Elizabeth's blessing, was only too happy to oblige.


Dr. Grotto's office was in the lower level of the massive building housing the English Department, down a staircase to a corridor in the north wing. This section of the building, separate from most of the classrooms, was quiet. Empty. No students or faculty wandering the halls. Most of the office doors, with their frosted glass windows, were shut and vacant, no light shining through the opaque panes.

Kristi screwed up her courage as she headed down the corridor, her sneakers silent, not making a squeak. So she was finally going to confront Dr. Grotto, one-on-one. She wasn't certain exactly how she was going to play this, but her mind was cranking out possible scenarios:

An innocent, just asking about her assignment, hinting about some kind of cult?

Straightforward, as if she were an investigator with the police department?

Coy? Flirtatious? Hoping to elicit information while stroking his ego?

Stomach acid burned up her throat at the thought.

*Play it by ear,* she told herself, though her nerves were tight as piano wires, her apprehension growing with each step. She checked her pocket: her cell phone line was open, but muted, and hopefully Jay would be able to hear all of her conversation, even though he might not like it. She hated relying on him, but decided not to be a fool. Grotto could be dangerous. She had no idea how her professor would react if he thought he was caught.

She reached the corner and, hearing voices, partially muted but loud enough for her to decipher, realized an argument was blazing.

"I'm telling you, this is dangerous," a woman was

saying, her voice rising with emotion. Kristi stopped dead in her tracks.

Lucretia?

"You have to stop." Yes, it was Lucretia and she sounded desperate. Kristi chanced peering around the corner and saw that the hallway was empty.

"I know what I'm doing." Grotto's voice. Angry. Deep. Coming from behind a door that was cracked just a bit, so little that they probably didn't realize it was open. Heart thudding, Kristi sneaked along the wall, getting closer.

"Don't you see they're using you? For the love of God, Dominic, get out now. Before it's too late."

"You don't know what you're talking about."

"I know something horrible is happening. Something evil. And . . . and I hate what it's doing to you. Please, Dominic, get out now. We can leave. No one will ever know." Lucretia was scared.

Panicked.

Kristi cringed inside at the thought of how much mental abuse her ex-roommate would take, for what? This creep that peddled vampirism?

" 'No one will ever know?' That's ironic coming from you," he sneered, his voice heavy with accusation. "Since you're the one who opened your mouth."

"I made a mistake."

"One that I have to fix."

Kristi could barely hear over her own thudding heartbeat. They were talking about her! About Lucretia's original request for Kristi to check into some kind of vampire cult.

"I was worried! About them! About you!" Lucretia was nearly hysterical. "About . . . about us!"

"You should have thought about that before you decided to talk to your friend."

"She's not my friend," Lucretia said quickly.

"A cop's daughter, for crying out loud. And not just any cop, but a homicide dick. Homicide, Lucretia. As in murder. What the hell were you thinking?" Grotto was really mad now, his voice rising. "The last thing we need is any more attention from the damned police."

"I—I just thought she could help."

"How? By exposing everything? Jesus Christ, Lucretia, you're supposed to be an intelligent woman. But talking to someone so close to the police, drawing attention to me, asking for help when you don't even understand what's going on?"

"Dominic, please—" Lucretia's voice broke and Kristi almost felt sorry for her.

"I told you it was over," he said more quietly, like a death knell. The declaration sounded cold and heartless, much worse than if he'd screamed at her, if there had been some tiny bit of feeling in his voice.

"You . . . you don't mean it," she said, sniffing.

*Get over him, he's a stone-cold loser,* Kristi thought, inching closer to the doorway. Sexy yes, but cruel, and obviously mixed up in something dark and dangerous, ultimately illegal, something to do with the missing girls, quite possibly murder. She wondered how she herself could face him after this.

Lucretia tried to defend herself. "I—I told her you were . . . innocent. Persecuted."

"But she didn't buy it, did she?"

Silence.

Damning silence.

"Now I have to deal with her. I've tried to avoid her since the beginning of the school year, ever since I realized who she was, but she's relentless and"—he drew a breath—"she's coming to see me in a few minutes. On some pretense about her assignment."

"Don't meet with her," Lucretia pleaded softly.

"I have to. So, go. Now. She'll be here any minute.

Use the back, in case she comes early. And call me in about twenty minutes. I'll use the excuse to cut the meeting short."

"Oh, no, please, Dominic—"

"Leave, Lucretia. Get the fuck out. Before you ruin everything for me."

She gave a little squeak of protest and Kristi started backing up, faster and faster, down the length of the hallway. Her heart was racing, a cold sweat running down her spine. There was no place to hide, no closet to slip into, no stairway she could climb. She had to pretend that she'd just arrived and hadn't overheard the argument. She reached the corner, backed around it and waited, running in place, already coming up with an excuse for being late.

In the distance, she heard a door bang shut and assumed that her ex-roommate had taken her ex-lover's advice and fled through the entrance that led to the back of campus, near Greek Row and away from the quad. A few other students came down the stairs and Kristi headed back up, plucking the phone from her pocket as she stepped outside. "You there?" she whispered, all the while jogging in place.

Jay didn't answer.

She realized then that the call had been dropped. "Great."

It didn't happen often, but when it did it was always, it seemed, at an inopportune moment. Just like in the commercials. Quickly she redialed Jay.

"What the hell happened?" he demanded, sounding frantic.

"Couldn't you hear?"

"What?"

"Never mind, I'll fill you in later."

"I'm on my way over there."

She searched the darkness, looking toward the library, but didn't recognize him in the groups of people hastening from one building to the next.

"Wait. I haven't gone in yet. Grotto had company. I'll tell you about it later. Where are you?"

"Just leaving the library." She squinted and recognized him hastening down the wide steps. He walked briskly under the security lights toward the English Department. Lamplight caught in his hair and she saw his expression was hard and intense.

"Good, then you can wait inside the doors of the English Department."

"Unless you want me closer. Like on the other side of the door to his office?"

"Only if you hear me say, 'I'm in trouble.' Then you can play Rambo to your heart's content."

He was now close enough to her that she knew he was looking at her. She gave him a little wave, then hurried into the brick building once more and down the steps. Before Jay could argue, she hit the mute button again, tucked the phone in her pocket and, glancing up at the clock in the hallway, noted that it was almost ten minutes after her scheduled meeting. No time to lose. Not if she wanted to catch Grotto. Kicking it up a gear, she hurried down the hallway, half running, as if she were trying to make up for lost time.

Rounding the corner, she spied Dr. Grotto at the door to his office, locking up. Dressed in black slacks, T-shirt, and jacket, holding his briefcase in one hand, he looked ready to split.

"Oh! Dr. Grotto, I'm so sorry I'm late," she said in a rush, hoping her cheeks were flushed. "I had a phone call from my dad, and he held me up." She rolled her eyes. "He's just a little overprotective." Breathlessly she managed an apologetic smile. "I had to tell him I had an important meeting with you to get him off the phone."

"Unfortunately, I, too, have another meeting," Grotto

said. Probably a lie, but she had no choice but to let it
slide.

"I just need to talk to you for a minute or two. Really."

He studied her for a second, then unlocked the door
again, straightening to his full height of six-two or
-three. "I was about to give up on you, but I suppose I
can spare one minute." His voice was calm, evenly
modulated, as if he hadn't recently been a part of an intense argument.

He made a big show of checking his watch, trying to
make her feel bad about being late, obviously already
coming up with excuses to cut out of their meeting as
fast as possible.

Fine. She'd make it quick.

"Have a seat." Waving her into a small rolling desk
chair, he settled into a worn leather chair on the other
side of a small black writing table and snapped on the
desk lamp. The entire room was cramped, little more
than a closet with a window cut high into the wall and a
computer desk crammed into one corner. A bookcase
covered one wall, every shelf filled to capacity with information on vampires, ghosts, werewolves, and anything the least bit paranormal.

"So, what can I do for you?" He folded his hands
over the desk and stared at her with an intensity that,
she suspected, was supposed to make her squirm. It did.
His eyes were deep set and mesmerizing, his face all
bladed angles, his mouth so thin it appeared a crease in
a strong, sharp-cut jaw. A handsome man, he seemed
used to banking on his looks and size to take control of
the conversation.

She decided to play it straight. Kind of. "I wanted to
talk to you about some of your students."

He cocked his head, his hair glistening black in the
lamplight. "It's against the policy of the college to give
out information about anyone. I assume you know
that."

"I'm talking about the ones who've gone missing," she said. "You remember? Dionne Harmon, Tara Atwater, Monique DesCartes, and Rylee Ames? All of them, while they were students here, were enrolled in your class on vampyrism."

"I said I wouldn't discuss them."

"I'm just talking about their curriculum," Kristi forged on. "They were all English majors. They had many of the same classes. Yours was one of them. It's a very popular elective."

"The most popular elective in the department," he agreed with a taut smile, his white teeth stark against his swarthy skin. He seemed to relax a bit. Except for the tiny, telltale tic that had developed near one eye. "Maybe even on campus."

"Even more than History of Rock and Roll."

"I couldn't say. Is this going somewhere, Ms. Bentz?"

"You were one of the last people to see Dionne Harmon alive."

He froze. "Are you saying she's dead? Did they find her body?" His cool facade cracked and something akin to panic washed over his face. "Dear God, I didn't know."

"I'm just saying that you were one of the last people to see her before she *disappeared*."

"Say what you mean the first time," he snapped. "That's a big difference. And yes, apparently I was one of the last people to see Dionne before she disappeared. But this is really no business of yours, is it, Miss Bentz? If you have some questions about your assignments, or class, please"—he waved in a "come on" gesture—"ask, but that's all I'll talk about." He no longer made any pretense at smiling. "I am a busy man."

"What do you know about a cult of people who worship vampires? Here, on campus?"

"I don't know what you're talking about."

"You've never seen one of these before?" She dug beneath her turtleneck to flash the vial of blood.

He glared at the vial as if it were the embodiment of evil. "What is that?" he asked in little more than a whisper.

"A vial of blood. Human blood."

"Oh, God." He closed his eyes for a second and drew in a long breath. For a long time she didn't think he would answer, but then he surprised her by admitting, "I've seen it, or one like it."

"Where?"

"A student. Her name is O." He looked about to confide in Kristi, then shook his head. "I can't discuss her or anyone else. But I know she's very outspoken and wears the vial almost militantly."

That much was true. Kristi's own father had interviewed the girl on an earlier case and she had proudly shown off her unique jewelry.

"Where did you get that?" Grotto asked.

"I found it in my apartment."

"Your *apartment*?"

"Tara Atwater used to live there."

"And you think it was hers?" he said, the corners of his mouth tightening, the temperature in the room seeming to drop ten degrees.

"I do. DNA will tell."

"You've had some of the blood tested?"

She nodded.

His gaze was cold. "If the police were going to run any tests, they would have taken the necklace. You're bluffing, Miss Bentz."

"I sent drops in . . . claimed they were my own. I have a friend who works in the lab."

"What does this have to do with me?"

"Don't you care what happened to your students, Dr. Grotto?"

"They're runaways." He said it as if he believed it. Or as if he wanted to believe it.

"You think all four just left town? All four who attended your class? All four who were English majors? All four just up and decided to take a hike? That's one helluva coincidence, don't you think?"

"It's more common than you think. They're young and, from what I understand, troubled."

"And missing."

"It's possible something happened to them, I suppose, but far more likely that they took off." Grotto seemed torn between the desire to throw her out and a need to talk about the missing girls.

"Without a trace?" Kristi questioned skeptically.

"Ms. Bentz, even in today's world, if someone wants to disappear, it can be done. Maybe not forever, but for a while. I think all of the girls will turn up. When they want to."

"That's such bull," she said.

"Easy to say. You had a loving family, right? Father and mother who doted on you?"

She didn't respond, didn't want this turned on her. She refused to mention that her mother had died years ago in a single car accident and that her father, after pouring himself into a bottle, finally pulled himself together. Neither did she mention that she was adopted. The less Grotto knew about her, the better.

At that moment, his phone rang. Lucretia.

"Excuse me," he said. Into the receiver, "Hello? Oh, yes . . . I'm on my way . . . sorry, running late. I'll be there in"—he checked his watch—"fifteen minutes . . . yes . . . bye." He hung up and stood, signifying the interview was over. "I really do have to go." He picked up his briefcase again, walked to the door and held it open.

She'd pushed it as far as she could.

And had come up with nothing.

"Say 'hi' to Lucretia for me," she said as they walked out, "and tell her I'd appreciate it if she'd return my calls."

He glared at her and in that second she witnessed the

paling of his complexion. Had she hit a sensitive spot? But the blanching went further than just a moment's shock. Grotto's entire face bled of color and she had the distinct hit that he, like so many others she'd seen on campus, might soon be dead.

"What?" he asked when he found her staring at him.

"Be careful," she said, and saw the questions in his eyes. "I don't know what you're into, Dr. Grotto, or how deep, but it's dangerous."

He half laughed. "You've made up your own myth, haven't you?"

Had she?

She could tell him that he'd turned gray—a signal, she was certain, of impending death or doom. But he would just laugh at her some more, think she was a real whack job, just like Ariel had.

What had she expected? That he would turn over and spill his guts, tell her about some dark, demonic cult? Admit that he killed the girls and what—drank their blood? Or drank it first and then killed them?

Grotto locked his door. If she'd thought she was going to get some soul-cleansing confession from him and break the case wide open or even gain information for her damned book, she'd been sadly mistaken.

She climbed the stairs to the first floor and found Jay seated on a bench near the stairwell. Less than fifty feet from Grotto's door.

"Way to go, Sherlock," he said, and she tossed him a don't-mess-with-me look.

"You heard," she said as they walked through the front doors and a blast of cool winter air hit them.

"I heard that you took the vial in there, taunted him with it, screwed around with evidence!"

"I thought it might be effective."

"Damn it, Kris, that wasn't part of the deal."

"I should have told you," she admitted as they walked along the brick path where other students were busily crossing campus. Bikes and skateboards whipped past and a jogger with two dogs on a leash raced in the opposite direction.

"But if you had, you knew I wouldn't let you mess with it. What were you thinking?"

She wasn't about to try to make excuses. Instead, she said, "I thought you were supposed to be waiting outside."

"Yeah, well, I wanted to be a little closer, just in case."

"Of what? That he might attack me?"

Jay shrugged, his hands deep into the pockets of his jacket. "Maybe. You did bait the hell out of him." He took her arm, pulled her closer to him as a bicyclist cut through the quad. "From now on, no secrets. If we're in this together, we have to be honest with each other."

She nodded. "Okay."

He looked as if he didn't believe her, but he didn't release her arm as they walked briskly toward the student union. Jay pulled open the door and they stepped inside. A swell of warm air hit them and the sounds of laughter, music, and conversation filled the open area where students were hanging out, some studying, some plugged into iPods, others meeting friends. They seemed so innocent, so unaware of the evil that Kristi believed lurked in the crevices and corners of the campus.

*Who would be next?* she wondered, and thought of how pale Dr. Grotto had appeared.

"Did you believe him?" Jay's voice brought her back to the moment.

"Grotto?" She shook her head. "He was hiding something." Despite the warmth of the low, well-lit building, she felt a whisper of cold deep in her heart. She looked up at Jay and saw that his eyes were troubled. "And he was lying through his fangs."

# CHAPTER 25

Jay sat in his office and, using a magnifying glass, studied a picture of the severed arm. He'd seen the real thing, of course, but it was being kept frozen in hopes the body from which it had been detached would be found. There were computer pictures as well, those that could be enhanced, but sometimes the old-fashioned way was most familiar.

He'd been in the lab for ten hours on Tuesday. It was nearly quitting time now and he was testy. Edgy. Hadn't felt right about returning to New Orleans despite Kristi's insistence the night before. She hadn't listened to any of his arguments, wouldn't consider living in his aunt's bungalow or even keeping his dog. She'd moved back to her apartment against all his protests. He was in constant contact with her, either by phone, text or e-mail, and so far she was all right.

So far.

*So how will you feel if something happens to her?*

He tried not to immediately go to the worst case scenario, but it was always there, looming in the background of his brain, ready to pounce on his consciousness again. He had to quit worrying about Kristi. As she'd told him time and time again, she was an adult. Could take care of herself. She swore that the idea her would-be video-taper might try to access her apartment didn't bother her. Said she almost welcomed it.

"Bullshit," he muttered, focusing again on a discoloration between the elbow and wrist.

"You talkin' to me?" Bonita Washington asked as she walked into the lab area, eyeing the microscopes and careful not to touch the gas chromatograph.

"Talking to myself, I guess," he said, rolling his chair back.

"Notice anything unusual about that arm?" She pointed to the picture lying on his work area.

"It's missing a body."

"Smart ass. Anything else?"

"Her fingernail polish doesn't go with her lipstick, oh, wait—"

Washington, usually stoic or grim, actually cracked a smile. "I was talking 'bout this," she said, stabbing a finger at a spot of skin in the lower arm. "What's it look like to you?"

"I'm not sure."

"How about freezer burn?"

Jay looked again.

"Like when you put chicken in the freezer and the package isn't sealed, or even if it is, if it's been in there a good, long time?"

He rolled his chair back to the desk area and, using his microscope, studied the blemish on the arm. "You think the arm . . . no, the body was frozen before being dumped into the swamp."

"Uh-huh."

"So our perp doesn't keep them alive," he thought aloud. His hope that they would find the missing coeds alive took a direct hit.

"Don't know what he does to them, but at one point, I'd be willing to bet my new Porsche that this woman was frozen."

"I thought you drove a Pontiac."

"So far. But if I had a Porsche I'd make the bet." She nodded, as if agreeing with herself. "Couldn't take a chance on losing the Grand Am."

Why would the killer keep the bodies on ice? Why not just dump them fresh, after the kill? Did he not want them to rot and smell, could he not get them to a dumping ground fast? And why was there no blood in the severed limb?

Jay tapped the eraser end of his pencil on the desk.

What kind of a nutcase was behind all of this?

Again, he thought of Kristi and this time, he couldn't keep his dread at bay.

By midweek, Kristi was no closer to the truth than before. No one had dared come into her apartment; her meeting with Dr. Grotto had left him unruffled; he'd even had the nerve to call on her in class and smile almost benignly. The chat rooms, which she frequented every night, hoping to catch DrDoNoGood or JustO online, were a bust. They'd gone fairly silent, maybe with midterms looming in the next few weeks. Things on campus were quiet.

Almost too quiet.

The calm before the storm, she told herself as she rode her bike through the quad, heading for her writing class. She locked her fifteen-speed in the rack, then hurried into the building, a few steps behind Zena and Trudie.

Perfect.

They were in no hurry and she walked briskly, closing the gap between them so that when they reached the door to the classroom, she was on their heels. Zena found an empty desk. Trudie took one next to it and Kristi snagged one nearby. She glanced around the room. Wasn't Ophelia—JustO—in this class? If so, she was nowhere in sight. Kristi definitely wanted to try and buddy up to her after their last meeting at the play. O, she thought, had secrets to spill.

Nor was Ariel anywhere to be seen. In fact, as Kristi thought about it, Ariel hadn't been in any of her classes all week.

And Kristi had witnessed her changing from color to black and white, which, recently hadn't meant much.

Still . . .

If it weren't flu season, Kristi might have gotten suspicious. Instead, she made a mental note to check on the girl.

As Preston started his lecture, she glanced over at Zena again but didn't catch the other girl's attention. She would have to wait. She pretended interest in Dr. Preston as he lectured on the importance of perspective and clarity when writing, and she hoped she didn't fall asleep.

Today, he seemed more content to rest his jean-clad hips on the edge of his writing table, rather than pace. Still, he flipped the chalk, his expression affable enough, but beneath his tan and California good looks, she thought she noticed a harder edge.

But then hadn't she experienced just that same feeling with Dr. Grotto and Emmerson? Even Professor Senegal, the mother of twins, seemed to have a darker side to her, one she hid behind her sleek glasses and burgundy-colored lips.

Most of the students seemed to be in the same Zombie-like state as she. Kristi was beginning to recognize some. A few desks over was Marnie, the blonde she'd followed into Wagner House. Marnie, it seemed, was also a part of the group of friends including Trudie and Grace. Then there was Bethany, another girl in most of Kristi's classes. She was busily taking notes, her fingers flying over the keyboard of her laptop as if Dr. Preston were giving out the answers to the universe.

One of *those,* Kristi thought as the girl asked a question to clarify a point on symbolism. A real suck-up.

Hiram glowered in his chair, and Mai was tuned into the lecture, taking fastidious notes.

*Save me.* This class was too basic for her taste. She'd already sold articles on true crime and she just wanted to hone her skills for the book she was putting together. She wasn't certain Dr. Preston was the answer.

He must've read her thoughts. "Miss Bentz?" he said, his voice simmering with authority.

She froze.

"Am I boring you?" he asked, and when he stared at her, she wanted to melt into the floor. "Or you?" he said, swinging his gaze back to Hiram Calloway.

"Yeah," Hiram said insolently. "You kinda are."

"Kinda?" Preston said, snapping his chalk into his fist.

"Okay, no, you are. You're boring me. I just want to write. I don't think we need to study symbolism or imagery. We all took that in high school. Isn't this supposed to be a college course? Sheeeiiiit." With that he closed his laptop, stuffed his books into his backpack, kicked back his chair, and left the classroom.

Kristi thought all hell would break loose. But the anger in Preston's face quickly disappeared. "If anyone else feels the way Mr. Calloway does, I invite you to leave at this time."

The room went absolutely silent. No one even dared cough.

Preston's glare traveled over each student and once he decided no one else was intent on leaving, he cleared his throat. "Good. Let's continue . . ."

Once again he began flipping his chalk and pacing.

Kristi tried her best to pay attention. But it was hard. Hiram was right, the class was seriously boring.

She glanced at the clock and spent the next forty-five minutes noting that Trudie and Zena pretended interest in the class while texting each other. They held their cell phones just under the desk and were adept enough at working the keyboards to effectively "pass notes" without getting caught, which was a little weird. This was college, not junior high. But Kristi did her part as well, trying her best to read the information they sent back and forth.

It proved impossible, for the most part. The screens were too small, but she did pick up a line or two and quickly jotted down the piece of shorthand she saw. WH came up frequently . . . *Wagner House?* Or was she just willing it so? She also saw: Grto, which she assumed was in reference to Dr. Grotto, and a series of numbers, which, she thought, referred to Friday, which was more than just the start of the weekend, it was also the date of the last performance of *Everyman*. The rest of the information made no sense whatsoever, but she jotted notes down just the same.

When class was over she was once again behind the two girls but saw no reason to break into their conversation, nor did she overhear anything worth noting.

It was as if the whole world were holding its breath.

Outside was the same. The air was still. The sky filled with pewter clouds that didn't seem to move.

The hairs on the back of her arms raised and though there was nothing obviously wrong, she knew, deep in her heart, that evil was lurking in the shadows.

It was after four on Friday and Portia was a little jangled from the eight—or had it been nine?—cups of coffee she'd had throughout the day. She *had* to ease back on that. Today, she'd stopped counting when she'd reached six, even though she'd switched to decaf in the early afternoon. She was still feeling the effects as she parked her car in the lot at the station. Probably more from lack of sleep than the caffeine. She'd been working twelve-hour shifts, eight on the clock, four on her own time. When she got home, she walked on the treadmill for forty-five minutes, ate some microwavable, fat-free, low-carb, vitamin-fortified, tasteless meal, then hit it again, only taking a break for a glass of wine with the news. All to get rid of the twenty pounds that had crept on once she'd turned thirty and given up cigarettes.

Sometimes she wondered if she'd made the right choice.

The rest of every evening, she was buried in her work and she didn't even want to think about what she really earned per hour. It would be too depressing. "Remember the benefits," she reminded herself over and over again as she sweated on the treadmill, cranking up the music with her increasing pace. And then there was the simple fact that she loved her work. *Loved* it. Nothin' better. Even if it meant sleeping in her big king-sized bed alone most nights.

She had to remind herself of that fact as she walked through the doors to the station house the following afternoon and made her way to her desk. She'd spent the past four hours talking to witnesses in a domestic violence case, and she was cranky from the conflicting testimony. Half the people at the party where the alleged incident had taken place insisted the wife was at fault; she'd baited her husband by flirting with his brother, then really heated things up by punching him in the gut. The other half said the husband, a possessive jealous type, known to use a steroid or two, had overreacted: he'd grabbed his gun and shot his wife dead.

Overreacting . . . no shit. How could people be so stupid?

Portia had about two hours of paperwork, and then she was going to call it a day. Shifts were about to change and there was a lot of activity in the office: phones jangling, computers humming, suspects in cuffs and shackles seated at desks protesting their innocence and bad treatment by the cops.

She passed by one of the young secretaries' desks. A

burst of color in the form of carnations and roses indicated that someone was thinking of her. Portia peeled off her raincoat and hung it on a peg near her desk while laughter erupted from somewhere near the fax machine. Then she stared at what appeared to be a mountain of reports to be processed.

So much for the whole "paperless society thing."

She plowed through some of the files. Reminding herself she did *not* want a cigarette, she sorted through the paperwork as well as a butt-load of her e-mails.

The phone rang sharply. She picked up the receiver, her eyes still on her computer monitor. "Homicide, Detective Laurent."

"This is Jay McKnight from the crime lab. I got your name from Sonny Crawley. I think he made a request for me."

"Oh, right. I've been wanting to talk to you." Her interest was immediately diverted from her paperwork and she started typing commands on her keyboard. "It just so happens I was gonna give you a buzz a little later. Just had some final loose ends to tie up . . . here we go." She found the correct file and brought it up. "Let's see. It's taken a little time but I've got a list of potential vans, all domestic and dark, Louisiana plates, owned by people who work at the college. I'll send them if you give me your e-mail address."

"Great." Jay rattled it off. Portia would verify it before sending, even though she recognized the URL as belonging to the state police.

"I'm driving up tonight," McKnight added. "I could stop by the station, exchange information."

"Good idea. Maybe by then I might have more info on the background checks you requested. Still working on those." She pulled up Jay McKnight's file on her computer. Though she'd never officially met him, she'd seen his name and observed him once at a crime scene. So far so good.

"It'll be late. I work until seven. By the time I get there it could be close to nine. As long as things stay calm and I don't have to pull any overtime."

"Doesn't matter, I'll be here," she assured him, grateful that someone in the department was starting to believe they had a problem at All Saints. A big problem.

"See you then."

Portia hung up and not only sent the list of vehicles to McKnight but printed out another copy for herself. She was surprised at how many of the workers there owned a dark van. Along with a gardener and a security guard, the parish owned a black '98 Chevrolet full-sized van; an assistant professor named Lucretia Stevens owned an ancient Ford Econoline that looked like it had once belonged to someone else in her family; another person named Stevens, Natalie Croft's husband, owned a dark green van that he used in his construction business; and Dr. Dominic Grotto's brother, too, owned a black van. Portia had widened the swath a little, just because she was suspicious of the guy. She'd interviewed him twice. He was too smooth for her. One of those who thought he was smarter than the rest. His conversation with her had brushed on supercilious, though he'd acted concerned, as if he wanted to help.

But Grotto wasn't the only person on campus she thought was hiding something. The whole damned English Department was filled with secretive sorts. Even the woman in charge, Natalie Croft, was a lofty, self-important academic whom Portia didn't trust for a second. The curriculum had been changed to add in the popular "hip" and "cutting edge" classes such as the vampire thing, a class on the history of rock and roll, and others to draw students to All Saints. Then there were the Wagner descendants. She could have a whole file on them alone. Georgia Clovis was a major pain in the backside, acted as if she were royalty. And her brother, Calvin Wagner, a rich bastard who didn't hold a job as far as Portia could tell, was certainly an odd duck. The third child, poor frail Napoli, was only one short step away from a permanent breakdown.

Beyond the Wagners was the clergy. Father Anthony "Tony" Mediera was a forceful priest with his vision of what the college should be, and Father Mathias Glanzer, the burdened priest in charge of the drama department, seemed riddled with secrets.

Portia would love to hear what each of them needed to confess.

There were others as well, new faces in the college. She was doing background checks on all of them, not that she had found anything even hinting of illegal activity. But then, she'd only gotten started and everyone had something they wished to hide. Everyone.

Besides, who was to say that the suspects were limited to the faculty of the college? What about other students? Or someone who wasn't enrolled but used the campus as his personal hunting ground?

*Slow down, you still have no bodies . . . just a single arm wearing nail polish that, according to the lab, was about as popular as grits for breakfast.*

She looked again at the list of dark vans and wondered if any of the vehicles could be connected with the missing girls.

She was about ready to run to the employee lunch room in search of a diet soft drink when her phone rang. Sweeping the receiver to her ear, she balanced it between her chin and shoulder. "Homicide, Detective Laurent."

"Yeah, this is Lacey, in Missing Persons." With the fire-engine red hair and tight clothes. The one with the attitude. "I was hopin' to catch y'all."

"What is it?" Portia asked, but she felt that tingle, that little sensation telling her more bad news was on the horizon.

"I figured you'd want to know 'bout this. We have another missin' person, over to the college. All Saints. A student. Ariel O'Toole. Her mother faxed over the report from Houston, that's where they live, well she and the stepfather. They're on their way. She hasn't heard from her daughter in over a week and none of her friends, the ones she knows, have seen her. The daughter's not returning her calls and that's supposedly unusual," Lacey said with a bit of sarcasm in her voice. "Imagine that."

"Are you sending a uniform over?"

"A car's already been dispatched. Thought you might want to tag along."

"You got that right. I'll pick up a copy of the report on my way." She hung up. *Another one. Damn it, another one.*

Sliding on her shoulder holster, she strapped in her sidearm, then threw on her coat, and grabbed her purse. She was heading toward the hallway to Missing Persons when she ran into Del Vernon. She gave him the abbreviated version of what was happening as he fell into step beside her.

"I'll come along," he said, jaw set, dark eyes cold. "I hate to say it, Laurent, but there's more to this than kids disappearing by choice," he said, holstering his weapon and grabbing his overcoat.

"Glad you finally got there, Vernon," she said as they walked toward the doors of the station together.


"We've got a floater." Montoya, coffee cup in hand, strode through the doorway of Bentz's office sometime after four. Wearing his trademark black leather jacket and diamond stud in one ear, he added, "A bit upriver from here. Still in the city limits. Female. African American. Been in the water awhile. They just fished her out."

Bentz looked up from his pile of paperwork and saw

that his partner was holding back. He dropped his pen. "And?"

"And she had a tattoo on her back, just over her buttocks. The word 'love' along with hummingbirds and flowers."

Bentz sat up straighter. "Dionne Harmon," he said aloud, and that bad feeling that had been with him ever since he'd heard about the girls missing from All Saints just got worse. Lots worse.

"Looks like." Montoya leaned a shoulder against Bentz's filing cabinet, one rescued from the aftermath of Katrina. Repainted and now rust free, it served as a constant reminder of how bad things could get. "They're sending divers, seeing if the victim was alone, or if she had company."

"Shit," Bentz muttered, already rounding the desk. He snagged his jacket off a hall tree. "Let's go. I'll drive."

"No, I'll . . . never mind, you drive. And there's more."

"More?"

"So you haven't heard of the arm they found in the belly of a gator?"

"What the hell are you talking about?" Bentz's gut twisted because he knew what was coming. The day took a nosedive.

"I'll explain on the way." Montoya finished his coffee and dropped the paper cup into a trash can in Bentz's office. They walked amid the cubicles and desks and Bentz caught sight of a TV monitor, where, sure enough, the local news was showing shots of a search and rescue boat on the Mississippi. It was getting dark, but the crew had set up lights and cameras.

"Son of a bitch," Bentz muttered. He reached into his pocket for a pack of Juicy Fruit, unwrapping a stick as they headed downstairs and outside to the parking lot, where rays of a fast-dying winter sun were struggling to pierce the clouds. A few managed to reflect in a myriad of puddles strewn across the asphalt, but darkness was coming fast.

Bentz took the wheel of the Crown Vic. As Montoya, over the crackle of the radio and thrum of the engine, explained about the arm discovered in the swamp north of New Orleans, Bentz drove to a spot in their jurisdiction where crews had taped off an area of the levee.

Camera crews had already gotten wind of the discovery and had set up shop. Overhead two news helicopters, blades whirring loudly, spotlights illuminating the gloaming, vied for a better view of the scene. Uniformed cops held back an ever-growing crowd.

Bentz almost wished for worse weather to keep the lookie-loos at bay. The water was thick and muddy, the dank scent of the Mississippi filling his nostrils, a cool breath of wind starting to pick up.

"Detective Bentz!" He turned to see a pretty woman reporter brandishing her microphone and making a bee-line for him.

"Can you verify that a woman was found in the river?"

"I just got here."

"But it appears as if a body had been pulled from the Mississippi and there's speculation that it might be one of the girls who went missing from All Saints College in Baton Rouge."

"That's a mighty big leap," he said, trying not to snap.

"And isn't it true that a body part was recovered in the swamp closer to Baton Rouge?"

*Son of a bitch,* he thought, but turned briefly and said, "I'm not at liberty to say, but I'm certain the public information officer will give some kind of press briefing." He offered the woman an all-business smile, then ducked under the crime scene tape.

"Detective Montoya!" the woman called.

"No comment." He, too, slid beneath the tape and together they approached the water's edge, where members of the crime scene and the coroner had already gathered. Bonita Washington nodded at them, her face a stern mask.

"Dionne Harmon?" Bentz asked.

"Tattoo's the same. African American. About the right age, size, and shape." Washington walked over to a body bag, unzipped it, shielding the contents from view overhead with her own body.

Bentz stared at the partially decomposed face of what had once been a pretty black woman. Someone's daughter. Sister. Friend. Though no one, especially not her jerk of a brother, seemed to care. Got herself involved with a snake of a boyfriend, too, from what he'd heard. Naked, her hands bagged by the criminologists in the hope that she'd fought her assailant and there was still a trace of DNA under her fingernails, she lay eyes open, lifeless inside the heavy bag.

Above them the copters hovered, disturbing the thick water.

Bentz held out little expectation of getting enough of the killer's DNA that wasn't degraded to do any good.

His stomach roiled. He looked away.

"Son of a bitch," Montoya muttered.

"Dionne Harmon went missing around a year ago," Bentz said, mentally calculating the state of decomp.

"Yeah, I know." Washington was way ahead of him. "This body, it only looks like it's been in the water a few days, and before that . . ." She shrugged.

"She was alive," Bentz said, his mind spinning ahead. "So he keeps her alive, locked away for a year, then decides to kill her?"

"Maybe." Washington was obviously as puzzled as he.

"Do you know the cause of death?"

"Not yet, but I did notice some puncture wounds on the body."

"From what"

"Don't know yet, but she's got what appears to be a bite mark on her neck." Washington pointed to two holes beneath the dead woman's ear. "And then another, larger and single, here, over the jugular. And another at the carotid." She glanced up at him, then rezipped the bag.

Bentz straightened. "What's that mean?"

"Nothin' good," she said, her face a knot of worry. "Nothin' good."

"Hey!" A shout from the boat.

Bentz braced himself as the helicopters swooped in for a better look. He knew what was coming. The officer on deck yelled over the whomp-whomp-whomp of the copter's rotors: "Looks like we got another one!"

# CHAPTER 26

Kristi cut through the water, swimming hard, her strokes even and quick as she tried to figure out a way to break into the inner circle of students she was certain were involved in the vampire cult. She'd even gone online and posted a plea: Searching For Lost Souls. Then, in want-ad fashion on the Internet, she made a request as ABneg1984 to link up with other believers in the reign of the vampire. She didn't know if she'd have any takers, didn't even know if her request would make any sense, but she was fishing and she would be interested to find out what she might catch.

*Probably nothing but weirdo losers, likely all of them under the age of thirteen.*

But the good news was that, so far, she hadn't seen any video of her apartment on the Internet. She'd searched through MySpace and YouTube and a few other Internet sites and hadn't found any grainy, dark movies of her and Jay making love. Hopefully that's the way it would stay. So who had put the camera there? She'd tossed it around in her mind hundreds of times and always came back to Hiram Calloway. Who else could it be? Someone posing as a repairman? She didn't know but it made her nervous as hell, a fact she kept from Jay as she didn't want him insisting she should move out.

At the far end of the pool she submerged, pushed off, and started her last lap. All the while she was thinking about her next move and how she was sick and tired of the waiting game she'd been playing. It was time for action, and she planned to start it at the final production of *Everyman*. Then she intended to have a face to face discussion with Father Mathias. He seemed to be on the fringes of all this somehow. She'd spotted him at Wagner House, coming up from the basement. And he was close with Georgia Clovis, as well as Ariel O'Toole, who had been missing all week.

When Kristi had spied Ariel's friends at the student union yesterday afternoon, she'd purposely stopped by Trudie and Grace's table to ask about her. Chomping on chicken strips and ranch dressing, they'd insisted Ariel's vanishing act wasn't in the least bit strange. Ariel liked her space and sometimes, especially when studying for a major test, she would disappear, only coming out for a needed Starbucks run. That piece of wisdom had been dispensed by Grace, the near-anorexic with traces and electric-shock red hair.

Trudie had nodded, agreeing with Grace's assessment. "Everybody needs some downtime," she'd said, dipping a fried piece of chicken into a small plastic cup of dressing. "Ariel just needs more than most of us." She'd bobbed her head, as if agreeing with herself.

Kristi had tried to strike up more of a conversation without turning the girls off, but they seemed more interested in their food than worrying about Ariel the Studious. But they'd been a little friendlier than usual, making room for her to pull up a hard plastic chair, so Kristi considered it progress. As she sat down they gabbled on about how they couldn't wait for the second performance of "hot" Father Mathias's play, offering up a few wishful, sighing comments about it being a "shame" the priest had taken his vows of celibacy. Then they mentioned meeting for drinks before the show.

They always had a drink or two at the Watering Hole, just off campus, before they watched the play.

"You should join us sometime," Grace said, obviously trying to be polite. Trudie shot her a look and Kristi lifted a shoulder as if the invitation wasn't a big deal.

"Maybe I will. Someday," Kristi agreed, ignoring the increased look of wariness on Trudie's olive-toned face.

"Good." Grace had been pleased, or so it had seemed.

Not so her friend. Trudie, obviously agitated, had yanked on her sagging ponytail with both hands, forcing the rubber band higher on her head, so that the thick black shank of hair hung higher and brushed her shoulders. All the while she fiddled with her hair, she glowered at Grace.

Kristi had acted as if she didn't care one way or the other. She wasn't sure how to take this thin olive branch of friendship, but Ariel's "friends" knew something; she was sure of it. She just had to gain their confidence, pretend to be like them. That would be a trick because the more she knew about the girls who seemed prime candidates for the vampire cult, the less she liked them.

She hoisted herself out of the pool, showered quickly, toweled off, and slipped into street clothes. Her muscles, which had been tight for two days, were more relaxed and the exercise had exhilarated her a bit, lifting her spirits, focusing her on what she needed to do to find out the truth about the four missing girls and the damned severed arm. It didn't hurt that Jay would be back tonight.

She'd actually missed him.

Who would have ever thought?

With minimal makeup, her hair twisted into a damp knot on her head, and the vial she'd sworn to Jay she wouldn't touch dangling from the chain surrounding her neck, she left the locker room and stepped into the night. In the time she'd worked out, the darkness that had been threatening had fallen and fallen hard. No stars were visible above the street lamps, and the wind, which had been quiet all day, was now blowing with force, rushing through the trees, chasing a few dry leaves across the campus lawns, and biting at her nape.

Shivering, she walked briskly through the alley near Greek Row, crossed one of the busier streets near the campus, and pushed her way through the glass doors of the Watering Hole. She spied Trudie, Grace, and Marnie, the blonde she'd followed through Wagner House, seated at a tall café-style table in one corner of a darkened room. All three girls were huddled over stemmed glasses filled with a brilliant red concoction.

Kristi headed in their direction, forced a smile she didn't feel, wending her way through the tables.

Ready or not, it was showtime.


Ariel O'Toole's apartment didn't look like anyone had been inside in days. Dishes were piled in the sink, the bed unmade, a bag of chips tucked into the bedclothes, the cheese dip in a container by the bed old and crusted over.

"Something's not right," Portia said as she, the uniformed officer, the apartment manager, and Del Vernon moved slowly through the studio with its wall of decorative bricks and a curtain separating the bedroom area from the living room. "Look at this place."

"No sign of a struggle," Del remarked.

That much was true.

"So she's a slob," Del said. "Hasn't cleaned up in a few days."

Portia opened the single closet. Everything was neatly organized, her clothes arranged by color, her shoes polished and kept in tidy pairs. Her drawers, too, were meticulous, books in the shelves straight and alphabetized. "Don't think so. This girl is a neat-freak who just hadn't cleaned up from a late-night snack." She opened the door of a small refrigerator, saw the contents were arranged carefully. She stepped aside so Del could see.

"Not a slob," he agreed.

Portia turned to the door where the apartment manager had slowly edged. "When's the last time you saw her?" Portia asked him.

Bald, with a fringe of graying reddish hair that matched three days worth of stubble, he was nervous having the police on site. "Don't know . . . uh, I saw her for sure last weekend, taking a load of trash to the cans outside and then again . . . oh, hell . . ." He rubbed his head and his scrawny shoulders jerked up and down as if pulled by strings. "I think she was hauling laundry up . . . Let's see, I'd been raking up some old leaves. Guess that was Sunday afternoon."

"And since?"

He shook his head. "I've got forty units here, I don't keep track of everyone. Do I look like a house mother?"

*Defensive,* Portia noted. "You got a key to her mailbox?"

"Well, yeah . . ."

"Let's check it." She glanced around. "No phone."

"Most of the kids just use cells," the manager said.

"Can't check her messages then, and she doesn't get a paper." But there was a smell to the place, an empty, almost musty smell, and a forgotten cup of coffee was sitting in the microwave.

They walked outside to the mailbox. Bills and junk mail were piling up. According to the report, Ariel didn't hold down a job, but she should have been going to class. Portia had talked to the mother, who was battling a case of hysteria and was flying in early in the morning, hoping to locate her girl. Portia had called the woman and explained that the police were on the job. They'd called all Ariel's friends, her neighbors, and checked with the local hospitals. She didn't have a car, but she did have a cell phone and a bike. Campus police were searching for the bike. Portia had also double-checked with the bank, seeing if there had been any activity on her credit cards, but so far there had been no new purchases.

Ariel's mother wasn't convinced enough was being done. She gave Portia the name of her daughter's cell phone company and said Ariel's phone was equipped with a tracking device, but she wouldn't be consoled.

"My daughter's not like those other girls," she argued. "I've read about them, those . . . those girls who have no one who cares about them. It doesn't matter that Joe and I are divorced, we both love our daughter and . . . and we'll do anything, *anything* to find her!"

"I'll call you as soon as I know anything further," Portia assured her, more determined than ever to find Ariel.

She just hoped the girl would be found alive.

Her cell phone rang as they were locking the apartment. Caller ID indicated the number belonged to the New Orleans Police Department.

"Laurent, Homicide," she said automatically as she walked outside, one step ahead of Del Vernon, who was still talking to the anxious apartment manager.

"Detective Bentz, New Orleans, Homicide," a low, serious voice informed. "I heard you were working on the missing girls from All Saints as potential homicides," he said without preamble.

Portia drew a breath as she stopped under an overhanging eave on the outside of the tired stucco building. Del was saying something to her, but she shooshed him with a wave of her hand.

"That's right. I am."

"It looks like you were right," Bentz said. "In the last hour, four female bodies, one African American, three Caucasian, all in the same state of decomp, all appearing to be in their twenties, have been pulled out of the

Mississippi down here. One of the Caucasian girls was missing an arm."

Portia's exhale was a sigh of resignation and dying hope.

"Physical characteristics, hair and eye color, tattoos and scars suggest that they are the girls who've gone missing from the college."

"Okay," she whispered. Though she'd suspected they had come to bad ends, she'd hoped she was wrong and that everyone else in the department was right, that Dionne, Monique, Tara, and Rylee were still somewhere safe and alive. "You said all in the same state of de-comp? But they were abducted months apart."

"We'll know more once the ME examines them," he said, his voice tightly controlled.

"Cause of death?"

"Don't know that yet. Preliminarily it looks like they haven't been in the water more than a few days, possibly a week. Hard to tell." He hesitated and she knew something was on his mind.

"What else?"

"There are strange puncture wounds on the bodies. You know that there wasn't a drop of blood in that arm you guys found in the swamp?"

"Yes." She suddenly felt cold inside. Steeled herself for what she knew was coming.

"It looks like these bodies might not have any blood as well."

"Severed arteries?"

"Not exactly," he said, and she felt his anger radiating through the wireless phone. "But it could be that the corpses were ex-sanguinated."

"Drained of blood," she said, thinking of the puncture wounds.

"You might want to see for yourself in the lab."

"I will, but now we've got another missing girl."

He drew in a quick, swift breath. "Who?"

"Student at All Saints by the name of Ariel O'Toole. Parents can't locate her and from the looks of her apartment, I'd say she's been gone for several days."

"Don't tell me, she's an English major."

"That's right."

"And she took that vampirism class?"

"Yeah."

He swore hard. "I'm on my way up there. The lab can call in their report. My daughter's a student at All Saints. An English major."

"I wondered if you'd show up," Grace said, sipping from her drink as she sat at a table in the noisy bar, where music was playing loudly and a band was setting up in the corner. "Join us."

Trudie's face tightened. She made fleeting eye contact with Kristi, clearly not as thrilled to welcome her as Grace.

Marnie tossed her hair from her shoulder and said, "Yeah, have a seat."

Kristi ignored Trudie as she settled into an empty chair, eyeing their drinks. "So what're you having?"

"Blood red martini." Grace lifted her glass and twirled the long stem in her fingers, the scarlet contents threatening to slosh over the rim.

"What's in it?"

"Blood, of course." She licked her lips, then took a long swallow. "Mmm."

Kristi nodded. "Yeah, right, like blood from a pomegranate or cranberry or—"

"It's human." Grace laughed at her joke, but Trudie's mood turned even darker. She shot her friend a "shut-the-hell-up" look, which Kristi guessed, from the glint in Grace's eyes, she was ignoring. Grace was enjoying this.

As was Marnie. "That's right, we're all into it. The whole vampire thing, you know."

Kristi decided to play along. "I'm in Grotto's class, too. Is he, like, the greatest teacher or what?" Before waiting for an answer, she added, "I guess I'd better have one."

She looked around just as a waitress dropped off a pitcher of beer and four frosted mugs at a nearby table. Once finished, the girl, a slight brunette with a streak of fuchsia in her hair, turned around and Kristi thought she looked familiar, as if she'd seen her on campus. "You're in some of my classes . . . ?" she asked her.

"Yep. Bethany," she said. "What can I get you?"

Kristi pointed at Trudie's drink. "I'll have one of those."

"Good choice." She nodded her approval. "My personal favorite."

"Really?"

"Blood red martini."

"Made with?"

"Gin, vermouth, cranberry juice, and just a hint of grape juice."

"No real blood?" Kristi asked.

"Sorry," Bethany said, one side of her mouth lifting. "The board of health frowns on that."

"I imagine."

She glanced at Trudie and Grace. "Refills?"

Trudie shook her head. "I've got to get to the theater before Father Mathias has a heart attack."

"You're in the production, right?" Kristi asked.

"Trudie's character is Death," Grace said, and Marnie nearly choked on a sip of her drink.

"Fitting, isn't it?" she joked.

"Whatever." Trudie finished her drink in one swallow and grabbed her purse.

Bethany was still waiting, and Grace said, "Why not? And make mine a double."

"Are you crazy?" Trudie said, horrified. "You have to go to the play!"

"I know, but I already saw it." Both Grace and Marnie seemed amused by Trudie's concern, as if they had already swilled down several drinks. "I know the whole gloomy plot."

"I'll be right back with those," Bethany said, heading to the bar.

"Why go to the play again?" Kristi asked.

"Required." Marnie picked up a few peanuts from the dish at the center of the table and tossed them into her mouth.

"It's required to see the same play twice?"

Trudie glared at Grace, willing her to shut up. "Not if you're drunk, it isn't."

"Oh, get over yourself, 'Death,'" Grace said, and she and Marnie laughed uproariously.

Trudie, flushed, muttered, "Screw you, bitches," then swept through the surrounding tables in outrage, nearly running into a busboy with a tub of dirty dishes.

"She's pissed," Marnie said, and they laughed again.

"You know," Kristi said, as someone changed the music from hip-hop to country. A Keith Urban ballad could barely be heard over the conversation, "I almost believed you. About the drinks."

Marnie exchanged glances with her friend, then whispered barely loud enough to be heard, "Grace wasn't lying. We doctor ours." To prove a point, she actually pulled a small dark bottle from her purse, then surreptitiously unscrewed the lid and added a few drops of dark liquid to her glass. "It's kind of salty."

"Like a margarita," Grace chimed in.

"Yeah, right."

Grace shrugged, as if she didn't care what Kristi thought, and took a sip. Either the two friends were certifiable, or they'd decided to have a little fun at Kristi's expense. Kristi didn't comment, but waited for her drink as the music changed again. There was a loud eruption of noise at the nearby pool table when one of the players missed a shot.

A few seconds later, Bethany returned, left fresh drinks, and swept up the empty glasses.

Marnie reached into her purse again and lifted her eyebrows, offering a bit of the "blood" to Kristi. Though she wanted to appear to be part of their group, Kristi wasn't about to drink down some concoction of unknown origins. She shook her head. Besides, both Marnie and Grace were already acting so giddy and drunk, Kristi wondered if whatever they were putting into their drinks might be a street or prescription drug that enhanced the effects of alcohol.

"Come on, Kristi. You've been asking all the questions," Grace said. "Don't you want Marnie to add a little bit of real blood?"

"Nah. Got too much to do tonight."

"You don't know what you're missing." Marnie shook several drops into her drink, then some into Grace's as well. Lifting her glass, she said, "To vampires," her eyes gleaming with mischief.

"To vampires," Grace agreed, clinking her glass to her friend's.

Kristi hoisted her stemmed glass. "To vampires," she intoned, and they all took a sip.

The drink was strong, tasting of cranberry and gin, warming its way down Kristi's throat. Marnie and Grace giggled all the more and licked their lips. They acted like they really believed in the vampire stuff, or at least found it incredibly hilarious. Kristi watched them as she sipped her drink, then put in casually to Marnie, "I thought I saw you go into Wagner House the other day."

Her own words "other day" seemed to reverberate a bit, and Kristi looked around toward the band, wondering about the sound. And was that right? Was it the

other day? Or, had it been at night? She couldn't seem
to rightly remember. "It was after hours," she added, for
clarification.

"Really?" Marnie's smile wobbled a bit . . . looked
like a snake crawling across her lips. A blood red snake.
No, it was just her lipstick running . . . or . . . ?

"We all go there," Grace said over the loud music,
and she seemed to be having trouble staying on her
chair.

"Yeah, we meet there."

"We're meeting at Wagner House tonight." Grace
again. "Maybe you'd like to come."

Grace's words sounded funny, as if coming through
water. And her image kind of wavered. Feeling uncomfortably warm and off balance, Kristi licked her lips and
tried to respond but the words felt stuck in her
throat.

"Oh, God, it looks like the drink really hit you hard."
Marnie seemed concerned. "Let's get her out of here."

"I'll pay," Grace said, and flagged over the waitress
. . . what the hell was her name? Bethany . . . the girl in
Grotto's class . . . She came over in a hurry and they
began talking together. They grabbed Kristi under her
arms and helped her toward the door. Lord, she was
drunk, her legs hardly working. She heard phrases like,
"Can't hold her liquor . . . we'll get her home . . ."

But that wasn't right.

She'd been drugged. She knew it.

Somehow, someway, they'd slipped something into
her drink and she'd been foolish enough to have trusted
the waitress. Damn it all . . .

No one in the bar seemed to notice as she was hus-
tled out a side door and into the dark, cold night. She
tried to yell, but no words came, and when she managed
to fling one arm out, nearly swiping Grace's chin, the
other girl laughed it off.

She looked like just another wasted college girl.

*Now what?* she thought, but even as the words crossed her mind they escaped again. Her mental acuity, at least for the moment, had disappeared. Blackness pulled at the corners of her consciousness and she thought she might pass out.

*Don't! Stay awake! You have to keep your wits about you!*

"Here ya go," Bethany said, opening a door as the two other girls guided her outside, keeping her moving while her own legs became less and less steady.

Outside the air was crisp, in stark contrast to the thick, noisy, warm atmosphere in the bar. "We'll take it from here," Marnie said.

"I've got to get back inside. . . ." Bethany, sounding pissed.

"If anyone asks . . ." Grace's voice, as if from a distance.

"I know what to say. Just get her out of here now, before someone comes."

Bethany had been the one to put something in Kristi's drink.

*Fool! You knew she was in Grotto's class as well!*

She tried to yell, to call for help, but only the smallest sound escaped her lips.

The door slammed behind them and Kristi realized she was being held between Marnie and Grace and she couldn't move at all, couldn't command her muscles to do what her brain was asking.

For the other girls, all the joviality, the silliness of the evening, seemed to have worn off.

"Stupid bitch," Marnie said, forcing Kristi along a dark alley. "Stupid, snooping bitch."

"You want to know about vampires?" Grace asked as Kristi's dread increased. "Believe me, tonight, you'll learn." She grinned down with a malice so cold Kristi's heart quivered. Behind her braces, just barely visible, were a set of glistening white fangs.

Kristi blinked again, tried to scream, made one last attempt to kick out at the two girls dragging her down the alley, but she was helpless as a kitten. Her limbs refused to move, her voice was mute, the world distorted, blackness threatening to overtake her.

She thought they'd shoved her into a car . . . but she didn't know if that was right.

She was lying across a backseat, headlights flashing on the ceiling of the car, Marnie and Grace in the front seat. Was Trudie dressed as the character of Death, with her in the back? Or, was it Bethany?

Her mind spun and, try as she might, Kristi couldn't find reality. Jay . . . oh, God . . . she thought of Jay. Where was he? Had she told him she loved him? And her father . . . was he alive? Hadn't she seen Rick Bentz's face in black and white?

Where the hell was she?

She blinked and realized the car ride, if that's what it was, was over. She was being half dragged again.

Where were they taking her?

What did they have planned?

The chapel bells tolled loudly . . . so close she knew they were on campus. . . . She blacked out for a second—or was it longer?—only to realize that she was alone.

And she was naked.

Lying on a couch of some kind.

A mist rising all around her.

How the hell had this happened? Her mind began to clear a bit, but she couldn't move, couldn't open her mouth to speak. There was a red light, basking everything in an eerie, reddish glow. She searched the area she could see, but aside from the ever-growing fog, she could make out nothing above or beyond this velvet-feeling couch upon which she rested.

How had she lost her clothes?

Was this a dream?

Vaguely she remembered being in a bar, sipping blood red drinks, talking and laughing with girls from her classes . . . who were they? Grace, yes, Grace with the spiky hair and . . . and oh, right, Marnie, the blonde. She thought she'd been so clever, trying to win their confidence and now . . . oh, God now . . . how was she going to get out of this?

*Think, Kristi, think! Don't give up!*

Closing her eyes, she strained, attempted to move her muscles, but nothing happened. No response. She was trapped here.

She heard the scrape of a shoe, a little sniff.

She wasn't alone?

Where? Where were they? She tried her best to see, but beyond the veil of the fog, there was nothing . . . not a damned thing.

Panic shot through her. Her mind, clearing, began to think. Obviously she'd been drugged, but certainly it would wear off. This paralysis couldn't be permanent.

Or could it?

New horror shot through her.

With supreme effort, she tried to raise her arm and though she strained, willed her heavy limb to move, it remained still and lifeless.

A tiny cough.

Reminding her that she was being viewed.

Laughed at.

*Goddamn it, Kristi, move your damned arm!*

Again she tried, pushing so hard inside she thought she might explode.

Nothing happened.

*Oh, God, help me. Help me!*

Her heart pounded erratically, spurred by adrenaline, echoing in her ears. This is what had happened to the missing girls, she was sure of it, just as she now believed for certain that they were dead.

And, she, too, would soon be.

Unless . . .

With all her might, she strained to move her muscles but nothing happened. The footsteps were louder now, echoing through her brain.

Slow.

Steady.

Approaching.

She tried to turn her head as the red light pulsed, a visual interpretation of her heartbeat.

What *was* this?

Again, she attempted to look over her shoulder, to force her immovable head to turn. She felt the slightest response, as if her shoulders had shifted minutely. Or was it her imagination? A hair's breadth shimmer in the cool air. Digging down, she tried again.

Nothing happened.

But she wouldn't give up. Damn it, she would fight as long as there was a whisper of life in her.

"This is Sister Kristi," a deep, male voice intoned.

She knew him! The voice was familiar. She just had to think, to place it. Why was he introducing her? To whom? She forced her gaze to the blackness beyond the shifting veil of smoke and fog but saw nothing. She sensed that there were more than one person hiding in the shadows, as if there were onlookers, an audience.

Her blood ran cold as death.

*Audience! Dear God, that was it!*

This was part of some macabre show!

Sweet Jesus, she had to get out and get out now. He was so close. So familiar, yet her mind couldn't grasp his name. She felt him stand behind her and a hand slid onto her bare shoulder.

She experienced a tingle.

Oh, how sick!

Strong fingers trailed along her skin.

What was this? A seduction? Onstage with who knew how many people staring on? Or maybe he was

just the first of many. . . . Kristi's guts revolted at the
thought and she tried to cringe, to draw away.

"Sister Kristi joins us tonight willingly," he said
with conviction.

*Willingly? What?*

Couldn't they see that everything he was saying was
a lie, that she was a prisoner in her own paralyzed
body?

*Of course not, Kristi. Remember: they want to be-
lieve.*

"She is ready to make the final, ultimate sacrifice."

Her mind flew to all kinds of torture, of rape, of
death. Ultimate? As in final? Jesus, was he going to
"sacrifice" her right here? Slit her throat like a sacrifi-
cial lamb? She struggled with all her might.

To no avail.

His fingers moved sensually against her skin and she
felt her body responding. Oh, God, this was so sick, so
damned sick! He had the gall to touch her breasts, to
watch her nipples respond and she knew in that second,
if given the chance, she would kill him. Despite the desire starting to pulse through her body. She would. She
would kill the sick bastard!

He was leaning downward now, his breath ruffling
her hair as his hands slid lower and harder.

If she could kick. Could bite. Could spit in his face.
Who was he? *Who?*

She felt her head rotate a bit, almost of its own ac-
cord, and in that moment her eyes met his, and she
stared into the dark eyes of Dr. Dominic Grotto.

Grotto . . .

Kristi fought to scream and flail, to hit or recoil, but
she remained motionless.

"I'm sorry," he whispered.

*Sorry? For what? Let me go, you miserable son of a
bitch!*

He leaned closer, his breath as hot as all the fires of

hell, his lips curling back to show off his fangs, bright and glistening in the thin red light.

She screamed, but no sound passed her lips as he bit into her flesh. Her skin was punctured by the awful fangs and then . . . oh, God . . . then, her blood pumped to the surface.

And he began to feed.

# CHAPTER 27

Vlad had his work cut out for him.

No doubt about it.

And Elizabeth was nervous as a cat, watching over his shoulder, certain that any second they would be "found out." Not that she didn't have some cause for concern, he thought as he slipped through the shadows of the campus, but he was handling everything. Didn't he always? It irritated the living hell out of him that she, the one whom he adored, couldn't, or wouldn't, trust him.

He'd been working on the details for a very long while. It was time she had some faith in him.

*Control freak,* he thought as he felt the shift in the atmosphere, the calmness of the night slipping away with a gust of wind. Wispy clouds rolled over the moon, becoming thicker and moving more quickly as the minutes passed. The promise of a storm was heavy in the air, and it sent his blood singing through his veins.

He crept close to Adam's Hall, hiding in the shrubbery as he made his way to the chapel. As he slipped quietly through the night-soaked umbra, he thought of Kristi Bentz . . . beautiful, frightened, supple Kristi . . . she'd had just a little taste of what was to come. He licked his lips at the thought of her blood, how sweet she would taste, and couldn't help imagining what he would do to her. The images in his mind caused an immediate response between his legs and he had to tamp down the lust that boiled through his veins.

But first, there was work to be done.

He couldn't be distracted.

Afterward he would savor her, all of her . . . alive and dead.

The storm picked up, gusts chasing across the campus, bending the grass and weeds, threatening rain and more . . . thunder perhaps. The bells began to chime and clouds swirled over the moon as he slipped into the chapel. Inside, the rush of the wind was muted and row upon row of candles, their tiny flames flickering in the vestibule, greeted him. He smelled their burning scent, noticed the wax turned liquid.

Yes, he thought, padding silently up the stairs that curved off the vestibule, he would take care of everything. As he had since he'd been a child. Elizabeth should calm herself and trust him. Had he not always provided and protected? Though often he'd been in the shadows, had she not been able to rely on him?

Yes, he thought, as he reached the balcony. Yes, he knew that four bodies had been discovered, and it pained him to think that the police were even now touching and cutting into the bodies of those he'd chosen so carefully. Yes, he realized that soon the authorities with their sophisticated equipment, trained detectives, dogs, and determination would eventually find their way here. They could no longer linger.

They had to leave.

But not until he tied up a few little loose ends. It wouldn't take long, but those that knew the truth, or suspected it, would have to perish.

To sacrifice themselves, little though they might be.

Now, he slipped between the folds of the heavy velvet curtain and waited. The final performance of the morality play was over and the priest would soon come to pray at the altar before taking the back path to his private residence, where he would pray for forgiveness, absolution, and mercy.

Vlad smiled in the darkness.

*Mercy.*

He kept his gaze trained on the door. As soon as Vlad was certain Father Mathias wasn't altering his routine, he would follow him and ensure that the priest's tormented soul was released.

Father Mathias would no longer suffer.

Jay whistled to the dog, opened the door of his truck, and once Bruno was inside, slid behind the wheel. He kicked himself up one side and down the other for being such a fool and tried to keep from panicking.

Checking the glove box, he found his Glock and shoved it into a pocket of his jacket, all the while thinking of Kristi—beautiful, athletic, sassy, and stubborn Kristi. How had he let her talk him into leaving her alone in Baton Rouge?

He switched on the ignition and, grinding the gears, threw the old Toyota into reverse, squealing onto the street. Then he rammed the truck into drive, hit the accelerator, sped out of the cul-de-sac onto the main street, and headed for the freeway.

He'd been delayed at the lab with the discovery of four bodies—the missing girls from All Saints. The evidence found with the bodies had taken quite a while to collect and process. And as he'd worked he'd tried, over and over again, to call Kristi, to no avail.

Where the hell was she?

One more time, he hit her speed dial number.

One more time he was thrown to her voice mail.

"Hell!" He nearly tossed the phone across the seat as he kept one eye on the road, skirting around a tractor trailer. Why wasn't she answering the damned phone?

Had she forgotten it? Had it run out of battery life? Or had something happened to *her*?

In his mind's eye he saw the bloodless bodies of the girls in the morgue and sent up a prayer that she hadn't become a victim of the psycho who was behind the killings. Why hadn't he insisted she go to the police when they found the damned vial of blood? What kind of an idiot was he to allow her to stay in Baton Rouge, alone, when they both suspected that a serial killer was stalking coeds. And that someone was videotaping her apartment!

*Like you could have stopped her! No way. Not that bull-headed woman.*

But he couldn't shake the guilt. He should have stayed with her. Now . . . oh, God, now . . .

"Son of a bitch," he bit out, driving like a madman, ignoring the speed limit, hitting the gas whenever a light turned amber. Bruno, unperturbed, stared out the window as Jay's headlights cut through the night.

He'd left three messages for Rick Bentz, too, none of which had been returned, but then Bentz himself was up to his eyeballs in this case, the press, and the resulting chaos. As Jay understood it, the New Orleans Police Department, as well as the Baton Rouge PD, had issued statements to the press and general public that there was a serial killer on the loose. The university had been contacted, so hopefully a warning had already been issued to the students to stay indoors or in groups, and a curfew had been imposed.

Jay had finally connected again to Portia Laurent, who had given him all the information she had over the phone. The upshot was that Dominic Grotto had access to a navy blue van, one he borrowed from his brother-in-law upon occasion. Jay was convinced the vampire-loving professor was their man; Portia Laurent was reserving judgment. She was still doing background checks and Grotto, so far, was clean. She had another couple of leads she was following up, something that was bothering her, but before she could explain, another call had interrupted her and she cut him off, saying she'd phone him later.

So far, she hadn't.

Jay was nearing Baton Rouge when his cell phone rang. He picked up before the second beep, his hand gripping the damned thing as if it were a lifeline. He hoped to God that Kristi was on the other end of the wireless call, that she was safe, that his worst fears were unfounded.

"McKnight," he answered.

"Bentz. You called." Rick Bentz's voice. Tight. Hard. Seething with fury—and maybe repressed fear.

"Yeah. I'm on my way to Baton Rouge, but I haven't been able to reach Kristi. I was hoping you had."

"No." The single, damning word echoed through Jay's head and until that moment he hadn't realized how much he'd hoped that Kristi had been in contact with her father. "I thought she might be with you," Bentz went on. "She's not picking up her goddamned phone and I'm on my way up there right now."

"Me, too. I should be there in about forty minutes."

"Good. I know the Baton Rouge PD is stretched to the limit, FBI's been called in. The public's being made aware, police working with the press to get the word out. I'm surprised you got out of the lab."

"I worked it out. I'm officially in the field." Jay had put in over forty hours in the crime lab this week and Inez Santiago had taken over for him. Inez had been insistent that he leave when she'd arrived and had assured him that she, Bonita Washington, and the other criminologists on staff could handle anything that came up.

Jay hadn't needed any more encouragement. Not after finding bodies drained of blood, their necks showing evidence of bite marks measuring the size of an adult male human, the puncture wounds consistent with razor-sharp cuspids. Bruising on the necks of all four victims was identical and the hope was that the police could match the mark on the victims' skin with the killer's teeth.

The work of someone trying desperately to make them believe that there were blood-sucking creatures of the night attacking girls at All Saints.

Jay's hand clenched over the wheel and he braked to avoid rear-ending a motorcycle that had cut into his lane. He said to Bentz, "You know that Kristi was in a class on vampires in society or some such crap." Checking his side view and switching lanes, he tromped on the gas and sped around a sedan driven by an old guy in a hat.

"Yeah?"

"I think someone's taken this vampire thing to another level." Quickly, he explained to Bentz about Lucretia tipping Kristi off about a campus cult, and how he and Kristi had found a vial of blood in Kristi's apartment—Tara Atwater's previous home. While Bentz listened silently, Jay explained about discovering the video camera and setting a trap. He added that Kristi was convinced Father Mathias, the priest who staged the morality plays, was somehow involved in the coeds' disappearances. Jay finished with, "Kristi believes that Wagner House is at the heart of the cult."

"Someone might have told me," Bentz stated grimly.

Jay didn't respond. Let Kristi's father make of it what he would.

"And you left her there?" Bentz charged quietly.

"My mistake."

"You bet it was."

Jay let it go. The exit sign for Baton Rouge caught in his headlights just as the first drops of rain pelted his windshield. He accelerated onto the ramp and decided he'd been the brunt of Bentz's rage long enough. "So where are you?"

"A half hour from Baton Rouge. With Montoya."

"Good. I'm already there. I'm going directly to Kristi's apartment. I'll call you when I get there."

Pushing the speed limit, Jay cut through town, past neighborhoods that had become familiar since the first of the year. But all the while he was driving by rote, spurred on by images of the drained, bloodless corpses dragged out of the Mississippi.

His hope was that the killer had kept them alive for a long time before taking their lives. The delayed decomposition suggested as much.

*Unless they'd been frozen.*

He couldn't forget Bonita Washington's assertion of freezer burn on the severed arm, which, as it had turned out, belonged to Rylee Ames, the last victim.

Unless Ariel was the last one to go missing.

Until Kristi . . .

He took a shortcut to the campus. The rain was heavy now, coming down in sheets. News vans and cop cars were parked around the gates of the All Saints grounds, where, it seemed, every officer on the campus security force was visible. Students were far and few between, but klieg lights had been assembled by the news teams, and reporters dressed in rain gear stood with microphones at the ready.

All in all it was a damned circus.

The campus of All Saints wasn't officially a crime scene, at least not yet, but the presence of the police and the news teams announced to the world that a killer was on the loose, one who considered the private school his personal hunting ground.

"Not for long, you prick," Jay muttered as he drove to the old house where Kristi lived and felt a second's relief when he spied her Honda parked in its usual spot. Maybe she was home. Maybe she'd lost her cell phone. Maybe . . . Oh, God, please. He shoved open the door of his truck before it had even stopped rolling. "Stay," he ordered Bruno, then ran up the stairs, taking them two at a time, his key already in his hand. He was on the third floor in an instant, unlocking the door, throwing it open.

"Kris!" he yelled, stepping inside.

It was dark and quiet, the smell of old candles in the air, the window over the sink open wide, a stiff breeze stirring the curtains.

His stomach clenched and he reached for a gun.

"Drop it! Down on the floor!" a female voice ordered. Mai Kwan stepped out of the shadows, directly in his path, the pistol in her hands leveled straight at his heart.

"Vampires?" Montoya, in the passenger seat, stared at Bentz as if the older detective had lost his mind. Light flashing, siren screaming, their Crown Victoria with Bentz at the wheel was flying up the freeway toward Baton Rouge. "Are you serious? Vampires? As in blood-sucking creatures that morph into bats and sleep in coffins and can't be killed without silver bullets or a stake through the heart or some kind of crap like that?"

"That's what he said." Bentz squinted into the night and drove as if Satan himself were on his ass. The rain was thick, his wipers slapping it aside as the police band radio crackled and spat. In the distance streaks of lightning sizzled through the sky.

"You believe this?"

Bentz felt Montoya's gaze drilling into him. "What I believe is my kid is missing and some crazed son of a bitch has her."

"But vampires?"

Bentz muttered tautly, "Those bodies pulled from the river had only traces of blood in them. Traces. And the puncture wounds. No one's reported finding any bloody crime scene without a body."

"Except for our stripper, Karen Lee Williams aka Bodiluscious. There was blood there. And she went missing." Montoya scratched at his goatee. "You think they're connected?"

Bentz scowled. "Don't know. There was blood there, yeah, but not six quarts. Not a whole body's worth."

"So, this fuckin' vampire worshipper probably drank the rest. And then turned into a bat and flew off on bat wings to a vault somewhere and slept in a coffin while he digested his meal." He reached into an inside pocket of his leather jacket and found a pack of cigarettes, the ones he saved, Bentz knew, for nights like this. His sarcasm couldn't quite disguise the hint of uncertainty he felt. Neither of them knew what they were up against.

Bentz saw the exit for Baton Rouge and angled the Crown Vic toward the ramp. "All I know is my kid's missing and there's a whole lotta weird shit going on." He thought of Kristi. Her smile. Her green eyes, so much like her mother's. The way she loved to bait him, or play up to him and call him "Daddy" when she was trying to wheedle something from him. Inside he felt empty. How many times would he have to go through this? She was the light of his life, and he suddenly felt a jab of guilt for the happiness he'd found with Olivia. Had he ignored Kristi, his only child? Shit, he'd even blamed Jay McKnight for abandoning her when he'd really been pissed at himself.

"Don't beat yourself up over this," Montoya said, lighting up, the smell of smoke drifting through the car. "And don't say you're not. I see it in your face. I've been through this with you before. We'll find her."

*Dead or alive.*

The phrase cut through Bentz's brain, but he didn't repeat it. Couldn't think that he'd never see his daughter alive again.

\* \* \*

"What the hell are you doing here?" Mai demanded, her gun trained on Jay, who'd immediately dropped to the floor.

"I'm the boyfriend, remember? I think I should be asking you that question. I'm with the crime lab, for Christ's sake."

"FBI."

"What?"

"You heard me. I'm a field agent with the FBI. I've been working undercover on the missing coed case ever since the second vic went missing."

He looked up at her and saw the hardness in her small face. She was dead serious as she pulled out a badge. "Get up." She motioned with the gun, then crossed to the door and pulled it shut.

As she slid her sidearm into her shoulder holster he got to his feet and examined her badge. He'd seen enough in his life to recognize its authenticity. "What's going on?"

"I'm not at liberty to say—"

"Kristi's missing," he snapped. "I don't know where the hell she is so don't give me any federal crap. What the hell do you know?"

"I can't tell you."

He pulled his cell phone from his pocket. "Then you can explain yourself to Rick Bentz."

"Stop it! You can't intimidate me."

"We don't have any time."

That seemed to get to her. She pushed a hank of black hair from her eyes, glanced at him, and mumbled something about a loss of protocol, but sat on the edge of the couch and said, "Tit for tat, McKnight. You spill everything you know, and we'll work this together." She held up a finger. "Just for now. I need clearance."

"Deal." He didn't hesitate.

"I've been working this case for months, undercover, and then your girlfriend comes along and starts screwing everything up, jeopardizes and threatens everything I've been doing for half a year!"

"You had the camera in here?"

"It was already in place. Hiram, the so-called manager, used to watch it for fun. His own private girlie show." She couldn't hide the sneer in her voice. "Should've run him in, but once again, I was working things out. We discovered the camera after the Atwater girl went missing and left it up, just in case the killer returned."

"You used Kristi as bait?"

"We did not put her in harm's way," Mai insisted.

"Nor did you warn her off." Jay was furious, ready to throttle the little woman.

"Couldn't blow our cover. You obviously discovered it, so I came back to adjust the books you put over the lens."

"You came in through the window," he guessed, and she nodded, a hint of a cold smile twisting her lips. "So where's Kristi?"

"Don't know. I thought she might be with you."

"You didn't have anyone following her?"

Mai met his gaze. "You don't know where she went?"

He shook his head. "She mentioned going back to see *Everyman,* Father Mathias's production—"

"I work on the crew," she cut him off. "We know something is up with Mathias, but nothing we can prove, and no, Kristi, wasn't at the performance tonight. We tape them."

"You tape them?"

"With the administration's approval." She was stone-cold serious. "We don't know everything about this guy, but we're pretty sure he's a whack job of the highest order."

"But you don't know who he is?"

"We're working on it."

"And you haven't arrested Dominic Grotto?"

"He's not our guy."

"He's the one who's into all the vampire crap!" The cat hopped through the open window, took one look at the strangers, and shot under the couch. Jay pulled the window shut and rain slid down the panes.

"I'm telling you we don't have a case against him."

"You mean you didn't," Jay pointed out. "That's changed. Now we have bodies," Jay said. "Bloodless bodies with evidence of homicide. Bite marks on the victims' necks. I'll bet my right arm those bruises match Dr. Grotto's bite impression."

Mai stared at him. Weighing her options, as if she might renege on her previous agreement. Finally, glancing at her watch, she said, "Okay, let's do this thing. We'll go talk to Grotto and see what the Vampire King has to say. On the way, you tell me everything you know and don't leave out a word."

"Forgive me, Father, for I have sinned," Father Mathias whispered as he knelt at his bedside. How had he been so tempted, so easily led astray? He'd thought it was all for the greater good.

Or so he'd tried to convince himself.

But God knew. The almighty Father could so easily view the darkness that was Mathias's soul and recognize the deceit, the evil, that lingered deep inside.

How many times had he attempted to confess all his sins to Father Anthony? How often had he wanted to seek the counsel of a wiser and more devout man than himself? And yet he hadn't.

*Coward,* he mocked, knowing his weakness.

He closed his eyes and bowed his head, his hands clenched in heartfelt supplication. "Please, Father, hear my prayer," he whispered, hearing the sound of the rising wind, the approach of a heavy storm. Already rain was beating on the windowpanes and running through the gutters, gurgling noisily in the downspouts.

Somewhere above, a branch was pounding, banging against one of the attic windows.

Evidence of God's fury.

His all-powerful rage.

A reminder of how small and insignificant Mathias was.

He lost himself in his prayer and missed the soft tread of footsteps slipping along the hallway. He was unaware that he was no longer alone. Absorbed in absolving himself of his wrongdoings, offering up his repentance, he didn't realize an intruder had entered until it was far too late.

And then, the creak of one floorboard made him freeze, his intonation lost. . . .

The hairs on the back of his scalp prickled as he turned, looking upward into the face of evil. Dark, soulless eyes stared down at him. Liver-colored lips drew backward into a hideous grimace. White fangs, seeming to drip with blood, caught in the dim lamplight.

Mathias gasped, but it was too late.

Lucifer incarnate had descended upon him. The devil to whom he'd sold his soul so willingly had returned to collect his due.

Mathias started to rise, but the creature lunged, its fangs bared.

Mathias screamed to the heavens, throwing up his arms to ward off the evil. But he was no match for the devil, this maniac with a thirst for blood.

Vlad bit down. His teeth ripped into the soft flesh of Mathias's throat, biting off another scream. Blood sprayed.

Searing pain tore through Mathias's body. He scratched and clawed but Vlad, having satisfied his taste for the priest's unholy blood, unsheathed his knife.

He raised it high in a deadly arc.

Lamplight glinted against the blade.

Mathias wriggled in fear. He was sweating, nearly urinating on himself. This wasn't supposed to happen.

No . . . he wanted God's forgiveness, expected to live long and repent his sins and—

Slash!

The blade sliced downward in a silver arc.

Father Mathias was dead in an instant.

The feds, Jay thought, of course.

The FBI had been at work all along.

*And still hadn't arrested Grotto.*

Jay drove with Mai Kwan on the seat next to him, Bruno relegated to the backseat. She knew Grotto's address, and as Jay told her everything he and Kristi had discovered, she showed him where to park, a block away from the vine-covered Victorian where Grotto resided. The house was fitting with its sharp angles and pitched roof and gargoyles decorating the downspouts.

"I just don't think whoever pulled this off would point a big red arrow at their head by teaching vampirism," Mai said. "Our killer seems too smart for that."

"Ego," Jay said, taking out his pistol. "God complex. He thinks he's brilliant, more clever than everyone else. Now he wants to rub our noses in it."

"Or he's being set up."

"Either way, he knows something."

Mai snapped a clip into her weapon. "Agreed. Let's go."

They didn't wait for backup. She had already phoned a higher up, asked for a warrant, and when told to "stand down" had said that of course she would. Which was a bald-faced lie. Jay figured the guy on the other end of the phone had known it.

"Looks like he's not alone," Mai whispered, frowning when she spied a car parked in the driveway. "We'll have to wait."

"No way. Kristi could be inside."

"We can't risk it."

"You mean *you* can't risk it. I'm going in."

Kristi woke up slowly.

Her entire body ached.

Groggy and disoriented, she opened one eye to darkness.

Pain slammed through her head and she wondered faintly where she was.

Shivering, she realized she was naked, lying on a cold stone floor, her hands and ankles bound, the dank smell of the earth deep in her nostrils.

The world spun a bit and she had to work to think clearly, if at all. As if through a long tunnel, she heard water dripping and muted voices rising in anger. An argument?

She started to cry out, then held her tongue as images—sharp, kaleidoscopic shards—cut through her brain so painfully she winced. She remembered being on the trail of a vampire.

Wait! What? A vampire? No, that wasn't right, or was it? Her skin pimpled at the thought.

*Think, Kristi, pull yourself together.*

She remembered a bright red drink, a dazzling concoction that someone called a blood red martini . . . and . . . and . . . there had been others with her. Her memories were coming back now, faster and faster. She'd been duped by two girls, Grace and Marnie . . . no three, that damned waitress, Bethany—she'd been in on it and then there was the surreal image . . . Dr. Grotto approaching her on the stage, bending over her in the mist, showing an unseen audience what he could do to her before he plunged his teeth into her neck.

She recoiled at that memory.

She tried to croak out a sound but her throat still

wasn't working. It was all so surreal. Maybe just a bad trip? Whatever Bethany had slipped into her drink had given her hallucinations . . . of course that was it.

*Then why are you lying naked on a stone floor?*

Her eyelids, at half mast, flew open and she tried to see, to gain some vision in the near-total darkness. . . . Where the hell was she? Why had she been part of that horrible ritual?

*Why are you still alive?*

Panicked, she tried to stand, but she wasn't strong enough.

She couldn't get her stupid limbs to do what she wanted.

Grotto's image came to her again.

He'd called her by name, told the unseen audience of one person? Five? A hundred? Told them that she was ready to make the ultimate sacrifice.

And then he'd apologized to her. Whispered that he was sorry. For what? Sticking his goddamned teeth into her? Abducting her? Holy God, what the hell had she gotten herself into?

So dizzy she thought she might throw up, Kristi forced herself onto her hands and knees. If she couldn't walk, she could damned well crawl. Head pounding, holding one eye closed against the incredible pain, she started to move. Maybe this was only a dream. A really bad dream. She stopped for a moment, wobbling on her knees, and reached up with her tied hands to touch her neck.

She bit back a scream when her fingertips came into contact with the wound: two holes in her neck, not bandaged, just crusted over with her own blood.

Her stomach revolted and she had to swallow back the bile that burned up her throat.

It hadn't been a bad trip or a nightmare. Dr. Grotto had actually bit into her neck and sucked her blood. She touched the tracks of the blood that had dripped down her shoulder and over her breast. Sick, sick!

Fighting the blinding headache, she told herself she had to find a way out of this dark, stone hole.

*A tomb, Kristi, you're in another tomb.*

Her skin crawled at the thought, the memory of the last time she'd been sealed away, certain of her death.

*Don't give up.*

It hadn't happened before and it damned well wasn't going to happen now. At least not without a damned good fight.

She eased across the cold rocks, moving slowly, feeling with her bound hands. She listened for any noise over the drip of water, but heard only the scratch of tiny nails, as if rats or mice were scurrying out of her way.

Inching her way, she finally ran into a wall. It, too, felt made of stone. There had to be a way out, she reasoned, her mind clearing bit by bit. Somehow she'd been placed in here and unless she was in some huge reservoir with only an outlet in the ceiling, there had to be a door. She just had to find it.

*Don't give up. You're not dead yet.*

She was just getting her bearings when she heard the footsteps, coming closer.

She scooted back and lay down again. She wasn't strong enough to fight, not yet. She'd have to feign that she was still unconscious.

This was it.

Her chance.

A key rattled in the door.

Kristi closed her eyes. *Give me strength,* she silently prayed, *and help me kill this son of a bitch.*

# CHAPTER 28

So it had all come down to this, Dominic Grotto thought as he sat, cell phone in hand, the ice cubes in his untouched drink melting. Even the Vivaldi drifting from the hidden speakers mounted on the bookcase of his study could not soothe his soul. What had begun as a unique way to get kids interested in all kinds of literature had ended up in death.

Four girls dead so far.

Probably more. No doubt Ariel O'Toole and Kristi Bentz had died and would be found in the river as well.

He knew it now. The blind eye he'd so willingly turned could now see perfectly. No more did he delude himself into thinking that he was doing the right thing and helping girls whose lives were a shambles start over.

Since returning from his own personal performance, his last performance to his private audience, he'd switched on the television and caught news reports of bodies being pulled from the Mississippi. There had been few details, no names listed until next of kin were notified, but he knew. Deep in his heart he knew exactly what had happened to those girls.

And it was his fault.

Even now, he tasted the blood of Kristi Bentz upon

his lips. All part of the show. All part of the plan. All for the greater good.

Like hell.

*All part of your own personal aggrandizement.*

He'd gotten to know the girls personally and told himself that they were willing participants, that the fear he'd seen in their eyes was all part of the show, that the reason they'd been paralyzed and weak was only their acting ability.

He'd convinced himself that nothing illegal had happened, that there were no victims, that no one had been hurt.

But deep down, he'd known.

But he might be able to save Ariel O'Toole and Kristi Bentz. There might still be time. He might be able to stop this horror from ever happening again. Even if he had to turn himself in for his part in the debacle—his very integral part.

Outside the storm was raging, rain lashing at his windows, and the flash of lightning lit up the sky in sizzling bursts, thunder rolling afterward.

He should have come clean when Kristi Bentz had visited his office, wanting answers. Oh, hell, he should have come clean a year ago, when he'd first heard that Dionne had gone missing.

He'd suspected that things had gone wrong then.

Over the soft music and angry storm, he heard the front door creak open and his heart clutched. He'd locked it, hadn't he? Or had he forgotten?

*They're coming for you.*

*They know.*

A drip of fear slid down his spine as he climbed to his feet to investigate. "Hello?" he said, disgusted with himself. He was a strong man. He'd never known real fear in his life.

Footsteps clicked determinedly down the hallway.

"Who's there?" He was at the den door when it swung open in front of him and the woman he'd claimed to love stood before him in trembling fury.

"No more, Dominic," Lucretia said, her voice hoarse, her eyes sunken, skin as pale as death. Her head was bare and wet, mascara tracking down her cheeks. Rainwater ran down the folds of a long black raincoat. She hadn't bothered closing the door and it banged open against the wall, cold winter air rushing through the hallway. "No more lies. No more disappearances. No more making me think I'm crazy."

"Lucretia, I'm going to the police—"

"Now? When they've found the bodies? *Now* you're going?" She shook her head from side to side. "I loved you," she whispered, tears filling her eyes.

"I know. I loved you, too—"

"Liar!" she spat, nostrils flared.

She pulled her hand from the pocket of her raincoat, her fingers curled around a small black handgun.

He froze. "Oh, Christ, Lucretia, what're you doing?" he asked, but he knew. In his heart, he knew. "Don't!" His stomach dropped as she raised a pistol, the one he'd given her months before.

"You killed them," she said, her voice trembling, her hand shaking.

"I tried to save them! I just put on a show for the others, but it was all an act, I swear!"

"No . . ." The pistol wobbled in her hands.

Maybe he could talk her out of this. Maybe he could take the weapon from her.

"Just listen. There might be time. Kristi and Ariel might still be alive."

"Kristi? Kristi Bentz? You dragged her into it? And Ariel? Her, too?" Her eyes hardened as she aimed the gun at his head. "She's missing. Has been since last week . . . and it's your fault. Oh, God, she's dead. I know she's dead. I should have warned them, told them."

He took a step toward her, but her fingers moved on the gun's trigger. He stopped. Held up both hands in an attempt to calm her. "We just have to find Preston. He's . . . he's the one who got to know the girls, who helped them. . . . He has a place, it's connected to the Wagner House by the old tunnels that Ludwig Wagner used."

"They've been sealed for a hundred years," she said dully. "This is another lie."

"No, no, I swear. Preston claimed he was helping them all start over, gain new lives, disappear. . . ."

"Helping them die."

"Lucretia, I didn't know. I swear, I did not know," he said, trying to keep her engaged in conversation as he thought of a way to strip the weapon from her, to tackle her and take his chances.

"But you suspected. Just as I did." She focused on him, the gun steady but lowered to his chest again.

His heart shuddered and for just a second, over the howl of the wind that shrieked down the hallway from the open door, he thought he heard something. Footsteps?

"You're guilty, Dominic. We're both guilty."

"No! Lucretia, just wait. Listen to reason. I'll call the police and tell them all about Preston, about the girls, about my part in it. I'll confess. Please, my love, just give me a chance," he said, changing tactics, smiling at her, stepping toward her. She wanted to believe he still loved her, so he would give it his all. "I'm so, so sorry," he said in the voice that always had made her melt. "I've always loved you. You know that. I'll tell the police about Preston and the plays and the tunnels from Wagner House. They might be able to find Kristi and Ariel. They could still be alive. Come on, honey. Trust me."

She flinched, then looked him straight in the eye.

"Lucretia, baby—"

"I'll see you in hell, and when I do, I'll remember to spit on you."

She pulled the trigger.

\* \* \*

Jay didn't wait.

He and Mai had seen Grotto's open door and considered it an invitation. They ran through the rain, up the steps of the front porch. Weapons drawn, they surged into the building. A light emanated from the end of the hall where voices rose in an argument that could be heard over the rise of the wind and the slamming rain.

Mai signaled to him to stay back, that she would handle it, but he was right beside her, hearing every word of the conversation, hearing Kristi's name and mention of tunnels running from Wagner House. Grotto's statement, "They could still be alive," propelled him. Glock raised, he pushed open the door.

*Bang!*

A gunshot boomed through the house.

Thud!

"FBI!" Mai yelled, rushing the room behind him. "Drop your weapon!"

*Bang!*

Jay watched helplessly, yelling to no avail, as Lucretia fell to the floor. The weapon slipped from her fingers, blood oozing from a self-inflicted wound to her head.

Grotto was down, bleeding from the chest, a red stain spreading over the carpet. His eyes were open, staring blankly toward the ceiling.

Jay punched 9-1-1 on his phone as he knelt beside Grotto. "He's still alive!" he yelled, finding a pulse as the emergency dispatcher answered.

"She's gone." Mai removed her fingers from Lucretia's neck and came to Grotto's side.

Jay stayed on the line with the operator, giving the address, explaining what happened.

"Stay with me, Dr. Grotto," Mai said. "Hang in there."

Sirens shrieked over the keening wind, and through the window Jay, still talking to the operator, watched police vehicles, lights flashing, screech to a halt in front of the house. An ambulance and fire truck arrived in tandem.

"They're here," Jay said into the phone, his mind still racing. "Thanks!" He dropped to a knee as footsteps thundered through the hallways.

"Back here!" Mai yelled.

"Where is she?" Jay demanded, leaning over Grotto, his face only inches from that of the wounded man. "Where's Kristi?"

"With . . . Preston . . ."

"Where?" Jay demanded.

"Tunnels . . ." Grotto wheezed, his voice faint.

"Out of the way. Step back." An EMT muscled in, taking over, trying to save the bastard's life. "Get these people out of here!"

Frustrated, Jay backed away from the wounded man, his fear for Kristi more acute than ever. He stepped into the hallway—right into the path of Rick Bentz.

"Where the hell is Kristi?" Bentz demanded.

"With Preston."

"Who's he?"

"Dr. Charles Preston. A professor at the college, English Department," Jay explained. "Grotto says Preston has her, maybe somewhere in Wagner House. I'm guessing the basement, which is always locked. It leads to old tunnels, at least that's what Grotto claims. Kristi was convinced there were some kind of weird vampire rituals taking place there."

Mai Kwan joined them. "Those tunnels have been sealed for a century. I know. I checked. We've looked into Wagner House."

"Who the hell are you?" Bentz demanded, ready for a fight.

"Mai Kwan, FBI. And you?"

Jay wasn't interested in pleasantries. While Bentz, Montoya, and Kwan straightened out jurisdiction, lev-

els of authority, and fucking protocol, he walked into
the night.

If he ran, and cut across campus, he could reach
Wagner House in less than five minutes.


Portia Laurent had spent all day going over information from the school concerning their employees. She'd
found several who owned dark vans and, of course, she'd
immediately thought of Dr. Grotto, Professor Vampire
himself, as the primary suspect. But it just didn't make
any sense. Why would he be so blatant? He'd never
struck her as an idiot. An egomaniac, yes, certainly, but
not a cretin.

So she'd dug deeper, finding nothing, hoping for another shred of evidence that hadn't come through. She'd
placed calls and e-mails, searched the Internet along
with criminal and banking records, DMV, anything she
could think of.

"Strike three hundred and three and you're out," she
told herself, and placed a call to Jay McKnight. He didn't
pick up. "Story of my damned life," she thought. Then
she glanced up and saw an e-mail that had been written
earlier in the day but, probably because of all the spam
filters, had taken hours to get to her.

She read the damned thing three times before she realized what it was saying. It was from a private college
in California and said simply:

> You must have made some mistake; the
> person you're asking about is deceased.
> We're sorry to inform you that Dr.
> Charles Preston passed away on
> December 15, 1994.

Portia immediately checked the Internet, finding the
obit and confirming the story. Preston had died in a

surfing accident. The photograph was clear and there was no way that he was the same man who taught writing at All Saints.

On her way to the car, she called Del Vernon and left him a message. No way was she waiting for him. She and Charles Preston—or whoever he was—were about to have a heart-to-heart.


The door to Kristi's prison opened silently. She didn't move. Her heart was slamming into her ribs and she had to force her muscles to go slack. Her eyes remained closed except for the tiniest crack that she allowed herself, just a glimpse of her surroundings.

Until a flashlight was trained on her face.

"Hey!" A man's voice echoed through the chamber. "Wake up!"

*Dr. Preston?*
*The surfer-dude writing teacher?*
*Not Grotto?*

Her head still pounded, but her mind was beginning to clear. She knew her arms and legs worked, but not completely. She'd never be able to overpower her captor. But Dr. Preston?

"Kristi! Wake up!" he yelled at her as he approached. He bent down, grabbed both her arms and gave her a little shake. "Wake up. Come on."

She let her head loll forward, then back as he shook her. Though she wanted to kick his teeth in, she knew she had to wait until just the right moment, when her faculties were sharp, when her body obeyed her mind.

*But what if it's too late? What if he kills you first? Are you going down without a fight?*

She thought about trying to overpower him and knew she should wait. She had to, if she wanted to escape.

"Dumb cunt," he muttered, and left her on the floor. He closed the door again and turned the key.

*You missed your only chance! You should have fought, tried to run!*

No . . . she knew that wouldn't have worked. Shaking inside, she took deep calming breaths. She had to outsmart the son of a bitch.

She remembered little of the previous hours. She had fuzzy memories of being nude on a stage of sorts and Dr. Grotto biting her neck, but after that, after she'd passed out from fear, from the drugs she'd been given, or whatever else, she remembered nothing.

She tried her legs again. They wobbled, bound as they were, but she could move her hands, and if she could somehow untie the ropes . . . no, not ropes or chains, but tape, thick duct tape that held her ankles together.

She sat on the floor and wished for the first time in her life that she had sharp nails. But her fingers were nearly useless as she tried and failed to tear at the plastic-coated tape.

She thought of Jay. Why hadn't she told him she loved him? Now, there was a chance, a very good chance, that she might never see him again and he'd never know how she felt, how she'd fallen in love with him.

*You have more important things to think about.*

Again she tried to rip at the tape, but to no avail. But her body was responding now; she could give it commands and her muscles did as they were bid.

She levered her legs upward, pulling her ankles as close to her torso as possible, then leaned forward. She was flexible from years of athletics. Tae kwon do and swimming had helped. She stretched her spine and positioned her mouth over the tape between her ankles. Then she bit down hard and flung her head backward. Her teeth skated over the tape. No purchase.

*Damn!*

She tried again.

Failed.

One more time, concentrating hard. Straining. Sweating. She had to get herself free before he returned. If so, if she could stand, catch him off guard, sweep his legs out from under him.

*Do it, Kristi, just effing do it!*

She bit down hard. Drew her head back fast. This time her tooth scraped through the plastic, caught and she was able to make a little tear. She grabbed both of the tiny ends with her fingers, which promptly slipped off the tape. Damn! She was damp with sweat, her heart knocking, time running out.

She grabbed the ends of the tape again and pulled.

*Rrrriiiip.*

She was through!

She flung herself to her bare feet just as she heard the sound of footsteps in the hall beyond.

*Come on, you cocksucker,* she thought, still slightly unsteady. She clasped her hands together, intended to use them like a club once she'd knocked the bastard off his feet. *Come on, come on.* She was keyed up. Ready. Every muscle taut when she heard keys rattling on the other side of the door.

As soon as the door swung open she rounded on him, her bare foot slamming into his shins.

He howled in surprise, but didn't go down. Kristi didn't bother hitting him, just sprang through the open door and yanked it shut behind her.

Locks tumbled into place.

Breathing hard, she felt a rush. She'd turned the tables on him! But for how long? She took off down a darkened hallway and didn't look back. She only had a few seconds.

He still had the keys.


Jay flew up the back steps of Wagner House and tried the door.

Locked.

No problem. He kicked in the nearest window and flung himself through just as he heard other footsteps clamoring up the porch: Bentz, Montoya, and Kwan. Jay found the doorway to the basement and tried it.

Another damned lock.

This time he kicked at the panels, but the door wouldn't budge. He swore, looked around the kitchen, and found a metal stool. He was about to crash it into the knob when Mai Kwan climbed through the window he'd just broken.

Mai rolled to her feet and shouted, "Stand back." Her weapon was already out of its holster. She shot at the handle of the door, springing the lock and shattering wood as Bentz, too, heaved himself through the broken window. Montoya was on his heels.

Jay didn't wait. Using a penlight, he hurried down the stairs, half expecting a sniper to be waiting, ready to pick him off. But with Mai one step behind, he made it unscathed.

Bentz hit the lights and everything came into sudden, sharp relief.

The large, open room was filled with crates, old furniture, boxes of knickknacks, even photographs. A behemoth of a furnace with ducts stretching upward like metallic arms filled one corner, an empty coal bin another, a fuse box, wires long cut, sat next to a newer electric panel.

"Search the walls," Mai ordered. "Look for another way out."

There were several doors, all boarded shut, dusty and obviously unused. None that would open. Mai shook her head in frustration. "I told you we already searched down here."

"There has to be a way." The dead air of the basement filling his nostrils, Jay shoved a hand through his hair and stared at the doors. He started trying each one again, more slowly and deliberately, but none of them would budge. Bentz was shoving boxes and crates, and Montoya stalked the perimeter of the room.

Had Kristi been wrong?

Jay checked his watch, felt time slipping away. He'd pinned his hopes that he would find her here, but now . . . what?

"We need to talk to Father Mathias. Kristi seemed to think that he knew something."

Mai nodded. "He lives just behind the chapel. I'll go." She was already heading up the stairs.

Montoya followed after Mai. "I'll back her up."

Jay and Rick Bentz looked at each other across the dusty, moldering basement. "If Kristi said something was going on down here, then something was," Bentz said. He squinted as he eyed the window casements placed high, near the rafters, where spider webs and old nails were exposed in the ancient beams.

Jay, too, was eyeing the perimeter of the building, looking for something they'd missed, something right under their noses. He studied the furnace and began to sweat as the minutes ticked by. Nothing seemed out of place. Bentz moved a stack of crates out of the way to study the floor while Jay made his way to the electrical box. Inside all of the circuit breakers were thrown to the "on" position. He tried a few. Nothing happened except that the basement was thrown into darkness for a second.

"Hey!" Bentz yelled.

Jay flipped the switch. Nothing there. And the old fuse box wasn't connected, its wires visibly cut. Nonetheless he opened the metal door and stared at the panel of old fuses, a thing of a bygone era, still in place. He pulled out the first and nothing happened. Waste of time. And then he noticed that one tiny wire, a newer wire, ran out the back of the box.

He felt a little spurt of hope just as he heard footsteps

overhead. More police no doubt, drawn by the gun-shots.

"Hey!" a big voice shouted as feet pounded through Wagner House. "What the fuck's going on here?"

He pulled another fuse plug. Nothing. Then another. And gears suddenly started grinding. Jay stepped back as a section of the wall, one devoid of doors, began to slide open.

Swearing, Bentz was across the room in a flash.

Without another word he and Jay walked into a tiny room with a narrow staircase. The door shut slowly behind them, plunging them into near total darkness.

Kristi had no idea where she was going. The tunnel was long, narrow, and lit by thin, flickering lights on a track overhead. She'd made it to a corner when the door behind her opened and she heard a shout.

Dr. Preston!

Adrenaline spurred her on, but she was still weak, her hands bound, her brain not firing on all cylinders.

*It doesn't matter. Just run. Until you come up to a dead end, just run. You have to escape.*

He was chasing her, his footsteps ringing on the cold stone floor, echoing through this narrow hallway, a tunnel of sorts. How did she get down here in the first place, she wondered, but just kept running.

"Stop, bitch!"

She didn't bother to look over her shoulder, knew only that he was gaining on her.

*Faster, Kristi, faster!*

Her heart was beating wildly, her feet slapping the uneven floor, scraping on the stones. She was a runner . . . she could do this!

And still he pursued her.

Oh, God, she had to get away from him. Ahead was

an opening, she saw it. Lights beyond. Maybe a way out!

With a final burst of speed she raced through the archway and found herself in a huge room . . . like a dark, underground spa. The dark cavern was filled with candles and mirrors and a stone tub filled to overflowing, water cascading over its sides.

A woman, a beautiful woman with dark hair and sharp features, was reclining in the water. She was taking a damned bath, for the love of God.

"You have to help me!" Kristi said in a rush, and again wondered if this was all some weird dream or if she were still hallucinating from the drugs she'd been given hours ago. Maybe this was all just a weird, horrible reaction.

"Of course I'll help you," the woman said, her eyes gleaming with a malevolence that made Kristi's insides curdle.

Wait. This naked bather was no friend.

Kristi started to back up, but couldn't; the doorway was now filled with Dr. Preston.

"So, Vlad, do you want to try something new?" the woman asked.

*Vlad?* She'd called Dr. Preston Vlad?

Kristi was damned sure, like Alice before her, she'd fallen into a nightmarish wonderland. "What is this?" she asked, afraid of the answer as she scanned the room wildly, looking for escape. There was only one doorway and it was firmly blocked by Dr. Preston or Vlad or whoever the hell he thought he was.

"Something new?"

"Let's pump her directly into the tub," the woman suggested. "Just contain her, slip her into the water with me, and slit her wrists. So much easier than pumping all the blood out and dripping it into the tub."

Kristi's mouth went dry as she backed away. Surely

she'd heard wrong. No way were they going to pump the blood from her veins.

Dr. "Vlad" Preston turned to Kristi. "Elizabeth wants to bathe in your blood."

Kristi could only stare, her brain devoid of rational thought as she tried to make some sense of this. "Elizabeth?" she repeated.

"The name I've taken. Of an ancestor. You might have heard of her? Countess Elizabeth of Bathory?"

Instantly Kristi recalled what she'd learned from Dr. Grotto's class. About the sadistic woman who had killed young girls, innocents who worked for her, and bathed in their blood in an attempt to rejuvenate her own flesh.

Elizabeth rested her head on the tiles and sighed as if she were in ecstasy. "She was right, you know. I've seen a difference since I've been using her treatment."

"Blood baths," Kristi said, scarcely recognizing her own fear-choked voice. From the corner of her eye, she saw Vlad approaching. He gave her wide berth, but closed in. "That's what happened to the others? To Monique? Dionne?"

"Yes, yes, and Tara and Ariel, those that are good enough." She sat up then and said, "But I wouldn't have the lesser. No tainted blood."

"Karen Lee wasn't tainted," Vlad said.

"Not good enough for me, then." Elizabeth settled back in the water and said, "Let's do this before I shrivel up like a prune."

Kristi wasn't giving that whacked out woman one drop of her blood. As Vlad approached, she reeled, kicking him hard in the shin again. She tried to sprint past him, but he was onto her plan. He threw himself at her and they went down in a heap, wrestling and fighting. He was strong as an ox and heavier, forcing her to the floor.

"Vicious bitch," he growled, grabbing hold of her

bound wrists and forcing them over her head so that she was heaving and sweating beneath him.

Elizabeth stood. "Don't ruin her! Don't crush her vessels . . . I want . . ."

"I know what you want!" Vlad spat out, but he was staring down at Kristi. To her horror, she felt his erection, stiff and hard, through his black pants. She fought the urge to heave as a smile slid snakelike over his lips and he pushed his groin down a little harder, making certain she knew what was about to happen.

She was going to be raped and drained of blood.

Oh, God, she had to fight. This couldn't happen!

She tried to squirm, but got nowhere, and within seconds he'd bound her feet again and forced a pill down her throat by holding her nose until she gasped and coughed.

Within minutes the drug, whatever the hell it was, started to take effect again and she was weak as a kitten, her brain disengaged as if she were drunk.

She tried to flail, but her swipes found only air as he cut off the tape surrounding her wrists. While she wanly protested, he hauled her into the warm, almost soothing water.

"About damned time," Elizabeth complained petulantly.

"I had to wait until the drug took effect."

"I know, I know." Elizabeth slid to one side, her skin slick against Kristi's. "Look at her skin. Flawless. Perfect . . ." She glanced up at Vlad. "She's the one. Her blood will do it."

Do what? Save her from aging? "Nope. You're done," Kristi managed to say, but they ignored her, and though she tried to wriggle away, she couldn't. To her disbelief, as if from a long way away, she watched as Vlad very carefully slit her right wrist.

In a swirling plume, her blood began to stain the water.

* * *

Mathias was dead. Murdered. Apparently while he'd been praying at his bedside.

A statement? Mai Kwan wondered as she called in a report to her superior, then searched through the priest's small rooms, trying to come up with a clue as to why the man had become a victim. And why did Kristi Bentz think he was involved with Wagner House and some kind of weird vampire cult?

No vampire had been at this murder scene.

Too much blood left behind.

Montoya was with her every step of the way, through the slashing rain as thunder cracked, backing her up as they'd entered Mathias's rooms. He hadn't said much but had taken in the entire gruesome scene.

"What do you think?" he asked as she bent over the body.

"He pissed off the wrong guy. Look at this," she said, pointing to the priest's neck. "His throat is slashed, jugular, carotid, hell, nearly to his spine."

"Almost decapitated," Montoya said grimly.

"Rage. Whoever did this was in a blind fury."

"At a priest?"

"*This* priest. It's personal."

Which didn't bode well for Kristi Bentz and Ariel O'Toole.

Mai stepped over the body, walked to the priest's desk and started going through his files, all the while wondering what Bentz and McKnight had found. If anything.

Mai hated to think it, but she sensed that Kristi Bentz was already dead. And, judging from the state of Father Mathias's body, violently murdered.

Kristi tried to force her eyes open, to find some energy to fight, but she could barely stay awake, her muscles refusing to aid her as she lay in the soothing bath, the water turning scarlet.

"I feel it," Elizabeth said into her ear as Kristi tried to move away from her slick, clinging limbs. "I feel it rejuvenating me."

*Oh, for the love of God. No way!* Again she tried to push away even though she thought that without Elizabeth's arm around her she might sink into the tub, slide beneath the murky surface and drown in her own blood. The mirrors in the room allowed her to watch in horror and disbelief as her own face went white. Vlad the Horrible stood at the edge of the tub, ready to climb in with them.

Her skin crawled at the thought and she wanted to scream, to rail at the heavens, to call for help. But it was too late. Her voice let out only the barest of whispers and Vlad, as he glared down upon her, knew it. The smile upon his wicked lips, the light of anticipation in his eyes, told her he enjoyed her suffering, her ultimate fate.

He was a monster. A mortal who envisioned himself as something more. Who was this sicko who licked at blood, who pretended to be a vampire, who taught a class at the college all the while preying upon his students? There was no doubt that he adored Elizabeth, who almost seemed to be his mistress. Almost.

"You're like a dog on a leash," Kristi said to him. "She uses you."

"As I use her," he replied, irritated. He reached down toward her neck and Kristi expected him to try and choke her. Instead one finger locked on the gold chain and he ripped it from her neck. "This belongs to me," he said, clasping the vial of blood in his hand much as he'd held a piece of chalk during his boring lectures. He slid a glance at Elizabeth. "We'll have to save a few drops for one more." His lips curled into an evil smile, revealing his needle-sharp teeth.

"You're such a fake," Kristi said, feeling dizzy, hardly able to concentrate. As Vlad leaned forward again, she spat in his face, the spittle dripping into the tub.

"What! No!" Elizabeth nearly freaked. "The water can't be tainted!"

Effortlessly, he scooped up the floating spittle and snarled, "It's fine."

"But—"

"Shhh. I said it's fine," he said more sternly, and Elizabeth, though irritated, quieted.

Light-headed, Kristi spat again. This time the globule landed on Elizabeth's leg.

The woman screamed, and Vlad showed his teeth once more. "I'll rip out your fuckin' throat," he warned, eyes blazing.

*Good! Get it over with!* But the words didn't form, with Kristi's strength seeping away. Vlad saw her weakness and he gloated over her, his smile triumphant, his wicked, fraudulent fangs glistening in the candlelight. "She is ours," he said, so loudly his voice echoed in the underground chamber.

Kristi opened her mouth to argue, to scream, but only a small sound escaped.

It was too late.

She saw her own skin leeching of color, knew she was shivering despite the warm bath, felt herself slipping out of consciousness. Darkness closed and in a way it would be a welcome relief from this torment.

No help was coming.

She couldn't fight.

Her blood flowed, coloring the water a darker hue.

She was, she knew, dying, slipping away.

She would never see Jay again.

Never argue with her father.

All was lost. . . .

As the black curtain slid behind her eyes, she wondered faintly if there was a heaven. Hell? Would her soul rise and would she see her mother again? Jennifer Bentz, who had become little more than a memory as faded as the pictures in the old album she'd found in the attic. Would she actually see her again?

Her throat clogged with unshed tears as she thought of the mother she barely remembered while being held afloat by a psycho who wanted, of all things, her blood.

Dear God . . . maybe she should just let go.

Never had she felt so alone.

*Jay,* she thought weakly, and nearly cried with the thought of how much she loved him.

She was cold inside and the blackness that was teasing at her began pulling her under. All her life Kristi had been a fighter; maybe, finally, it was time to succumb.

Voices.

Jay heard the sound of voices.

He lifted his hand to Bentz, who nodded.

Nerves strung tight, crouched and ready for an attack within the darkness, they each took one side of the long tunnel that opened to a large, dark chamber. The room was empty except for half a dozen chairs placed in an arc around a raised platform, like a stage, upon which a worn velvet lounge rested. A hazy mist rose from the floor and a red light pulsed, almost throbbed, as it illuminated.

The voices emanated from an open doorway that led back to the tunnels.

Without a word they split, each taking one side of the next tunnel. There were offshoots, doorways that appeared locked. But at the end of the darkened hallway a room glowed in flickering light, as if lit by a hundred candles.

On silent feet, they headed toward the doorway, and the voices reached Jay's ears.

"Her blood flows, Elizabeth . . . washing over you . . . it's almost finished."

Jay's heart nearly stopped.

Jaw set, he exchanged glances with Bentz, nodded, and they burst into the room where Kristi lay, white as a sheet, in a tub that overflowed with thick red water and was occupied by another woman who was looking upward at a naked man who was about to step into the tub.

"Hands over your head!" Bentz roared.

Dr. Preston's head snapped up.

The woman turned and Jay nearly faltered.

Althea Monroe? The woman he'd replaced? The professor who was supposed to be taking care of her frail, displaced mother? She was in a blood-filled tub with Kristi?

"On the floor!" Bentz ordered. "Now, cocksucker!"

"Vlad!" Althea screamed. "Kill them!"

As if she had complete control over him, Preston whirled, knife in hand. With incredible precision, he threw the knife at Jay and in the same motion, launched himself across the room, straight at Bentz. Hands outstretched, teeth bared, he leapt.

Jay ducked, the knife glancing off his shoulder, pain shooting down his arm.

Bentz fired, unloading into the naked man as he fell upon him. Jay was at the tub in an instant, dragging Kristi from the murky, red water. She was unconscious, her body limp and pale, the slits on her wrists dark with smears of crimson. He tore at his shirt, making strips for bandages. He couldn't lose her now. No way. He had to save her. Frantically, he wound the fabric over her right arm.

"No!" Althea raged. "I need her!" Climbing from the tub, she pounced, her eyes bright with her madness.

*Blam, blam, blam!*

A gun fired and Althea's body jerked as the bullets ripped through her flesh.

She gasped, covering her wounds as she fell, screaming, "No, no . . . oh, no . . . Scars . . . I can't have . . . scars. . . ." Blood bubbled from her mouth with the final words.

Montoya stood in the doorway, his weapon still aimed at her.

"Call 9-1-1!" he yelled as Jay wrapped the strips of cotton over Kristi's wrists.

"They're on their way." Mai was already at Bentz's side as he pushed Preston's body away. "You okay?"

"Fine." He was on his feet and crossing the room to kneel beside Jay, who was cradling Kristi. The slightest pulse was visible at her neck, but Jay knew she'd lost too much blood.

"Hang in there, Kristi, you just hang in there. Don't you dare leave me." His throat was thick and though he knew Bentz wanted to touch his daughter, to hold her, Jay couldn't let her go. She was breathing, but just barely, and he willed her to survive as Althea Monroe breathed her last.

Through the veil, Kristi heard the crack of gunfire, smelled the acrid odor of cordite, and heard voices . . . frantic voices. People shouting. People running. People screaming. She felt herself being dragged from the water and one voice was louder than the others.

*Jay?*

She tried to open her eyes but couldn't, and though she felt his arms around her, heard his muffled voice telling her to hold on, it was impossible.

"*Don't you dare leave me. . . .*"

Another voice. Her father's?

If she could just pull back, if she could find the strength to open her eyes, to push back the curtain to . . .

"Kristi! Stay with me, darlin'! Kristi!"

Jay's voice was steady, determined, as if he were

willing her back to him, but it was too late. She wanted to tell him she loved him, that he shouldn't worry about her, but her lips wouldn't move, the words wouldn't come, and she felt herself slipping ever deeper, floating away . . .

It seemed to take forever for the paramedics to arrive, but when they did, Kristi was still breathing. Shallow breaths, but still alive. The EMTs administered to her, placed an oxygen mask over her face, and carried her out on a stretcher.

"I'm going with them," Jay insisted.

"Me, too." Bentz was covered in blood, Charles Preston's—Vlad's—blood, but otherwise unhurt. Jay's wound was slight and he assured the EMT that he would be fine until they reached the hospital. He asked Mai to check on Bruno in the truck, then hurried to keep up with the stretcher.

Outside the storm howled and keened, lightning striking wildly. Bentz watched as Jay climbed into the ambulance with Kristi, then walked to the front of Wagner House, where he'd parked the Crown Vic. Rain poured from the heavens, the wind screamed down the streets.

"I'll drive," Montoya said as Bentz paused to take one final look at Wagner House.

In that instant, lightning forked in the sky. As if thrown by angry gods, a bolt struck a huge live oak in the front yard.

"Watch out!" Montoya yelled.

Bentz dived as the wood cracked and smouldered. The tree split in two and as Bentz and Montoya scrambled out of the way, a huge branch crashed to the ground.

Bentz dived as the limb struck, heavy wood cracking against his back, a broken limb piercing his clothes and flesh. Pain sizzled up his spine and for a second he couldn't breathe.

Then there was nothing but blackness.


Kristi opened a bleary eye.

Jay was staring at her.

"Welcome back," he said, managing a smile.

Her lips were dry and cracked, her tongue thick. "You look like hell," she croaked out, and realized she was in a hospital bed, IVs strapped to her wrists.

"You look beautiful."

She started to laugh, coughed, and managed to ask, "What happened?"

"You don't remember?"

"Not everything, not what happened earlier, but last night . . ." She looked at him and he shook his head.

"Three nights ago. You've been out awhile."

"Tell me. Everything," she insisted, and felt his hands touch her fingers.

He did. He explained that Althea Monroe, who had died of her wounds at the scene, had been in league with Dr. Preston, killing girls for their blood in an effort to keep Althea young and beautiful.

"Elizabeth of Bathory," Kristi said.

"Exactly." Jay told her that Dr. Preston was a fraud. He'd been DOA at the hospital, but his fingerprints had identified him as Scott Turnblad, a man with outstanding warrants in California, where the real Dr. Preston had resided before his death.

Dr. Grotto had been a part of their plan. He'd been involved up to his pointed eyeteeth, though he, still alive, insisted that what he'd done was for the greater good, that Preston had convinced him that he would help the troubled girls disappear and start new lives. In exchange, Grotto got to stage his weird production and play out his own sick vampire fantasies. His audience—the girls he played to—were just as bad as he was and under his spell, finding "new blood" and not caring that the unwilling participants disappeared.

"You mean Trudie and Grace and Marnie?" she asked.

"And a couple of others, including the waitress who added a little something extra to your drink. They all were half in love with Dr. Grotto and got off on his fantasy."

"More Elizabeths in the making," she said, and he squeezed her fingers.

"More jail time in the making. They'll be up on charges, too."

"What about Father Mathias? And Georgia Clovis?"

"The Wagner heirs are apparently innocent, but Mathias is dead, probably killed by Vlad because he knew too much. We're not certain but it looks like Mathias might have turned troubled girls toward their deaths. Probably inadvertently. The conjecture is that he heard their troubles during confession or maybe counseling. He tried to help, gave them parts in the plays and allowed Dominic Grotto to 'guide' them, and I use the term 'guide' loosely. Even though Grotto might not have known about what ultimately happened to the girls, he was no saint. He probably had affairs with them."

She shuddered, thinking of the innocent victims.

"But the real maniac in all of this was Vlad, aka Dr. Preston aka Scott Turnblad. We're guessing that too many people knew too much. Lucretia took care of Grotto, but that left Father Mathias. Vlad couldn't let him escape."

"He was beyond sick. And Elizabeth."

"Althea. Yeah. She duped us all. Turns out her mother never even lived in New Orleans. She just wanted to spend more time being Elizabeth."

"Where does that come from?"

"She was a distant relative of the countess, I guess."

"And crazy."

"Certifiable. She got all caught up in trying not to age. We found her diaries. Besides being related to the Blood Countess, Althea was convinced she could turn back time, regain any lost youth by bathing in the blood of younger women."

"Nutso."

"Yeah, on top of that, she'd been married and the husband left her for a younger woman, just as her father left her mother twice for trophy wives."

"So what? It happens to a lot of women. They don't turn into homicidal maniacs."

"You said it yourself. 'Nutso.' Althea aka Elizabeth found her soul mate in Vlad. Their relationship started young. We've been digging into Turnblad's sordid past. His killing may have started young, with his own parents. And he got away with it."

"So he learned from a young age that he could."

Jay's lips twisted at the thought, the way they always did when he encountered a problem he couldn't understand. "Turns out he and Althea—"

"That would be the nouveau Elizabeth of Bathory?"

"You *are* paying attention," he said with a wink. "We found out that they've known each other since they were kids."

"I can't imagine what kind of games they played."

He grimaced. "Don't even go there. Anyway, Detective Portia Laurent put two and two together and found Vlad, er, Preston's lair under an old hotel. Ariel's body was there, on ice, as was another woman, a stripper from New Orleans by the name of Karen Lee Williams, whose stage name was Bodiluscious."

"Does everyone have an aka?"

"At least one," Jay said with a smile, then explained to her about Mai Kwan and the FBI, and the camera in her apartment. It was Mai they'd chased that night because she hadn't wanted to reveal her true identity.

Kristi absorbed this with disbelief. "I knew that

Hiram was a first-class creep, but Mai . . . FBI . . ." She shook her head and started to smile, but then saw Jay's taut expression. "What aren't you telling me?" she asked, her smile disappearing. When he didn't immediately respond, she urged, "Jay?"

"It's your dad."

Her heart froze.

"He's in a hospital in New Orleans. Back injury."

"Back injury?" she repeated slowly, remembering how many times she's seen his face turn from color to black and white.

"He's going to be okay."

"You're sure?" Dear God, no . . . she couldn't imagine life without her father. She held Jay's hand in a death grip.

"I think so." But he was hedging; she saw it in his amber eyes.

"Damn it, Jay, tell me!"

He sighed. "Okay, here's the deal," he said. "Your father's spine is bruised—"

"What?" Oh, God, no! Her father could never stand not being able to get around on his own.

"Hey, slow down. I said 'bruised,' not severed, so he'll be okay eventually."

"Eventually?" she asked.

"The paralysis will be temporary."

"Oh, God."

He held her hand a little more tightly. "The doctors feel confident that he will walk again, but it'll take some time."

Kristi couldn't believe her ears. Had her father survived death only to be paralyzed? "But . . . he will walk on his own again," she said anxiously.

"That's the prognosis."

"Then I want to see him. Now." She looked up, trying to find a nurse. "I need to be released."

"Kris, you'll have to wait until you're better."

"Like hell! This is my dad we're talking about. He was there, right? He came to save me! And . . . and what, he gets shot and . . ." Her voice failed her. "Oh, God . . . there was a storm that night." She saw the image as clearly as if she'd witnessed it herself. "A tree was struck by lightning, that's what happened, right?"

Jay just stared at her.

"Right?"

"Yes, but—"

"And a limb hit him?"

"I said he's going to be all right."

"I know what you said," she admitted. "Now do what you can to get me out of the damned hospital. I need to see my father."

"Okay, okay . . . hold your horses. I'll come with you."

"You don't have to—"

"I know," he snapped. "I don't have to do anything, but I want to, okay? And I'm not letting you go through whatever it is you have to go through with your dad alone. I'll be there."

She was already out of the bed, reaching for her clothes when she stopped short. "Jay—"

"I love you, Kris."

She turned and saw that he was smiling. "You do?"

"Uh-huh. Just like you love me," he said confidently.

"I love you?"

"That's what you kept saying over and over while you were out of it."

"Liar!" she charged, but couldn't help but nod. "So, yeah, okay, I love you," she tossed back at him. "So what're you going to do about it, McKnight?"

"I don't know."

"Well . . . like maybe ask me to marry you?"

"Mmmm. Maybe."

She laughed. "You're bad, McKnight," she said, and reached for her jeans.

"Perfect for you, then, right?"

"Humph."

"Come on, let's go see your dad and on the way, you can try to convince me to marry you."

"Yeah, right!"

# EPILOGUE

" . . . he's holding his own. . . ."

Rick Bentz heard the words but couldn't open his eyes, couldn't move a muscle to indicate to those around him that he was waking up. He'd heard them, of course, the doctors and nurses with their hushed voices, and his daughter, Kristi, who must have recovered, thank God, because she'd been around often . . . talking to him, insisting that he was going to get better, that he had to walk her down the aisle because she was going to marry Jay McKnight and write some damned book and . . .

Dear God, how long had he been here? A day? Two? A week?

He tried to open an eye. Montoya and Abby had been by and Olivia, of course, who'd been ever vigilant. He'd heard her soft voice, known she'd been reading to him, noticed every once in a while her words had faltered or her voice, that sweet dulcet voice, had quavered a bit.

Jay McKnight had been by as well, and he, like Kristi, had talked about marriage, asking for Bentz's blessing or something like that. Or had he dreamed it?

It was about time his daughter settled down, stayed out of trouble. . . .

The doctor left on squeaky shoes and he was alone again. He heard a steady noise, a soft beep, beep, beep, as if he were hooked to a heart monitor, and he wanted to move, God, he wanted to stretch his muscles.

His mouth tasted like crap and he was vaguely aware of footsteps in an outer hallway, a cart rattling, people talking . . . he drifted for a minute . . . an hour? A day? Who knew? Time, for him, was suspended.

Kristi was there again, talking softly to him about the wedding . . . the damned wedding. He wanted to smile and tell her he was happy for her, but the words wouldn't come.

Her words slowed, her voice softened, and then was gone entirely. Had she left? If he could only open his eyes.

He tried and failed.

There was a slight stirring. Just a breath of cool air.

In that second he knew he wasn't alone.

There was someone else in the room, someone other than Kristi.

His skin prickled. The temperature plummeted, as if a soft gust of wind had slipped through an open window. Within the cold was a fragrance . . . something familiar and vague that teased his nostrils, a woman's perfume with an underlying scent of gardenias.

What was this?

He felt someone take his hand, then link smooth, slim fingers through his. "Rick," a woman whispered in a soft voice that teased his psyche. A familiar voice. A faraway voice. "Honey, can you hear me?"

His heart nearly stopped in his chest. The room seemed suddenly silent, all noises of the hospital muted.

The fingers slipped from his and the stirring gust of wind kicked up again, brushing his cheek, as if someone had left an icy kiss upon his skin.

The perfume floated past him . . . the same intriguing scent Jennifer had worn whenever they'd made love. . . .

Jennifer!

His eyes flew open.

His breath fogged in the coldness. He blinked his eyes several times, wondering at the phenomenon. He couldn't move his head, but out of the corner of his eye, he saw the doorway to the room and beside it a chair. In the chair, Kristi slept, her head lolling forward.

In the doorway, backlit by the outside hall, was a woman in a black dress.

Tall.

Slim.

Mahogany-colored hair falling down her back.

Oh, God! It couldn't be. . . .

She looked over her shoulder and smiled.

That sexy, come-hither smile he knew so well crossed her red lips.

He felt as if he'd been thrown back in time. His heart nearly stopped.

"Jennifer," he whispered, saying his dead ex-wife's name for the first time in years. "Jennifer."

He blinked.

She was gone.

"Dad?"

He slid his eyes toward the only chair in the room. Kristi was staring at him, her own eyes anxious, a line of worry creasing her smooth brow. Jesus, she looked like her mother!

"You're awake!" Kristi was out of the chair in an instant, tears catching on her lashes. "Oh, God, you're okay!" she said, standing over the edge of his bed, taking his hand and squeezing it. "You old fart, you nearly scared me to death!"

"Your mother," he said anxiously, wondering if he was losing his mind. "She was here."

"Mom?" She shook her head. "Wow, what kind of drugs are you on?"

"But she was here."

"I'm telling you that's the morphine talking." Kristi was laughing through her tears.

"You didn't see her?"

Kristi shook her head. "No one was in here, I was here all the time. Yeah, I dropped off, but . . . Jesus, it's cold in here." She shivered. "But I'm just glad you're back," she said. "I was so afraid . . . I mean, I thought you might not make it . . . But then you're tougher than most."

Bentz wasn't deterred. "But she was here . . . your mother . . . I saw her . . . just walking out the door. . . ."

"No way, Dad, it's me. You're confused." She eyed him a little more critically, then glanced to the doorway. The empty doorway. "You know," she said, turning back to him, "you've been in a coma for nearly two weeks and I know what it's like. Weird as hell. Sometimes when you finally wake up, you're all messed up in your head."

"You didn't see her?" He tried and failed to pull himself into a sitting position. His arms were weak and his legs . . . Hell, they still weren't working. He couldn't even feel them, not like he could his arms and shoulders.

"She wasn't here," Kristi said anxiously, and quickly. As if she, too, knew something odd had happened. "Look, I need to call the nurse and the doctor. And Olivia. She's on her way back here already, but she'd kill me if I didn't call her. And the staff. I need to let everyone know you're awake." She was already walking to the door, the very doorway in which Jennifer had stood only seconds before.

"She was here, Kristi," Bentz said, certain he was right. This was no hallucination. No bad trip. No confusion from medication. Whether anyone believed him or not, he knew the truth.

Jennifer Bentz was back.

Dear Reader,

I loved writing Kristi Bentz's story and it was a lot of fun to walk through the halls of All Saints College again. From the epilogue you know that there's another book coming in the Bentz/Montoya/New Orleans series. That book is MALICE and I think it's one of my best yet. I've never written anything like this before, but I think it's an interesting concept.

You all know Detective Rick Bentz of the New Orleans Police Department. He's Kristi's dad and Detective Reuben Montoya's partner. He's also one of my most popular characters and right now he's in a heap of trouble. If you've followed the series, you know that Bentz was first introduced in HOT BLOODED. In the next book, COLD BLOODED, he was the hero of the story. He met his future wife Olivia in the pages of COLD BLOODED, but we, as the readers, never really saw how he dealt with the death of his first wife, Jennifer.

That's changed. In MALICE, Rick faces his most deadly enemy yet in a psychological game of cat and mouse. Jennifer Bentz seems to be back, even though Rick was the man who identified her body when she was killed in a single car accident.

So who is the woman he swears is her? Is Jennifer dead? A ghost? A figment of Rick's imagination? Just who is the alluring female who takes him back to a time he'd rather forget? And how does his new-found obsession with this woman who's haunting him affect his marriage to Olivia just when she wants to have a baby of her own?

Rick Bentz is torn and tortured. He's determined to get to the truth behind "Jennifer" but he has no idea that he's in for an emotional roller coaster that leads from the bayous surrounding New Orleans to secrets hidden beneath the glitter of Los Angeles. What he doesn't expect is an enemy so seductive and deadly, everyone he loves is suddenly in mortal danger.

You can read on for an excerpt as well as visit *www. lisajackson.com* for more information on MALICE, which will be available in hardcover from Kensington Publishing in April 2009. While you're visiting my website, you can learn more about MALICE as well as my other books. I think you'll like this new book. It's a bit of a twist for me, but I can tell you straight up, MALICE is truly one of my favorite books. I hope you agree.

Lisa Jackson

# PROLOGUE

*A suburb of Los Angeles*
*Twelve years earlier*

"So you're not coming home tonight, is that what you're getting at?" Jennifer Bentz sat on the edge of the bed, phone to her ear and tried to ignore that all-too familiar guilty noose of monogamy that was strangling her even as it frayed.

"Probably not."

Ever the great communicator, her ex wasn't about to commit.

Not that she really blamed him. Theirs was a tenuous, if sometimes passionate relationship. And she was forever "the bad one" as she thought of herself, "the adulteress." Even now, the scent of recent sex teased her nostrils in the too-warm bedroom, reminding her of her sins. Two half-full martini glasses stood next to a sweating shaker on the bedside table, evidence that she hadn't been alone. "When, then?" she asked. "When will you show up?"

"Tomorrow. Maybe." Rick was on his cell in a squad car. She heard the sounds of traffic in the background, knew he was being evasive and tightlipped because his partner was driving and could overhear at least one side of the stilted conversation.

Great.

She tried again. Lowered her voice. "Would it help if I said 'I miss you'?"

No response. Of course. God, she hated this. Being the pathetic, whining woman, begging for him to see her. It just wasn't her style. Not her style at all. Men, they were the ones who usually begged. And she got off on it.

Somewhere in the back of her consciousness she heard a soft click.

"Rick?"

"I heard you."

Her cheeks burned and she glanced at the bed sheets twisted and turned, falling into a pool of pastel, wrinkled cotton at the foot of the bed.

*Oh, God. He knows.* The metallic taste of betrayal was on her lips, but she had to play the game, feign innocence. Surely he wouldn't suspect that she'd been with another man, not so close on the heels of the last time. Geez, she'd even surprised herself.

There was a chance he was bluffing.

And yet . . .

She shuddered as she imagined his rage. She played her trump card. "Kristi will wonder why you're not home. She's already asking questions."

"And what do you tell her? The truth?" *That her mother can't keep her legs closed?* He didn't say it, but the condemnation was there, hanging between them. Hell, she hated this. If it weren't for her daughter, their daughter . . .

"I'm not sure how long the stake-out will be."

A convenient lie. Her blood began a slow, steady boil. "You and I both know that the department doesn't work its detectives around the clock."

"You and I both know a lot of things."

In her mind's eye she saw him as he had been in the

bedroom doorway, his face twisted in silent accusation as she lay in their bed, sweaty, naked, in the arms of another man, the same man with whom she'd had an affair earlier. Kristi's biological father. Rick had reached for his gun, the pistol strapped in his shoulder-holster and for a second Jennifer had known real fear. Icy, cold terror.

"Get out," he'd ordered, staring with deadly calm at the two of them. "Jesus H. Christ, get the hell out of my house and don't come back. Both of you."

He'd turned then, walked down the stairs and left without so much as slamming the door. But his rage had been real. Palpable. Jennifer had known she'd escaped with her life. But she hadn't left. She couldn't.

Rick hadn't returned. They hadn't even fought about it again. He'd just left.

Refused to answer her calls.

Until today.

By then it had been too late.

She'd already met her lover again. As much out of retribution as desire. Fuck it. No one was going to run her life, not even Rick-effin'-Bentz, super-hero cop. So she'd met the man who was forever in her blood.

*Slut!*

*Whore!*

The words were her own. She closed her eyes and hung her head, feeling lost. Confused. Never had she planned to cheat on Rick. Never. But she'd been weak; temptation strong. She shook her head and felt black to the bottom of her soul. Who was she so intent on punishing? Him? Or herself? Hadn't one of her shrinks told her she didn't think she deserved him? That she was self-destructive.

What a load of crap. "I just don't know what you want," she whispered weakly.

"Neither do I. Not anymore."

She saw a swallow left in one martini glass, and drank

it down. Did the same with the second. The noose tightened a notch, even as it unraveled. God, why couldn't it be easy with him? Why couldn't she remain faithful? "I'm trying, Rick," she whispered, gritting her teeth. It wasn't a lie. The problem was that she was trying and failing.

She thought she heard a muffled footstep, from downstairs, and she went on alert, then decided the noise might have been the echo in the phone. Or from outside. Wasn't there a window open?

"You're trying?" Rick snorted. "At what?"

So there it was. He did know. Probably had seen that she was tailed, the house watched. Or worse yet, he himself had been parked up the street in a car she didn't recognize and had been watching the house himself. She glanced up at the ceiling to the light fixture, smoke alarm, and slow-moving paddle fan as it pushed the hot air around. Were there tiny cameras hidden inside? Had he filmed her recent tryst? Witnessed her as she'd writhed and moaned on the bed she shared with him? Observed her as she'd taken command and run her tongue down her lover's abdomen and lower? Seen her laughing? Teasing? Seducing?

Jesus, how twisted was he?

She closed her eyes. Mortified. "You sick son of a bitch."

"That's me."

"I hate you." Her temper was rising.

"I know. I just wasn't sure you could admit it. Leave, Jennifer. It's over."

"Maybe if you didn't get off bustin' perps and playing the super-hero, ace detective, maybe if you paid a little attention to your wife and kid, this wouldn't happen."

"You're *not* my wife."

*Click.*

He hung up.

"Bastard!" She threw the phone onto the bed. Her head began to pound. *You did this, Jennifer. You yourself. You knew you'd get caught but you pushed everything you wanted and loved including Kristi and a chance with your ex-husband, because you're a freak. You just can't help yourself.* She felt a tear slither down her cheek and slapped it away. This was no time for tears or self-pity.

Hadn't she told herself a reconciliation with Rick was impossible? And yet she'd returned to this house, this home they'd shared together. Knowing full well it was a mistake of monumental proportions; just as it had been when she'd first said "I do," years before.

"Fool!" She swore under her breath on her way to the bathroom where she saw her reflection in the mirror over the sink.

"Not pretty," she said, splashing water over her face, but that really wasn't the truth. She wasn't too far into her thirties and so far, her dark hair was thick and wavy as it fell below her shoulders, her skin was still smooth, her lips full, her eyes a shade of blue-green men seemed to find fascinating. All the wrong men, she reminded herself. Men who were forbidden and taboo. And she loved their attention. Craved it.

She opened the medicine cabinet, found her bottle of Valium and popped a couple, just to take the edge off and hoped to push the threatening migraine away. Kristi was going to a friend's house after swim practice, Rick wasn't coming home until God knew when, so Jennifer had the house, and the rest of the evening to herself. She wasn't leaving. Yet.

*Swoosh.*

An unlikely noise traveled up the staircase from the floor below.

The sound of air moving? A door opening? A window ajar?

What the hell was going on? She paused, listening,

her senses on alert, the hairs on the back of her arms lifting.

What if Rick were nearby?

What if he'd been lying on the phone and was really on his way home again, just like the other day? The son of a bitch might just have been playing her for a fool.

The "stake-out" could well be fake, or if he really were going to spend all night watching someone, it was probably her, his own wife.

*Ex*-wife. Jennifer Bentz stared at her reflection in the mirror and frowned at the tiny little lines visible between her eyebrows. When had those wrinkles first appeared? Last year? Earlier? Or just in the last week?

It was hard to say.

But there they were, reminding her all too vividly that she wasn't getting any younger.

With so many men who had wanted her, how had she ended up marrying, divorcing, and then living with a cop in his small all too middle class little house. Their attempt to get back together was just a trial and hadn't been going on long and now . . . well, she was pretty damned sure it was over for good.

Because she just couldn't be faithful to any one man. Even one she loved.

Dear God, what was she going to do? She'd thought about taking her own life. More than once and she'd already written her daughter a letter to be delivered upon her death:

*Dear Kristi,*

*I'm so sorry, honey. Believe me when I tell you that I love you more than life itself. But I've been involved with the man who is really your father again and I'm afraid it's going to break Rick's heart.*

And blah, blah, blah . . .

What a bunch of melodramatic trap.

Again she thought she heard something . . . the sound of a footstep on the floor downstairs.

She started to call out, then held her tongue. Padding quietly to the top of the stairs, held onto the railing and listened. Over the smooth rotation of the fan in her bedroom, she heard another noise, something faint and clicking.

Her skin crawled.

She barely dared breathe. Her heart pounded in her ears.

*Just your imagination—the guilt that's eating at you.*

*Or the neighbor's cat—that's it, a scraggly thing that's always rooting around in the garbage cans or searching for mice in the garage.*

On stealthy footsteps she hurried to the bedroom window and peered through the glass, seeing nothing out of the ordinary on this gray day in LA where the air was foggy, dusty, and thick. Even the sun, a reddish disc hanging low in the sky over miles and miles of rooftops, appeared distorted by the smog.

Not the breath of a breeze from the ocean today, nothing stirring to make any kind of noise. No cat slinking beneath the dry bushes, no bicyclist on the street. Not even a car passing.

*It's nothing.*

*Just a case of nerves.*

*Calm down.*

She poured the remains of the shaker into her glass and took a sip on her way to the bathroom. But in the doorway she caught sight of her reflection and felt another stab of guilt.

"Bottoms up," she whispered and then seeing her own reflection with the glass lifted to her lips, she cringed. This wasn't what she wanted for her life. For her daughter. "Stupid, stupid bitch!" The woman in the mirror seemed to laugh at her. Taunt her. Without thinking, Jennifer hurled her drink at her smirking reflection. The glass slammed into the mirror, shattering.

Crraaack!

Slowly, the mirror cracked, a spider web of flaws crawling over the silvered glass. Shards slipped into the sink.

"Jesus!"

*What the hell have you done?*

She tried to pick up one of the larger pieces and sliced the tip of her finger, blood dripping from her hand, drizzling into the sink. Quickly she found a single, loose Band-aid on the shelf in the cabinet. She had trouble, her fingers weren't working as they should, but she managed to pull off the backing and wrap her index finger. But she couldn't quite staunch the flow. Blood swelled beneath the tiny scrap of plastic and gauze. "Damn it all to hell," she muttered and caught a glimpse of her face in one of the remaining jagged bits of mirror.

"Seven years of bad luck," she whispered, just as Nana Nichols had foretold when she'd broken her grandmother's favorite looking glass at the age of three. "You'll be cursed until you're ten, Jenny, and who knows how much longer after that!" Nana, usually kind, had looked like a monster, all yellow teeth and bloodless lips twisted in disgust.

But how right the old woman had been. Bad luck seemed to follow her around, even to this day.

Spying her face now distorted and cleaved in the shards of glass that remained, Jennifer saw herself as an old woman; a lonely old woman.

God, what a day, she thought thickly.

She needed the broom and dustpan, and started downstairs, nearly stumbling on the landing. She caught herself, made her way to the first floor and stepped into the laundry room.

Where the door stood ajar.

*What?*

She hadn't left it open; she was sure of it. And when her lover had left, he'd gone through the garage . . . so . . . ?

Had Kristi, on her way to school, not pulled it shut? The damned thing was hard to latch, but . . .

She felt a frisson of fear skitter down her spine. Hadn't she heard someone down here earlier? Or was that just the gin talking? She was a little confused, her head thick, but . . .

Steadying herself on the counter, she paused, straining to hear, trying to remember. Good God, she was more than a little out of it. She walked into the kitchen, poured herself a glass of water and noticed the hint of cigarette smoke in the air. No doubt from her ex-husband. How many times does she have to tell him to take his foul habit and smoke outside? Way outside. Not just out on the back porch where the damned tobacco odor sifted through the screen door.

*But Rick hasn't been here in two days . . .*

She froze, her gaze traveling upward to the ceiling. Nothing . . . and then . . . a floorboard creaking overhead. The crunch of glass.

*Oh, God, no.*

This time it wasn't a guess.

This time she was certain.

Someone was in the house.

Someone who didn't want her to know he was there.

Someone who wanted to do her harm.

The smell of cigarette smoke teased at her nostrils again.

Oh, Jesus. This wasn't Rick.

She slid on silent footsteps toward the counter where the knives were kept and slowly slid a long-bladed weapon from its slot. As she did she thought of all the cases Rick had solved, of all the criminals who had vented their revenge upon him and his family when they'd been arrested or sentenced, how they had vowed back at Detective Bentz in the most painful ways possible.

He'd never told her of the threats, but she'd learned from other cops on the force who had gladly repeated all the horrid threats.

And now someone was in the house.

The back of her throat turned desert dry.

Holding her breath, she eased into the garage and nearly tripped on the single step when she realized that the garage door was wide open to the driveway, an open invitation. One the intruder had used.

She didn't think twice and slid behind the wheel where the keys were in the ignition.

She twisted on the keys.

The engine sparked.

She threw the car into reverse and gunned it, tearing out of the driveway, nearly hitting the neighbor's miserable cat, just missing the mailbox.

She glanced up to the master bedroom window as she crammed the van into drive.

Her heart froze.

A dark figure stood behind the panes, a man with a cruel, twisted smile.

"Shit!"

The light shifted on the blinds and the image was gone—maybe just a figment of her imagination.

Or was it?

She didn't wait to find out, just hit the throttle, racing down the street as old Mr. Van Pelt decided to back his ancient tank of a Buick into the street. Jennifer hit the brakes, her tires screeched, and then once past the startled old man, floored it.

"There was no man in the window. You know that," she tried to convince herself. "No one was there."

She reached for her purse and, while driving with one hand, searched for her cell, which, she now remembered was lying on the rumpled bed in the bedroom where she'd seen the tall man standing.

"Just your imagination," she said over and over as

she drove out of the subdivision and onto the main highway, melding into traffic. Her heart pounded and her head throbbed. Blood from her hand covered the wheel. She checked her rearview often, searching for a vehicle following her, looking through the sea of cars for one that seemed intent on chasing her down. Metal glinted in the sunlight and she cursed herself for not having her sunglasses with her.

Nothing looked out of the ordinary. Tons of cars heading east, silver, white, black sedans and sports cars, trucks and SUVs . . . at least she thought that was the direction she has going. She wasn't sure. She hadn't paid a lot of attention and she was starting to relax, to think she'd eluded whoever had been after her. If anyone really had.

Just another Southern California day. She spied a dark blue SUV coming up fast and her heart jumped, but it sped by, along with a white BMW on its tail.

She flipped on the radio, tried to steady her nerves, but she was sweating, her finger still bleeding, her mind numbed. The miles passed, nothing happened and she started to relax. Really relax. She drifted a bit, nearly side-swiping a guy who laid on the horn and flipped her off.

"Yeah, right, whatever," she said, but realized she shouldn't be driving, not in all this traffic and at the next exit, she turned off . . . dear Lord where was she? . . . in the country? She didn't recognize the area, the sparseness of the homes, the stretches of brush and farmland. She was inland somewhere and the Valium had kicked in big time. Blinking against the sunlight, she looked in her side view mirror and saw another big blue SUV bearing down on her.

The same one as before?

No!

Couldn't be.

She yawned and the Explorer behaved, following her at a distance on the two-lane road that led into the hills.

It was really time to turn around.

She was so damned tired.

The road before her seemed to shift and she blinked. Her eyelids were so heavy. She'd have to slow down and rest, try to clear her head, maybe drink some coffee . . .

There was a chance no one had been in the house. Geez-God, the way she was imagining things, the way her nerves were strung tight as guy wires these days, the way guilt was eating at her, she was probably letting her mind play tricks on her. Her thoughts swirled and gnawed at her.

She saw the corner in the road and she braked, and as she did, she noticed the dark Explorer riding her ass.

"So pass, you idiot," she said, distracted, her eyes on the rearview mirror. The rig's windows were tinted and dark, but she caught a glimpse of the driver.

Oh, God.

Her heart nearly stopped.

The driver stared straight at her. She bit back a scream. He was the same intruder she'd seen in the upstairs window of her house.

Scared out of her wits, she tromped on the accelerator. Who the hell was he?

Why was he following her?

She saw the corner and cut it, hoping to lose him, but her judgment was off and one of the van's tires caught on the shoulder, hitting gravel. She yanked on the wheel, trying to wrestle the car onto the road, but the van began to spin.

Wildly.

Crazily.

Totally out of control.

The van shuddered. Skidded.

And then began to roll.

In slow-motion certainty, Jennifer knew she was going to die.

More than that, she knew she was being murdered.

Probably set up by her damned ex-husband, Rick Bentz.